Jack Curtis was born in Devonshire. He now divides his time between London and a remote valley in the West Country. CROWS' PARLIAMENT is his first novel.

Crows' Parliament

Jack Curtis

CORGI BOOKS

During the writing of this novel I called on a number of people for advice and information. My thanks to all who helped – but in particular to Richard Erskine who supplied invaluable answers to some crucial questions.

CROWS' PARLIAMENT

A CORGI BOOK 0 552 13081 8

Originally published in Great Britain by Bantam Press, a division of Transworld Publishers Ltd.

PRINTING HISTORY
Bantam Press edition published 1987
Corgi edition published 1988

Copyright © Jack Curtis 1987

This book is set in 10/11 pt Baskerville
by Colset Private Limited, Singapore.

Corgi Books are published by Transworld Publishers Ltd., 61–63 Uxbridge Road, Ealing, London W5 5SA, in Australia by Transworld Publishers (Australia) Pty. Ltd., 15–23 Helles Avenue, Moorebank, NSW 2170, and in New Zealand by Transworld Publishers (N.Z.) Ltd., Cnr. Moselle and Waipareira Avenues, Henderson, Auckland.

Made and printed in Great Britain by
Cox & Wyman Ltd., Reading, Berks.

To Vernon and Sue

Crows' Parliament

Part One

1

In a desert landscape there is always movement.

The untutored eye wouldn't find it. Knowing where to look and how to look is always the specialist's secret, although a visitor to some barren place, who had missed the tiny rumplings of sand as creatures burrowed before his footfall or the snapped fractions that make up the passage of insects, might observe how the dying of the light brings change. The sky darkens abruptly, leaving a pale fragile band of aquamarine stretched on the horizon like watered silk. Everything goes blue. Rocks and scrub trees take on a clean sharp edge for a brief time, then soften as if they had gathered a coating of dark moss; and soon, like the whole landscape, they settle into themselves as if finding a stillness deeper than the bleached immobility of noon.

In Sardinia, in the early autumn, the sun goes quickly. The deep granite ravines of the Barbagia hold the heat, though; warm bowls ringed by boulders like sentinels and by the misshapen skeletons of trees, their bones warped by the *maestrale* that blows for almost half the year. The trees turn their backs to it, their raddled arms stretching always towards the south-east as if in supplication. Rooted in granite, they have no escape.

The eyes that scrutinized the skyline, inch by inch, knew what to look for. As the light drained out of the vast arc of the sky, they took in the line of skinny trees that resembled a procession of penitents, the low scrub, stiff as coral, the outcrop rock, the four boulders furred by dusk and looking, from a distance, like a gathering of tribal elders. The watcher let his gaze travel the entire length of the ridge, slowly, then back again at the same pace. Finally, when he was sure, he tossed his rifle into the air, turned and, without looking back, caught it by the webbing strap and slung it on his shoulder – a flamboyant practised movement. Then he walked back into the pool of yellow light that came from the window of a small single-room hut, slammed the heel of his hand against the door where it always jammed on the frame, and went inside.

One of the three men would check every hour or so. Each knew what to listen for, what to look for. The landscape couldn't hide much in any case, so it was perfect for their purpose. And it was as familiar to them as streets and traffic and buildings to a city-dweller. The man who had just gone inside was reasssured. Scanning the lip of the ravine, he'd found only the expected. He'd seen trees and ragged granite and three boulders.

The other boulder was a man. He hadn't seen that.

It was growing cold up on the ridge. The *maestrale* had been blowing all day, monotonous, insistent. Now it was nearly dark, the wind was bringing the temperature down rapidly. Guerney held the position he'd been maintaining for most of that afternoon: hunkered down on his heels, his knees almost brushing his chin, head down, arms circling his calves. He seemed to be in a mild daze: eyes unfocused, his breathing slow but shallow. Apart from the scarcely perceptible rise and fall of his chest, there was no movement about him. His dull khaki shirt and pants were tight-fitting; leaving the wind nothing to tug at; his hair was cropped; his balance hadn't broken since the moment he'd found the place and settled on the skyline – out in the open where he would be seen but not identified. He knew what the eyes would be seeking: a flattened shape, a silhouette behind a silhouette, any errant vertical motion from the desert floor. Anything furtive.

He'd come on the ravine and the hut some five hours

before, and begun to wait, letting his mind drift into a trance, not looking towards the hut, barely thinking of it. Knowing the men were down there, along with the woman and the boy, was all he needed; and Guerney knew that to look for too long – to concentrate for too long – was to run the risk of prompting that animal intuition that makes someone turn to match a stare.

Now, over the low snuffling sound of the wind, came a ragged laugh from the hut, and a shadow danced crazily for a moment against the light from the window. Guerney pivoted slowly on his heels and stared down the dark slope.

It had taken him four days. The Lear jet had set down at Olbia's Venafiorita Airport at dusk the previous Monday. He'd come in from Milan, deliberately dog-legging and choosing the domestic airport, timing the flight so that he could make the long drive south to Orgosolo during the hours of darkness. The first twenty kilometres or so on one of the island's major roads had been smooth enough. After he'd turned south towards Monti, the road quickly deteriorated: narrow, often rock-strewn, and bordered on both sides by a void. Guerney had made a lot of use of the umbrella-handle gear-shift on the old Renault he was driving as he pushed on into the high granite plateau. He'd driven with utter singlemindedness, never once taking his eyes from the patch of rutted road illuminated by the headlights, never allowing his thoughts to stray from the job in hand.

Three and a half hours later, and four kilometres outside Orgosolo, he'd glanced down at the instrument panel, noting the distance he'd covered. Precisely half a kilometre further along the road he'd swung the car to the left, bouncing over the pitted ground for a short while, then cut the motor. The man had been waiting, completely masked by darkness. Guerney had started to walk towards him before the matchflare bit into the intense blackness. They'd faced each other for a moment, seeing nothing, then the man had taken a few paces forward.

11

'Mr Guerney.' The accent was strong, leaning on the vowels, but the use of 'Mr' had indicated a preciseness. 'Let us walk a short way further from the road.' They'd moved side by side for a couple of minutes, neither man stumbling or hesitating; then the Sard had stopped and sat down abruptly. Guerney had squatted, waiting while the man lit a cigarette.

'Of course you are right. They are here in the Barbagia. I do not know exactly where. Do you know the' – he'd sought for a word – 'the terrain?'

'I haven't walked it. I've studied it with great care.'

'Yes.' The man had seemed thoughtful. 'There are many places to be found and searched. The Gennargentu – the mountains – are a wilderness.' There had been a brief rustling sound, and a small square of white had seemed to float in the dark between the two men. 'I have drawn for you a *carta*. The villages you must avoid, so I have marked them. Otherwise I draw only the tracks. Places I think you should look – search – I have arrowed. This is all I can do. I can think of nothing more.'

Guerney had taken the map, which floated a moment longer, then disappeared like a medium's illusion. The Sard's hand had remained extended to take the envelope that Guerney had produced from a pocket inside his windcheater.

'Mr Guerney' – a meditative tone, as if the unseen eyes might have been narrowed, the invisible head cocked slightly to one side – 'you are a professional man, I know. A man of special qualities. I do not know how you think, or what you will do here – not exactly. But you should understand something of my people.' He'd spoken rapidly, in a low tone, as if eager to get the words said; but a thread of passion had grown in his voice.

'In this province, Nuoro, there has always been abduction. Some would not even think it criminal – a way of *finding* justice, they think. They are bandits and they are shepherds. Both. It is not against nature for them to be both. They think in straight lines. There is the *codice barbaricino* –

code of honour; they do not break it. They will give freely if they desire to; they will not have things taken from them.' Guerney had listened to what he already knew; but he'd listened carefully none the less. 'The Nuorese, these shepherds, will kill you happily. In the villages everyone is watched. They watch each other. There is always one *basista* – the spy – who watches and watches and tells who the victim should be.' There was a pause. Then: 'For years I have fought them . . . opposed. I have no power. I am a policeman. I sit here with you in the dark, take money, tell you these things. I am one of them. What can I do?'

Guerney had waited for several seconds after the man had fallen silent, then stood up. The policeman had got to his feet a moment later and begun to walk back towards the road.

'You'll take the car, as arranged?'

'Yes.' The Sard had taken two or three more paces, then stopped. 'Mr Guerney.' His voice had been low, but carried on the wind. 'You must kill them all. You will almost certainly have no choice. But it is necessary to kill all of them.'

'Yes,' Guerney had told him, 'there is nothing for you to worry about.'

He'd squatted down again to wait for the dawn.

Four days later, he'd found the ravine and the hut. He'd watched from a kilometre away as a pair of hawks hunted along the ridge, quartering the ground, locking on to their prey, then dropping out of sight. Their victims were unnaturally plentiful, so there must have been easy foraging for them, as for the executioners. Scraps – waste food – in surroundings as scoured and barren as those mountains could only mean a human presence. Only humans could afford to be wastrels.

Like a shadow moving on a shadow, Guerney went down the slope towards the hut, his body slung in a crouch, arms loose. Not for a moment did he take his eyes off the door and the window next to it. Twenty yards away he stopped and listened. At first there was nothing to hear. Then there came a breathy drawn-out *Aaaaaaah*, then another, then another, rhythmic and monotonous, the sound a mother makes to soothe a fretful child. Guerney circled to the window, waited motionless for another full minute, then edged his body up to the frame and looked in.

The woman was belly up across the table, her buttocks on the edge, her legs trailing down to the floor. She was wearing only a blouse that was torn down the seam on one side, exposing most of one breast. There was a fading bruise on one side of her face, and her nose looked a little out of true. She was staring at the ceiling, offering no expression; tears were trickling from the corner of the eye that was visible to Guerney, running into her hair and blackening a lock by her temple, but she made no sound of sobbing and no movement.

One man was standing close to the window with his back to Guerney. Another was close to the woman. He was holding a rifle in one hand, gripping the stock; the tip of the barrel was probing between her legs. Like a child prodding a small animal with a stick, he gave the gun a little push, laughing, then turned his wrist. The woman's legs jumped, and she turned her head to one side; her hand, on the rough wood of the table, fluttered as if calibrating the pain. The shepherd laughed again, looking over to where the boy was standing. Behind the boy was a third man, his hand fastened in the child's hair, painfully tight, as if he had dragged his captive to his feet that way and maintained the grip. He was forcing the boy to look, shaking the blond head every now and then by its hair to keep him attentive, to remind him to keep his eyes open.

The noise Guerney had heard was coming from the boy. He stared at his mother fixedly and made the cooing pained sound over and over without closing his mouth. His nose was running, but he made no effort to clean himself. His hands stayed where they were, convulsively kneading the flesh on his stomach.

Guerney moved back from the window and unfastened

two of the buttons on his shirt. Beneath it, he was wearing shoulder-holster strapping that supported a long-barrelled handgun. He edged up to the window again.

The second man had put down the rifle. He was standing in front of the woman, and untying the cord that supported his pants. As they dropped, he shuffled forward a pace and caught the woman at the back of her knees with bent forearms and hoisted her thighs so that her shins were trapped by his shoulders when he leaned forward. He yelled as he pushed into her; then he gripped her upper arms, stretched his neck so that he was looking over her, beyond her, at the far wall, and began to pump.

Guerney let five seconds pass, then moved to the door. He judged the place where the wood stuck, hit it left-handed and stepped inside. His first shot took the woman's assailant in the side of the neck. The man's body convulsed massively, then went rigid; he neither moved nor collapsed; still bowed over the woman, still supporting himself on her arms, he opened and closed his mouth reflexively.

Guerney went past him. The shepherd holding the boy had time to thrust his captive away, but no more. Guerney fired twice, hitting his target high in the chest. He turned again, dropped to the floor, rolled once, took the third man's half-raised rifle to one side with his left hand and brought the gun under his chin so that a line of blood was drawn where the skin grazed. The kidnapper let his rifle drop. Four seconds had passed since Guerney had come into the room.

As if she were removing a mote from her eye, the woman eased out from under the dead man – bracing herself, turning her lower torso as she pulled back; then, when she was free, she raised a foot and kicked him to one side. He went over like a sack of wheat. Before she went to the boy, she pulled on the skirt that was lying on the floor, and looked for a moment at the streaks of blood on it. Then she picked the boy up, pulled his face into her shoulder and went out of the door.

Guerney hadn't taken his eyes off the man he was holding

at gunpoint. When the woman was clear, he turned the barrel so that the sight drew a little more blood, then took the man by the upper lip, painfully, and led him into the open. The woman was waiting, still holding her son. Guerney looked at the shepherd – holding the expressionless stare that was fixed on him – but spoke to the woman. 'Montez jusqu'au sommet de l'arête et attendez-moi là-bas.'

She nodded, but transferred her gaze to the shepherd. Carefully, she set the child down, turning him away to face into the night. Then she walked over and spat, carefully, into the man's face. She continued to look at him but seemed to expect no reaction. Hawking slightly to summon more spittle, she put her face close to his, paused, and spat again. The second time, the man flinched from the venom.

Guerney raised his free hand as if to ward her off. 'Dépêchez-vous,' he snapped, 'nous sommes pressés.'

She stood still, as if there were something else she had to do, then nodded again, picked the boy up, and made for the top of the ridge as she had been bidden. A few minutes later, Guerney joined her. He took the boy in his arms and turned to the woman once before leading off across the high plateau.

It was late the next morning before the dead men were found. A couple of islanders passed the place and were drawn to the hut by the sight of a body in the ravine. This corpse, in particular, puzzled them and they paused to look at it again after they had entered the hut and found the other bodies there.

The man had been shot, cleanly, through the back of the head, but his body had not been left to lie. It was lashed by the ankles to one of the ravine's stunted trees. It hung utterly still, seeming to curl stiffly in the heat, as if some flexion had been trapped by death. It was a ragged dishevelled thing; head down, it appeared awkward and in some way obscenely undignified. It had the abused look of the crows and weasels that English gamekeepers hang from a gallows-branch.

16

2

The river looked lovely in the rain. Each drop plucked a tiny
pock in the sleek surface, so that the entire sinuous length of
water was dimpled like beaten copper. Houses on the bank
seemed dank and sodden; they huddled together and bore
the downpour like horses wintering out.

Guerney looked up at the overlapping sheets of rainwater
cascading along the Plexiglass roof of the riverboat, then
peered out at the drenched chestnut-trees along the redbrick
lip of the Seine. The man sitting opposite him hadn't put a
fork to his *omelette fines herbes*. He was crying discreetly, turning his face so that the tears almost merged with the wash of
water on the angled panes. Now and then, he would collect
errant drops on the side of his left hand. His right hand held
the fork loosely, as if he were uncertain of its true purpose.
Finally he cut the omelette and pushed the forkful to the
edge of the plate.

He said: 'Monsieur, on s'est occupé de ça. C'est fait.' As
he turned his face towards Guerney, he lapsed into English,
as if from politeness now that they were eye to eye. 'In the
name you gave me. To the Geneva bank. All as our agreement. Today it was arranged.' The short sentences prevented his tears from forcing a lesion in his speech.

Guerney nodded. 'As arranged; I'm sure. I thank you.'
He wanted to give the man something, some support, but
there was no convenient gap in his misery. They sat for
another half-mile or so, the engines throbbing remotely
under the brass-riveted planks, the torrent above their
heads echoing the sound. For the most part, the Frenchman

kept his eyes averted, but from time to time he would look up and fix on Guerney, his eyes wide and defiant, like those of a coward meeting his adversary's stare full on in an attempt to face him out. Then the gaze would slide away, glutinously, as the tears returned.

Guerney sighed and looked up the length of the boat. Fat matrons clucked over the *coupes chantilly* while tourists doggedly pressed the shutter releases on four-hundred-dollar Nikons; Paris gave them nothing back. He took the fork from the Frenchman's hand, placed it alongside the plate, put the salad-dish atop the omelette and pushed the whole thing to the edge of the table.

'Monsieur Durand' – his voice was soft and married with the deep flutter of rain – 'you must think of the boy. Your wife . . . it is all in the future, but your wife can be restored. There are many tortures. For her, one was no worse than another. They hurt her, but what difference does it make now? For the boy it will have been worse. Ask her help. Enlist her that way. Both of you must think of the boy.' He felt stupid as soon as it was said.

Durand retrieved the fork, turning it over and over in one hand. He said: 'It is ironic. My wife leaves me; she takes the boy. Not for a lover, not from hatred. She is bored. No, perhaps not that; I should believe her, believe what she said: that love had gone, that she could not recognise the person she had grown to become.' He paused and looked across at Guerney. 'You understand this?' Guerney nodded. 'Yes, I also. I feel it myself. But in loving her I have not changed. That is funny – odd, I think. But the irony – it is that she is now returned to me; that she can go nowhere else.' His attempt at a smile came unstuck. He asked: 'You killed them all, m'sieur?'

Guerney knew it wasn't enough. 'It was necessary,' he replied.

'Yes,' Durand set the fork down softly and looked out at the city – distorted, wavering behind grey slanting rain. 'C'est fait.' He snapped it out. 'I have credited your account. Geneva, as instructed.' He rubbed his hand along

18

his jawline brusquely and smiled a frosty smile. 'You have my gratitude.' Then he pulled back the cold remnant of his lunch and began to eat as though he were famished.

Guerney allowed himself to be drawn into one of the huge hollow Plexiglass tentacles of De Gaulle Airport, giving himself over to the inevitable boredom and inefficiency of air travel. There was little enough about him to make him stand out among the slowly flowing ramp-load of people. The strong narrow features and crisp black hair could have belonged to a Spaniard, an Italian, an Argentinian, and the well-cut casual clothes were as anonymous as a business suit. He was above average height – clearly in good trim as someone might be who paid regular visits to a gym – and his accent hadn't quite enough of a burr in it to turn heads.

Fifty per cent or more of the people who stood on the ramp with him were probably professionals of one sort or another: specialists. A banker or two, a computer engineer, a fashion designer, perhaps, or a linguist. Like them, Guerney had his profession. He specialised in a peculiar, though not at all rare, disease: kidnapping. He had studied it carefully, knew its symptoms, its causes, the forms it took, knew how it was likely to progress. In this he wasn't alone; there were others who did his kind of work. Some were buccaneers, ex-mercenaries, romantics; others were careful negotiators, men whose most effective weapon was the telephone. Guerney was a craftsman. Just as a master carpenter will adapt his technique to the grain of the timber, so Guerney would use instinct to test each situation, inventing a method as he went along. None the less, there were certain ground rules. Guerney wouldn't take on a hopeless case; he wouldn't get involved with officialdom in any guise; he wouldn't offer his services – people came to him when other methods had failed or when they didn't want to involve the forces of law and order. Either way, Guerney would be starting from scratch.

Kidnapping couldn't be called a modern disease. The word was first coined in the seventeenth century, though the

19

lack of a precise term hadn't discouraged those who practised it before that. The Greeks had been good at it. In medieval England abduction had been a common-place revenge on the thwarted suitor; and the Italians have excelled in it through all ages. Kidnapping, hijacking, sieges: they had remained fashionable because, more often than not, they worked. Guerney was a specialist in a growth industry.

3

At Heathrow the inefficiencies were greater and, being English inefficiencies, lacked any humour or style. By the time he'd retrieved his car from the long-stay carpark, Guerney was high on adrenalin and low on patience. He drove snappily to the motorway, overtaking fast-lane cruisers on the inside, then headed west, settling the car down at a steady 100 m.p.h. Less than ninety minutes later, he crossed the Somerset border.

Guerney had been born there, and it was the place he would always come back to. His father had farmed some steep acres in the west of the county. Guerney had lived with his father until he was eighteen. His mother hadn't lived with them. She had been alive then, but she hadn't lived with them. They never spoke of her. There was nothing sentimental about his attachment to the county, nothing winsome in his affinity with the hilly acres and woodlands and the people who lived there. He inhabited his patch with the naturalness of one who instinctively understands country rhythms and country ways and knows where he can best be himself. The isolation was looked for; and, since he never knew how long it would last, carefully conserved.

His house, Druid's Combe, lay a mile back from a minor road on the fringe of the Brendon Forest. It had been a keeper's home: stone-built, square, constructed on high ground looking directly out at the immense, fir-covered, barrow-shaped hill from which it took its name. From the windows at the front of the house, you could look directly down on the delicate swaying tips of conifers and beyond to the twisting rope of white water that wound across the valley. The sound of fast water was always present if you wanted to listen for it.

The house was difficult to find, even if you knew where to look for it; and viewed from outside it was nothing special: squat, solid and workmanlike, it was well-suited to its original purpose. Inside, it was full of small surprises. The furniture was unobtrusive, antique and expensive. The pictures were modern, good and expensive: the best of them a small Bonnard that hung in an alcove, squarely above a walnut bureau. In one corner, set on a slender plinth, was a Giacometti – a group of three-inch figures locked in arrested motion. It could still hold Guerney's attention, despite the fact that he'd owned the piece for a long time.

Now, however, he went past it without a second glance, heading directly for the bedroom. Stripping off the clothes he'd worn for the last thirty-six hours, he balled them up and tossed them into a corner, then walked naked to the shower. He emerged fifteen minutes later, but the water had failed to ease the tension and travel-weariness. For a while, he allowed images and recollections and words to filter through his mind. Then, as if he had actually made a physical gesture, swept them away. After that, he slept for fifteen hours without stirring.

He woke to broad day, the sun high and casting hard bars of light through the bedroom shutters, and lay perfectly still for five minutes. Then he got up and pulled on a pair of running-shorts and a loose T-shirt. He carried his shoes to the door with him and sat on the steps to lace them: fell-runner's shoes, light, with a high padded ankle and spikes for the tufted hillsides. There was a mild breeze that seemed to stir a mist of dust from the topmost branches of the firs.

Guerney walked a couple of paces, then immediately fell into an easy loping run, heading for the hilly pasture behind the house. It wasn't exactly a discipline. It certainly had nothing to do with concessions to fitness or the building of stamina. It was more a kind of separation, a means of withdrawal from all but immediate sensation or whatever the eye might light upon. He felt heavy for the first mile or so. The terrain tested him. Then the metronome of his stride pattern became self-governing, his body collected, and he dwindled to a rhythm, an abstract shape that repeated and repeated against the green and red backcloth of meadow and ploughed field.

Joggers in a city park, bearing the burdens of their paunches round a statutory mile, find the world closing in on them: other joggers, dogs, the haze of traffic fumes, sightseers, the responsibility of the run. They plod dutifully on, each step taking them further, so they believe, from the heart-attack that will otherwise erupt in the quiet of 3 a.m. or at a boardroom lunch. They know that death will come on a day that starts just like any other – toast, tea, inconsequential chatter on the train, a neighbour calling to return the Black & Decker – and they retreat from it, as best they can, in a panicky pattering of expensive shoes, counting their circuits as a child being punished will count the strokes of the cane.

Guerney had known fell-runners who couldn't have told how far they ran, nor could they have told why. Their running was a tradition, and tradition needs neither impetus nor purpose. They weren't hard men, or even men of substance; but now and then they inhabited a place that most people couldn't know of. It lay beyond the limitations of most.

Guerney felt high. He'd been running for eight miles, and his mind was washed of everything, almost dazed. The pain had fallen away first, then thought had stopped chattering at him until the only print he allowed was what his eyes focused on. He traversed the swell of a long low slope below a spinney and then stopped to rest, lying flat and facing away from the sun so that he could look straight up.

A pair of buzzards were quartering the ground, drifting at about a hundred feet and crossing, one just below the other, as they traced the lines of some invisible grid. He watched the broad wings taking the thermal and felt as light, as untrammelled as the birds. He believed he could sense the casualness of their hunting, the easy slide from meadow to meadow, the certainty of success. He watched them until they left, then ran back to Druid's Combe.

He showered, made himself a light lunch, then spent much of the afternoon at his desk in the sitting-room. He phoned his bank and his broker; he attended to paperwork like a good and diligent clerk. In common with many people who choose to live alone, Guerney was a good cook and neat in his habits.

He was solitary by nature, but rarely felt lonely. His past was no more a burden to him than his future. He'd chosen the life – aware that his existence and his nature couldn't admit the trappings that encumbered, or enriched, other men. By choosing one thing, we lose another. Guerney had chosen against wife, children, a sense of continuity, the happy clutter of that way of being. Not that he despised those things in others; he often envied them. But he knew he lacked the talent for ordinary living.

Images came back to him of the journey out of the Sardinian mountains. The woman had been in pain. Walking had been difficult enough, and the forced jog-trot he'd pushed her to must have been well-nigh unbearable, but she'd come through. The child had sat astride Guerney's shoulders, silent, his hands locked around Guerney's forehead. It wasn't until they'd reached the car that the woman had broken down. He'd concentrated on his driving, knowing that he could provide no answer to her anguish and shock. At that moment, her role was that of victim. For her captors, she had been a token, a unit of exchange, something negotiable. That was the thing about codes of honour: they generally protected the people who formulated them, and advantaged them, too. Guerney had no time for such pathetically transparent devices. What had happened in Sardinia didn't oppress him, though. The parts he might learn from had been stored and filed, ready to be drawn on if the occasion demanded. That selectivity was one of the attributes that made Guerney good at his job. He was not devoid of compassion – far from it, but he reasoned that his role demanded, more than anything, an efficient and clinical approach, an attention to the mechanics of kidnapping. The aftermath – therapy, counselling – he left to others, though he knew a great deal about how that worked and why it was necessary.

If he'd retained anything, it was a sense of cold outrage. He'd never defined it, but there existed in Guerney a kind of moral sternness that he'd have laughed at in others. It co-existed with a quirky social anarchism; he accepted no one's rules but his own. The idea of affiliation to society's structures seemed ridiculous, in the same way that politicians and other guardians of our welfare appeared irrelevant. He always assumed such people were lying for gain.

He retreated from all that when he could. The ways of the countryside were known to him by instinct; he'd had to learn the ways of men. And if, at times, there seemed to be little to separate them Guerney knew that, in truth, the difference was great. Animals did what they did unaffected by hatred, or greed, or ambition.

In the early evening, with the horizon thickening and beginning to smudge, he hiked back over part of his route, leaving it, at one field's edge, to climb over a stile and take the lane that led to the village. A dozen houses and three farms: he made for the furthest farmhouse, looked first in the yard then, finding no one, walked through a musty doorless barn and crossed a pathway to the kitchen door. The woman who answered his knock smiled at him, but didn't bother to stand aside, knowing he wouldn't want to go in. As they walked back through the barn, she asked him if he'd had a good trip. He said he had. The weather, she informed him, had been uniformly good. Had it been like that where he'd been? He told her it had been perfect. They were approaching a large pen – thirty feet by twenty – with a shelter at one end.

'She's been fine.' The woman smiled at him again. 'We ran her every day, as usual. She's very fit.'

'Thank you, Mrs Davies.' Guerney was looking directly at the pen. Fifteen yards from it, he whistled softly and the dog turned and bounced towards the gate, reaching it at the same time as her master. She was the classic gypsy lurcher – a collie-greyhound cross with greyhound dominating her shape and colouring. The ears that stood like assegais when she was hunting lay back, close to her head; her deep narrow chest rose steeply from a massive ribcage to narrow hind-quarters. The tiger-stripe of her brindle grew closer and darker about her eyes.

The farmer's wife unlatched the gate of the pen, and the dog emerged, chattering with delight, whipping herself into S-shapes by Guerney's knees, then hopping up to rest her forepaws on his chest. He lowered his head, briefly, so that she could lick his ear. 'Lady,' he said, 'get down, now.' They returned to the farmhouse where Guerney paid the boarding fee. Mrs Davies handed him the slip-leash.

'When you're going away again . . .'

He nodded, and bent to leash the dog. 'Yes, thanks. You look after her wonderfully well. I'm grateful.'

She smiled and half-closed the door. Both were looking for some convenient signing-off remark. Guerney wasn't well known in the village, nor was his presence remarked on any more than his absences. It was too small a place for there to be a round of gossip. He wasn't aloof, however. He'd been seen, from time to time, in the local pub, or buying provisions at the store, where he'd pass the time of day and have something to say about the subjects with which farmers preoccupy themselves: weather and money. He was civil, they said to one another after he'd finished his drink or loaded his groceries into the car, and knew a bit about country ways. They understood him to have business interests abroad and imagined that he must be wealthy. Though he was tall, he had a Celtic look about him: a West Country look. He was dark and blue-eyed, sufficiently attractive for Mrs Davies to wonder whether he'd been married, whether he had a girl in London, girls overseas.

'Well,' she said, 'any time, as I say . . .'

He raised a hand and said goodbye.

The dog walked easily on the leash, keeping to heel through the village, her head held on a plane with her shoulders so that she appeared to have to glance slightly upward in order to look ahead. The posture gave her a look of melancholy surprise which was accentuated by a slight furrow in her brow. When they crossed the stile and came into the meadow, her head lifted a little. Her ears came up to form two loppy right-angles and she began to look around, spot-checking the two or three acres that sloped away from her.

With the first sighting came the transformation that thrilled Guerney every time he saw it happen. Her neck appeared to lengthen, to grow slender and upright, like a gazelle's, and the long leaf-shaped ears stood straight up. Her body assembled along the line of itself: something loose-knit suddenly locking and finding a truer shape. The bevel of her head jutted from the neckline so that the whole resembled an adze.

She was up on her toes, taking slow strides, never once looking away from whatever was fixed in her sight. Guerney tried to look down the beam of her gaze to find the prey himself. While he sought it, he allowed the dog to guide him, feeling the tug on the leash and remaining careful to stay close so that he could keep his thumb on the spring-clip.

Shortly, he found the rabbit. It was upwind some sixty yards away, feeding close to the hedgerow. He altered their line of approach to take the dog a little nearer to the field's edge and gained another ten or twelve yards while Lady leaned on the double thickness of leather that held her. Guerney stopped, eased back on the leash with his right hand as if to lend the dog impulsion, then pressed the release with the thumb of his left.

It seemed, as the collar fell open, that the creature passed him at full stretch. There appeared to be no transition between the dog at his side and the dog in pursuit: so fast that it was the speed of an accident when there's not time to duck, or swerve, or even cry out.

27

She ran a perfect line to the prey, her torso banking at a sharp angle to follow its course, and closed on it in a flurry of screams, then went in over the top to take its neck and put in a couple of paralysing bites. She brought it back and let Guerney take it from her. He put the heel of his hand under its chin and pushed upwards. It flexed, then went immediately limp.

'Good girl. Good girl.' He fondled her ears and slipped the loop of the leash over her head. Then they made for the house, leaving a line of tracks in the dampening grass.

Next morning, he hunted her again, before his run. Later in the day, he drove in to Wellington and visited the post office to see whether any mail had arrived for him *poste restante*. There was none.

This was the pattern of his days for the better part of three months. He ran, hunted the dog, waited for mail. Each evening he would listen to music or reread something from his library. He used his radio for the sole purpose of keeping up with the news: a sort of research. International events might sometimes be of importance to him.

The weather sharpened imperceptibly. One night there was a gale and he went out, at 4 a.m., to stand above the trees, watching their dark spear-shapes roll and unfurl against a clear moonlit sky. The night seemed to shake and howl round him, masking the roar of the stream, and he knew he was where he most wanted to be. In the morning, he found a tree was down, leaning elegantly on its neighbour, roots half-canted out of the red soil. It would help stock his stove during the winter, he thought.

Ten days before Christmas, a letter came.

4

The youth's skin was the dead colour of marble and translucent with sickness. About the jawline and cheekbone, under the eyes, were touches of yellow that made his pallor, if anything, more noticeable. He was lifting a bunch of grapes, not to eat but to offer them, and it was clear that the gesture withered him. His eyes were hot and bright with fever; they regarded the watcher excitedly. His mouth, though, told the real story. It was a satyr's mouth, broad-lipped, turned down slightly for emphasis, the Cupid's bow a heavy sensual cleft. His illness was the illness of excess. He would always offer more; always want more. He was dying of pleasures viciously given and taken. The man who had painted him, Guerney reflected, had known a lot about that particular form of trade. He looked at it for a few more minutes, then strolled to one of the museum's ground-floor windows.

It was a cool, dull day. A thin wind turned leaves on the lawn and lifted the fringe of the mohair scarf worn by the man who sat, reading, on a bench that faced the museum. He was a slim edgy-looking type, balding in the particularly ugly way that occurs when a large circle of hair goes from the crown, though the rest stays thick. Guerney sighed. He wondered when they would make their approach.

He decided to do one more slow round, then move on; and he decided to give Rome two more days. The childish cat-and-mouse business was beginning to irritate him. He stopped by the Caravaggio again. The youth still invited with a trace of a leer, his body made wan by decadence. You

29

could hear the soft corrupt laughter. His naked shoulder glowed like tallow before it falls into the winding-sheet. Guerney looked at it for a while, then went to the door. When he emerged, the slim man was standing by one of the pillars, smiling, extending a hand decorated by two small rings and a delicate identity-bracelet which lay lightly on the hairs circling his wristbone. The hand was small and fastidiously manicured and, when Guerney gripped it, dry like sacking.

'Mr Guerney. How agreeable. I had a feeling I might find you here. I'm so glad I was correct.'

After the handshake had been given, the man held on to Guerney's hand in a manner that was at first annoying for being Roman and fey, then became mildly threatening. He extended his free hand in an overelaborate gesture. 'We can walk this way, perhaps. Would you like to do that?'

Guerney nodded but stayed where he was on the lower step of the doorway. It almost seemed that if he were to step down to the other man's level before unclasping they might set off like that, walking crablike, hand in hand through the Borghese Gardens.

The man released him and immediately set off along one of the narrow paths. Guerney followed, not hurrying, so that the other was obliged to slow his pace before they could continue side by side.

'You are comfortable in your hotel, I trust?'

'It's fine, yes.'

'Good. I am glad. You have been seeing something of the city?' The syllables were fractionally separated – *see-ing, ci-ty* – and clicked in the man's jaw like tumblers. 'The museums, you will have discovered, are closed in the afternoons.' *Clo-sed*. 'The churches also.'

'I'd noticed, yes.'

'It is silly, with so many unemployed.' He shrugged, and lifted a palm in a gesture of resignation. Neither man looked at the other as they walked and spoke. Guerney was looking straight ahead, not knowing where they were heading. His companion cast an occasional glance to left or right. They continued along an avenue lined with statues, each splashed with red paint about the head and shoulders. The man caught Guerney's look of curiosity. 'Children,' he said. 'Young people.' Then, to amplify this: 'Communists.'

'Ah.' Guerney nodded.

They emerged from the avenue by a flight of wide stone steps that led down into the street. A limousine was parked some twenty feet away, and the man made for it, getting there fractionally ahead of Guerney and opening the rear door. A second man sat on the far side of the back seat.

'Well, Mr Guerney, it is good that you could come.' He was still holding the door open, waiting for Guerney to climb in. 'Please sit in the back with my friend.' The pleasantry and the command were seamlessly joined.

They drove in silence, heading north from the city through a muddle of new tower blocks which had sprouted alongside the stained façades and ornate balconies of once elegant houses. The older houses had a shuttered dignity about them, like captives in a place that has fallen to siege, waiting for the end, looking with distaste at a barbarism they have no wish to survive. There was a freeway for a mile or two, then trim suburbs. The first man, now driving, finally spoke.

'I am Joseph. My friend is Peter.' He anglicised the names carefully. 'Soon we are there . . . will be there. Mr Paschini is anxious to see you now.' Joseph had removed his scarf and laid it on the seat beside him; his thin overcoat sported a velvet collar. He was, Guerney decided, dapper; that and meticulous. The care he took in correcting his own English lent a certain weight to 'now'.

The houses became fewer, but larger. After a further half-mile, Joseph swung the car off the road into a well-screened driveway. The house was partly hidden by a row of trees that bisected the acre of lawn. But when they came closer Guerney could see the figure of a man standing four-square in front of the double doors. As he climbed out of the car, Paschini advanced to meet him, his hands clasped behind his back.

31

'Mr Guerney,' he said, then turned immediately to lead the way into the house. 'We will go straight in to lunch, I think. You have not eaten? No. We have something prepared.' He said this over his shoulder, then opened a door and walked into the room first, holding the door open for Guerney. As he closed the door he waved a hand towards one of the two place-settings, occupied the other himself, and at once poured wine into their glasses. Paschini was businesslike rather than hurried or impolite; he had the air of a man who had chaired many meetings. He took a sip of wine, gestured towards the dishes of food set out on the table, and sat back in his chair. 'So, Mr Guerney.'

It was a rich man's house, decorated with great taste and selectivity. Guerney didn't need to look more closely at the pictures in order to identify the painters. He put Paschini at about fifty: a short man, slightly built, greying hair swept back from a narrow face and high forehead. He was dressed casually: jeans and a pale lamb's-wool sweater. His hands, as he helped himself to salad, were delicate and quick.

Guerney allowed a silence to endure between them for a while. Then he asked, 'When was the boy taken, Signor Paschini?'

'Six days ago. Thursday.' He spoke without looking up from his plate. 'On his way to a lecture. At least, he left the house where he lives with other students in order to attend a lecture. He did not arrive at the University. Then came the telephone-call.'

'To his mother.'

'Yes.' Paschini pushed his food to one side, lit a cigarette and looked at Guerney through the smoke. 'What will happen next?' In asking the question, he seemed to lose a little of his assuredness. He pecked at the cigarette, then rotated it nervily, using his thumb and first two fingers. 'What will happen?'

'Why did you wait three days before contacting me after I reached Rome?'

'I was told to wait. Not to wait to see you – of course, they know nothing of our meeting. They said I would hear

32

nothing for some days and should wait for instructions. It gave me the opportunity to . . . regard you?'

'Look me over.'

'Yes, if you like.'

'Why?'

'Why not?'

Guerney smiled briefly and picked up his wine-glass. 'And now you *have* heard from them.'

'Yes, that's right.'

'And they've told you what they want.'

Paschini rolled his cigarette in the ashtray until the tip detached, then crushed it. 'Ten million dollars.'

Guerney tried not to show surprise. 'Have you got ten million dollars?'

'Oh, yes.' said Paschini. 'What will happen?'

'And are you willing to pay it?'

'They might kill David anyway, is that not right?'

'Yes,' said Guerney, 'it is.'

Paschini nodded. He folded his arms on the table and leaned against them as if he were suppressing a sudden pain. 'That is why you are here, Mr Guerney.'

'When I ought to be in America. That's where the boy is, where his mother is. From what you said when we spoke on the phone last Sunday, you've been getting all this at second hand. Your wife has had the direct contact. I'm wasting time here. I've wasted three days.'

'No.' The response was sharp. 'It was necessary for us to see one another. It is not . . . and I am not being callous. David means a great deal to me. He . . . we seldom meet.' He paused and lit another cigarette, then waved it to and fro as if clearing the air of irrelevances. 'In any case, you would not raise ten million dollars from his mother.'

'And you'll get the money if I need it?' Guerney asked.

The other man nodded as if irritated. 'What will happen?'

'I need to know more.'

'You will have done your homework, I suspect.'

'And I need to know more.'

Paschini spread his arms, twisting this way and that on

33

his seat as if to indicate all that lay around him. 'I am a wealthy man, Mr Guerney, as you see. Recently, I have become wealthier. I made my money – you will laugh – by trading in fish: fishmeal, fish products.' He paused, looking across the table for a response.

Guerney shook his head. 'I won't laugh at the fish any more than at the wealth, Signor Paschini.'

The other man held his pose for a moment, like someone weighing objects one in either hand, then let his arms fall to his lap. 'It is easy with a commodity – with fish, for example. You must have a good financial brain. I have one. Apart from that, one needs nothing. A little money. It is not necessary to be artistic or sensitive to what is being produced. It is not necessary, even, to take many risks. One need not please people, or gain their admiration. You produce and sell and manipulate money; and you must be clever with markets sometimes.'

Guerney's eyes strayed to the picture that hung behind Paschini's chair.

'Oh, yes.' Paschini glanced over his own shoulder and back again, to show that he'd taken the point. 'They are good, I know. And safe. Anyway,' he sighed, as if accustomed to admitting a lack of adventurousness, 'recently one of my companies made a successful offer for a competitor. A takeover. The share price of the smaller company went up very considerably. Now I am much richer. It is simple. The newspapers wrote of it, of course; and these people might have learned of it that way. It made my son a victim.'

There must have been a bell under the table or a means of observing what was going on in the room, because a man-servant came in bringing coffee. He cleared the dishes and set their demitasses before them. They both watched him, and he was conscious of that – of having broached their talk.

Guerney was aware of a mild headache flickering behind his eyes. He tilted his head and ran the fingertips of one hand across his forehead, while Paschini poured coffee for the pair of them. The conversation which had lapsed with

34

the arrival of the manservant seemed momentarily lost. They sat in silence, Paschini smoking a cigar – leaning heavily against his chairback and watching the line of smoke make oxbows and curlicues as it rose. Now and then he would break it with a slow cloud from between his lips. Guerney looked towards the tall french windows, fingertips still resting on his brow. Shafts of sunlight entered the room through a high window, and swathes of cigar smoke rolled voluptuously in each, enveloping a scribble of dust-motes. The silence was neither embarrassed nor companionable. Each man had fallen, for a while, into his own thoughts.

'Let us walk, Mr Guerney.' Paschini wagged his cigar towards the french windows. They emerged onto a broad expanse of sparkling lawn, broken here and there by topiaried hedges. Beyond the furthest hedge lay a swimming-pool with a small bar built across the near angle at the shallow end. A teenage boy was patrolling the tiled edge, trawling for insects and leaves with a net attached to a pole. They skirted the pool and came into an ornamental garden: shrubs, vast stone urns crammed with flowers, statuary, little sculpted pools here and there with carp shivering and darting just below the surface. In their walk through the garden, the fish were a constant flicker in the corner of Guerney's eye.

'They say you are good.'

'Who?'

Paschini shook his head, as if to indicate that Guerney should have known better.

'It is said you have always been successful.'

'So far.' Guerney peered into a pool where the fish were congregating, head on, around some tiny object, darting at it in awkward little rushes, backing away, then bumping in again. 'It doesn't have much significance. Each time is dif-ferent. There aren't any averages. If I'm to help, I must go to America tomorrow. Can you arrange that for me?'

'If you like.' They were reaching a part of the garden which would give a full view of the city. With each step, a new segment fell into sight, houses and domes thickly clustered, with a blue line of haze scoring the skyline. Paschini put out a hand, not to grasp Guerney, but simply to bring him to a halt, then half-turned, looking upwards at the taller man, intending this time not to be denied an answer.

'What will happen?' he asked.

'They will give instructions about how the money is to reach them. I will ask for proof that David is still alive . . .'

Paschini broke in. 'Is he?'

'I don't know. I suspect so.'

'He could be dead already?'

'Yes.'

'Will you tell his mother of this possibility?'

'Probably not.'

'I would sooner you did not.'

Guerney shrugged. 'Then, I won't; unless it's necessary for some reason. I can't think of one.'

'Please try to avoid it.'

'I promise I will.' Guerney turned and started back along the path.

'After that?'

'I really don't know. It's never the same way twice. There are signs to look for. Spoor. They will have to talk to David's mother, relay orders; they will behave this way or that – give something of themselves away. I will try to get close to them without their knowing or getting jumpy. I won't know how until I've listened to them – what they say, how they say it. There will be traces of them – every mortal thing leaves some trace. I must get close to them; that's the way it works.'

They had emerged by the pool. The youth was still trailing the net, and flicking it, from time to time, in a neat professional sort of way, to ensure that his catch stayed trapped in the narrow part of the mesh. As Guerney watched him, he pulled lengthily on the pole one last time, then raised it from the water with a flourish, slapped it down on the poolside and walked briskly away. The two men started across the lawn towards the car. Peter and Joseph were waiting there, lounging against the bonnet. Paschini glanced from side to side, then briefly back towards the pool, as if he were assessing the value of the property they had walked through – as if he were the visitor.

'When David was a child,' he said, 'I mean eight, or perhaps nine – before his mother and I parted and she went home to the States – we all lived here. It was pretty much the same: the house and the grounds. We went – I took him – shooting once. Not the usual Italian shoot – you know, songbirds, anything that flies – more the English style of thing. He cried all the time that birds were being killed, and finally we came away. I lost my taste for it after that. Is that right?' He was querying the idiom. 'Lost my taste?' Guerney nodded. 'He is seventeen now, and he speaks like an American – which he really is, I suppose.'

As they got closer to the car, Joseph and Peter straightened up. Joseph opened the driver's door and retrieved his overcoat with the velvet collar. They were still out of earshot, though, when Paschini asked: 'Will they hurt him, Mr Guerney, do you suppose?'

'It's not possible to know.' Guerney was aware that his enunciation and the way in which he was emphasising words echoed Paschini's own rather prissily correct English, as if he might be better understood for speaking that way, and he was annoyed with himself for having fallen into that trap. He supposed it had not gone unnoticed. 'It is better not to think of things that way.'

Paschini said nothing, but clapped him on the back in a surprising genial gesture, and they continued to the car. This time it was Joseph only, his hands already resting lightly on the steering-wheel, but Guerney still elected to get into the back. He pressed the switch that activated the window.

Paschini bent slightly at the waist, looking in at Guerney. 'The fee is agreeable?'

'The fee is agreeable.'

'You will communicate with me?'

'Of course,' said Guerney. 'So long as it's possible.'

37

Paschini bobbed his head in agreement, then stepped away from the car and walked backwards up the steps until he stood within arm's length of the door. As the car began to move, he turned and went inside.

He had always stayed at the same hotel in New York: a rather dull, efficiently run, faintly antiquated place in midtown, too small for conventions or charity dinners, not quite fashionable, and discreetly overpriced. She had left a message in the name of Caroline Rance, her maiden name, as she had said she would. No one had called her Paschini for eight years. The call-back number was that of the Plaza.

He took the phone over to the window and looked towards Fifth Avenue. The weather was bitter. On the cab ride in from JFK, he had looked out at a pale steely sky that seemed to press luminescence down into the precise geometric gaps of the city's silhouette and remembered how you were always conscious of the frenetic, exhilarating, violent life of the place – the sheer volume of energy packed in and barely contained. It was like a vast generating plant, those gigantic glittering towers and the grid system below humming day and night. A few snowflakes rocked past his fourteenth-floor window, followed by a flurry which was borne up by the wind for a moment so that it fell and rose and danced on the spot just in front of his eyes.

He made the call, and they rang through to her room, and she answered seeming a little breathless even though she'd picked the phone up on the first ring. Yes, she'd been waiting for his call; she was anxious to see him. No, she hadn't heard any more from the men who had taken David. She was waiting to be told what to do. Would he come over to the Plaza – could he come right away?

He walked the eight blocks through a thicket of late-afternoon shoppers, roller-skaters in leg-warmers and ear-muffs, beggars, assorted Santas and a liberal sprinkling of Yuletide crazies. Down at street level, the snow was thinner and less playful. The stores were laden with consumer durables, all replaceable in a second. Jewellers' windows were part-masked with trickily cut templates, showing off just one or two pieces. The exquisitely dressed dummies in Bonwit Teller looked over their shoulders, frozen-faced with superiority. There was nothing in the city so expensive that it could not be bought.

Her suite at the Plaza was spacious and overlooked the park. She ushered him in much as a secretary might have, taking his coat and hanging it tidily in the closet, offering him a drink, instructing him to take a seat. It was almost as if she were about to say: 'I'll be out in a minute if you'd care to wait.' But after she'd settled him she went back to the drinks-tray and poured herself a stiff Scotch before sitting down to face him, and the illusion of brisk efficiency was lost. She was haggard about the mouth: a raggedness that had come from tears and weariness. She was blonde and slim and naturally pale – attributes that made her frailty more apparent. After each sip of Scotch, she put the glass down so that the slight tremble in her hands wasn't given away by the chiming of ice.

'It's been a week, Mr Guerney. A week. They told me to come to New York, to this hotel. They know where I am. They said that something would be delivered – instructions, something. Nothing has happened. What does it mean?'

'It needn't mean anything.' Guerney made his tone businesslike. He wasn't there to console. Thus far, she had borne her burden alone and she would have to go on doing that. He couldn't afford to become her support even though he knew what it must be costing her to stay in the room, waiting to be contacted, able to talk to no one or seek reassurance. She was seeking it now. She said: 'You're an expert at this. Cesare told me.'

'Yes.' He lifted his drink. 'There are things that both of us must do. I have one or two people to see. You will have to stay here and wait. I'll let you know where I am, always. As soon as they are in touch with you, you must let me know. You've told them you will pay what they're asking?'

'Cesare has guaranteed it, yes.'

'Then, it's likely that they will be working out how best to

39

lay hands on the money – systems of transfer. It's a large sum. Did they let you speak to David?'

She shook her head. Her eyes were fastened on Guerney's face, as if she expected to find there the certainty that her son would be returned to her: as if his lips might move to form the words that would make it plain to her that soon, very soon, everything would be as it once was, her life normal again, and the boy's, and this suite, this furniture, this view of the park, all things that she could begin to forget.

He said: 'You haven't been sent anything? Any evidence that David is still alive?'

She winced, but continued to look at him. 'They just said to wait. And that if I told anyone . . . the police . . . that David . . . that I wouldn't see him again.'

'Who told you this?'

'It was a man. I don't know . . . there wasn't anything special. An American accent. New York, I think. Ordinary. He was calm; he didn't shout. He sounded like a businessman doing a deal.' Finally, she switched her gaze and picked up her drink. 'When he'd finished, he just hung up. It wasn't a conversation.'

'This was in Woodstock?'

'Yes.'

'And you came directly to New York?'

'I told people that Cesare was going to be here – that it would be a chance for David to see his father. Mr Guerney . . .' She paused, looking for a casual tone, reaching for her glass with a casual gesture, but she was shaky, her timing was out. Her voice snagged in her throat, and she rapped the glass with her knuckles, almost catching it before it tumbled to the floor spilling whisky and ice.

The mishap broke her. She began to weep as she went down on her knees, pointlessly scraping the chunks of ice back over the lip of the glass, then abandoning both to rock to and fro on hands and knees like an autistic child, her tears falling straight from her eyes on to the spillage. She was saying something hoarse and incomprehensible, something not

40

meant to be deciphered, a lilting wail of vowels becoming sobs.

Guerney waited while the anger and fear churned in her; he neither spoke nor moved to help; and eventually she righted herself, feeling backwards with one hand for the edge of the chair and shuffled on to the cushion, wiping at her eyes and nose with the underside of her wrist, taking a little series of indrawn breaths as she recovered. She sat for a moment staring at her knees, then said what she had meant to say: 'What will happen now?'

'I've told you,' Guerney answered. 'You wait. I shall be seeing a couple of people. We need to have instructions.' He got up and collected his coat from the closet and walked over to the door. She didn't follow; she stayed where she was, but looked up at him with a final question already formed on her lip.

'What will they do to him?' she asked. 'Will they hurt him, Mr Guerney?'

It was snowing more thickly as he walked back to his hotel. Although darkness had fallen, the city was never dark. Above the band of poisonous-looking sodium light, the snowflakes were invisible; if you looked up, you could see what appeared as a ceiling of snow and a fall of orange feathers apparently issuing from a point not thirty feet above the streets. On shoulders and hats, in shuttered doorways, it became white again. In the streets it quickly merged to a grey pulpy slush.

Back in his room, he poured himself another drink, half-dialled a number, then had to ring off to consult his book for the correct placing of the last two digits. He was answered on the eighth ring. A slightly muffled voice said: 'Yes?'

Guerney smiled at the accustomed abruptness. He said: 'Hello, Rachel. It's Simon Guerney.'

'So there you are. Hang on a minute.' There was a pause, after which her voice came through more clearly. 'I'm eating a peanut-butter sandwich. Sorry. I got your weird cable. Where are you – at that bijou hotel as usual?'

'That's right.'

41

There was another gap in the conversation while she filled her mouth again. 'So', she said indistinctly, 'business or pleasure, Simon?' He said nothing, and she didn't press the point. 'I won't be in the city tomorrow,' she continued. 'I'm taking a break – going to Long Island. Beyond the Hamptons, you'll be pleased to hear. I've got some vacation that has to be taken before the solstice. Whaddya think?'

'I'd like to stay in Manhattan.'

'OK, stay. I'm going to Long Island. I've paid. Is it that urgent?'

'It might be. I need to see you, though.'

'Need to. So it's business. OK, I'm not insulted. But that's where I'll be tomorrow noon, Simon.'

'I'll come,' he said.

They took the Jitney bus from Grand Central Station next morning. Snow had fallen heavily during the night, but the weather was now clear – so clear that the sky's piercing blue was hard to look at. The light was refracted from windows and from snow-piles the Sanitation Department's ploughs had compacted on the avenues. Those in the know were wearing down coats and sunglasses. Rachel was wearing just that. A pair of reflector shades and a hip-length, gunmetal-grey padded jacket that made her torso ridiculously bulky. When they boarded the bus, she took the coat off and crammed it into the overhead rack, then flopped down next to Guerney, looping her arm through his.

They had known one another for six years or so, their friendship surviving several attachments and one near-marriage. Their meeting, at an embassy party in Washington, had led to a swift intense affair which both knew couldn't last. He'd thought that Rachel Irving was one of the most beautiful women he'd ever met; he'd also thought she could be useful to him – even then, most of what passed across her desk in the course of a day's work had been classified. Since that time, Guerney's work had changed; he stood well outside the world of diplomacy and daily intrigue. She was still useful, though, from time to time; and still beautiful.

During the ride, they caught up on their news. She knew better than to ask him leading questions. It wasn't until they had checked into the beach-front hotel and colonised their cabin with cosmetics, tooth-brushes, his razor and the few clothes they had brought for the weekend that she asked: 'Is it local?'

'More or less.' He'd conceived the vague notion of going for a run on the beach: the tide was out and there was enough firm sand. He shrugged out of his clothes, apart from his briefs, and threw an aged tracksuit, some shoes and a pair of Nike socks on the end of the bed.

'I'll go a mile with you,' she said.

'OK.' He looked up in surprise as she took a warm-up suit out of her bag, together with some expensive New Balance shoes.

'It's become fashionable, Simon – hadn't you heard?' He looked up at her and smiled wryly, picking at a knot in one of his laces. Then he watched her uncover her body and set the shoes aside, knowing that they weren't going for a run – not quite yet.

She was (he remembered each characteristic just before she displayed it) the shape of a Modigliani: small, high perfectly globular breasts; a long narrow body showing the ribcage sharply as she lifted her arms; sloping hips and rounded thighs, a crisp neat pubic triangle. Noticing his eyes on her, she walked over to where he sat on the edge of the bed and stood before him, letting him encircle her waist. He dropped a palm to either buttock and she followed the pressure, jutting her pelvis towards his face. She grinned down at him as he rimmed the tiny tight declivity of her navel with his tongue, then stepped over him to sit half-upright against the pillows, cupping his head as he turned and drawing it down, again, to her navel, then lower, watching him at work between her jacked-apart thighs, then not watching, her eyelids drooping with pleasure. Only her fingers were busy, making it easy for him, and her hips sawed slightly, echoing his rhythm. When she'd taken enough, she let him brace her thighs with his forearms and move into her. She said, 'Take a long time,' and he dipped his face to hers, kissing her lightly, then running his tongue around the back of her lips and across the gums, to leave there the strong saltiness of her own taste.

Guerney had put on his tracksuit, run four miles in an icy wind and returned to find her still lying there, her thighs loose and spread, dozing in the half-light.

He showered and emerged, snapping on an overhead light to see her the better. 'You look wonderful,' he said. 'You look like a whore.'

She squinted up at him and dropped a hand, the forefinger extended, between her legs. 'I've often thought,' she said dreamily, 'that, had I been guaranteed rich, young, clean, athletic tricks, I'd have made a terrific whore. Sadly, life isn't like that. You have to take the smooth with the rough, as it were.' She turned over, displaying a sweet, firm, white bikini-patch. 'I'm hungry.'

'It's four-fifteen,' he told her. 'Too early and too late for everything.'

'An outmoded concept in a consumer's Valhalla, chum.' She rolled off the bed and stretched. 'There are no discreet pauses in consumption here in the Land of the Free. If you want it, and you can pay for it, someone will sell it to you – any time, eight days a week.'

He lifted the bedside phone and looked questioningly at her. 'No,' she said, waving an arm and making for the shower. 'I'll be less hungry by dinner-time – all to the good.'

She spent no more than five minutes in the bathroom, emerging with a scrubbed look, her hair slicked back behind her ears. She'd wrapped herself in a long white bathrobe and arranged its skirt about her knees as she sat cross-legged on the bed. 'OK,' she said, 'now it can be business. You said it was local.'

'New Hampshire – in so far as that matters.'

'Tell me.'

'A week last Thursday, a boy – a teenager – was kidnapped on his way to college. His father is Cesare Paschini.'

44

He paused, waiting for a nod of recognition, and got it. 'His mother lives in Woodstock. The boy lives near campus in a student rooming-house. They've asked for ten million dollars.'

'All news to me.'

'I'm glad to hear it. Paschini summoned me to Rome, spent some time rather clumsily circling me, finally put me on the case.'

'The mother?' She got up for a cigarette, rooting round in her bag.

'Sitting in a three-hundred-dollar-a-night suite at the Plaza, waiting for a phone-call and going quietly crazy. They've been separated for years. The boy lives with her. Father's a stranger.'

'But prepared to shell out.'

'Sure.'

'What about the police?' She asked the question a trifle sharply.

'You know I almost always tell them to do that.'

'Unless . . .'

'Unless it's not going to help for some reason or another.'

'And in this case it wouldn't?'

'You tell me.'

She thought back over what he'd told her. 'The phone-call the mother's waiting for – it's the follow-up call, instructions about money where and when.'

'That's right.'

'And the boy was taken' – she paused a second – 'eight, nine days ago?'

He raised an eyebrow and lifted one hand, palm out: *Voilà.*

'He's dead?'

'No' – Guerney shook his head – 'no, it doesn't feel like that. Too professional. A murdered victim doesn't usually result in silence. There'd be a flurry of phone-calls, attempts to get the money quickly, other evidence of panic. They certainly wouldn't have stayed silent at any rate. You didn't use to smoke.'

'No.' She looked down somewhat ruefully at the cigarette clipped between her fingers. 'Evidence of pressure: it's hard on the way to the top. What *do* you think?'

'I'm not sure I know what to think.'

'What do you want of me, Simon?'

'Paschini's rich, and lots of money usually means lots of complexity – irons in fires, clandestine connections, unlikely involvements. I need to know more about him. Your people are going to have something on a man as powerful as that: someone at the Rome embassy, maybe.'

'Sure,' she nodded, 'I can ask . . . You mean it might be political – what?'

'It could be anything; I might be wrong and find out it's a straight-forward ransom job that's gone wrong for some reason.'

'But you doubt that.'

'Yes, I doubt that.'

'OK,' she said. 'I'll ask. I guess I can take a couple of hours out of my vacation to make some phone-calls. It shouldn't be difficult. It'll mean the risk of a few people becoming curious. Questions might be asked.'

'I know.'

'When are you going back to the city?'

'Tomorrow afternoon, I expect.'

'OK. I'll call you Monday night.' She had smoked her cigarette to the stub and was holding it delicately upright, balancing a tall pillar of ash. 'They have a gym in this place – but I gather that if you walk straight through it there's a steam room and a jacuzzi beyond. I'm for that.' She tossed her stub into a waste-basket. 'Then a drink, then another, then dinner.' She smiled at him. 'I may have neglected to say this, but it's good to see you – despite the fact that your motives are pretty shabby.'

They had an early dinner at the less fancy of the hotel's two restaurants. Like most other people there, they were dressed casually in warm-up suits – it was the style of the place, a so-called spa that offered a week of fitness programmes to the well-fleshed well-heeled. Pear-shaped women could be seen at all hours of the day, beached in leotards on the floor of the workout room. Middle-aged execs carried their bellies from one Nautilus machine to the next, puce with effort but glowing with virtue. And just the same people would be seen, not long afterwards, forking cannelloni into their mouths with a stoker's action, clearly believing that their day-time flirtations with fitness permitted evenings of excess.

Guerney and Rachel went back to their cabin to raid the mini-fridge for their after-dinner brandies. Despite the cold, they took the drinks out on to the tiny porch that screened them from their neighbours and faced directly out to sea. Earlier, in the bar, they had sat at a table near the window to watch the sunset: an event so spectacular that it had provoked timeless responses of deep cynicism in them both. There had been a line of brilliant red at what seemed the sea's lip. Clouds like ostrich plumes had been stained with the same colour on their undersides, and the massive mauve blush in the sky became a band of pure aquamarine, brittle, and falling through nameless shades to its brightest hue, just above the horizon. 'Well,' Rachel had remarked, 'the old clichés are the worst, wouldn't you say?'

Now she stooped to rest her forearms on the rail that bordered the porch and looked at shifting tracks of moon-light on the sea. 'I'm hunting for something mystical in all this,' she observed. 'I'm waiting for some tiny revelation to come skittering across the wave-tops – some sudden insight into the mysterious relationship between Man, the music of the spheres and a Bloomingdale's account.'

Guerney didn't reply. He moved behind her and eased down the waistband of her warm-up pants until it was around her lower thighs and ran his fingers lightly between her legs. She chuckled and made an awkward shuffling motion with either foot to stand as spraddle-legged as the constriction would allow. He held her hips and slid into her, looking over the slope of her back at the vacuum of the sea and the tracers of light, then took up a slow casual rhythm,

almost absent-minded, the half-attentive attitude of someone pushing a child on a swing while holding a conversation. Now and then she would mutter briefly, or make a tiny
mew of approval. After a time, though, her breathing
quickened a trifle and there came an almost imperceptible
countermovement: her buttocks nudged the tops of his
thighs and she began to make a tiny circling motion from the
waist. Finally, she used one hand to push the pants to her
knees and leaned further out across the rail, lowering her
head between arms that were all but outstretched; then she
moved her feet further apart and tilted her ass up.

She said something and moaned, and spoke again, but
her voice was muffled and had the same timbre as the sea.
He saw a light go on, briefly, in a back room of the main
hotel building, and a shape passed to and fro by the curtained window. Somewhere, a generator that must have
been humming all the time shut down.

The boy had been conscious of the darkness, then light, and
now darkness again. The light had been hard and white,
almost filling his vision; but at its edges had been the almost
recognisable shapes of things, as if he were viewing a sun-
shot lake through a fisheye lens, so that objects on the shore
receded and were distorted.

He knew he was lying down. He was cold and, though he
didn't know it, they had given him a blanket. Sentences that
he might have been speaking passed through his mind, but
he couldn't make sense of them.

There had been a short journey – he retained sensations
of being jostled and jolted. There had been a house. The
memory of these things came and went like the little myths
of childhood. His body felt insubstantial – hands and feet
too remote to be accounted for, head a helium-filled balloon,
paper-thin, that wafted on its tether with the slightest
draught.

There was a noise, a vibration of sound, that drummed
on the taut skin of his forehead. Someone a few feet away
laughed and looked out of a window, then accepted a

cigarette with a preoccupied air. A second person struck a match for both of them, kindled the cigarettes and extinguished the flame with a fierce exhalation of smoke. A remark was made about the boy, then a question asked. The answer was a slow shaking of the head – reassurance. The boy was aware of none of this. He sensed a change in the noise. It seemed to him that it was a piece of music, but he could only hear the opening chord endlessly extended, a fluctuating monotone trapped in his skull and excluding everything else. Soon, though, he was not even conscious of knowing this. The sound enveloped him and he might as well have been sleeping.

5

The snow had disappeared almost without trace. The bag
ladies were back on the streets, mingling with the last-
minute shoppers whose arms were laden with expensive
trifles that would burden them only for a day. New York,
Guerney had long ago decided, reinvented itself on a daily
basis. Because nothing grew, nothing seeded. Its inhabitants
emerged each day remembering their lines, their stage
directions. Some were deadly ad-libbers, fired by the anticipation of stealing the show.

When he collected his key from the hotel desk, they gave
him a message timed at half an hour earlier. He went
straight to the Plaza and, when he got no reply from her
suite, settled down to wait in the lobby. He knew there was
nothing amiss – or knew, at least, that no one had harmed
her. She arrived in less than ten minutes, trailing a shopping bag, looking this way and that across the lobby
expecting to find him; but when she did, her face lost its wan
look and took on the expression of someone who had already
detected betrayal and has found the culprit. She walked past
him to the bank of elevators.

He got up and went to stand behind her as she watched
the numbers tick off. Her blonde hair was spread thickly
over the collar of her mink coat, dragging sideways against
the fur when her head moved, just slightly, to make sure
that he was in attendance. They rode up in silence – she
staring straight ahead as others got in and out at various
floors. He followed her down the corridor, waiting patiently
while she juggled with bag and key, then followed her into

50

the room. She put the bag down on a table by the window and stood there, motionless, resting her hands on it as if to trap her purchases.

'I phoned the place on Long Island, and they said you'd checked out.' She was anxious, not angry, and they both knew it, but she had to try the role.

'I was on a bus when you called,' he said. 'I had to go there. I'm sorry.'

Her head went down, and she let her arms fall to her sides. The bag toppled over, spilling a few packages. 'Look at these.' She nudged them with her hand, making room for a seccond little avalanche of bright wrappings and bows. She lifted the bottom and gave it a shake, emptying the whole thing out.

'Look at these. I went to your hotel: they said you'd just gone out. I knew you'd be coming here. Coming back up Fifth, I – ' She gestured miserably at the heap of gifts.

He held out a hand for her coat, and she shrugged out of it meekly like a child and asked for a drink. Like a child, she was avoiding the subject that would make Guerney the person he was, would make his purpose in her life what it was – delaying things just for a second or two, at least until she got the drink.

When he brought it over to her, she spoke before sampling it. 'Someone called about an hour and a half ago. He said they would call again later – tonight, tomorrow morning, some time soon. He asked who you were. He was angry.'

'That was all?'

'Yes, all.'

'No instructions, no threats?'

'The call only lasted . . . it couldn't have been above twenty or thirty seconds.'

'What was said about me?'

She laid her glass alongside one cheek, to cool it down with the ice. He thought that she looked wearier than before: this new contact with the kidnappers hadn't revived her. 'He said: "Who is this man Guerney? What is he doing?" Something of that sort.'

'What did you say?'

She chewed her lip. The telephone-call had been so crucial

51

to her that she'd let it slip without remembering much of what had been said. It hadn't gone as she'd hoped – there had been no promises, no bargaining, no bidding up and down in order to reach an agreed solution that would give David back to her. For days, she had prowled the rooms of her suite, moving in a complex pattern that drew the shape of a pentagram between the points in each room where a telephone stood. Its lines were overscored by her restless to-ing and fro-ing. A telephone was always in her vision, it seemed. Its false alarms (calls from the desk, from room service, one call from Cesare) had left her fizzing and nauseous.

She ached for the one event. She had so willed it to happen that her strength had all but gone; and when the call came its effect was to leave her more desperate than before. It had been cruelly brief and inconclusive. Her senses, over-pitched, had blurred everything.

'I've been thinking about that. I think my words were: "He's a friend; he's just a friend of mine." I've tried to remember exactly. Then he said, "Be careful," and he used my married name. "Be careful; lies won't help David." And then he put the phone down. I think that was it.' She shook her head – uncertain – and turned towards the window in an effort to check her tears.

Guerney said: 'We'll wait. I'll wait here with you.'

She nodded and smiled brightly to let him know that he had said the right thing. 'A drink? I'm sorry.'

He asked for a Scotch and soda, and she moved briskly to the drinks-table to mix it, then put it into his hand as she passed back to the gaudy cornucopia of the bag and its tumbled gifts. One by one, she restored them, packing them cleverly in order to find a space without stressing the bag. Now and then, she would remove a rectangle or a sphere and replace it with something that fitted more neatly. Her movements were too jaunty to be evidence of recovery. Eventually, the package was just so, and she took it into the bedroom to store it somewhere out of sight. When she returned, she collected her own drink, and switched on the television before joining Guerney on the long sofa.

They sat at opposite ends. Five women, and a man who was obviously the star of the show, were singing carols in voices so oily that it was almost blasphemous. The women wore red mini-dresses with fur-trimmed hoods. They sang through their smiles, moving their arms and long legs in unison behind the star who was doing 'Silent Night' as if it were a ballad, lifting his arms and his eyes in reverence, injecting little trills or a mellow vibrato into the drawn-out notes. He was wearing a dress shirt and a tan that seemed three skins deep.

Caroline was making a little home, Guerney saw; a nest. It was a frail gesture and, like him, she saw the sadness in it. Easing off her shoes, she looked across at him briefly, then tucked her feet up on the sofa. They watched television for an hour or so, and from time to time she cried discreetly, bowing her head and raising a hand to shield her face.

Guerney had telephoned her before leaving Rome – a few instructions, details of his arrival-time – and had asked for photographs of the boy. She had compiled them but was reluctant to let them go: they made a talisman, and she wanted to hold on to her luck. Now she took one or two out of her bag, together with the cigarette that had been her original intention, and leafed through them. She wasn't ready, yet, to talk about David; but, then, Guerney thought, there was little he really needed to know.

The call came early on Christmas morning: at about seven-thirty.

From the sitting-room, Guerney said, 'Caroline,' sharply but there had been no need. In the bedroom, she lifted the receiver on the third ring, as he'd instructed her, and in the same instant he lifted the extension.

After she'd spoken her name, there was a pause; then a man said: 'We don't have much time, so try not to interrupt. I'm calling to report on David. He's well.' Caroline began to say something, but the man spoke across her. 'Listen. We've moved him. He's no longer in the country.'

This time he didn't talk her down immediately.

'What do you mean – out of the country? What do you mean?' There was panic in the words – only contained by the need to know what would be said next.

'It's safer for everyone, including David.'

'Is he all right?' The pitch of her voice rose to an edgy thinness at the end of the question, despite what she was doing to control it.

'Yes,' said the man. 'There isn't time for that. We want to be told about Guerney.'

She said what Guerney had instructed her to say. 'He's a friend; I told you. It's the truth. But I want him to help. I can't do this on my own.' She started to cry, and through her sobs, said: 'I really can't.'

The caller didn't speak for a few seconds – not out of any concession to her tears, it seemed, but to take a short while to think. 'OK,' he said; but she'd spoken on top of his response and didn't hear it, and there followed an awkward gap in the conversation – farcical and inappropriate, threatening to be the first in a series of clashing words followed by shared pauses while each waited for the other's remark.

'Are you there?' She was terrified that the man's reaction to what she'd said about Guerney had been to hang up. 'Are you there?' she asked. 'Oh God, oh God . . .'

The man's voice said: 'OK, you want him to be your representative, right?' She said she did. 'OK. If he's not listening to this call, tell him we'll phone back to tell him what he must do. We know you haven't told the police or anyone so far. Tell him to do the same. We're not having any trouble. David's fine right now, but we don't want any trouble – do you understand that?'

She nodded as if she could be seen, but didn't speak. The caller didn't insist on her reply: there was no need. 'OK. We might call today, or maybe tomorrow. It will be about the money – and how to pay it. Then David comes back to you, right?' She said yes; but either he didn't hear her, or wanted some stronger response, because he raised his voice a little and asked again: 'Right, Mrs Paschini?'

'Yes,' she said weakly, 'please,' and sat holding the phone to her ear listening to the dialling tone until Guerney came in, took it from her and placed it back in its cradle.

He was thinking what an odd, starchy word 'representative' was. He wasn't surprised that they knew of him, though he was mildey curious about how they had come to know his name. He moved to the bedroom window and looked down through the gap that Caroline had left in the drapes. There was little traffic: cabs cruising the outskirts of the park, a few cars on Fifth Avenue. The cross-town streets looked almost deserted. Runners entered the park at the rate of about one every thirty seconds. Two beggars had staked their pitches – one on either side of the approach to the hotel. There was the usual percentage of people just hanging out – kids, bums, others with nowhere special to go. For the most part, the few New Yorkers on the streets appeared, as usual, to be full of purpose: getting there, or hurrying back. He looked intently for a minute or two, but couldn't find anything that mattered.

She had thrown back the bedclothes and turned to sit on the edge of the bed when she'd answered the phone, but hadn't changed her position since then. He wasn't searching any more, though he stayed with his back to her, peering out. She asked him what the call meant.

'It looks as if they want to move things along.' He wasn't at all sure that it was true, but it was what she wanted to hear. 'I think that the next call will be today, not tomorrow.'

'They were happy with what I said about you?'

'It seemed that way, didn't it?'

'We ought to call Cesare.'

'Yes,' he said, 'you do it. Say that I'll contact him soon – when I know about the arrangements for the money.'

'Why have they taken him away?' It was the question she had most wanted to ask.

'It's never the same way twice,' he told her. 'There's no real pattern. Sometimes they make it up as they go along; it depends on what happens – how events change actions. I don't think moving him was spontaneous, though; probably part of their way of organising things from the onset – they'd always meant to do it.'

'Will it make difficulties?' she asked him. 'I mean, does it put David at greater risk?'

He shrugged slightly. 'I don't see why it should: no.' That much was true. He didn't believe much of what he'd been saying, though. The delays were wrong; so was the way the kidnappers prevaricated over their instructions concerning the ransom. Of course, the boy could be dead; he wondered for the first time whether that really might be it. But they'd have to know that evidence to the contrary would be asked for: that man on the phone hadn't sounded panicky or stupid or unsure of how to act.

Guerney didn't know what it meant, or how to progress matters. He felt like a climber working on a familiar pitch, who discovers that where his handholds should be is a wall of utterly smooth rock. He didn't know why they'd moved the boy out of America. He didn't know how in hell they'd managed to do it.

'I'm going to shower.' Caroline's tone of voice required a response. It meant: I shan't be by the phone.

'Yes, OK.' He didn't turn as she got up and went through to the bathroom. Before she emerged, there was another call. Caroline reappeared immediately, wrapped in a towel; but it was Rachel, who had been given the number according to Guerney's instructions, when she'd tried him at his hotel.

'Merry Christmas, Simon.' She sounded chipper. 'I thought maybe you'd want me to touch base.'

Guerney looked up at Caroline and shook his head. 'Thanks, Rachel,' he said, using her name to underline the point. 'Anything?'

'I've made two calls. There are more to make, but people are away – Christmas and everything. I could get the other numbers I need, but that would take more explaining than would be wise, I suspect. Can I have two more days on that?' Guerney said yes, but that he'd probably have to call her. Would she still be on Long Island? 'Yes. But where will you be? What's happened?'

'They say they've taken the boy out of the country.'

'Christ.' Rachel sounded mildly alarmed. 'Why would they do that?'

Guerney didn't answer. He said: 'Can it be no more than two days?'

'Yeah – I don't see why not. But I've got to tell you, Simon, so far it looks harmless. At least, what I've heard hasn't yet produced any evidence of skeletons in Paschini's closet. It's true that he's rich beyond the dreams of avarice – even mine – but neither of the people I spoke to seemed to know of any dubious connections. His business rivals might wake up to discover that they're short of a company or two, but they *do* wake up. He collects paintings, but he pays for them. Why not? He could probably make a bid for the Museum of Modern Art. One of the guys I spoke to had scouted an international trade conference and met Paschini there. He likes sex, but he takes it straight up, as it were.' She giggled at her own joke. 'He usually has a couple of goons in tow but, then, they all do. He made his money out of fish, did you know that?'

'Yes,' Guerney told her. 'I did know that.'

Rachel laughed again. 'Well, who cares?' she said. 'I once knew someone who'd made a million out of condolence cards for bereaved pet-owners. Paschini has charities, and so forth – endowed a home for handicapped kids somewhere in southern Italy a year or two ago. Not a recluse, but not gregarious, either. All in all, that's about it.'

'No family connections?' asked Guerney.

'Give me a break,' she said. 'I wouldn't have forgotten to mention that.'

'No, I know; silly to ask. You'll make those other calls as soon as you can?'

'As soon as I can.' She sounded good-humoured, like someone assuring a child for the tenth time that, yes, Santa

Claus will come. 'Call me in a couple of days. So, meanwhile, how is it?'

'I'm not sure,' he said.

She paused, as if puzzled by his abruptness, then said: 'Oh, she's there – the mother?'

'That's right.'

'Is she going to hold up?' Again he didn't reply.

Rachel said: 'She must be in hell. Jesus.' They were both silent for a moment, then: 'In two days, Simon. I'll get all I can. It would be really good to see you again before . . . if you're leaving.'

'Yes, it would,' he said. 'I don't know.'

'Listen, it's OK. If you want to call, around noon is a good time. I'm taking the aerobic beach-walk every morning. Can you believe it?'

'I believe it.' He smiled. 'Take care, Rachel.'

He hung up and turned to where Caroline Rance was still standing in the doorway by the bathroom. Because she always slept naked, she had been naked when Guerney had first walked into the room and taken the telephone from her, but until she had appeared in the towel neither of them had realised it.

Of course he continued to wait with her, but he didn't find it an easy thing to do. Like most singleminded people, or those whom circumstance requires to adopt tunnel vision, Guerney found it difficult to be active while waiting for something to happen, found talk and company and the world's daily demands irksome. He would have preferred to be in the limbo that he usually organised for himself at such times – a speechless hibernation that didn't even require the summoning of a gesture.

It was clear that the next phone-call would tell him whether or not the kidnappers were serious about the ransom demand – and possibly tell him whether or not David was alive. There was no reason for further delays; the more protracted the business became, the more likelihood there was that the machinery of barter would overheat and break up. Whoever had David would know this. Until the call came, there was nothing to be done. It would have suited Guerney had he been able simply to unplug and put his systems into neutral, but Caroline Rance had her own needs and he couldn't turn his back on them – principally for fear that her small reserves of faith and expectation and courage would be used up in isolation. Her way was to be near someone and to look for reassurance. So they ordered food from room service, she flicked the televison on and off, he showered and carried on a conversation through the door while towelling off, she timed her first drink and, later, ordered more food which neither of them wanted to eat. They moved from room to room while the maids cleaned. They spoke about what had happened, but not about what might happen.

It was he who made the call to Paschini while she hovered anxiously nearby. She didn't want to speak to Paschini, and Guerney kept it short. He made his report and said he'd be in touch as soon as he had been told how they wanted the money transferred. Before they hung up, Paschini said: 'I'm concerned that they know about you.'

'Yes.' Guerney paused to allow for the delay on the line. 'I'm not overjoyed about it myself.'

'How did it happen?'

It was an odd question, Guerney thought. 'I don't know,' he replied, stating the obvious. 'I wish I did. I suppose the likeliest explanation is that, since they picked your wife's hotel, they also had a good deal of opportunity to stake it out efficiently.' He knew 'wife' was wrong, but couldn't think of how else to describe her. 'I'm not happy about it but, then, I'm not sure it matters that much, either. They say they'll negotiate with me. My camouflage is the lack of need for camouflage.'

'Will they require you to go to wherever David is being held?'

'I don't know.' Guerney was growing impatient. 'I think I ought to keep this line free.'

'Of course, of course.' Paschini didn't put the phone down immediately, and Guerney wondered whether he was expecting Caroline to come on the line. He said, 'Goodbye, Signor Paschini,' and broke the connection with a finger.

At once she said: 'Why isn't he here?'

Guerney could understand that she'd want to blame someone for something. 'As things have turned out, it wouldn't have helped much,' he remarked. 'David's not in the country, or so they tell us. Who's to say he's not in Italy?' She stared at him, startled by the notion and resentful, too, that he should deflect her bitterness. 'Unless,' he continued, 'you want him here for yourself.'

'No!' She drew the word out to three syllables, staring hard at Guerney – refuting an accusation. Then she took a cigarette and lit it before shaking her head and saying it again, sharply, decisively: 'No!'

Since he'd provoked the response, Guerney was prepared to hear more, but she held her peace and he was glad of it. She padded about the room for a bit, coming to rest now and then on a chair or a sofa, or by the window. From time to time, she fiddled with the cap of the whisky-bottle, each time knowing that she was going to give herself the drink. Finally, she fell asleep, just as dusk was gathering over the city, and didn't wake until, at about ten-thirty, the phone rang.

Before picking it up, Guerney gave her time to get to the extension. When he spoke, a man's voice said: 'Are you Guerney?'

'Yes.' It was a businesslike voice, Guerney decided – that of someone practised and tough.

'Let's keep this short, OK? David Paschini is in Britain. He's well, but he's kind of homesick. You are to go there. To London; but he's not in London. Understand?'

'I understand.'

'Check in to the Connaught Hotel. Paschini can afford it, even if you can't. Reigster under your own name and wait by the phone. We want to get this deal done without any mishaps – and soon. I'm sure you want that, too. I don't have to tell you not to talk to anyone, leave trails, anything cute like that?'

'No. I understand.'

'You're just a friend, Guerney, right?'

'That's it.'

'We don't care who you are. Don't foul up is all. There's a boy's life in your hands.'

'Don't worry.'

'Just go to the Connaught and wait there until we call you.'

'No,' Guerney said.

Neither man spoke for a couple of beats. Then the voice said: 'Did you say "no"?'

'I need to know that David is alive.'

'Don't give me that shit. He's alive.'

Guerney counted to five, slowly, before replying. There was nothing to guarantee that things would go his way. There was nothing to guarantee that what followed would be evidence that the boy was not dead. He thought of Caroline, out of sight, listening in on the bedroom phone, and prayed that she would stay silent.

'That's what you tell me. I need to know.'

'What the hell do you want, Guerney?'

'Supply some evidence. And you can forget about cutting pieces off him. I'm sure you know how it's done. If you don't, or say you won't, I'm going to assume he's dead and open the whole thing up, right now: police, papers, everything.' He waited.

Finally the voice said: 'I'll get it to you in London.'

'Yes,' Guerney said, 'that will do,' and he put the phone back in its cradle.

Some time passed before Caroline emerged from the bedroom. She looked pale and was running a hand shakily through her hair. *Drowning*, he thought. *She's drowning in it*. He wondered whether she was coming up for the second or third time.

'Wasn't that dangerous?' Her voice wavered between fear and anger, then anger took the upper hand. She walked

61

over to where he sat and half-pushed, half-clubbed his shoulder with her fist. 'Suppose they'd called your bluff?'

He caught her hand quickly and held it, pulling on her arm, gently, to emphasize his words. 'It wasn't a bluff. They have to have something to trade with. The response to my asking for evidence means that David's almost certainly alive.'

Her body seemed to lose its weight. She almost toppled over when he released her. 'Had you . . . had you doubted that?'

'Now and then, yes.'

She sat down and said, 'Oh,' very quietly. Then she asked: '*Almost* certainly?'

He didn't give her an answer. Instead, he got up and began to collect the small number of his possessions that were here and there in the room. Then he said, 'Go back to New England. Reassure people – tell them that David's on a short vacation with his father, perhaps.'

She looked at him. 'I can't come?' She was really asking for confirmation of what she already knew. He had taken his coat from the closet; now he put it back on the rail.

'I'll stay here, if you like,' he said. 'Until I get a plane.' She nodded mutely. 'Or until you get one. Tomorrow morning will do.'

It wasn't what he wanted. He poured her a drink, and she sipped it, holding the glass in both hands like someone taking broth, as he lifted the phone to try for reservations.

Hers was easy; his not so. Eventually, he managed to secure a first-class seat on a British Airways flight that left at seven the next evening. Caroline was to fly from La Guardia before noon. With her second drink, she began to rehearse her return, giving herself a role. He agreed with her plans; he promised to let her know what was happening if he could; and while she was speaking he suddenly understood that it was wrong – the whole thing was wrong.

He knew what he found puzzling and he knew where the expected pattern was out of kilter. It hadn't to do with those things. Quite simply, the understanding stemmed from his being with her, acting almost domestically. Somehow the past two days seemed farcical. The very situation – this woman, this room, the sad swing of her breasts as he'd taken the phone from her that morning, her tiny, manic shopping spree, the visits from the room service, the too-familiar chintz of the upholstery – all this was his evidence. He tried to quarry meaning out of it, but was left with impressions.

Next morning, he felt the same. Caroline had slept for no more than two hours at a stretch, and each time she woke he'd been conscious of it – hearing her snap on the light and shift restlessly in the bed, then go through to the bathroom, or strike a match for her cigarette. Once, she put the television in her room on, very low, for ten or fifteen minutes. On two other occasions, she had padded past the couch where he lay, bumping into chairs, using the knife-edge of light from her door-jamb to go to the fridge for mineral water. Although he didn't stir, she'd whispered, 'Sorry, sorry,' as she sidled across the room.

He waited while she checked out, then hailed her a cab. Before she got in, he handed her a piece of paper on which he'd written the telephone number of the Connaught, together with the number of the room he'd booked the previous night. She responded by giving him photographs of her son. They were like shipboard lovers, exchanging addresses at the end of the cruise.

He watched the cab turn towards Sixth Avenue. It was still just in sight when the bell captain emerged carrying the bag laden with gifts. He looked from side to side, tensed as if to wave or yell, his arm half-raised, then let his breath escape in a rush and the arm fall when he realised he was too late. As he made to go back inside, his eyes met Guerney's, and there was a half-recognition in them. He raised the bag slightly, unsure, a gesture that was almost a question. Guerney looked straight through the man, turned, and began to make his way downtown.

* * *

He packed and paid his bill before calling Rachel. 'Where are you?' she asked.

'In transit. I'm just leaving.'

'Leaving town?'

'London,' he told her.

'That's where the boy is?'

'They say he's in Britain. I've been told to go to London.'

'Good luck, Simon.'

'Thanks.' He lodged on the side of one of the beds. 'What have you got?'

'I managed to contact one other person – this time in Italy. I don't think he was *too* curious about why, but – '

'It can't be helped,' Guerney reassured her.

'Well . . . interesting. It seems that Signor Paschini may not be white as the driven snow after all. He doesn't get close to it, you understand, and I don't have a hell of a lot more than heavy hints, but it's possible that some of the things Paschini peddles might be fishier than others. It seems he's freelance, if at all, by the way: I mean no Cosa Nostra so far as anyone can tell. Just a little dabbling. He doesn't run things: just invests here and there for a good return.' Guerney waited. 'At first it looked like nothing. A few houses looked after by one of Paschini's heavies, it seems. It could have been that Paschini didn't even know. Some people consider running a few hookers is the Italian male's birthright. But some pretty high-grade smack is getting mixed in with the fishmeal from time to time, and that's out of the hired help's league. There's only one clearing-house – overseas. There are a few whores on the premises, too, but mostly it's a place for stashing, cutting and reselling.'

'Who buys it?' Guerney asked.

'Dealers, I guess. I'm not too sure. I mean, the guy I spoke to didn't really say. I don't suppose much of it comes down to street-weight.'

'Where?'

'London, as a matter of fact.' She paused briefly, then said: 'I've got an address. It was just luck – something

Rome had picked up. It doesn't matter to them. Frankly they couldn't give a flying fuck. He's too well covered and too VIP to hit even if he is involved. Anyway, I wouldn't be surprised to hear that the Pope's got a piece of the action – you know what it's like. Even so, Simon, I'll deny I ever told you.'

He said: 'Of course.'

She gave him an address in Cheyne Walk.

There were two who were with him most of the time and one who came and went. They wore business suits and ties, discreet dark material, and had neat haircuts. Apart from their differing builds, they were indistinguishable from the back, so David had named them Tom, Dick and Harry.

Harry was the gofer. He'd disappear from time to time, returning with food and booze, or clothes. On one occasion, he had made a special sortie for galoshes and a flashlight. It was easy to tell, from the labels and wrappings on things, that he did his shopping in a town. David wondered how far the place was from the house he was in. They had a car, but it was garaged on the side of the house opposite to the two rooms where he was kept – two rooms with three windows between them. The view from each was of trees and meadows, rising on one side – the east, he calculated – to a beechwood on a hill. He supposed it wouldn't help him to know about the car, in any case. Harry was thin and dark, and sometimes smoked a cigar. David could tell when he was around from the smell of his smoke. He puffed away, each evening, while he cooked.

Tom was stocky and blond. He had a nervous manner and spoke rapidly, breaking his sentences into uneven segments. Often, it seemed, he couldn't find the word or expression he wanted, and he'd spread a well-manicured hand, palm downwards as if to say: 'Don't give it to me; I'll get there in a second.'

Like the other two, Tom rarely spoke to David except to issue instructions, even though they slept in the same room. Tom chain-smoked and drank the Southern Comfort that

Harry fetched with little, neat, repetitive sips, holding the glass just below his lip, his little finger angled outwards. Sometimes the men told jokes – *There was this guy, see* – and Tom would laugh in a lengthening staccato after each of his punchlines, as if to encourage the others.

It was Dick who would go into a further room to make the phone-calls – sometimes a couple a day, sometimes many more. He was blond, too, but slight and a fraction taller than Harry. Like Tom, he smoked, but sparingly. He had traces of a Southern accent, a minimal rounding of the vowels, especially 'o' sounds. He had given David the shot of whatever it was before they'd gone to the plane, injecting him in the back of the hand and placing a swab over the entry-point before withdrawing the needle in a fast fluent manner and holding the cotton-wool in place for a short while. David was pretty sure that Dick and Harry thought Tom a bit of a klutz.

Each of the men was clean-shaven. Dick bore a small Y-shaped scar that started just below the bridge of his nose and disappeared into the thick part of his eyebrows. David wondered whether any of this mattered. Whether it did or not, he had stopped bothering to observe after they had moved him.

The drug had been disturbing: a long fever of nightmare images that still hadn't quite receded. They'd left him anxious, hag-ridden. He felt he might, at any time, slip back into that world of demons and sulphurous landscapes: the country of worst fears. There was a part of him – and he'd always known it – that contained mechanisms more delicate than most people owned, a system of hair triggers that often made it necessary for him to walk through the world with a delicate tread. Things could get out of control. David knew the signs. At present, the air was alive with them.

He wasn't sure that he would dub it 'gift', though 'talent' was a word that some people had used and he supposed he could see the sense in that. Scenes that the drug had brought would return without warning, vivid episodes in full colour, so sharp-edged that the places seemed inhabitable and full of noise and the cast of humans, demi-humans, winged things, almost familiar. Voices and animal cries and the thudding of feet rang through the room. If he worked at making it fade, then sooner or later it would. It exhausted him, though; and he was still full of fear. He didn't know what the men would do with him. He couldn't see how things might turn out well: their lies, their indecisiveness would bring everything to grief.

His defence – his only defence – was to sleep. It had worried the men a little at first. His ability to sleep self-protectively made them wonder whether, maybe, the kid was sick. Tom was irritated by it too: it made him feel like a goddam babysitter; but there was something unnerving about it as well, as if David were retreating from them, going AWOL, or taking some sort of obscure advantage. They had made a phone-call about it and been told, rather sharply, just to do their jobs. If the kid was sleeping a lot, then that was all to the good, wasn't it?

Tom remained edgy. 'This Christ-awful place,' he said. 'It's full of' – he searched for the word – 'spaces. The kid's in a coma half the time. Who's this goddam Guerney?'

'They're checking him out.' Dick spoke without turning round. He was sitting at a dining-table, cleaning a gun – a short-barrelled .38.

'Is he a pro?' Tom wanted to know.

'They're checking.'

David heard none of this; he was sleeping. They had positioned the bed so that it could be seen through the open door. The single window in the bedroom was fitted with locking bolts. He'd been nervy and morose for two or three hours, asking for food that he didn't eat and coffee that he didn't drink. He had discovered that they wouldn't hurt him, but by and large he didn't trade on the fact.

He slept, and sometimes he dreamed dreams that he'd remember. Not the horrors the drug had brought – they haunted his waking hours. His dreams remained what they

67

had always been: clear, easily remembered, yielding their meanings too glibly sometimes; and sometimes almost tractable for the way he could enter and control them, knowing them to be dreams.

He was dreaming as Dick reassembled the gun and replaced it in the holster positioned over his kidneys – as Tom leaned forward in his chair to get a clearer view of the bed.

After the first few images had come at him, he saw that it was a dream and he began to observe, interestedly, storing what pictures he could. One was a house in a place he'd never been to. It was built of stone, perfectly square, and had chimney stacks at either side. It stood on the flank of a hill and looked out at another hill. Fir-trees grew in ordered lines below the house, looking trim and well brushed. From the road, they resembled ranks of pikemen, advancing on the place. A faint breeze stirred their tips, and it was as if the whole army, on some command, had wheeled. The windows facing the far hill reflected the day's brightness – except one, which appeared dimmer than the rest. David knew that this was because someone stood behind the glass, looking out; but, apart from being able to register that it was a man's shape, he couldn't distinguish much. He tried to get closer, but for some reason the terms of the dream wouldn't permit it.

He moved to the meadow behind the house and saw that the man had preceded him, almost gaining the crest of the hill. As David watched, the other's head and shoulders rose above the brim and came clear against the sky. The shape beside him was a dog at close heel. They walked the skyline for fifty yards or so, then began to descend, the dog disappearing almost instantly, while the outline of its owner fell gradually out of sight in a jerky, piecemeal way, like a man going downstairs. David watched him sinking in sections but didn't follow. Nearby was a well – a broad brick-built structure that was clearly fed from a high spring and was close to overflowing. He listened for the sound of running water and, before long, heard it.

Now he could see through one of the back windows into a stone-flagged kitchen with a large dresser along one wall to hold crockery and a pine table with plain wooden chairs. The dog's basket was close to the stove. As he watched, the image faded and modified. It became something he couldn't make sense of, and then it seemed that he was in New York, and then by the sea, and next Tom intruded, speaking inaudibly, or scything his hand to prevent interruptions.

That was all he wanted of the dream, but it continued, lapsing from time to time into grey, taking him back to some crowded scene on campus. He heard again the engines of the plane as music. An entire orchestra, in a packed concert-hall, were stalled on one note.

When he woke he was intrigued. He pictured the house, its surrounds, over and over, leafing through his memory's library of snapshots, becoming surer by the minute that he'd never visited such a place before and knowing that he now wanted to go back. He asked if he could have some coffee and was told they'd be eating soon, he'd get coffee then. Tom slapped his thigh and wandered from window to window, looking jumpy. He was waiting for the phone to ring. Dick asked if he had slept well; he said he had.

The man came back to him, lofting his outline above the hill's brink. David felt no anxiety when he recalled how the shape had diminished and finally vanished to the far side. After all, he reasoned, the man could only have been leaving the house for a short while.

6

Rachel let her gaze wander around the room, taking in the hessian wall-covering, the unimpressive abstracts, the leather-backed chairs spaced evenly round the oval table. She wasn't particularly avoiding the eyes of the two men who sat at the table with her, but she didn't much want to talk with them – not yet – so she refrained from looking at them. She felt uneasy and impatient and a little angry.

A third man entered the room, opening one of the double doors and swinging it shut behind him without looking back. He had the brisk bustling air of someone who comes late to meetings which can't start without him. Rachel listened to him saying sorry, graciously, reflexively, and watched as he sat down and squared some notes on the table, then circled them protectively with his arms, locking fingers on the polished surface.

Ed Jeffries was getting set to rule a certain roost in Washington, and his body language let you know it. At least, thought Rachel, his suit was repellent and his tie too obviously understated. A lock of hair, oddly boyish in its effect, had fallen over his brow, and he swept it back with an automatic flick of the hand. He made a needless show of scanning a few lines of the notes while the others sat in silence. Finally, he looked up, all alertness, and asked: 'So – where do we stand? Guerney has left for London, is that right?'

'He's there by now, Ed.' The man who had spoken flexed his arm and consulted his watch. 'The plane will have decked about two hours ago.'

'And someone's keeping tabs?' Jeffries looked down the table to the second man, whose baldness was compensated for by a heavy moustache.

'Sure. We'll know when he farts in the bath.'

'OK.' Jeffries looked across at Rachel, who sat on the far side of the table, the apex of an equilateral triangle. 'I just want to go back over a point or two. You gave him the information about Paschini?'

'Before he left, yes.' As she was called on to speak, she dug into her bag for cigarettes. Long before the action was complete, she realised it betrayed her and for an instant her biceps twitched to counter it. She registered that it was too late; and then she thought *Damn it, why has this bastard got me so strung out?* and lit the cigarette with studied care.

'Good. Good.' Jeffries was glancing down at his notes again, as if he were working from a script. 'And he believed you?'

She shrugged. 'Who knows? Yes. There was no reason that he shouldn't. He asked me for information in the first place, after all.'

'Sure, I know. It's just the initial stuff you gave him made Paschini harmless.' He tapped the table with his fingertips: a gesture of annoyance. 'I wish a few connections had been made before you made those first phone-calls.'

'I'm sorry,' Rachel said testily. 'No one had said a damn thing to me about any of this. It was known that he's a friend of mine – at least, it's on file. How in hell was I supposed to know – ?'

Jeffries cut her off, waving an open hand and smiling. 'No. No, look, you're not to blame for anything. Someone loused things up – didn't make the connection, neglected to check . . . whatever. Forget it. Let's deal with what we've got.' Rachel felt patronized and resentful. 'Our guys have been told to sit tight for the time being?' Jeffries asked this of the moustache.

'That's right.'

'And where are they?'

'A safe house. Buckinghamshire. It's about an hour from London by car.'

'And the boy's OK?'

'The boy's fine.'

'OK.' Jeffries turned back to Rachel. 'That brings me up to date. Let's have something on Guerney.'

There was nothing, she thought, absolutely nothing that she could do. She had worked harder than most at her career, scarcely putting a foot wrong. Now things had gone haywire. It was always possible that something like this would happen. Her job, her role, touched everything in her life: it was the same for all of them. There was something permanent in their lives – a way of being that she had identified as stealth. *Damn it all to hell! Why Guerney?* And, though she hadn't meant to, she said: 'I don't like any of this, Ed.'

'No. He was part of their embassy here, that right?'

'Six years ago; maybe a little more.' She pondered what she knew about him. 'He was at Oxford as a student, very good at sports, read history. That's . . .' She waved a hand, interrupting herself. 'You don't want me to go back that far?'

'No. There's a file.'

Yes, she thought, half-smiling, there's always a file. In Guerney's case, though, it wasn't likely to contain much pillow-talk. What Jeffries wanted to know could be compiled from mere observation. He wanted to get close: close enough to touch his man, to be walking on his heels, a shadow. He wanted to be there in the passenger-seat, alongside the bed like a night-nurse, dining at the same table. He wanted to be the shaving-mirror.

She lit another cigarette and sighed the smoke into the air. 'His father was a farmer in the West Country of England. Guerney tried the diplomatic service. He was, as they say, brilliant but wayward. Unsuitable, in other words. He probably knew it as well as anyone, but he hung on for quite a while, all things considered. He had a problem with authority – that'll be in the file. Too much of a loner. I think I remember him once saying to me that he couldn't sit

72

still for taking dumb orders from assholes in sharkskin suits – something like that.' Guerney had never said any such thing, but she allowed herself the indulgence. Jeffries didn't give any sign of having registered it. 'I met him at a party and we became lovers for a while.' She smiled. 'I was only there as makeweight: one of our elder statesmen needed a new ass to pat. Anyway' – her tone became brisk – 'it lasted a few months; it was fine; no one got hurt.'

'But you still screw him?'

She winced. 'When I see him.' It was said in a soft voice that did nothing to mask her anger. She felt she'd had enough for the time being and launched a tiny counter-attack. 'Why has David Paschini been taken to England?'

Jeffries shook his head and steered her back. 'There are reasons. England isn't America . . . we have a good set-up there . . . we have friends. After the affair?'

'We didn't see each other for a while – some weeks. Then we stopped deliberately avoiding one another and found that was OK.'

'And that's the way it's been?'

'That's the way; except he lives in England now and we barely meet. He usually calls if he's in New York. Sometimes I'm there, sometimes I'm not.'

'OK.' Jeffries' tone was that of someone who had just ticked off one item on an agenda. 'So what have you learned about him?'

She tried for a deflection and, surprisingly, it worked. 'You know how he came to do what he does?'

Jeffries assumed that the answer to his question lay behind her own. He did know, but he said: 'Tell us.'

'It was when Massey was taken – their first secretary. He was on vacation, fishing somewhere upstate. The IRA had been working with some of our home-grown psychopaths whose ancestors had once read Sean O'Casey, or whatever; it doesn't matter – some sentimental garbage that provided an excuse to play cops and terrorists. Their initial intention, or so it seems, had been to get a bunch of people released from H-Block under the threat of killing Massey. They'd

probably intended to waste him anyway – more publicity.'
She realised she was reporting what Guerney had told her
and, in that instant, recalled the flash of anger in his voice.
'Anyway, they collared him efficiently enough.' She
dropped in another piece of Guerney's unofficial version.
'They even had time to eat the trout he'd caught that
morning, before taking him across two state lines. There
were a couple of factors, though, that made the business
even less amusing for the Brits than having a senior diplomat
held to ransom: two things that went along for the ride.
Massey had taken some work on vacation with him; he
shouldn't have, but he did. All classified, all dangerous as
hell – embarrassing in a dozen different ways, lethal in
several others. The other thing was probably thought
expendable at the time. Guerney had a secretary he was
very fond of; not sex or anything – he just liked her an awful
lot.'

The moustache, who had been sitting with an arm flung
over the back of his chair and listening with the air of
someone so well informed that he could scarcely hold boredom at bay, nodded without looking up and said: 'Fiona
something . . .'

Rachel let a few seconds elapse and then made a tiny show
of sitting back in her chair, as if signalling the end of her
contribution. 'You know all of this,' she said.

'I think we'd like to hear it from you,' Jeffries said. He
didn't look at the moustache, but his voice was tight with
anger. The moustache turned to face front, awkward with
arms and legs for a moment, and found himself almost
sitting to attention. He looked as if he might speak, then
changed his mind. Rachel watched his reaction. *Winged one
of the sons of bitches.*

'Yes,' she said, 'Fiona something. The kidnappers didn't
know quite what they'd got, but they could see that the
papers were important, so they started bidding up. The
Brits knew they couldn't afford a syllable of publicity, so
they agreed to just about everything; but they also said that,
if the kidnappers contacted the press, they could kill their

hostages and the H-Block prisoners would rot there. It was bluff, but it worked temporarily. The Brits said that things would take a little while to organise – you know how it goes – and sat down to think. Meanwhile Fiona Something was being gang-banged around the clock, but no one seemed to give much consideration to that. She'd been sent up to Massey's cabin, wherever it was, by Guerney – messenger work at Massey's request. Maybe she was supposed to ferry back some of the papers. It's not unusual for them, apparently. Foreign Office secretaries are often seen buzzing around London in the backs of Daimlers, doing courier work.

'All in all, it wasn't a happy situation. I gather that their security people were about as much use as a tit on a boar. The short story is that Guerney went Injun and solved the problem himself. Sort of. It's odd how random, how unprepared systems like ours are for something like that. No one knew what in hell to do. Guerney just took over – did a lot of the negotiating, insisted on a meet to ensure that the hostages were alive and to have sight of the papers. The boys in green weren't exactly pro and they went along with most of it – what mattered, in any case. He managed to build in a day's leeway and, by that time, was sufficiently in control to insist on doing it on his own. He convinced everyone who mattered that it was simply an interim move: playing for time, making sure the papers hadn't been mailed to the press already – and that Massey and the girl were still alive, in so far as that mattered to them. It was agreed. Other, more important types were doing other, more important things: calling London, calling Belfast, drafting letters of resignation . . . Guerney got up there and took them out. Trouble was he went a tad above and beyond the call of duty and killed them. It seems he was angry. What else he was supposed to do was never made clear, but those in authority thought it was a little excessive. Massey got in the middle of it all and was pretty badly hurt, although he survived to ride in a wheelchair for ever after. I gather that Fiona Something wasn't in great shape, either. That was the grand finale to Guerney's career. I don't think he cared a great deal. Anyway, one way or another, he'd lost a job, but gained a reputation among those who knew. He went freelance. I don't think he intended to; then, again . . .' Her tone wavered, and she realised that she didn't at all know how to say what she meant. Looking at her audience, she decided to try flippancy. 'He'd sort of gotten religion.' That didn't work, for her or for them. 'The kidnapping affected him. It's a vile thing. He saw exactly *how* it's vile.' She was putting it together from the few – very few – things Guerney had ever told her. 'And he was good at it. I guess you could say he had the chance to become a specialist in a specialist's field.' That, she imagined, they would understand.

'Not long after the Massey thing – six months maybe – someone approached him for help. He took the job. Mostly he doesn't, because mostly there's nothing he can do that the police can't. He was never . . .' She paused, suddenly understanding that she was looking for reasons herself. 'There are things about Guerney that are odd. He can play the civilised game, but he's not. You think I know a lot about him – stuff that isn't even between the lines in a file – but I don't. I'm not sure I know who does. He's good at his job, but he doesn't talk about it. I'm not sure he even *likes* it. The few things he told me . . .' She lifted a hand. 'Like describing a hectic day at the office.' She thought of something and chuckled. The laugh grew, with little shruggings of her shoulders, until it became full-blooded. 'Jesus,' she said, 'he's probably a nut.'

Jeffries watched her till she'd finished laughing, then waited a second or two to make sure that she'd also finished speaking. 'Yeah,' he said, 'that's what worries us.'

'Why is the boy in England?' Rachel asked.

Jeffries glanced at the moustache, then back again at her before dropping his eyes. 'He's too hot for this country. The English people know how we work; and we're calling in a few dues.'

'You mean you might have to kill him? America doesn't want the corpse?'

'You can't be told everything, Rachel; you know that, God damn it. Stay in touch – with Guerney, with us. Go back to New York.' The remark wasn't meant as a dismissal. 'What is he going to do?'

His sudden abruptness stung her; the pulling of rank. She saw how vulnerable Guerney had become.

'You know what.' As she spoke, she slapped the table in anger.

He held her eyes and saw the defiance there. His look said: *Don't even think it. I'll put your ass in a sling.* And again she realised there was nothing she could do.

'I don't know,' she said. 'Would he tell me? Anyone? Think about it.' She felt weary. 'I'd imagined that it would be more likely that you'd be telling him what to do. Isn't that it?'

Jeffries picked up his notes and eased his chair away from the table. 'Stay close, Rachel. If he calls . . . anything . . .'

'Sure,' she said. 'Sure.'

As they rose, he reached across the table and – it seemed a curious gesture – shook her hand. 'We'll tell you what to do.' She nodded. The other men leaned forward, smiling formal smiles. 'Rachel,' they said; and she found herself shaking hands with them, too.

Guerney had stopped looking over his shoulder. It seemed right to invite them – to appear unguarded. As things stood he was on call to them. Almost nothing was of his devising, and he was prepared to acknowledge it. His only edge had been asking for proof that the boy was alive, and he didn't award himself any points for that – a light blow with the flat of the glove, nothing more. Far better to let them lead. And, although things seemed random and wrong, he believed that the disadvantage was not all his. Some of what was odd didn't feel entirely dangerous. There was a sense of improvisation on their part. They were several steps ahead all right, but Guerney wasn't convinced that they knew

77

where their steps were taking them. If that were so, he reasoned, it would be better to be drawn than to attempt to overtake.

The Connaught, as always, exuded impeccability from every oak panel. It was a place where matters would always be just so. Men without ties and women wearing trousers would be barred from the dining-room with stern civility. The place amused him vastly on every visit. He could count the times; and each had had a distinct sexual purpose. Until now, he had always connected the Connaught with gentle salacious sparring, with anticipation over dinner, with someone undressing and the discovery of that body, those ways; with love-cries and urgency and other sorts of nakedness.

He checked in and went to bed and instantly fell asleep. Four hours later, he came awake with sluggish reluctance wondering if the phone had woken him. The desk said that it hadn't. He started to run a bath and sat alongside on the bathroom chair, dozing in the steam and watching the tub fill. A piece of the dream he'd been dreaming just before he awakened was lodged in his mind. He started to dismiss it then, on a whim, decided to let it replay, knowing that if he concentrated on the fragment he'd retained it would be possible to retrieve the rest, hauling it in hand over hand. By the time the bath was full and he'd started to soak, the dream was almost entire so far as he could recall it.

He was walking away from the house, coming clear of the fringe of trees that lay at the meadow's edge and conscious of moving from that dankness to the bright edge of sunlight beyond the fence. In a single surreal moment, he could feel the plush of pine-needles beneath his feet and then the corrugation of furrows under a thin patina of grass. The dog was with him. In one sequence of frames, she pursued some creatures and returned. As he dreamed it, the chase seemed at first instantaneous – as she left, so she returned, bearing her prey; but, then, if he looked at what lay beneath the

78

picture, he could watch her in graceful slow motion: the compression of hindfeet between forefeet, the sinuous unleashing of full stretch.

The next sequence put him higher on the hill and the dog at his side. Three feet or so away from where she walked to heel, there was someone else. He thought it was himself at first. Then he realised that whoever it was appeared as a profile that barely nudged into vision with each upward step – snagging the corner of his eye, then falling back maddeningly. For some reason, he wasn't able to turn sideways to identify the person, but he knew that it was some dream convention that prevented him, so he didn't fight it.

He followed the route of one of his usual walks: across the crest of the hill and down to the lower slopes where the hedgerows gave good hunting. An hour's walking made a dreaming second or so, but somehow the time wasn't lost, nor the sensation of someone with him all the way.

Next, he was back at the house, crossing the stile by the well and, he realised, alone. He looked up and saw a figure peering into the kitchen window – the someone, who had come home before him. He discovered that he had positioned himself so that he stood directly behind whoever it was, waiting to confront him as he turned.

He saw the scene as if from behind and above: his own back, the back of his head, the same view of the person in front of him, like an image that might suddenly proliferate and extend infinitely. Then he looked past his own shoulder and saw David Paschini's face reflected in the azure of the window-pane.

The logic of the dream wouldn't permit the boy to turn, but the reflection began to contort slightly and Guerney could tell that David was speaking. Because it was a reflection, the words made no sounds. The futile effort of lip-reading was the last recollection Guerney had – a terrible straining for sense – the silent mouthings seeming like the bottled-up volume of a record that's playing though some bad connection prevents it from being heard.

As he bathed, he reflected on the dream's symbolism:

rather obvious, he thought. He recalled the three photographs that Caroline Rance had given him. In the first, David had been laughing – sitting at a trestle table with a group of friends during a skiing holiday. The table was set outside in what looked like bright cold weather; skis were stacked nearby. Two of the friends were clowning for the camera. David was sitting in the left foreground, his hand resting on the shoulder of a pretty blonde girl who was caught only in profile.

The second had been taken on a trip to Europe; in the background was the Lagoon and the tall spindly prows of a dozen or so gondolas. It was one of those organised poses: the subject is told to look away, slightly, to his left – no, not too much, perhaps *down* just a little.

The formal studio portrait – the third – gave the best detail. It was a handsome face, and friendly. The characteristics of the child were still evident, here and there, in the face of the adolescent. And you could guess how the features would fare in the man. David Paschini had the look of someone who wouldn't age until he was into his fifties. It was an open face, lacking guile and ill-temper. It also, Guerney remembered, lacked the resolution that hardship sometimes brings. It was the face of a contented, generous, rich boy.

The three poses, the three faces of David Paschini, fell on one another without blurring. Guerney shrugged into the towelling robe and walked back to the main room to take the photographs out of his wallet. His memory of them had been correct; but as he studied them he became aware that the dream-face hadn't quite matched up to any of these and he wondered why he should have invented a change in the boy's appearance – why he should have made the cheeks a little thinner and have given the whole face more angles; why he should have burdened the eyes with knowledge and fear that hadn't been there before.

He resummoned the moment in his dream when he had seen that face hovering in the sky's reflection. There had been something distinctly eerie about it. He understood

80

now that it was not to do with the disembodied face in the blue backwash, or the futile mouthings. It lay in something gauche and fearful about David's stance and the way he'd held his head, in the way his mouth had worked and in the silent pauses between the silent words. It had about it the shocked clumsy gesture of someone whom fear has taken by surprise.

Guerney wondered, briefly, about the power of dreams to invent. The image, now that he had worked on it, was astonishingly precise. It was a fourth photograph, he decided – one that he had somehow taken. He had little doubt that it was the most accurate.

He waited for two hours for the phone to ring and, when it didn't, assumed he knew what that meant. To be certain, he waited another half-hour, then made a call himself. A voice at the other end informed him that George Buckroyd was unable to come to the phone, but would return his call if he cared to leave his name and number. He hung up, left it for a further thirty minutes, then tried again.

'Buckroyd,' said a voice, swooping down the long slope of the final syllable.

Guerney smiled. 'George,' he said, 'it's Simon Guerney.'

'Hello, Simon.' The tone was genial and warm. 'Good Christ . . . how are you? *Where* are you?'

'I'm in London. George, could we meet? I need to talk something over with you.'

'Brain-picking,' said Buckroyd. He made it sound positively bloodcurdling.

'That's right.'

'Something's afoot.'

'That's right.'

'Well, well.' Buckroyd appeared pleased. 'I won't ask you where you're staying; and I don't suppose you'll want to come here. You tell me where.' As an afterthought he said: 'It's a lovely day.'

They met at the Spaniard's Inn. Guerney had arrived first, having zig-zagged through a few miles of the West

End. A large anti-nuclear demonstration had snarled up the traffic in Park Lane and Oxford Street – five or six thousand people carrying banners and placards. Guerney had used the demo for initial cover, weaving through the slowly moving ranks and eventually emerging close to an Underground station. He'd caught a train going south, then doubled back. Three times in all he had alighted from a train, walked part-way along the platform towards the exit, then squeezed between the doors as they moved to close. It was standard stuff and risky. Leaving the hotel at all was risky. Nothing could be done about that.

From the back of the pub he saw Buckroyd come in and buy a drink. He was a tall man, dignified. A shaggy mane of white hair fell back from his broad forehead. The face was full of good humour, but not without a generous measure of wryness. When he moved away from the bar Guerney stood up – in part to be seen but also, he realised, out of a regard that incorporated a good deal of respect.

'Well, Simon.' They shook hands and smiled at one another in genuine pleasure. 'You probably haven't got much time for chit-chat.'

None the less, they made a little time. Buckroyd was amusing about his life: 'I'm writing a book about London's churches,' he told Guerney, 'references to them in literature together with potted histories. Ridiculous undertaking for a Catholic, really. Every so often I fail to repress my indignation, and a rather pleasant girl with large breasts who's editing me has to find a new way of pointing out that my brief doesn't include being polemical. You know, of course,' he said, 'that I'm really out of it now.'

'But you hear things.'

'Sometimes, sometimes. Not often. Old habits die hard, I suppose, but I have to admit that I don't listen much any more, or try to read between the lines. The corridors of clandestine power always contained a high proportion of idiots, but it seems that nowadays they amount to a throng. The witless rich looking for a political *piste noir*, professional hard-liners ossifying with every passing minute, and none of them with as much sense of the subtle as a dockside whore. They do their thinking by computer. History isn't so much a closed book to them as a defective VDU. Dangerous to have no sense of history. Anyway' – he flapped a hand, as if clearing the corridors – 'what can I very probably not do for you?'

Guerney related the story and waited for a reaction. Buckroyd looked pensive and toyed with a beer-mat for a while. 'I'll get some more drinks,' he said.

Guerney took over the beer-mat, testing his reactions by flipping it up from the table's edge and catching it before it landed. He slid it under his fresh drink when Buckroyd returned and took a sip or two before asking: 'Well?'

'I see the imponderables. Or, at least, I see *some* imponderables.'

'But nothing sounds familiar?'

'No,' Buckroyd shook his head. 'Nothing. You're convinced that it's not what it seems?' He corrected himself. 'What it seemed at first.'

'Would you be?'

'From what you've told me, no.'

'Why not?'

'You're testing me, Simon.' He made a show of looking affronted.

Guerney smiled. 'I want to see if we agree.'

'The transfer, principally. The plane, the getting here, the organisation – all of that. They must have intended to move him – don't you think? – or it would have been impossible to fix. It could hardly have been impromptu. If they came by scheduled airline, they'd have had to reserve seats, what – drug the boy or something of that? – have made provision with the airline for an invalid, or however they intended to work it. It's a bloody difficult operation to mount; it's also risky as hell. What's more' – he paused and swilled Scotch round the circumference of his glass – 'I'm not sure I see the point.' He looked at Guerney. 'Do you?'

'No.'

'You've done the obvious things?' Buckroyd asked. 'Been the concerned uncle who missed his sick nephew's arrival?'

'No.'

'Ah.' Buckroyd rested an elbow on the table between them and cupped his chin in his hand. 'Because you don't think he came in that way.'

Guerney nodded. 'I don't think it's possible.'

'No,' said Buckroyd slowly, 'I suppose I'd be inclined to agree. It's occured to you that he might not be here at all?'

'Yes, it's occurred. I'll find out soon enough. I think he is, though.'

'In that case, if he is, then – yes – it might be that something will filter through to me. I could try to do a little homework, if you'd like.'

'I'd be grateful, George, yes.'

Buckroyd nodded, then widened his eyes and shrugged his shoulders minutely. 'Though God alone knows why . . . I mean, it seems a terribly long shot, Simon; not plausible, in fact.'

'My problem', Guerney pointed out, 'is that very little of it is plausible from start to finish. It's not running right. Last autumn, I had a job in Sardinia – that went haywire after they'd got the money: the point at which I was hired. It wasn't too easy, because they'd got what they wanted – or mostly wanted. Someone had trusted them to do the most dangerous thing – hand over the hostages. Stupid, of course. It's always easier to kill them. But this . . . they're retreating all the time. It's off the rails.'

'Ten million,' Buckroyd said. 'Yes. Shall I call if anything turns up?'

'Fine; but don't leave messages. I'm at the Connaught.'

Buckroyd laughed. 'Good grief,' he said, 'they *have* staked you out, haven't they?' He paused. 'They must have booked in advance, don't you think? The Connaught . . .'

'Or have influence in odd places,' Guerney said. 'Yes, I'd thought of that.'

* * *

It was 3 a.m. when the phone rang in Guerney's hotel room. The timing constituted the first piece of manoeuvring he really recognised. It was the voice he'd heard in New York. 'Listen carefully,' it said. There was a pause.

'Yes,' Guerney replied. 'OK.'

'The documentation you want will be delivered to your hotel in three hours. It's just a regular taxi-cab delivery, so don't get ideas – you'll be wasting your time. Don't even trouble to ask him for the pick-up address – we're going to give it to you. The money's going into a Swiss bank. We'll tell you how; you'd better make sure Paschini can come up to the mark. Understand?'

'I understand.'

Guerney's words were followed immediately by the dialling tone. He lay back in bed and stared at the ceiling. They might know, he reasoned, that he'd left the hotel; in any case he was assuming that they were professional enough to know. And they'd know that he knew that – his tube-train waltz would have made it clear, even if they'd had doubts before. Maybe he'd shaken them, maybe not; either way, it hadn't been mentioned.

I don't have the first idea what this is, he thought. It was like looking at a picture of some creature he had never seen before: processes of elimination could do nothing to make identification possible. It's not an elephant, it's not a tiger, it's not an antelope . . . easy enough to determine what it was not.

He rinsed his mouth at the bathroom tap, put on a track-suit and running-shoes, and took the lift down to the lobby. The night porter emerged from his glass-panelled cubby-hole, shrugging into his uniform jacket, and accompanied Guerney to the door, managing not to show surprise. Guerney smiled at him as if owning to the eccentricity. 'Just ring the night-bell when you get back, sir.' The man held the door open and sniffed the air. For an instant, they stood side by side on the steps.

'Jet-lag,' Guerney explained. He glanced to and fro, casually checking doorways.

The night porter pointed to the bell. 'Just give it a tap,' he said.

Guerney fell into an easy lope, turning out of North Audley Street into Berkeley Square and heading for the river. The air was damp. Little gusts of wind buffeted between the walls of side-streets like tobaggans on a downhill run. Despite the earliness of the hour, Guerney could feel the scorch of carbon monoxide at the back of his throat. The sodium glow of the street-lights made the city look pallid, as if it suffered each day from having to rebreathe its own atmosphere: a soup of thinned-out remnants, the invisible detritus from trucks and furnaces, from chimneys and demolition sites.

The city's other sweepings were more evident. Men and women, most of them old, lay in doorways here and there, or across pavement grilles to take the warmth from kitchens. The newspapers they had used for insulation sprouted from tattered jackets and trouser-legs, and their faces were turned inwards to a wall or a doorway's recess as if they could preserve some sort of privacy. As he ran past the expensive hotels and the entrance-halls of luxury office-blocks, Guerney noted them. They were the city's discards. Their usefulness had gone. They had lapsed, like their own histories.

He ran along Piccadilly and down the Haymarket, then through Trafalgar Square into Whitehall. The government buildings had a fortified look, as if each room were a cubicle, battened down, and inside each cubicle a safe, and inside each safe a strong-box containing papers and letters, orders and responses, reports and memoranda that told how the world would fare, though the world would never know. The keepers of the boxes knew, but it was their privilege. They traded this for that; they struck bargains; they stole a march; they staked what they didn't own, bluffing, with impassive faces, on a broken flush. They cranked the world's machines while the world slept or married or mourned, while it bought and sold, brought cattle in from pasture, queued outside cinemas, played with children on

86

the beach, read an evening newspaper in the pub. There was nowhere to go, Guerney thought; there was nowhere you could go.

The river was empty of traffic. The tide was high, and the wind stronger along the Embankment. Reflections of riverside lights puckered and skipped in the backwash. He ran east towards the City, feeling the rhythm taking him now, and the initial heaviness beginning to leave his calves and thighs. He ran until his brain stopped manufacturing thought and, after forty-five minutes or so, turned instinctively back towards the hotel, not even conscious any more of the low hum the city seemed always to emit, although his mind had tuned to it as if some vast dynamo regulated his pace.

A bellboy brought the package to his room a few minutes after six o'clock: he'd told the desk that it was urgent and that he'd be expecting it. It contained a polaroid and a sheet of paper. The paper gave a time – 8 p.m. – and the address in Cheyne Walk. Guerney wasn't surprised. The photograph was of David Paschini. He was sitting on a straight-backed chair, looking straight at the lens and holding a copy of *The Times*, positioning it, with extended arm, to his right, so that his face wouldn't be obscured. He would check, he supposed – but Guerney knew it would be a reflex thing; the headlines would show it to be that day's paper. The boy's face was expressionless; it had the look of a face picked at random from a crowd of onlookers. He seemed wan and pinched. There was nothing in the eyes.

Guerney lifted the phone and asked for a copy of *The Times* to be reserved for him, then he spent ten minutes talking to Cesare Paschini before dialling Caroline Rance's number in Woodstock. She sounded distant and washed-out and a little drunk.

'It doesn't mean that David will be released.' He said it again, to make sure she'd understood: 'They won't release him until the money's secure.'

'Will you be able to see him, talk to him?' There was a

sudden urgency in her voice, as if the notion of some contact, even by proxy, had begun to excite her.

'He won't be there,' Guerney told her, making a positive statement out of a supposition. 'I'm quite sure they won't have him there.' He waited for her to ask why, in that case, they should want a meet at all, but it didn't occur to her.

'He's alive?' It was the third time she'd asked the question. 'You know he's definitely alive?'

'Yes, Caroline.' And he told her again about the photograph because it was what she most wanted to hear. He didn't say that he hadn't yet seen a copy of the paper. He was sure.

'I want to come over there.'

'No,' he said sharply.

'Jesus Christ, Simon.' She started to weep. 'I'm going crazy here. Please. Please let me come. How can it hurt?' He didn't reply, and her voice grew angry and wild, though she was still sobbing. 'Do you know what I'm going through, you bastard? Do you care? I can do as I please. He's not your son, not your son. You're the fucking hired help. You can't tell me what to do. Who are you? Jesus Christ, I'll get a plane if I choose. You bastard. Who are you?'

He put the phone down and waited for five minutes, then called again. She was still crying. 'Listen,' he said, 'we have to play this by the letter. Their terms. Right now, that's what we have to do. It seems that something is happening; they're letting me get closer.' He talked to her gently. 'I don't know what's going to happen, do you see? It wouldn't help – your being here. I don't know it's going to work. It might be important for you to be in Woodstock – who knows? He's alive; they've let me see that. They're talking about the transfer of the money. They want a meet. I don't want to disturb the balance.'

He thought of the suite at the Plaza, their strange claustrophobic domesticity, the air electric with suppressed hysteria. He thought of how, when he had answered the phone in the bedroom, her nakedness had meant nothing to her because fear had driven everything else out, and of how she would trek from chair to bottle, to and fro, until finally she gave up the pretence and kept the bottle by her.

'OK,' she said it weakly. 'OK. I don't know how I'll last. Please call me as soon as you can.' The words and tears ran together, making her voice a low drone. 'I don't sleep. I don't go out. What can I do, Simon?'

'He's alive,' Guerney said. 'Hang on to that.'

He breakfasted in the restaurant, scarcely bothering to scan the paper. The headlines matched, as he had known they would.

As he lifted a forkful of food to his mouth, Guerney was taken by a sudden flood of rage so intense, so unexpected, that he had to set the fork back on his plate and lean forward, his elbows on the table and his fingers rigidly interlocked, in order to contain it. He looked straight ahead, not registering what he saw, while the riptide of fury coursed through him. His fingers pressed on the backs of his hands with such violence that the steeple of his arms shook. The anger had struck him so quickly that he was scarcely able to rein it back. It was murderous and black and wholly useless.

They had run him. They had run him ragged. They were working his strings. He was out in the open and they were under cover, behind hides, doing whatever they did every day, guarding the boy. He thought of the man he had killed in Sardinia, of lashing his ankles to the low branch, of how his hands had slapped the ground as the bough swung back and bits and pieces had fallen from his trousers pockets. He thought of the woman: how she could only breathe through her mouth and how she had cried out each time the Renault hit a pothole or a rock. In part his fury had been kindled by compassion, and in part by fear – not his own, but that of the victim. The woman's fear; David's. More than anything, the threat of powerlessness appalled him. The panic and mad struggle of a snared animal.

Apart from the quaking tension in his forearms, he remained motionless for a full minute. Then, without there seeming to be a transition, continued to eat his breakfast. When he'd finished he went back to his room to wait, lying on the bed and leafing mechanically through the paper. George Buckroyd called him a few minutes after noon.

'I've got as much as I'm going to get,' he said, 'short of going round Century House with a questionnaire. There's not much. In fact there's damn all that's conclusive. You might well be on the wrong track, you know. I'd think of checking the possibility that the boy came in on a scheduled flight. I spoke to two people. Neither of them seemed to find the questions I asked anything but mildly puzzling, really. No signs of alarm, no slack-jawed astonishment, no threats. I'm not sure how much will get back, of course. There are still one or two people in the place who call me "sir" and value discretion. Well, two as it happens . . .'

'Anything that might help, George. What was said?'

'Well, I trailed various lures concerning the boy: was anyone under wraps at present, anyone been taken out of circulation recently, anything we might be helping Grosvenor Square with – an import, maybe, someone who'd been landed within the last few days? Had blind eyes been turned, or a little discreet help been requested? I even got risky and hinted at kidnap. Blank looks.'

'Genuine?' Guerney asked.

'I think so. I'm nigh-on certain. They're people who used to be on my staff; I think I know them well enough to pick up any signs. There's still a certain amount of loyalty involved, too, however unlikely that might seem; and they're old school. It's possible that they're the only two surviving human beings in the building. They were pretty curious, though. There's a deal of difference between soaking up the gossip over a drink now and then and actively seeking information. No way of avoiding that, I'm afraid.'

'How much risk, do you think?'

Buckroyd laughed. 'To you or to me?'

'Both. Either.'

'Not much, I suspect. Unless it's something that's going to shake the world. Anyway, since nothing seemed to be

90

connecting, there didn't seem any danger in getting a bit nearer the knuckle, so I filled in a few more pieces of the jigsaw – I mean, I was less vague about dates and geography. That's when I got a couple of faint echoes from the radar. Might mean nothing.' Guerney waited. 'The first is utterly unsurprising, but it is relevant so you'll want to know. It's not a secret that some of Paschini's consignments to this country contain a certain amount of funny stuff. It's also known that it finds its way to a knocking-shop in Cheyne Walk where it's cut and dealt. What wasn't clear was whether or not the Excise boys and the Drugs Squad know. Either way, it wouldn't really be anything to concern the faceless chinless down at Waterloo. The impression I got was that we're talking about a relatively small amount of heroin and that, in any case, Paschini is sufficiently powerful to be left alone even if he knows about the shipments – and that's by no means certain. He owns a large piece of the Italian business world; the days of powdered fish or whatever are far distant. There's no reason to believe that he's taking time out to organise some fairly penny-ante drug traffic. It's just something that Rome station happened to ferret out.'

'What about the brothel?'

'Christ knows, Simon. I'd doubt it, wouldn't you? One of the sidelines of whoever's selling the stuff this end, I imagine. I gather the girls are expensive, but value for money. I'd like to know who did that piece of research.'

'The second?' Guerney asked.

'Might be nothing. Who can say? You told me that the boy had been lifted when he was on his way to a lecture at his college. Dartmouth, isn't that right?'

'Yes.'

'Well, Dartmouth did bring a tic to the eye of one of my erstwhile staff. It seems that we had a presence up there for a while; in July, then again in September.'

'Alone? Just us?'

'No, no. The CIA were plodding about: it was their business, primarily.'

'What business?'

'I thought you'd ask that. I don't know. The person I spoke to was simply organising the bed and breakfast. They had a house in a place called North Pomfret, in Vermont, just across the state line and used to shuttle back and forth to Boston.'

'And now?'

'Yes, quite,' said Buckroyd drily. 'Our fellow hasn't gone back, I'm told. All in all, he was over there for about a fortnight.' There was a pause. 'It's probably quite coincidental,' Buckroyd went on. 'We're always sending odd bods to the States, you know that. And this wasn't fieldwork, so far as I can judge. There must have been crimes galore during that time: no reason to suppose that any of them relates in any way. Except for the rapes, of course,' he added.

'What was it, then?'

'Sorry?'

'It wasn't fieldwork, you said.'

'The chap was a technician of some sort. That's as far as I got. My man didn't know any more.' He waited for a response and got none. 'Remember, Simon, none of this might be particularly significant.'

'Not even if it's got up to look that way,' Guerney commented.

'Yes, there's that, too. Well, you know what I know; your guess is as good as mine.'

'And what's your guess?' Guerney asked him.

'The same as yours,' said Buckroyd, 'and what would that be?'

'No,' Guerney agreed, 'I don't know, either.' He was on the verge of telling Buckroyd about the latest phone-call and the instruction to be at Cheyne Walk at eight, but on second thought couldn't see what he might gain from doing that. Instead, he said: 'You know I'm grateful, George.'

'Be in touch if you need me: though, the way things are, it feels as if I've gone about as far as I can comfortably go . . . without having the dogs of Cold War sniffing round, I mean.'

'I know what you mean. Thanks again, George.'

'Yes. Take care, Simon.' There was warmth in the voice. 'Who knows – you could be right.'

Like someone opening a book at the marked page – someone whose eye falls at once on the next sentence to be read and remembers the image he last conjured – David Paschini took up the dream where he had left it. That was what he had wanted to do.

He was standing so as to face one of the back windows of the house. He could see straight through the room and beyond to where the fragile pinnacles of the firs, just visible above the sill, were whipped by the wind, seeming to furl and unfurl. Neither the man nor the dog was in the house, though the dog's basket was where he'd last seen it – by the stove – and a small reading-lamp had been left on. The kitchen had the look of a room that was lived in.

He dreamed he was dreaming it, and that made it possible to provoke an appearance. High in the top right-hand corner of the window-pane, he could see the reflection of the man, dropping, step by step, back down the nearside of the slope just as, before, he had vanished step by step. The dog ran ahead of him, coming down the hillside in little drifting runs, zig-zagging across the furrows. Although they were some way off, David allowed himself to see the man's features: a strong narrow face, slightly foxy like a gypsy's, a long nose, a high forehead. The wind had been at his hair and there was a slight curl to it: almost girlish.

The tiny image, occupying a fraction of the glass, was razor-sharp on its constant background of blue. David watched the scene descend the pane for a while, pleased by the notion of someone coming home. Then he moved things along. The man's form grew until it blurred, soon diminishing to a face that lay directly above the reflection of his own, the chin seeming to rest on his crown, and the features became, once again, hard-edged and perfectly in focus.

The eyes were on his. They could see each other's reflection, but not each other's true appearance; and David knew, as he was speaking, that his voice would make no sound. His mirror-image, drowned in sky, had no substance. It could ape speech, but couldn't speak. If the man could have brought himself face to face, or could have turned David, it would have been different. He knew it was futile, and he told himself to stop, but he continued to allow his reflection to mouth his story; what had happened, why, where he thought he might be and how frightened he was. He talked about his talent. He talked about what they had wanted from him.

He could see the man struggling to comprehend but failing, and he talked and talked, his stomach and chest muscles rigid with the effort to be audible, his throat thick and constricted with backed-up sound, until the terrible frustration of it brought him close to hysteria and he let the man go. He watched them both enter the kitchen, the dog nosing its bowl, asking to be fed. For a moment or two he controlled it still, but his strength was sapped. The dream fixed him where he stood until he became aware of someone else closing on him from behind. A face swam into focus and it was Tom, standing very close and grinning like a conjuror whose best trick has just worked perfectly. Tom's hands came into view, then circled David's head to cover his eyes. He was playing 'Guess who'. Then the hands fell to rest lightly on either side of David's neck. The fingers stroked his throat.

The man set the dog's bowl back on the floor and walked over to the window. Looking out, he was peering directly at David, their faces separated by little more than the thickness of the glass, but David knew the man could see no more than the hedge, the hill, the skyline and the sky.

And just before he turned away, perhaps, the ghost of himself.

7

A poacher's moon had risen, seeming to hang just above the buildings on the far bank of the Thames. It gave the water a thick yellow rind that glistened and undulated with the swell; the backwash from river-traffic looked like copper corrugation. Guerney thought of the animals quickening to the moon as it rose – foxes, badgers, owls – London's hidden nightlife.

He had found the Cheyne Walk address at seven-thirty and had been watching the place for almost half an hour. It was close to the house where the Getty heir lived his shuttered life, never emerging, never communicating. Apart from that one shabby façade, the whole row had about it the air of discretion, almost mystery, that wealth brings. Those doors and windows seemed to conceal events of importance that would be calmly and cleverly conducted by men and women who inhabited a world in which power and good breeding were no more than the starting-point.

The door Guerney had been watching hadn't opened. The windows were covered by heavy curtains that permitted no more than a dull glow to indicate that the house wasn't in darkness. The girls, he thought, must have been given the night off. He hadn't expected that his thirty-minute watch could give him much of an edge; nor had it. He'd seen and heard nothing helpful; and, in any case, they were expecting him. They had all the advantage. It was just instinct: a desire to study the terrain. Perhaps he'd hoped to get a glimpse of someone – the voice on the telephone, or any of those who were holding the boy. In some obscure

95

way, that always helped, and far beyond the simple advantage of having a face on file – a face to look out for, to track and run to earth. It had to do with the way primitive tribes fear a photograph.

He'd been watching from a position close to one of the stanchions of the Albert Bridge. A small boat puttered by, its wake silver and gold. He watched the effect for a few moments, then crossed the road and went straight to the dark front door. He pressed the bell and turned to face the grille of the entryphone. A woman's voice said: 'Yes?'

'Guerney,' he said, putting a hand to the door. A buzzer sounded. He pushed and went in. The door swung behind him, and clicked.

The woman was standing halfway down the long hallway that led into the house. She was pretty and young, and expensively dressed. She looked at him appraisingly, then indicated the door on her left. As he advanced on her she backed off a little to make it clear that he should enter the room first, then followed him in and closed the door.

'They're not here,' she said, crossing to a drinks-table in the centre of the room. 'You've to wait. Can I give you a drink?' Guerney shook his head. 'Sit down.' She didn't gesture to the chair, she pointed to it.

He sat with his back to the window and the heavy curtains. The woman made herself a gin and tonic, turning from him unconcernedly to scoop ice into her glass, then walked round the low table and lodged on the further arm of a sofa. They regarded one another in silence for a short while; then she asked: 'What do they want with you?'

'You don't know.' It wasn't really a question.

She sipped her drink. 'No, I don't.'

'Who are *they*?'

She made a circle with her glass that took in the room, the house. 'The people who run this place.'

'Who are you?'

'I work here. I'm a prostitute.' Clearly it amused her to tell him this. She smiled and put down her drink in order to take a cigarette from a box on the table. She lifted a table

96

lighter, but didn't use it immediately. 'Except that I'm not working tonight. No one is. Because of you. So I'm curious.' She paused. 'You don't seem taken aback.'

'I'm not,' Guerney said. 'How much do you sell for?'

She smiled again, and lit the cigarette. 'Should I be angry?'

'Of course not. Like you, I'm curious.'

'Lots of money,' she said. 'Lots and lots.'

'Expensive whores and heroin,' Guerney reflected. 'You must see many famous faces.'

She laughed aloud – genuinely amused. 'And a little gambling,' she said. 'Twice a week. No limit, no markers.'

'It all sounds very exciting.'

'Yes.' She spoke the word slowly, as if musing on the notion. 'Yes, it is. I hadn't thought of it that way for a while.'

'Will they be long?'

'I don't know.' She smiled. 'I was simply told to entertain you.'

Guerney grinned.

'What?' she asked.

'It's amusing – watching a whore being flirtatious.'

The girl narrowed her eyes and set her drink down on the table. 'Well, well,' she said. 'There's not much of the punter in you, it seems.'

For the next five minutes, they sat in silence, the girl taking an occasional sip from her glass, or letting her eyes wander round the room. Guerney watched her. Finally, she looked at her wristwatch. 'We've got another ten minutes or so,' she said. 'I was told to put out for you if you wanted that. Do you want that?'

Guerney shook his head, continuing to look at her. Then he said: 'Ten minutes' worth, on the house. It's a bit patronising, don't you think?'

'I hope you don't come to grief,' she said. 'I think I rather like you.' Guerney laughed out loud and the girl looked at him unblinkingly for a few seconds. 'Do you think I'm beautiful?' she asked.

'You know you are.'

'Do *you* think I am?'

He nodded.

The girl sighed and lit a fresh cigarette. 'Sometimes,' she said, 'I look in the mirror . . . just look and look until it's not my face any more; then I take my clothes off, piece by piece, and look at my body. I use two mirrors, so that I can see everything. I want to know what it's like to stand behind me. My spine, my waist, the way my hips curve – you know? It staggers me, how beautiful I am. I look at my breasts and my legs and my face and the slope of my back when I half-turn . . . The saddest thing in my life is that I can't make love to me. They're not coming here.' She checked her watch again, and crossed the room to take a piece of paper from beneath a clock on the mantel. 'You have to go to them.' She handed Guerney the paper. On it was the name and address of a trading estate in south London, and beneath that: *Unit 37*.

She took him to the front door, and he paused for a moment after he'd stepped outside. 'What's your name?' he asked her.

'Stella. It's a beautiful name, isn't it?'

'Yes,' he said, 'it is,' and watched as she closed the door, slowly, inch by inch.

In Cheyne Walk he hailed a cab and told the driver to drop him in Earls Court. From there, he walked to Kensington, zig-zagging, doubling back, holing up in a pub from time to time and watching the door. Next he took a series of tubes, beginning at Kensington High Street and ending at Marble Arch, using all the techniques he'd employed when going to meet George Buckroyd. Finally, he walked to Sussex Gardens and checked into one of the small anonymous hotels there. He called himself Peterson. The room was chilly and meagre. Because there was nothing left that he could usefully do, he lay down on the narrow bed and slept.

It was as if he were the lens of a camera, or a disembodied eye. He could see a forearm and hand ushering him from room to room in a house he'd never visited before; he was being shown the layout. There was a functional bathroom off a wide corridor, then a number of rooms that, for some reason, he wasn't permitted to see into. A broad staircase led down to a spacious hall and two rooms with a connecting door. The smaller of the two was being used as a bedroom. There were bars at the window. Guerney didn't care for the place. It had about it the air of a house that had never been occupied for long. Nowhere was there any evidence of an individual taste or style, nothing that showed a preference, none of the bits and pieces that knock around in people's lives.

The hand indicated the barred window. Looking out, Guerney could see a chestnut-tree and guessed it must have looked glorious in full leaf. Beyond the lattice of branches was a hill. A large cross had been cut out of the turf. It was, maybe, a hundred feet in height and stark white; the hillside must have been solid chalk. Towards its base, the upright cross broadened, like the Maltese cruciform. Apart from this one landmark, the hill was thickly wooded with beeches. His gaze shifted to the bed, then to the room beyond the open connecting door. He was aware that when he looked here or there, this way or that, it wasn't entirely by his own volition. He was being instructed, though not bullied; was being helped to garner information.

He said: 'I understand, David. I understand.' He couldn't see the boy, but felt his presence and sensed his complicity. David's hand, palm uppermost, motioned him to the door. Three men were seated at a table, playing cards. Guerney concentrated on their faces. The gesturing hand closed into a fist with one finger extended. It was pointing not at the men, but at the table and the deck of cards that lay in its centre, as if to say: 'Watch this.'

Guerney felt a charge of energy pass him: as if it were possible to detect the jolt from an electrical current, but at a distance. One by one, cards began to peel off the deck, rising into the air in an even flow, starting slowly then quickening until the whole deck was in space and travelling towards the wall. One by one, with a rapid staccato of taps, they struck the wall and fell.

One of the men yelled, and they all got to their feet, their eyes fixed on the airborne train of cards and the litter that followed the crash. Someone else came into the room from a door to the left of the table. Another of the men pulled a gun, then lowered it. The new arrival stared at them as they, in turn, stared at the muddle of playing-cards near the skirting-board.

There followed a moment when Guerney was outside the house, looking in through the barred window. David Paschini was lying on the bed and appeared to be asleep. Two of the men were in the room with him, one looking round, gun in hand, the other bending over the boy to see whether he slept. Before he woke, Guerney registered that the house had white shutters.

'Where are you now?' Buckroyd asked.

Guerney trapped the phone under his jaw and tied the lace of one shoe. 'Sussex Gardens. I discover that I've been sleeping in a bed with purple nylon sheets.'

'Corrupting,' replied Buckroyd. 'You're sure it was a set-up?'

'Oh, yes. No question. Unmistakable smell of fish.' Guerney's tone was light and tense.

'Which means they're not interested in barter?'

'Probably. They might know more about me than I'd imagined.'

'They kill you, then re-open negotiations.'

'Maybe that.'

'Or maybe the boy's dead.'

'No.' Guerney started on the other shoe-lace.

'You can't know that,' said Buckroyd.

'George, the real reason I phoned was to ask you whether you can identify a landmark for me. It's a cross cut into a chalk down, among beechwoods. Quite large. Cross-shaped except for the lower part of the upright; that goes into a sort of delta-shape. Not in moorland, not in a deserted place. Near a village, I should think. A well-to-do area. Big houses, big gardens.'

'It rings a bell.' Buckroyd paused. 'No, it's not going to come that easily. I'll rifle through some books and get back to you, shall I?'

'I'll phone you,' Guerney told him. 'An hour? At eleven?'

'Should be long enough.'

'OK, George,' Guerney said. 'Thanks.'

After he'd put the phone down, Guerney thought through the dream for a while. He tore the endpaper from a Gideon Bible that lay on the bedside cabinet and made a rough ground plan of those parts of the house that he'd been shown. As he sketched in the door that connected the two downstairs rooms, he recalled the sizzle of energy that had flipped the cards, without touching them, and made them fly. David Paschini's fist and pointed finger were indelible on his mind's eye. *Watch this*. He wondered what the hell was going on. He tested the business along his nerve-endings, failing to get back a damn thing he recognised or could put a name to.

It was Rachel. Rachel had entered through the door to the left of the table. Scared, disorientated, one of the men had drawn his gun, then lowered it when he'd seen who the newcomer was. She had paused by the doorway, not understanding the reason for their alarm. Uncomprehendingly, her eyes had followed theirs to the jumble of cards, and she had frowned. She'd had jeans on, and a sweater that she'd worn often during their short time on Long Island.

For the next fifty minutes, Guerney sat cross-legged on the bed, backed up to the pillows, and built himself a little nest of quietness; a vacuum. He breathed as if he were asleep, and his mouth sagged. One by one, he allowed his limbs to become insubstantial, then his hips and ribcage, then his head, until he could feel only the fatness of his tongue, a soft sleek weight that slowly evaporated as his pulse rate dropped. On the hour he emerged and telephoned Buckroyd.

'I remembered,' Buckroyd said, 'almost as soon as I'd

put the phone down. But I looked it up anyway. How much do you need to know?'

'What is there?'

'The theory is that it was a vast phallus at one time – pre-Christian. The reason that it deltas out like that at the bottom is that the church fathers were appalled by it, and changed the upright of the phallus to a cross by widening the shaft and adding a cross-piece. They couldn't efface the balls, though; not by leaving the – ah – upright as it was. So they broadened the base to obliterate them. I can't help thinking that the act is laden with errant symbolism. Do you know anything about the Fisher King myth?'

'Where is it, George?'

'The Home Counties. Mid-Bucks. A place called Whiteleaf. The marker itself is called Whiteleaf Cross. The village is about a mile off the A4010 between Princes Risborough and Aylesbury. Is the boy down there, d'you think?'

'In some ways,' Guerney said, 'I hope not. I think he is.'

'OK, I won't ask.'

'George,' Guerney hesitated, 'I'm not being evasive. There are things that I can't get a fix on. Chinese boxes, mazes, dead ends, dreams . . . I don't know.'

'Well, well,' Buckroyd said reflectively. 'Our Lord taught in parables. Just take care, Simon. Check in from time to time.'

'Is that dangerous?'

'I don't think so, no. I'll know if they bug me. If I tell you it's a wrong number, get off the line.'

'I'm very grateful, George; you know that?'

Buckroyd chuckled. 'I'm having fun. Hadn't you imagined I might?'

8

He took the M40 to the High Wycombe exit. For the first few miles, he had tried to apply his mind to what was happening to him. He reconstructed the dream in which he and David had met at Druid's Combe, the way the boy's face had not quite resembled his photographs, the frustration of his stoppered speech. He went back to his meeting with David's father and saw the nimble fingers manipulating the cigarette and the haze of smoke rising. He pictured Rachel's face in the cabin bedroom on Long Island, the way her eyes widened just before she came and how, afterwards, she lay looking straight up at the ceiling, her tongue arrowing out to take droplets of perspiration from her upper lip. He heard her voice on the phone giving him the address in Cheyne Walk. He recalled Caroline Rance's fingers trembling as she scooped the spilled ice back over the rim of her glass and the way her hair dragged in the nap of her fur coat as she waited for the elevator.

They all seemed dream images. He felt dangerously detached from the world. Driving through London, and now through the Buckinghamshire town, he found himself looking at people in the streets as if their actions, or appearance, might possess some oblique significance. A tramp lying on a patch of grass by the roadside; two men wheeling bikes; a pair of teenagers with coxcombs of pink and green hair pecking at one another's lips as they waited for a bus; a woman in a green tracksuit jogging on the verge. Maybe they added up to something: fragments of the pattern that had brought him this far. He felt dazed by their presence, by the randomness that made them a part of his drive to Whiteleaf, and by what he was doing – going to a place he had seen in a dream in the expectation of finding there someone who had both appeared in the dream and stage-managed it. Someone who drew him on in his pursuit, who visited him while he slept, who could shuffle a deck from a distance.

Guerney knew that there was more at risk here than mere failure. Something dark and limitless and unguessable was involved. It nudged his mind's moorings. He switched his thoughts to the men who had been at the table. He considered the things he could recognise: a voice on the phone, bargaining, sending him to the Connaught, telling him to expect evidence that David wasn't dead. Even in the dream, there had been the drawn gun; it seemed a reassurance. Then he remembered the pile of cards and Rachel entering the room.

He found the place easily and stopped the car, briefly, at the foot of the cross. The wide chalk scar came right down to the narrow road. He hadn't been at all surprised to have passed the house with white shutters half a mile earlier. Shocked, but not surprised. He drove a circle of something like four miles, skirting the town of Princes Risborough and driving back along the main road until he neared the turn-off that led to Whiteleaf village. A pub – the Black Horse – stood near the junction. It offered accommodation, and Guerney booked a room for that night. From his window he could see the four footpaths that led to the beechwoods and the dome of the hill where the cross was carved. He went down to the bar for a drink, as he knew he must. It was risk: it was all risk. No one spoke to him, or gave him a second look.

An hour later, he lodged himself among the bare branches of a beechtree and looked down at the house with white shutters. There were little stingers of sleet in the wind; they grazed his cheek. He could see the chestnut-tree and, beyond it, the barred window. A dark green BMW stood in the driveway. There was no detectable movement inside the house, and no one came or left.

Guerney worked out an approach and two escape routes, judging that it would be better to leave his car some way off. He stayed in the tree until the early dusk, circling the house in his mind, like a dog looking for a safe place to lie. Then he returned to the Black Horse, let the landlord know that he wouldn't be in for supper, went to his room, set his watch alarm for 3 a.m. and stretched out on the bed. From his bedroom window, he would be able to drop on to the porch above the pub doorway and swing himself down to the ground. He had brought with him a small grip that contained some dark clothing and a slender-bladed knife that fishermen use for gutting. He lacked a gun; there hadn't been time for that.

His technique would be to draw them out, somehow, one by one. He'd rehearsed a method of doing that during his observation of the house, but it wasn't quite the clear-edged thing it should have been; its details were blurred by a distraction – the dream image of Rachel, her possible presence in the house. He couldn't have said quite why, but he believed she was in there; and he wanted, somehow, to be able to talk to her.

He had already come to terms with the fact that he might have to kill her.

They ate early – at seven o'clock. Harry had made meat-loaf. In their bizarre domestic routine, it was one of the house specialities. Tom uncorked a bottle of wine and set it down at the centre of the table. The wind had risen. Each could hear it, splitting somewhere on an angle of the brick-work, a low sonorous noise that climbed in pitch now and then when it was answered by a small billow from the chestnut-tree.

Rachel looked towards the locked door of David's room. 'The boy doesn't get any?' she asked.

Dick cut his food with his fork and shook his head. 'Not tonight.'

'We're moving.'

'Yes.'

'You'll have to drug him?'

'Yes.'

'You don't think I might have been told?'

'I'm telling you now.'

'Why?'

'You asked.'

'Are we moving?' She let the annoyance show. Dick had known what she meant.

'It's time. We've been here long enough.'

'And?'

'We've been told to.' He saw the next question coming and provided the answer. 'Another safe house – in London this time.'

'Me, too?'

'You, too, Rachel. For the time being.'

She looked across the table to where Tom and Harry bent slightly to their food, and felt a strengthening of her dislike. In the three days that she had been with them she'd kept her distance, and they resented it. She had recognised Dick's senior status from his indifference to her; from the way, too, that it was he who made the phone-calls and passed their instructions on. To him, she was one of the team: there to do a job. Tom and Harry, though, had colonised the house in some small way – had almost made a home of it. Harry would set off in the car to fetch provisions, asking everyone, before each sortie, whether there was something they specially needed. He'd return with his packages, having remembered Tom's Southern Comfort. Once back, he'd potter round the kitchen putting the groceries away and planning a menu. She had watched him breaking eggs into a glass bowl, then tilting the bowl to beat them, his sleeves rolled back on his forearms, and had wondered how many people he'd killed.

On the first day, he, like Tom, had been talkative and flirtatious – eager to involve her in their household. After dinner, they had tried to make a night of it. Tom had sat at the table, opened his bottle of rye and rather too ostentatiously stripped his gun to clean it. The obviousness of that made her want to guffaw. Harry had said just enough to allow her to infer that Tom was thought to be a mild pain in the ass. She'd frozen them out by persisting with questions they didn't want to answer. She wouldn't flirt back and she wouldn't become one of the guys. It was as if she had disrupted an incipient cosiness. She could tell that Dick was vaguely amused by this and didn't like him any the more for it. He's a supercilious bastard, she thought, and wondered whether he knew that she'd already been given answers to her questions.

It had been clear that, although Ed Jeffries had travelled to New York rather than summon Rachel to Washington, this didn't make him a supplicant – a fact which he had underlined by motioning her to a chair before going to the long window of the upper East Side apartment where they'd met and gazing out for some time before turning to confront her. The technique had wearied her. She'd known who had the *wah* – and imagined that he'd think of it that way. Holy Christ, she thought, 'I'm beginning to develop a low tolerance for all this shit.'

Ed had fallen into the armchair and hooked a leg over one side, then run a finger along his jawline while he'd regarded her. She'd looked back, enjoying the silent speech that was running through her head: *Who are you, motherfucker? What do you want – an Oscar nomination? You're full of it, know that? It's coming out of your ears and staining your collar, asshole.* She'd smiled at him while letting the insults run out, allowing a tiny apprehension to weaken her smile.

After a few more seconds of silence and level gazes, Jeffries had spread a hand, palm towards her, as if measuring something, and said: 'Rachel, we're going to have to take him out.'

'Guerney.'

He'd made the hand a fist and tapped his knee with it, gently. 'It was always likely.'

Rachel hadn't stopped to think about how the information

affected her; there wasn't time for that. Later, there would have to be. She'd merely asked the obvious: 'Why are you telling me?'

'We need you; or we might . . .'

Fuck you. She'd nearly said it; it had almost passed her teeth. Instead she'd laced her fingers in front of her face, as if about to rest her chin on them, and tried to look thoughtful. 'Why?'

'I'm not sure Guerney is going to be that easy to kill.'

'I'm not sure you're wrong. What am I – a Trojan cow?'

'If necessary.' Jeffries had got up from the chair and gone back to gazing out at the East River. To some, he might have looked like a man burdened by an unpleasant task or a life-changing decision, weighing the pros and cons, trying to do the best for all concerned; knowing that, though it might be painful, you just had to tough it out, pick your pick and go for it. The dialogue wrote itself.

'What's the deal?' she'd asked.

'Go to London tonight.' He'd wheeled round, an expression of firm resolve on his face. 'We'll move on him in a couple of days. You might be useful. If he slips the people over there, you'll certainly be useful.'

Rachel had decided it was time to modify her role a little. 'What makes you think I'll do it, Ed?'

He had been expecting this – or so it seemed. 'What makes you think it's a request?'

'Even so.'

He'd sat on the arm of his chair and regarded her with what was supposed to be a mixture of sternness and compassion. Now he was the general, persuading the timid rookie to go over the top.

'Do you know what's at risk for you here, Rachel?' She'd waited for an answer. Jeffries had made a quick gesture of crumpling something and throwing it away. 'Everything's at risk.' He'd nursed a pause, then said: 'You don't want that.'

His jaw jutted. Although he'd been across the room from her, his faced had seemed close to her own.

George C. Scott, she'd thought, holding his glare for a second or two before letting her eyes drop. Ed's tone had softened as he told her about the arrangements for getting her to the safe house and sketched the set-up there – Tom, Dick, Harry, David Paschini. Then, because it was likely that she would be more involved than any of them, he'd told her about David and about why they had wanted him. Or, rather, he'd told her something like that. Finally, he'd given her instructions about how she was to handle Guerney if the need arose. As she'd listened, she'd realised that she hadn't the slightest idea what she was going to do.

'Let's make it thirty minutes, OK?' Dick's slight Southern burr was fey and somehow sinister for that. They were casual about their preparations for leaving, checking that they were taking out all personal possessions, but worrying little about any other trace of their stay that the house might still hold. Evidently the place was secure.

After she had packed her few clothes, Rachel crossed her room to look at the chestnut-tree that lay squarely in her view. The wind was moving the branches so that they opened and closed on ovals and sickle-shapes when they crossed. The full moon made the sky a rich dark blue; the black branches circumscribed it and the wind changed the shape of what they held. If she half-closed her eyes, it was a blue-black kaleidoscope. She could hear the keen of the wind on a gable-end.

Witchery, she thought, *the night is full of witchery* – then immediately wondered what on earth it was in her that could have responded to such an idea. She laughed, but what she really felt was intense irritation. A porch light came on, and someone walked out to the car. Rachel turned and snatched her bag from the bed. She wished to Christ she were back in New York behind the five locks on her apartment door, listening to music and smoking a slow joint, looking out at the barbaric neon.

David Paschini was being supported on either side by Tom and Harry. He was conscious, but barely. They loaded him into the back seat, then sat one on either side of the boy. David was muttering incomprehensibly, a monotone that occasionally rose to a whimper of exclamation when he would flinch and roll his head. Rachel got into the passenger seat alongside Dick.

'Is he OK?' she asked.

Dick glanced over his shoulder before putting the key into the ignition. 'Sure,' he said offhandedly, 'he's fine. He'll be out soon.'

By the time they reached the main road where they would turn to the motorway, David had fallen silent and his eyes were closed; from time to time, though, he would twitch, and his breathing was rapid. Rachel turned to look at him again.

'Don't worry,' Dick told her, 'he's just fine.' As he spoke, he was looking left and right at the junction. The road was clear, so he pulled out, passing the Black Horse on his right. It was nine-thirty.

To begin with it was like picking up on a television serial: the same characters taking the drama on from where they'd left it, the pack of cards their focal point. Rachel walked over to where the cards lay on the floor. Tom put his gun away. All three men left the table and joined Rachel, who crouched and reassembled the pack, finally handing it to Dick, who looked at it, then riffled the edges and shrugged. It seemed that they had been shaken by the incident but, oddly, not surprised.

He wanted to let David know that he was close, so he formed a picture of the cross, then another of the house as he had seen it from his vantage-point in the tree. Immediately he experienced a small surge of energy, like a gust of wind at his back. His mind-picture changed, becoming a daytime scene. Rachel and the men were drinking coffee and talking. It occurred to him that, if he could see their faces clearly, he might be able to hear them. Then the picture fogged, going slightly out of focus.

A zoom lens took him in on Rachel's mouth as she spoke,

though nothing was audible. He could see her tongue moving as she mouthed words. As he watched, the tongue swelled and distorted until it was the head of a snake, slithering between her teeth, its own tongue flickering at her lip. Guerney tried to draw back but couldn't. The snake began to emerge, slowly, stretching Rachel's mouth and belling her cheeks obscenely. Inch by inch it came, its body growing ever thicker until the lips it issued from were forced so far it seemed they must split and the jaw dislocate.

Rachel's face became frog-like. She hopped on to the table and squatted there, flanks palpitating. With a gulp, she swallowed the snake. Instantly, its flat bevelled head emerged from her vagina, worming out between plump, cantilevered thighs, dragging its bulk along the table in a thin glue of slime. Rachel's vulva gaped as the vast sinewy sleekness flowed out, thickening and thickening. She croaked. Her eyes swivelled with pleasure.

The men watched, attentive as thrushes. Their noses had sharpened and toughened to beaks. As the snake began to slither over the edge of the table, they darted in, one by one, and pecked at it, removing chunks from its side. They clapped the hot red meat under their tongues and squawked. The frog-Rachel grinned and made liquid gobbling noises in the pouch of her throat. The men strutted forward and fed her the gouts of flesh, disgorging them into her slitted mouth.

In the back seat of the car, David Paschini whimpered and flung out a hand, striking Tom lightly on the chest. In the same moment, Guerney turned in his damp sheets, striking out but not waking. Images of his own devising mingled with David's in a cross-transmission of terror. For two hours he ran the gauntlet of such images. He visited Hell with no notion that he might ever return.

A cyclops bore the head of a prophet on a spearpoint, the flesh seething with maggots, the beard matted with honey. Caravaggio's wanton youth melted like candle-wax, hair and eyeballs, lips and teeth, sliding in a formless clogged gobbet until only the glistening bones were left, meatless

111

and wet. A barren yellow landscape sputtered and cracked like lava-flow. Soldiers dragged themselves across it, pursued by long-legged birds. Those they caught the birds disembowelled, yanking out the purple coils of gut and shaking them like worms.

A raw featureless form that was Caroline Rance seeped droplets of blood like sweat-beads, and pointed to where her flayed skin was nailed to a wall. Behind a mask lay another mask and behind that another and behind that the face of David Paschini himself, which was yet another mask and came free with a fibrous ripping sound to reveal a network of nerves like filigree wires, each crackling with voltage and giving off a smell of scorch.

Four Dobermanns ran stiff-legged with malice in the space between a high wall and a wire-mesh fence. The wall was topped with shards of glass; and, in any case, no one could have cleared the fence from the wall. The dogs' domain was twenty-five feet wide. Anything inside it would not last for long. Tom closed and padlocked the gate that let into the fence, then walked back to the house. Rachel was standing at the door, watching him.

'Are those things lethal?' she asked.

Tom grinned. 'Chew the ass off anything stupid enough to get in there with them.'

Rachel watched the beasts trotting back and forth, streamlined like sharks and tense with backed-up energy. She turned to go into the house, and Tom chuckled, patting her on the rump as he did so. 'If I was a Dobermann, I'd sure as hell chew yours.' Rachel quickened her pace slightly and went into the main room.

Dick was using the telephone, saying little more than 'Yes, OK, sure,' and 'Right.' Harry was beyond in the kitchen, making coffee. When Dick had hung up, Rachel asked after the boy.

'Drug's pretty much worn off now, I guess.' Dick drew a hand across his eyes and yawned. 'He'll just sleep until morning.'

'What does it do to him?'

Dick gave her a look of surprise. 'Keeps him quiet.'

He was closing the subject, so Rachel switched to another. Nodding at the phone, she asked: 'What did they say?'

'I was just touching base.'

'And?'

Dick shrugged.

'Oh, for Christ's sake!' Rachel strode into the kitchen and helped herself to some of Tom's rye.

When she emerged, Dick shrugged again. 'We're on hold for a while.'

'Sure,' Rachel replied. 'OK. Screw it.'

She took her drink upstairs and went into the room that had been prepared for David. It was windowless, save for a skylight with a grille bolted across it. No one had bothered to lock the door: the boy was out cold. Rachel watched the almost imperceptible rise and fall of his ribcage. His face was placid, but seemed very pale in the dim nightlight. She sipped her whisky and stared at the boy until his features blurred in the gloom, and wondered whether she felt anything and, if so, what? Tired, mostly. It had occurred to her that their reason for moving must be connected to the attempt to kill Guerney, so presumably that had failed. She knew she was doing no more than reading the signs, but that was what seemed most likely. They'd missed. *Good*, she thought.

There came into her mind a vision of Guerney, moving silently through the undergrowth like a fox, while loud clumsy feet trampled the bracken. The image pleased her, and she tinkered with it, adding a full moon, putting the wind direction in Guerney's favour, giving him a sharp nose for scents and a knowledge of the terrain. The pursuers clattered about amateurishly, while Guerney lay low, second-guessing them and circling away from their line of approach. He went belly down, ears cocked to their clamour, their scents hot in his nostrils.

She enjoyed it for a while, seeing the scene with increasing clarity – ferns silvered by moonlight, the sweating, clumsy hunters tripping and swearing and labouring after their quarry, the night-breeze carrying their stink directly to the lithe soundless shape that flickered downhill and away, gaining a small stream in the valley and wading along it for a while before entering the featureless dark of a wood. Guerney as a fox.

Then she remembered why Ed Jeffries had ordered her to London.

For half an hour after he woke, Guerney continued to battle with the nightmare. Shapes squatted in corners, or scuttled across the floor to disappear in pockets of shadow; the ghosts of cries rose like miasma and echoed from the high ceiling. At times, the land of nightmare asserted itself so strongly that he wasn't sure whether he'd really woken or not and toured the room touching objects, or glancing out of the window at the soft Buckinghamshire countryside, or whispering reassurance to himself: *the window, trees, a road, a table, the bed, the Black Horse, my feet on the floor, my hand against the wall, nothing else, nothing else . . .*

Eventually, the horrors began to dissipate and that, for a while, was almost worse. As his mind emerged from the shadow, Guerney began to understand what had happened to him, and the knowledge was all but overwhelming. The fear of madness touched him like a dark wing. It was all the more frightening to realise that what he'd been through had been inflicted on him – an invasion. He'd been a host for someone else's parasite.

He lay full length on the bed and consciously relaxed, tensing each set of muscles in turn, then releasing, deliberately filling his mind with a procession of tranquil images: the trees below Druid's Combe, buzzards circling, the dog loping over pastureland. After ten minutes or so, he sat up and checked his pulse. It was more or less normal. He sat on for another five minutes debating with himself the option of pulling out. *I just visited a place*, he thought, *that I don't ever want to go back to. I could get trapped there. I could become a resident.*

He shuddered, paused, then got up and took a dark

blouson from his grip and put it on; he also took out the gutting-knife and threaded the sheath on to his belt. He'd slept in his clothes and they gave off a thin sour smell of sweat that was three parts fear. The odour acted as an *aide-mémoire* and took him back for a second, so that he shook his head, violently, like someone emerging from a dive into deep water.

He'd planned to go at 3 a.m. It was close to midnight, but he reasoned that he dare not wait any longer. Looping the long strap of the grip over his shoulder and chest, he opened the window, eased out on to the sill, then down on to the porch. There were lights on somewhere beyond the bar area, but no one was close. Guerney swung down into the forecourt. He had deliberately parked his car close to the road. He didn't switch his headlights on until he was clear of the pub by sixty yards and travelling along the side-road that led to the house with white shutters.

Dick was on the phone again, but this time taking a call, not making it. He made virtually no contribution, just listened and muttered 'Uh-huh', or 'Yes', as if he were being told how to get from one place to another. Harry was asleep in an armchair. Tom had tried to maintain a conversation with Rachel for a while, until Harry had waved him to silence.

After five minutes or so, Dick hung up, wordlessly, and looked at Rachel. 'They've had time to consult,' he said. 'It looks like your turn now.' He got up and dry-washed his face with his hands, making for the door. 'We'll talk in the morning. I'm bushed.'

Tom watched him leave the room and let ten seconds elapse before going to give Rachel another shot of whisky, standing close to her while he poured it. He patted her shoulder, letting his hand linger. 'Field-work,' he said. 'How do you feel about that?'

Rachel concentrated on not pulling back from his touch. She smiled as he nudged the glass a little nearer to her hand. 'I'll have to find out. It's new territory for me.'

Tom went back to his own chair and sat on the edge,

leaning forward in a manner meant to be friendly and conspiratorial. 'Maybe I could give you a few pointers,' he offered. 'You know, some technique. Help to give you an edge.' His grin was supposed to be boyishly crooked, but it spread like a leer. 'I wouldn't want that pretty ass to wind up in a sling.'

Rachel raised her glass in salute. 'Sure,' she said, 'maybe some time tomorrow. I'd like that. Thanks.'

'No sweat.' Tom tossed back his drink manfully. 'No sweat.' He glanced over at Harry, poleaxed in the chair. 'I'll make sure you stay out of trouble.'

Guerney could tell the place was empty long before he came close; even so, he went in, using a credit card on the front door that they hadn't bothered to double-lock. He took what he could from the place: a few sense impressions based on the traces they'd left. It was clear that he'd missed the boy by a matter of no more than an hour or two. In David's room he could detect the remnant of their nightmare. The same shadows. The same sulphurous smell. The sort of heaviness in the air that comes before an electric storm. He backed off from it, like an animal from fire.

They had left nothing that might give him a lead on their destination. An empty Southern Comfort bottle stood on the draining-board in the kitchen. Someone had doused a cigar butt under the tap and dropped it into the sink. In one of the bedrooms he found a tissue smeared with make-up. He held it to his nose for a moment as if taking the scent of a flower.

9

The same chintzy furniture, the same view of the park. The same suite of rooms and the same props. A bottle of Scotch on the coffee-table, an ice-bucket, her fur coat visible through the open door of the closet, the telephones lying just where they had lain. It seemed to her that, somehow, in this suite of rooms, things would be easier to bear. It was the site of her anguish, but also of her hope.

Many people would have stayed there since the day after Christmas. The rooms would have been cleaned many times; the sheets stained and replaced, stained and replaced; the chairs sat in; the drapes drawn and parted. Different bodies would have stepped into and out of the shower, used the same door-key, flipped through the television channels, lounged in the armchairs. Caroline felt as if she had never been away.

She ran the shower, but forgot to get into it. When room service arrived with the *noisette d'agneau* and salad that she'd ordered, scarves of steam were rounding the bedroom door and wafting just below the ceiling. The waiter looked curiously at them as he lifted the leaves of the portable table, set the struts to support them, and rearranged the food. After she'd tipped him, he nodded towards the building fog and said: 'Shower, lady?' His English was heavily accented, and she didn't catch the remark; she smiled, assuming he was thanking her. The waiter shrugged and put the five-dollar bill into the top pocket of his stiff white jacket. What did he care?

Caroline sat down to eat. She cut a piece off the lamb,

then cut another, then a third, and went on cutting until the meat lay in bite-sized pieces on the plate. She drank a couple of glasses of wine, then forked a lettuce leaf and put the fork, with the lettuce still on the prongs, down on the plate among the meat.

The steam crawled in slowly from the bedroom door, then eddied violently as it met the updraught from the room-heaters. It circled in nacreous streamers round the lamps. A pearly light suffused the room, glowing like a morning mist over meadows just before the sun breaks through. She went to the window and noticed that the panes were opalescent with moisture. She wiped them with her palm and peered out into the city's dusk. There were people and cars and lights and the faint susurration of noise that was all she could hear, at that height, of the street-level clamour.

Walking jauntily, she went to the telephone and lifted it from its cradle but then made no move to dial. She listened to the dialling tone for a while before going back to the table and sitting down in front of the plate of food. For a full ten minutes, she stared at the table and what it held until everything grew two-dimensional. It was an enjoyable effect that reduced the objects to mere representations of themselves. Steam flooded the room. Caroline left the table and went towards the couch, switching the television on as she passed it. Mysterious characters, warped by the cloudy shimmer, appeared and disappeared without logic or warning. After watching the succession of colours and faces for a few minutes, Caroline leaned slowly forward, put her forehead on her knees, and wept. Steam buffeted her in billows, and condensed, and settled on her like dew.

David felt light and brittle – bird-boned, his skin papery. He shivered and looked around his new prison. This time there was no view, nothing to fix on.

Close – Guerney had been so close, his presence almost palpable, and David had drawn strength from that. For a short while, he had even permitted himself to hope. Maybe he had inadvertently given something away, had provided the men with a reason for suspicion. Flying the cards, perhaps, or sleeping so often. If only his gift were strong enough to be a means of escape. But that wasn't its nature. He couldn't control minds with it, or fell trees, or spring a locked door. He could tune in to someone who was receptive; he could switch a light on and off or start a vacuum cleaner; he could make cards travel across a room or close a door. Sometimes he could bend metal or make things disappear for a while. That was how they had first noticed. His childhood temper tantrums would occasionally result in some object disappearing for a few minutes – salt-cellar, a cigarette-box. When they 'came back' the metal parts would be hot to the touch.

To begin with his mother had been distressed by it, and frightened. She'd sought help. Their local doctor wasn't sure whether he should pass David or Caroline over to a psychiatrist – both perhaps. They went from consulting-room to consulting-room and from sceptic to sceptic until, eventually, they found someone who thought them neither mad nor deluded.

A man from a government department made an appointment to see them in Woodstock. A little later, both Caroline and David went to New York, and a number of men ran tests over the course of a week. Mother and son were installed at the Waldorf-Astoria in company with a woman named Annette, who made sure they had what they needed and took Caroline on shopping and sightseeing expeditions while David was switching lights on and off and bringing hairdriers to life without moving from his chair. He had found the tests tiring and more than a little boring, though the men who had worked with him had been encouraging and endlessly patient.

Annette slept in the smallest of the three bedrooms. She and Caroline would often stay up late, drinking and chatting. Caroline grew to like her. It was Annette who persuaded her to allow David's daily performances to be filmed – a process he'd rather enjoyed. It was Annette who told her, after the week was up, about the nature of David's talent – how it was not so unusual, how many children with David's ability had been identified and that there was certainly nothing particularly abnormal about the boy. These were powers, she told Caroline, that many people possess, though they are latent. In David, and others like him, they were a little stronger, a little more obvious: that was all. The boy wasn't disturbed or dangerous; he was a lot like any other kid who could run faster, jump higher, calculate more rapidly or read much sooner than his friends. There were prodigies in music, in chess, in maths, Caroline was told; David's gift was comparable. Did anyone think of Mozart as a freak, or Einstein?

David and his mother went home to Woodstock and continued to live their life. Now and then, David would amuse her by switching on her reading-lamp to save her the trouble, or annoy her by changing the television channel to a sports programme when she was watching something else. By and large, though, Caroline had thought little more about her son's strange gift.

Close, he thought, *so close*. He felt depressed and fragile.

The grey glow beyond the skylight told him that it was probably mid-afternoon. A pitcher of water and a glass stood on the table by the bed. He wasn't hungry; he didn't want to see anyone. They'd bring him food eventually – probably the woman. Why had she suddenly appeared on the scene? he wondered. Tom, Dick, Harry. . . . He couldn't devise a name for her and didn't particularly want to. She spoke little, though there was clearly something about her that set her apart from her companions. She was brighter; she was edgier; she sometimes looked at David with something resembling concern. *Big deal*, he thought.

The light at the window grew progressively greyer. The house was quiet. There was no traffic noise – or any other, it seemed. David lay on his back and stared straight up. Now and then, he would be drawn back into the realm of the nightmare and would struggle against it until he emerged.

Ghouls, gargoyles, a liverish light, shrieks and cacklings, the fox-demon, a frog eating a snake, the smell of sulphur. He kept his eyes open and resisted sleep.

The dogs leaped against the mesh of the fence, rattling it, as Tom lobbed meat over the top, scooping the chunks out of a deep metal bowl. They didn't bark, though there was some muted growling as they fought for possession. Rachel watched from the door as the beasts pounced on the food, their shoulders and lowered heads jerking violently as they bit. Tom returned with the empty bowl, wagging a blood-stained hand under her nose and laughing when she recoiled. *Neat*, she thought. *Positively girlish.* Perhaps she should have added a tiny shriek.

She followed Tom to the kitchen and stood nearby as he rinsed the bowl. 'How much of that stuff do they get?'

Tom put his hands under the tap, then picked up a towel. 'Enough to keep them fit,' he said, rubbing his hands briskly, 'not enough to – ah' – he sought the right phrase – 'make them happy.'

'They're really killers, huh?'

'Oh, sure. You wouldn't stand a prayer. Don't worry' – he came closer and threw an arm round her shoulders – 'you're safe if you stick with me.'

She grinned at him, but moved away from the arm under the pretence of looking out of the window at the dogs feeding. 'Is it in the breed?' she asked him.

'No,' he replied. 'It's the training.'

'How is it done?'

'They get kicked in the slats on a regular basis. They expect humans to hurt them, so as soon as they stop being little dogs and start being big dogs they – ah – work out a method for – ah – not letting that happen. They attack first.'

'And never discriminate?'

'Shit, no. One throat's pretty much like another.' He stood close behind her and dropped a hand on to her neck. 'Yours, mine, this – ah – Guerney: his; they don't ask

121

whether you're friend or foe.' His fingers nipped, as if demonstrating a bite, just above her nape.

'You think Guerney will come here?' She thought she might as well start there; but it wasn't Guerney she wanted to know about. Dick and Harry had gone out about an hour ago – she guessed to a briefing meeting at the embassy. She also guessed that, when they returned, she'd be told that Guerney was her assignment for a while. She'd be given instructions. She didn't know what she was going to do, but there was no point worrying about that until the moment arrived. Right now, and for reasons that she hadn't properly examined, she wanted to know about the boy. It was clear that they were in a bind. They'd never intended to trade him; the ransom was nothing more than a stalling device. A mistake had been made. The boy wouldn't cooperate. He'd heard them out, then threatened to blow the whistle. She couldn't see a way they could hand him back; she couldn't see a way they could keep toting him from place to place, banged full of drugs and locked away like a dirty secret.

Tom shrugged. His hand moved to her shoulder as if absent-mindedly. 'I don't see how he'd find us. Who knows? He's working alone, isn't he?'

'Usually does.'

'I hear he's good.'

'That's what they say.'

'Maybe, then. If he gets in, he won't get out. I hear you and he had a thing going.'

'Before the Flood.'

'What?'

'A long time ago.'

'Oh, right.' The hand moved to her neck proprietorially. 'And what? *Is* he good?' Tom chuckled, trying to keep his tone light, but something thickened in his throat as he spoke.

Rachel moved away and walked out of the kitchen into the main room. When she sat down on the sofa, Tom came to sit next to her. 'Who can say?' She laughed. 'I was younger then.'

122

'Let's hope he does track us down,' said Tom. 'The bastard's beginning to be a pain in the ass.'

'Supposing he did manage to get the boy out?'

Tom looked at her and laughed. 'Are you kidding? How's he going to do that? If he found a way past the dogs, there are four of us here. We'd blow the mother's ass off.'

'Sure.' Rachel suffered Tom's arm to thread itself between her back and the sofa. 'Sure, I wasn't really speculating about his chances of success. I mean what if the boy – somehow, I don't know, Guerney, whatever – got out. It's that I was wondering about.'

'He won't.' Tom leaned over and nuzzled her neck, then kissed her just above the jaw – as if to offer reassurance. 'No chance.'

'Something'll have to happen to him some time, I guess. Isn't that so? He can't be put on file or left in an out-tray.'

Tom had shifted his position so that he was sitting sideways to Rachel, his free hand resting lightly on her stomach. 'Well' – he kissed her again, on the side of the face – 'if I was him, I wouldn't be thinking too hard about what I wanted for Christmas.' He chuckled, then again, louder. His hand closed on Rachel's breast, paused, then kneaded rhythmically.

'How long has he got?'

'I don't know, honey' – the hand went to her thigh, then back to her breast – 'I take orders is all. I'm guessing. I hear things said on the phone. I put two and two together, I come up with four. The kid's dead weight now, isn't he?' As he spoke, he was nuzzling and kneading.

Rachel took his wrist and pushed his hand away, standing up as she did so. 'I don't think so,' she said. 'Not a good idea.'

'What?' He looked up at her in astonishment.

'I don't think so,' she repeated.

The astonishment turned to anger. 'What the hell's wrong here? You weren't objecting a minute ago.'

'I'm sorry. I should have stopped you sooner. I wasn't really thinking.'

123

'Not *thinking*? What in hell *were* you doing?' He got to his feet and grabbed her breast, gripping it painfully. 'What was all this about?' To let her know what he meant by 'this' he yanked on her breast a couple of times. She tried to move away, but couldn't. 'You cock-teasing bitch. Funny, was it? Give you a kick?'

'I thought you were just being pally. I got it wrong. It went too far. I'm sorry.' There was nothing in her tone that spoke of an apology.

'The hell with it.' He closed in and clutched her at the back of her thigh, still holding her breast, and used both grips to draw her in. She turned her face from side to side as he tried to kiss her. His fingers dug into her thigh. The other hand started to delve into the neckline of her blouse. Rachel lifted a foot and stamped down hard on his instep. He swore and released her. She stepped back.

'I outrank you, you son of a bitch.' She lifted a finger and pointed it at him. 'And they need me right now. Stay in line or I'll get your ass busted.' She turned and went to the door; he didn't follow. 'A mistake,' she said. 'Forget it. And lay off me, OK?'

'Frigid bitch,' he spat. 'Just like all women. Cock-tease.'

'Sure,' Rachel replied. 'That's right.'

'Bitch,' he said. 'You sat there and let me. . . .'

'A mistake. I'm sorry. I said that.' Rachel put her hand on the doorknob.

'Sorry. That's terrific. She's sorry.' Tom's fists clenched and flexed. 'It's great to know you're sorry.' He gestured. 'What am I supposed to do with this?'

Rachel looked at the bulge in his crotch. She remembered what he'd been talking about while he'd squeezed her and gnawed at her cheek.

'Throw it to the dogs,' she told him, and went out, shutting the door behind her.

People congregated in John Stocker's small sitting-room much as they would have done if waiting to see the doctor; indeed, few of them would have made any distinction. They passed the time of day, or leafed through the magazines that had been left on the dining-table, while John worked in the kitchen.

Two of those waiting were suffering from arthritis, another had a badly sprained ankle that neither strapping nor liniment would cure. A child had been brought by her mother in the hope that there might be some solution to the asthma attacks that kept her in bed for days at a time. A shepherd had brought his collie because nothing seemed effective against the dry cough that afflicted the dog. One other, a man, had been told some days before that he had an inoperable cancer of the throat. Each believed that John's skills would help; in fact, they expected it. And it might well have been their belief that would make it possible. John Stocker administered no medicines, took no X-rays, gave no injections. He'd have found it difficult to locate a plaster. John was a healer. He cured people – sometimes – by putting his hands on them.

It wasn't an ability that he had worked for, or wanted, or anticipated. He didn't have the first idea of how it worked. Guerney had known him when Stocker was a relatively young man. Then, as now, he'd lived on Exmoor; in a cottage on the outskirts of Withypool. Guerney's father had visited him at times and taken his son along. The child had accepted completely what his father had told him of Stocker's skills: there seemed no reason to doubt it; and now, as a grown man, he could find no reason. He'd seen it work and seen it fail, much the same as any form of treatment. He knew, though, that what lay behind it was more mysterious than scalpels and drugs and the other paraphernalia of orthodox medicine.

Stocker was a West Country man. He lived simply, but was far from simple. He never took anything in payment save, perhaps, the gifts that people sometimes brought him: a pheasant, a bottle of whisky, some farm produce. Twice weekly, he opened his front door to whoever wanted to see him and worked patiently until everyone had been attended to. He neither advertised nor talked, ever, about what he did. Even so, people came from all over the country, sometimes from overseas, to sit in his tiny sitting-room, waiting to go through to the kitchen with its iron range and scrubbed pine table, so that they could talk to him and feel the power that he held flow through his hands and be absorbed. He never told them that he would heal them; he only said that he would try.

Guerney had telephoned before leaving London. Stocker had sounded pleased, if surprised, to hear from him. 'I'll be working till about seven-thirty,' the older man had said. 'It'll be grand to see you, Simon.'

A wind had risen, making the short springy furze tremble so that the entire moor appeared to quiver as if held by taut hawsers that might, at any moment, snap. It had been Guerney's deliberate intention to arrive there early, so that he could spend an hour or so on the high ground during daylight hours. The moor's boundless bleakness drew in him something that he couldn't name. He'd walked it in many directions and on many occasions, but had never tired of it. It was best in winter when it was left to the deer and the sheep, the raptors and the foxes. In summer, hikers tramped to and fro across the heather, ten of them in a square mile making the place crowded.

Under a bright cold spring sky, the outcrop rock would gleam like tin and the furze flash chlorophyll-green when the wind turned it. But the moor came into its own under the fogs of autumn and the winter snows. It was most beautiful then. Fog made the place limitless. You'd hear running water, but never find it. You'd hear your own footfall, and the rustle and drip of moisture from stunted trees. Winter blizzards would leave the moor as featureless as the ocean: no landmarks but the beacons and high tors. Ice-winds would scour the fall's topmost powder, sending little twisters of white hissing over the crust. The animals would endure it, turning their backs. The death-count was often high: of sheep, deer and starved birds, of unwary humans who didn't know that the moor could be lethal.

Guerney walked for almost an hour, making a slow circle back to where he'd left the car. When he arrived at John Stocker's cottage, everyone had gone. Stocker was in the kitchen, sprinkling some herbs on to a couple of trout that lay in a baking-tray. Guerney had simply walked in by the kitchen door, just as he always had. Stocker smiled and held out a hand.

'Hello, Simon,' he said. 'Well, it's nice to see you.'

Guerney shook the hand, wondering briefly, and somewhat irreverently, whether Stocker had to switch off, for a handshake, whatever it was that he switched on for his patients. For a while they talked old times: Guerney's father, Guerney's boyhood, the farm, the way things had changed. Stocker fetched two glasses of whisky and put the trout in the oven. It was clear that he expected Guerney to stay for supper, and Guerney was glad to.

They went through to the sitting-room and sat in armchairs on either side of the open fire. Guerney nursed his Scotch for a while, then said: 'John, there are some things I need to know. Nothing sinister's going on, but I can't tell you why, or tell you everything about what it is that I want to know. Is that all right?'

'Yes,' Stocker nodded.

'I'm looking for a boy who's missing from home. I've been looking for some time. A while ago I started having dreams in which the boy appeared – not just appeared, it was as if he were engineering the dreams in order to let me know where he is. Like a film-director. In one of them, he showed me round a house and pointed out land-marks from the window. I found the place. It exists. He'd been there. He made some playing-cards rise up in the air and fly across the room. I don't know what's going on. You were the only person I could think of.'

'Do you know that boy?'

'No. I've seen photographs.'

'It's your job,' Stocker concluded. Guerney neither confirmed nor denied it. 'Tell me about the dreams.'

Guerney told him most of it, missing details like the

127

men's appearance, and Rachel's. He let John know that there was a threat to David without being at all specific. There were parts of the dream about Whiteleaf that John wanted to hear twice. When Guerney had finished, John went into the kitchen and took the trout out of the oven and slid them on to plates. He served potatoes and peas straight from the saucepans and carried the plates back into the sitting-room, motioning Guerney to a chair at the table.

'You think the boy's a sensitive?' he asked.

'What do you think?' Guerney slipped his knife in behind the fish's gill and took the flesh away from the bone.

'Yes, you're probably right. There's a facility called lucid dreaming. You know how, sometimes, you'll dream and while you're dreaming think: "This is silly; it's only a dream"? It's a sort of ability to enter your own dream-world and recognise it as just that. Some people can take it further. I imagine many people could, if they really wanted to. The idea is that you can control your own dream-life. Experiments have been done where sleepers are told they'll get a prearranged signal when they start to dream – a pinch, or a mild electric shock. Not to wake them, simply to let them know that a dream has started. You know what REM is?'

'Rapid eye-movement. It's how an observer knows that someone's begun to dream.'

'Yes, that's it. What happens is that when the person conducting the experiment detects REM in the subject he gives the signal: whatever stimulus they've decided on. This tells the subject that he's dreaming. What's supposed to happen next is that the dreamer, aware that he's dreaming, observes the dream and controls it. In theory, he can make anything happen. And experience it with the immediacy of a dream. Whatever he wants to happen: that's what he'll experience. It's not a fantasy. To all intents and purposes, it's as potent as dreams usually are.

'At any rate, it sounds as if this boy owns the facility already. He's been using it to communicate with you. I've forgotten the beer. Do you want some beer?'

Guerney nodded, and Stocker went to the larder with two

glass mugs. When he returned, Guerney asked: 'How is he able to?'

'Communicate with you?'

'Yes.'

Stocker shrugged. 'You must be receptive. Many people are, but without knowing it. During the height of the Geller business, a number of carefully controlled experiments were run using children as subjects. It turned out that an unbelievably high percentage could bend metal by simply rubbing it softly – like Geller does. Ordinary kids; they didn't know they could do it. By all accounts, many of them weren't that surprised. It's the same thing. I'm not that taken aback to discover that there's a bit of the sensitive in you, Simon.' Stocker smiled and drank some beer.

'Geller's not a fake, then?'

'Lord, no; very talented. Good at teleporting, too, among other things. As might be your boy.'

'Why do you say that?' Guerney asked. Then said: 'Oh, the cards.'

'Yes. That's more telekinesis, but the two often go together. Geller can turn lights on and off – that sort of thing.'

'What's the principle?'

'It's not easy to say. No one knows, in fact. Suppose he's making a lightbulb glow. You couldn't claim that he was directing some sort of electrical charge at it: the energy would dissipate. In any case, how would it enter the circuit? No, he sort of *puts* it there. He doesn't claim to understand it – or be able to control it, sometimes.'

'Meaning?'

'I gather it can get out of hand. Occur spontaneously. Most often, he controls it, I imagine. Certainly for the purposes of experiment.'

'But he does put an electrical charge into the object some-how?'

'That's what seems to happen. None of these things is very well understood, Simon. I don't know how I do my stuff. It just seems to work somehow. I can feel something – power, energy, it's hard to explain. It cures people who can't be cured by other methods. While it goes on being successful from time to time, I'll go on doing it.' They had finished eating. Stocker got up from the table and went back to his armchair. Guerney followed suit, taking his beer with him.

'Would people know that the boy had these . . . abilities?'

'Yes, I'd have thought so.' Stocker nodded. 'Yes, someone would be likely to know. The boy's parents, relatives – some friends, maybe. It would depend how the boy – and his people – felt about it. I suppose some people think they might be mad, or be frightened of themselves. They'd keep it quiet, I imagine. But someone would know.'

'The parents?'

'I'm guessing,' Stocker told him. 'It seems reasonable, though, don't you think?'

'Who conducts the experiments? I mean, who checks on Geller and the others? Who's looking into the lucid dreaming business?'

'Oh, I think university departments, independent researchers, some medical men. It would appear that there's quite a bit of interest, one way and another. Rumour has it that both the American and the Russian governments have been funding research into psychic capability for some time; rumour also has it that the funding is very substantial.'

'I've heard that,' Guerney said. 'I've never quite understood what they thought they had to gain.'

'Who knows? If they consider it a powerful facility, then I suppose they'd imagine there would be a way to tap it for their own ends. A plague on both their houses. One common aspect is an ability to reproduce shapes that others have drawn and are concentrating on. You know what I mean – it's virtually a stage trick, the commonest sort of mind-reading. Someone makes a drawing, well away from the person who's to reproduce it, then concentrates on the shape. The psychic draws it on his own piece of paper. Geller's very quick at it. Most psychics are.'

'Can you do it?'

'Oh, yes.' Stocker got up and fetched two pieces of paper

and two pencils. Then he went into the kitchen. 'OK,' he called.

Guerney drew a cross of Lorraine inside a circle and outside that, circumscribing it, a triangle. To make things less easy, he then drew another cross the shape of the chalk carving at Whiteleaf, and put that inside a square.

'Right,' said Stocker. 'Just think around the outline of what you've drawn, then visualise it entire.'

In his mind's eye, Guerney rapidly traced the lines of what he'd drawn.

'No,' said the voice from the kitchen, 'a little slower.' It brought the hairs up on the back of Guerney's neck, but he obeyed, taking the configuration at a more leisurely speed, as if dragging a stylus. Then he concentrated on picturing first the one shape, then the other. A little less than a minute went by.

Stocker returned from the kitchen and handed Guerney his piece of paper. 'Sceptic,' he said, and grinned. Both drawings were rather stiff, as though their outline had been traced through something barely transparent. Both were entirely accurate.

'You didn't mind?' Guerney asked.

'Of course not. I haven't done it for a while, so the two similar images confused me for a bit. Then I saw what you'd done.'

'How?'

Stocker raised his hands, palms uppermost. 'Saw. I don't know. Just saw them.'

'I've heard about it,' Guerney said.

'It's not difficult, Simon. Many people have some facility for this sort of thing. You get better at it by flexing the muscle. It's a parlour game.' He shrugged as if to indicate its triviality. 'I was just suggesting a reason for governments being interested. In a café in Istanbul sits someone reading a document he's just picked up from a dead-letter box. Nearby sits a beautiful raven-haired woman: an operative for the other side. She has a tremendously strong talent for this kind of thing. Letters are just shapes that make words.

131

She also has total recall. I don't know. . . . If I make it sound ridiculously melodramatic, that's only because I find the whole idea of psychics being used that way a repellent one. Who knows what the masters of war are up to?'

'No,' said Guerney, 'I can't pinpoint anything that might be useful to a government.'

Stocker took their glasses out for a refill, talking as he went. 'The point is, Simon, that few people can think of a purpose of any sort for psychic ability. Although it's a startling thing to possess, and disturbing to witness sometimes, what the hell is it for? In some ways, it's a bit like having electricity but no concept at all of how to make use of it. There's this force knocking about, but no one's going to come up with the lightbulb or the electric kettle for a thousand years. So the owner of the secret makes sparks arc across two points and everyone says, "Wow"; but that's about all. I'm lucky. My ability seems to take some useful direction, but it's part and parcel of the same thing.

'Governments have been researching psi for years because there's hard evidence that it exists. What they want to do is find a use for it; to harness it for their own ends. There's evidence, and there's faith.'

Guerney raised an eyebrow.

'Healers are more common than you might think – and better respected. Most work unobtrusively, as I do. There are showmen, of course – all religious fervour and careful public relations – but many are consulted privately by some very well-connected people. It's not so odd that the Russian budget for research into parapsychology is a high one, when you know that Brezhnev used to consult a healer.'

'Did he?' Guerney looked surprised.

'A woman called Djuna Davitashvili. Nikolai Baibakov is a patient, too – the chairman of the State Planning Commission. Half the Politburo, for all I know. The Academy of Sciences has given her official status; she's one of a number of healers and sensitives who're being studied at the Academy. By all accounts, she's amazingly talented. Here – I've over-filled this.'

Guerney accepted the brimming glass and sipped quietly while John stacked logs on the dying fire. Without looking up from his task, he said: 'It sounds as if the boy's in real trouble.'

'Yes,' said Guerney, 'I think so.' He detected the weight of concern in Stocker's voice.

'I don't need to know, Simon – the details, I mean. I'll trust you. But if there's a time when you need me; if I can help. . . .'

'Yes.' Guerney looked at the man and remembered why, as a child, he'd liked him so much; why he still liked him. 'I won't forget. Thanks, John.'

During the three hours that he had spent with Stocker, the wind had shifted. The air was intensely cold and seemed to bear some light metallic taste that lay bitter, cleansing, on the tongue and gums. The moor was dark and silent, waiting for the snow. He drove the fifteen miles to Druid's Combe rehearsing his conversation with John Stocker.

What would it be? he wondered. *What use had they found for the boy?*

He recollected Buckroyd's snippet of information: 'The chap was a technician of some sort.' And before that: 'The CIA were plodding about; it was their business, really.' Suddenly he felt a rush of fear for David Paschini. The whole thing was a mess. The boy could be anywhere – even back in the States. And Guerney's true intentions were no longer covert. In leaving the Connaught and preserving himself, he'd let David's captors know exactly what he was up to. But, then, he reflected, since Rachel was their ally, they couldn't have been duped for long – if at all.

For an instant, the scent from the discarded tissue he'd found at the safe house came back to him, a pungent musty odour. It lay, indelibly, on other memories: Rachel next to him on the jitney bus, her arm linked loosely with his; Rachel's face looking directly up at him, her eyes wide with pleasure, her mouth slack; Rachel's fingertips resting loosely on his wrist as they mocked the extravagant sunset beyond the restaurant's plate-glass window. It lingered in the creases of the bed-linen. It mingled with the faint waft of iodine from the ocean as she leaned over the rail of the porch, arms extended and rump up, like a dog stretching. *Rachel*, he thought; and an emotion took him, a feeling so foreign that he had to work at identifying it. Sadness, threatening to become depression.

He opened the house and switched up the heating system, then built a log fire in the main room and sat before it with a tumbler of whisky.

Blown – all coming apart. They wouldn't contact him again. But they would, almost certainly, want to kill him. He realised that was his only way of coming close to them again without David's help. In tracking them, now, he was relying on their desire to have him dead; on that and on the interpretation of dreams. He smiled humourlessly at the notion, wondering what sort of control he could preserve in all that. Little, he concluded. As if to underline the fact, the nightmare came back to him in tiny vignettes of undiluted horror.

He knew he should phone David's father. Instead, he dialled the number of Caroline's Rance's house in Woodstock, checking his watch and calculating that it would be six o'clock in the everning, her time. There was no reply. Over the following three hours he sipped more whisky and leafed through a pile of books he'd carried in from the library, concentrating on this or that passage for a while, then turning to a new volume. He telephoned on the hour and the half-hour. There was never any reply. It became imperative: almost obsessive. He stayed up all night, making the last call at nine the next morning, then slept in his chair for five hours.

When he woke he called again. It was 8 a.m. in Woodstock. No one answered the phone.

10

Of the five men in the room, one was senior to Ed Jeffries, and it made him edgy. The two who had been present when he'd first talked to Rachel were there. The other was some-one Ed had never met before – a guy named Ben Ascher who'd flown down from New York. The ranker was called Howard Prentiss. He was leaving the talking to Ed and Ascher; that made Ed even edgier.

'I don't know,' Ascher was saying, 'there are so many aspects to this. I'm not sure that anything I tell you will be of use – or even accurate.' He was dapper – dressed in a neat dark suit and a white shirt; a pin drew his collar together under the knot of his tie. His fingers were thin, with almost translucent nails, and moved precisely round the right angles of his sheaf of notes, though the papers were already carefully aligned. A small oxbow of a frown let them know that he was concerned to be accurate about what he was tell-ing them.

'You've seen the films?' Ed asked him.

'Oh, yes. Sure. Yes. They don't say much. They resemble many other such experiments. The boy obviously has psi abilities. He's strongest on telekinesis and teleporting.'

'We know that.'

'Yes, yes. Well . . . there's not a great deal more to know. I've never worked with the boy. Those who did, I gather, are dead.'

'Coronaries.'

'Yes, naturally.' Ascher allowed himself a moment of wryness. 'It's difficult, you see, to predict how someone will

135

react under the circumstances that David Paschini is now experiencing. There's no difference from trying to imagine how *anyone* would react – do you follow? The fact that he's psi-prone doesn't prevent him from having – ah – normal human feeling. As far as the psychic part of his nature, I'd have to know him to be able to make a guess. To some extent, it depends on the strength of his powers and his ability to adapt them. No one's sure about that. It's as much psychology as anything else, you know. Like I said, the boy's still human. He might become lethargic and fall into a depression; he might become time-urgent; anxiety attacks, perhaps . . . It's a lottery.'

'What about Guerney?'

'Guerney?'

'The guy who's – '

'Oh, yes,' Ascher cut in. 'I'd forgotten his name. I don't know – that's the answer. You say you think he almost got to the boy?'

'There was evidence that he'd been to a safe house where David was being held.'

'Yes, I see.' Ascher spread his arms wide – an extravagant shrug. 'I'm sorry to keep saying it, but I don't know. Is there any evidence that he might be psychic? Why was he employed?'

Ed looked down at the folder on the table in front of him, but didn't bother to consult it. 'Nothing that we know of, no. He was used to keep the mother quiet; he's supposed to be the best. We thought about putting our own man in and decided against it. Guerney looks genuine because he *is* genuine. It's important to have the Rance woman feel reassured. There's no chance that. . . .' His voice petered out.

'Really?' Ascher steepled his hands, fingertip precisely to fingertip. 'He seems to have come pretty close.'

Jeffries swept back a thick lock of hair. 'It wasn't a decision made in this department.' The remark, as everyone knew, was for the benefit of the fifth man.

Ascher felt that Ed's disclaimer made it possible for him to offer an opinion. 'I can't help feeling,' he said, 'given what I've been told, what I've learned here today, that someone has gone off half-cocked. Surely it wouldn't have taken much research to find out whether the boy was likely to be suitable – psi apart, I mean. There seems to be a pretty bad case of tunnel vision at work here. He's seen to be suitable in one respect, and without any delay he's approached. He declines. But not just that – he's outraged; he threatens to blow the whistle. So he's lifted. All this kidnap subterfuge; everything played by ear. And you're stuck with him. What now?'

The question didn't receive an answer. There was silence in the room. Ascher was conscious of having spoken out of turn. He lowered his eyes and squared his papers fussily. 'Sorry,' he said, 'it just seems like such a mess; and unnecessary.' Then he fell silent. Like the others present, he was more than able to predict 'what now'.

Prentiss said: 'Thank you, Mr Ascher.' His voice was soft and unhurried, as if he were half-thinking of something else. Ed Jeffries got up and opened one of the double doors that led into a carpeted corridor. Wordlessly, Ascher lifted his papers from the table, neatened them by tapping the fore-edges against the polished wood, transferred them to an attaché case and left the room.

Before Ed got back to his chair, Prentiss said: 'He's right.' The same soft tone.

'I know it. The body isn't buried under *this* carpet.'

'There are those,' Prentiss said slowly, 'who don't give a good God damn where it's buried. The fact is it's beginning to smell.' He paused. 'The girl's going to run Guerney down.' It wasn't a question.

'That's right.'

'She's secure – not a risk?'

'She's secure.'

'You couldn't be mistaken about that?'

'Not a chance,' Jeffries said, then held Prentiss's eyes and said it again. 'Not a chance, that's a promise.'

'Yes, it is,' Prentiss told him. 'Where is Guerney now?'

137

'We're waiting for him to surface.'

'Will he?'

'Sooner or later, yes. He must.' For the second time, Jeffries hoped to Christ that he was right.

'What about this Buckroyd?' Prentiss looked at his own set of notes. 'George Buckroyd.'

'Nothing,' said Jeffries. 'M16, retired. We leave him alone. He's under surveillance, so we might get a lead on Guerney. Other than that, the Brits know. They might decide to wag a finger under his nose when it's all over. Their choice.'

'The mother?' Prentiss wanted to know.

'OK, well, she's back at the Plaza – in the same suite as before.' Jeffries looked a trifle embarrassed.

'What's that about?'

'Fuck knows,' Jeffries shrugged. 'It's nothing to do with us. In fact, it's a pain in the ass. Things were a whole lot easier when she was in Woodstock. As it is, we've had to tap the goddam Plaza. Received opinion is that she's cracking up.'

Prentiss tapped his pen on the pile of notes and looked thoughtful. 'Dangerous,' he said. 'Keep someone close to her.' He put the pen into an inside pocket and stood up. 'OK, that's about all, I guess. Keep me informed.'

'Sure.' Ed stood up, as did the other two. Prentiss left without bothering to close the door.

'Jesus Christ,' breathed Jeffries, 'what a shit-storm.'

For what must have been the twentieth time, Guerney listened to the single long trill of the telephone bell in Caroline Rance's house. He let it ring for three minutes before hanging up. Then he lifted the receiver again and dialled George Buckroyd's number. When he came on the line, Buckroyd didn't speak his name as he usually did: he said the number.

'Sorry,' said Guerney, 'is this 8413?'

'You've got a wrong number,' Buckroyd told him evenly, and put the phone down.

Guerney thought it through, then waited for half an hour before calling back. After Buckroyd had repeated the number, he said, 'Hello, George, it's Simon. Nothing special, but I thought I'd better call to let you know where I am, just in case you need me, or pick up something I might like to know.' He spoke rapidly, to prevent Buckroyd from having the chance to interrupt. 'I'm not making much headway, I'm afraid. Nothing new with you, I suppose?'

There was the slightest of pauses. Buckroyd said: 'Nothing. But I'll let you know.'

'OK. I'm at Druid's Combe. I'll be here for a day or two. A little research. You've got the number?'

'Yes. I'll call if there's anything. *Bon chance*, Simon.'

''Bye, George.'

Guerney fetched some logs and stacked them beside the fireplace after adding a couple to the blaze. He put a Mozart piano concerto on the hi-fi. He sat down to wait.

The mosaic covered more than half the wall. The colours were bright, but there was no real pattern. Blues, yellows, pale greens, reds, an occasional patch of pure white. It was composed of almost two hundred separate fragments – a painstaking job. If someone had looked through the open door facing the wall, it might have seemed that there was some design logic about the arrangement: a tracer of red here, a strip of yellow there, in the top left-hand corner a broken line of white and, lower down, an uneven circle of green beside irregular smudges of blue that ran out to the edge of the mosaic.

As you went closer, though, you'd have laughed at what had deceived you. The white was snow: ski-slopes, mountains, fields of snow between woods. The blue was the sky: clear in almost every case; looking sometimes hot and at others icy. The green was water: pool, lakes, the ocean. The yellow was sand. The red was many things: a sweater, a ski-hat, a warm plaid coat, a scarf. In one instance it was the colour of David's swimming-trunks. He knelt up on the yellow sand and looked straight at the camera, smiling.

Caroline used a map-pin to fix the last photograph to the wall. She'd brought with her every last one in which David figured. The plundered albums still lay on the floor of her bedroom in Woodstock. Then she sat cross-legged on the bed, holding a pillow to her stomach, and looked at them. She looked for an hour, after which she went to sleep.

It was never dark in the city; but it was night-time when she woke. There were lights in the streets surrounding Central Park. Lights and people. The people went from place to place, thinking thoughts that pleased or preoccupied them. She watched them doing it and wondered how it was done.

In the bathroom, she peered into the mirror, a lipstick poised in her right hand. The face looked back at her that she supposed to be hers. She didn't decorate it; instead, she tossed the lipstick into a waste-basket and leaned forward to squeeze a pimple that had emerged on her cheek. At the closet, she lifted an arm to take the fur coat from its hanger, then paused to sniff delicately at her armpit. A sour earthy smell. She noticed a small circular bruise close to her wrist and tried to remember how it might have happened. Two days before, walking back to the hotel from a bar, she had stumbled in the street and put a hand on a wall to steady herself; the wall's grime still showed as a dim grey newmoon shape on her palm.

She walked downtown to Fifty-Fourth Street, then turned right, crossed Sixth Avenue, and found the jazz club. In there, the noise was very loud and the drinks very expensive and no one wanted to talk to you. Later, she'd go down to the Village and drink a little more. Maybe she'd get something to eat in one of the restaurants that David had always liked to go to. As she sat down they were playing 'Basin Street Blues'. They played it every night.

She phoned at 1 a.m., which, thought Guerney, was a nice tactic and one he believed he recognised. He put down his glass of wine and stood over the phone, counting the rings. After eight, he lifted the receiver and muttered a question.

140

'Simon, hello.'

'Rachel?'

'I'm sorry. I guess I woke you up.'

'It's all right.' He paused, picturing himself sitting up in bed, dragging a pillow behind his back. 'What time is it with you?'

'One a.m., same as with you. I'm in London.'

'Really?' said Guerney. He allowed an alertness into his tone. 'What's to do?'

'Nothing. It's a result of coming up in the world. I've become a Slightly Important Person. It seems that I've got something in London called an opposite number. It was decided that we should be put together, just briefly, to see whether we added up.'

Guerney played along with the banter: it was something familiar to them both. 'And do you?'

'I hope not. The number in question was bright of eye and downy of beard. It had two names neither of them its first. It took me to lunch in a place that had damask napkins, weighty cutlery and Regency wall-paper. It talked in abbreviations.'

'It sounds like something I've met.'

'Only in England,' she said. 'Look, Simon, I've wangled a few days' leave. I've also unearthed one or two little-known facts about something you're interested in. Should I come down there? I'd like to. Or are you planning on being here soon?'

'No,' he said. 'Come here. When?'

'Tomorrow? Today, that is.'

'Fine. There's a train – oh, maybe you're driving.'

'No, no. I'll come by train.'

'OK. From Paddington to Taunton. Morning or afternoon?'

'Make it afternoon.'

'Get the five forty-five,' he said. 'It's called the *Golden Hind*. I'll pick you up.'

'Not for the first time,' she said, adding: 'Ho-ho-ho.'

'Ho-ho-ho,' he echoed. 'See you tomorrow.'

He waited until she'd hung up before putting his own

141

phone down. He looked at it thoughtfully and sipped some wine. 'Ho-ho-ho,' he said. Then he lifted the receiver again and tried Woodstock. This time, he gave it five minutes.

Somehow, Caroline had managed to stray on to the Bowery, but because she barely knew that, and wouldn't have cared much anyway, the bums did no more than stare, or call after her, or weave round her clutching their bottles swathed in brown-paper bags. One threw an empty that smashed just behind her heel, but she assumed it wasn't meant for her. Five cabs ploughed straight through before she managed to stop one. The driver was Italian and chatty.

'At this time of night, lady, that's no place to be. Know that?'

'I'm sorry,' she said.

He laughed. 'Jesus, don't apologise to me. It ain't my business. I'm just tellin' ya.'

'Thank you.'

'That's OK. No, listen, it's no place. Lotsa guys wouldn't stop, you know?'

She said: 'I hadn't thought.'

'You on vacation?' he asked. 'Listen, New York can be a rough town, you know that?'

'Yes.' She felt very lightheaded. The neon seemed to make circles in the air, like the fluorescent hoops kids buy at summer fairs. The cab hit ruts and potholes on the cross-town streets, and she flopped with the bounce. Once, she almost fell off the seat. 'I'm drunk,' she told the cabbie.

'Are you, lady? Terrific, I sure wish I was.' He chortled. 'Yeah, man, I could go for a coupla beers right now. Don't worry. We'll get you home. You're OK in this cab.'

'Thank you,' said Caroline. And his kindness moved her so that she started to cry. She careered from side to side with the jolting from the potholes and wept noisily.

The driver didn't speak again. When they reached the Plaza, she put a ten-dollar bill in the swivel tray that was let into the thick glass that separated them. He took it wordlessly.

'Thank you,' she sobbed. 'Thank you.' A man in uniform came to the kerb and opened her door.

Rachel was wearing the same down coat that she'd taken to Long Island. 'It's cold,' she said, and kissed him hello.

As they drove to Druid's Combe, the first few flakes began to fall, whipping past in the slipstream or colliding fatly with the windscreen to leave freckles of moisture as they melted. It was warm in the car, and the warmth accentuated Rachel's perfume. She told him how much she was looking forward to seeing the house.

'I've often imagined it – from the little you've told me.' She sounded genuinely eager; it was as if he were taking a bride home. After a while, she settled into talking about the conference she said she'd attended in London – the preposterous opposite number, the skeins of red tape, the proliferation of suede shoes and woolly cardigans under suit jackets. 'The Brit intelligence service sure has an odd style,' she observed.

She was patching it together quite well, he thought; though, knowing what he knew, he could detect the scraps of briefing. She worked at it deftly; anyone would have believed her. In order to make his response credible, he pictured the hapless man she'd supposed to have been teamed with and saw them lunching – the Gavroche? – before going back to the conference room. He imagined a table there, and gathered round it a bevy of lethal old duffers sucking at well-worn briars. He invented the agenda and heard the discreet coughs of those about to take the floor.

'It was boring,' Rachel assured him, 'but I suppose it was useful.'

'The result of getting an extra pip,' Guerney observed.

'What?'

He tapped his shoulder where an epaulette would have been.

'Oh, I see; yes. Well, whatever else, it's given me the chance to spend a day or so with you. Can't be all bad, can it?'

143

He smiled and shook his head, and asked when she'd have to go back.

'Work's over,' she said, 'so I can manage a few days. It's Wednesday today, isn't it? I guess I could stay on until Sunday. But will you be here till then? I mean, how's your business coming along?'

'Not good.' Guerney let a few seconds pass before adding: 'I've lost the boy.'

'How – lost? I thought the next move was to organise the money and take delivery.'

'So did I. It looked as if that was about to happen. Then they tried to set me up, so I went underground. There's no contact with the kidnappers any more and, in that sense, I've lost David.'

'Set you up? They tried to kill you?'

'Would have, I think, if I'd done what they expected me to.'

'Simon, that doesn't make sense.'

'I know.'

'What does it signify?'

'That I don't know.'

Rachel took a cigarette out of her bag and pressed the lighter on the dashboard. When it sprang back, she removed it and held the glow to the tobacco, puffing energetically. Through the puffs, she asked: 'What's your next move?'

'I don't seem to have one at present. That's why I'm down here. The only positive action I can take is to open it up – press, television, police and so forth. That would be complicated, to say the least of it. For one thing, I'd be hard put to explain that David was taken several weeks ago. Still . . . it's all I can see.'

Rachel expelled a stream of smoke and coughed. 'You've never done that before, have you?'

Guerney shrugged. 'I've never needed to. It's never been like this before.' He turned his head to look at her. 'I don't know what's going on.'

She nodded. 'I see the problem. Maybe you should hold on for a while – to see whether they try to make contact again.

There's the chance, I suppose, that you misread things – the set-up, I mean.'

'I doubt it. Who knows? It's certainly true that my reactions are shot to hell.'

She laid a sympathetic hand on his thigh. 'Is it far?' she asked.

The fall had thickened. Lines of flakes pattered against the car like a soft machine and silted where the windscreen-wipers left them. Fields, and the tops of hedgerows, already bore a thin covering that seemed startlingly bright against the darkness beyond, and a wind was beginning to build drifts in hollows and ditches.

Twelve miles later, Guerney pulled into a small semi-circular parking-place at the foot of a steep slope. He got out, and Rachel followed suit, looking at him enquiringly as he went to the back of the car and hoisted out a box of groceries which he left on the roof while he took a torch from the car before locking the doors.

'Where are we?' she asked.

'Home.' He pointed straight up the slope. Just above the brow, the sharp angle of a roof and its chimney were silhouetted against the dark sky. From road level, a series of posts were ranged up the hill, with a grab-rope linking them. Guerney shouldered the box and switched on the torch.

Rachel looked up past the tangle of bracken to the thicket of conifers beyond, then further, to the glimpse of rooftop. 'You're kidding?'

Guerney handed her the torch. 'We'd never have got the car up the track,' he explained, 'or, if we had, there would have been little chance of getting it down.' He grinned. 'Where's your sense of adventure?'

The steps cut into the slope were rudimentary and slick with snow. She fell three times before they had climbed the hundred-and-fifty-foot slope to the house, and four times had to stop to gain her breath. Her last fall came within twenty feet of the house. She lay there, laughing and panting, covered in a thick fleece of snow. 'There's little

145

doubt in my mind', she said through her laughter, 'that you're a true eccentric.'

Guerney watched her as she lay there, noticing the handful of snow she was gathering to make the snowball that she'd pitch at him before they got to the front door. Her mood appeared genuine. She was behaving as if her purpose were nothing more than to spend a few enjoyable days in the country, as if nothing more preoccupied her than the comedy of the climb up from the road, the tumbles in the snow, the little adventure of a house so inaccessible, the brandy she'd probably ask for when they went indoors. He had seen it before – this ability in women to deceive, to betray; to set aside, when they chose to, the burden of such things in order to take what they wanted from life – even to savour the pleasure to be had from time spent with the person they betrayed. It was done, or seemed to be done, guiltlessly. It never failed to puzzle him and make him afraid.

As he reached the door, the snowball clattered against the box on his shoulder. 'Missed,' he called and went indoors, switching on lights as he made for the kitchen. Rachel followed him in, delving into the box as he lowered it on to the table.

'It's all pretty basic,' he told her. 'There are steaks and whatnot in the freezer. We won't starve.'

'Looks terrific. Is there some brandy?'

He pointed the way to the main room. 'In there, on a table near the fireplace. Fetch me one, too, will you?'

She brought him his drink and watched him while he stored the groceries. 'It's a great house, Simon. Aren't you worried about leaving the fine art knocking around when you're away?'

'No one ever comes here,' he said. She had taken off her coat and draped it over a chair near the kitchen range. Her jeans were soaked, and there were patches of wet on her sweater. 'Perhaps you ought to get out of those. The bathroom's beyond the bedroom, which is beyond the room where you found the brandy. The water's always hot.'

'Wonderful,' she said, swallowing a large mouthful of her drink, then setting the glass down. 'I'll take you up on that.'

She was gone for five minutes, then returned, clad in Guerney's bathrobe. 'Guess what?' He looked at her, inviting the information. 'My luggage is on the back seat of the car.'

He smiled, heading for the front door. As he shrugged into his topcoat, he said, 'Have your shower,' then went out into the snow.

He took it slowly, letting the beam of the torch wander idly from side to side. It would be a matter of three or four minutes to make a call – he assumed that was what the diversion was about – and he'd be at least ten minutes fetching her luggage; but he didn't want to appear to hurry. After he'd taken the bag from the car, he reached back in to make sure that the spare key was where it should be: taped to the underside of the driver's seat. He slammed the door, but didn't lock it. Before climbing back to the house, he swept the accumulation of snow from the windscreen and threw across it a piece of sacking that he took from the boot.

At the top of the climb, he paused to look round. It was unlikely that anyone had followed them back from Taunton – he'd been alive to the chance – but that didn't rule out the possibility that they'd gone on ahead. The snow lay in crisp undulations between the narrow boles of the firs. Everything seemed wholly still against the slanting snowfall. The only sounds were those of the wind and the intermittent rush and soft *phlock* of snow dropping from an overladen bough. He circled, glancing through each window. The house appeared empty. When he came to the kitchen window, he saw the table and the dog's basket. For the briefest of moments, but with complete clarity, he recalled the dream-view of David Paschini's face reflected in the glass, his mouth desperately working, his features rigid with effort. It was there and gone, but as he moved back to the door its shadow floated on his retina, like a flashbulb's after-image.

He dumped the bag on the bed and stood there a minute listening to Rachel's singing in the shower. When he walked to the bathroom door and lodged himself there, one shoulder against the jamb, she stopped. Some sixth sense made her call out: 'Simon?'

'No,' he said. 'It's the demon of the stairs.'

An arm came round the shower curtain, clutching a long-handled bath-brush. 'Do my back.'

He took the brush from her and pulled aside the curtain. She was facing the shower-nozzle, her head tilted back to take the spray. He worked the brush in small circles over her shoulders and back, then concentrated on her buttocks for a while, pressing harder until they grew pink. She turned round and handed him the soap.

Guerney lathered his hands and passed them over her body, beginning at her collarbones and upper arms, then moving on to her breasts. She put her hands over his, leading him into a slow upward motion that began on her ribcage, lifted her breasts and then let them slide, soapily, across his palms. When she released him, he reached behind her and slid his hands from her waist to the tops of her thighs, then back, pulling on the upstroke, and cupping her, so that she unbalanced and fell against him for support.

Her arms went round his neck; strings of water ran from the fall of her hair and dampened his shirt. He shifted one hand and brought it between her legs. She gave a tiny hop, then stood flat-footed to take the pleasure, keeping her face buried in his neck even when she came, though, in that moment, he felt the hardness of her teeth against his skin. They stayed still for a while, like rescued and rescuer standing exhausted on a beach, just beyond the spray from breakers. Finally, Rachel pushed herself upright. Reaching down, she unbuckled Guerney's belt, pulled the zipper on his jeans, and eased them over his thighs. Then she drew him towards her, kneeling under the full force of the water, and took him in her mouth. Guerney stood and looked down at the dark sodden hair, the shoulders slick with cascading droplets, the wet shining breasts moving slightly as she worked.

Who are you? he thought. *Who the hell are you?*

Three a.m. *Vargtimmen*. The hour of the wolf. The time when most people die: a time of lowest ebb.

The wolves of New York City were out there: the predators, the carrion-eaters, in the Bronx, on Eighth Avenue and Times Square, in Harlem, at the wasteland fringes of the East Village, circling in the park just below her window. She stood at the window, bottle in one hand, a half-empty glass in the other. A terrible rashness lay in her. She half-remembered the lines of a poem that conjured a picture of something lithe and feline and murderous descending on the bright back of its prey. Beyond her window, unseen but surely there, were the outlaws, the rogue males, the scavengers hunting the badlands. They were hungry and desperate; they had nothing left to lose. The notion stirred and excited her, as if she were recognising for the first time an affliction in others that she'd thought she alone owned and must bear in isolation. It was an affinity; the shared instinct of the pack.

What lay around her in the room seemed trivial artifice. The television, the journals and papers, the tasteful lamps, the fussy expensive furniture, the room's controlled warmth. She took another drink and walked through to the bedroom, weaving slightly as she went. The photographs seemed to glow in the subdued light, like icons. She looked at each in turn, scrutinising them as if she might garner some piece of crucial information, or crack their code.

David as a baby. David as a first-grader. David wielding a little-league baseball bat while Cesare pitched. David on the nursery slopes in Vermont and Aspen. David in Disneyland. David on the Circle Line tour during their weeks in New York with Annette. David in Venice, in Florence, in Rome, in Paris. At a barbecue, at a Thanksgiving supper (his head thrown back, laughing at someone's joke), blowing out the candles on his sixteeth-birthday cake, on a beach in Greece, on a beach in California, on a beach in Brittany. Each memory made her wince. Sometimes she would turn her face slightly and look at a photograph askance, as if too direct a confrontation would be more painful than she could bear, but she went through them all, from time to time whispering place-names and dates and her son's name like someone telling a rosary.

Eventually, she retreated to the bed, still clutching bottle and glass, and lay there letting the cluttered wall go in and out of focus. Twice she lifted the phone but stopped short of dialling. She slept for an hour or so, and dreamed she was back in Woodstock. David was there, but she couldn't manage to find him. She went from room to room, knowing that he was just ahead, moving innocently from one preoccupation to another: close, but out of earshot. Each room had to be searched; and by the time Caroline realised that he wasn't there he would have abandoned the next room also, in pursuit of something more intriguing. The house became a maze of walls and doors. His restlessness, though she knew it to be blameless, annoyed her, and she woke with a feeling of irritation still intact. The whisky-bottle had fallen from her hand, staining the coverlet with liquor. She poured herself a drink from the remnant and went back to the wall to begin afresh the litany of where and when.

They ate sitting in armchairs close to the fire, balancing trays on their knees. Rachel hadn't bothered to dress; she was wearing Guerney's robe, her damp hair bunched in a loose pony-tail and fixed with a rubber band.

'Terrific,' she said through a mouthful of steak. 'Just right.' She forked a potato and dabbed it in the wetness, watching the pink seep in.

Guerney leaned from his chair to pour wine into their glasses. 'What was it that you found out?' he asked. 'You said you had some new information – is that right?'

She nodded, drinking. 'It's not much. Might help, though. The house in Cheyne Walk – did you check it out?' Guerney nodded. 'Like I told you, it's a cat-house and a temporary store for the heroin shipments that come over with Paschini's fishmeal. More interestingly, it has been used, now and then, as a safe house.'

'Yours or ours?'

'Both, I think. It didn't seem a good idea to appear too curious. The information came from one of my Washington contacts. He wasn't even aware of telling me something new, so far as I could judge: just mentioned it as if it was information we'd both have. I took it in but didn't push for more.'

Guerney gave the impression of thinking about it, then asked: 'And?'

'The other thing concerns Paschini himself. It seems he's on the missing-list. His house is locked up – just a couple of staff in attendance. The fishmeal man is nowhere to be found. It's not a holiday or a business trip. It'd be pretty odd if it were, with his son under lock and key. God knows where. I organised one or two very discreet enquiries. Nothing.' She paused. 'What could it mean, do you think?'

Guerney shook his head. 'What's your theory?'

'Don't have one.' Rachel set aside her tray and empty plate and took a long swallow of wine. 'Just what have you got on your hands, here, Simon?'

He took the dishes out to the kitchen and peered through the window towards the crest of the hill. The snow hadn't let up; if anything, it had quickened – driven now by a stiffer wind. The encrustations at the edges of each pane were frozen on. The temperature had probably dropped to five or ten degrees below. For as far as the house lights reached, he could see nothing but the pines standing in a tumult of white that fell like a cataract on the eye.

Rachel had moved from the armchair on to the floor in order to be closer to the brisk yellow and orange of the fire. Guerney leaned past her to heap more logs on to the flames, then sat behind her in the armchair, letting his hands fall beneath the lapels of the robe and over her breasts. She said, 'Mmmmmm . . .,' and wriggled her back to be more upright against the seat of the chair. He leaned forward and untied the belt, then parted the robe so that it fell from her shoulders. She freed her arms from the sleeves and half-turned, lifting her face to be kissed.

'Just a moment,' he murmured.

The wine-bottle was empty, and he took it with him as if intending to return with a replacement. In the hall, he removed one of the dog's slip-leashes from its hook. When he went back into the main room, she was sitting with her knees drawn up, staring at the blaze. He went behind her, wrapped the double thickness of collar round her throat and locked the ring-clasp at the back of her neck.

'What . . .?' She looked startled; then when she saw the length of leash in his hand, she grinned. 'Well, well, this is new.'

He drew her up, and she came willingly, taking a line for the bedroom. He checked her, giving a sharp tug on the leash, and walking quickly to the front door so that she had almost to trot to keep up, looking awkward because she was naked. When he opened the front door, she gave a cry and pulled back, her hands trying to locate the trigger-release at her neck, though she didn't know what she was looking for or how it worked. He yanked her through and past him, making her stumble into the snow so she landed on all fours; then he kicked the door shut and started to tow her towards a small clump of young conifers some twenty feet from the house.

She slipped and slithered in his wake, falling sometimes on her side and rolling, sometimes coming down hard on her rear. She yelled at him and, when he didn't answer, screamed.

'What are you doing? *Simon*! Christ! Have you gone mad? For Christ's sake. What the hell is this? *Simon*!' – and she went down in another flurry of snow, shrieking, then crawled madly on hands and knees to stay with him as the leather cut at her throat. When she fell, he didn't pause.

'*Simon*! In God's name, what're you doing?' But she knew what was happening – of course she did – and the screaming came from fear, not from puzzlement.

Guerney hauled her to the nearest pine and pushed her against it, winding the length of leash round her throat and the tree until it was used up. He trapped the loose end with his hand, standing behind her, his mouth close to her ear.

'We'll stay here for a while,' he said. 'Then *you* can tell *me* what's going on.'

'How the hell should I know?' She spoke through clattering teeth.

He didn't reply. He'd put her on the windward side of the

152

tree; billows of snow whipped towards her along the hill's flank.

'You've got it wrong,' she told him. 'You're making a mistake.' The words came shakily, and her whole body quivered. He could feel it through the leather as an angler can detect a fish's vibrations when it threshes on his line.

For more than five minutes, she kept up the pretence. 'What do you think? That I'm in on this? Is that it? You're wrong. Christ, I was trying to help, remember that?' After a while she started to cry. 'I'll die, you bastard. You're mad.' At one point she screamed: 'Stop it, stop it, stop it' – the last word rising in pitch until it climbed higher than the shrillness of the wind, and she rolled her head from side to side against the restriction of the leash, then let it fall forward as her shriek collapsed in a wild sobbing.

Guerney waited for another minute, then went round the tree to confront her. Her head wore a helmet of snow; her eyebrows were thick with it. Snow had gathered in a thick patina on the tuft of hair at her legs' apex and silted icily on the slopes of her breasts; lines and ridges had coagulated on the sharpness of her shinbones, along her shoulders, in the hollow of her throat. It capped her nipples. A tiny plug of ice filled her navel. She was blue: her lips showing almost mauve, her skin tinged lightly, her cheekbones dabbed with purple smudges. She looked bruised; her entire body was shaking convulsively as if she were dancing on the spot.

He looked at her and waited. She nodded and managed to say: 'All right. All right. All right.'

He unwrapped the leash, and she fell on him. He ducked, letting her slide over one shoulder, then gripped her under the buttocks and carried her back to the house where he dropped her into one of the armchairs in front of the fire. The fresh logs he'd added to the blaze were sending a steep flow of flames into the chimney. Guerney went through to the bedroom, returning with a duvet which he threw on to her. From the bathroom, he fetched two large towels and wrapped one round her head. Then he put a glass half-full of brandy close by and sat opposite her, waiting.

153

Rachel drank the brandy, spluttering because her hand wasn't steady enough to control the glass. She didn't speak for a long time: the sudden warmth was painful, and she dropped her forehead against her drawn-up knees to endure it.

Finally, without looking up, she asked: 'How could you possibly have known?'

He said nothing. She looked up to meet his gaze and saw that he wasn't going to tell her that. She held the glass out for more brandy and started to speak while he poured it. She told him about the first summons to Washington, about Ed Jeffries, about her subsequent briefing, about getting to Heathrow and being driven to the safe house to join Tom, Dick and Harry. She talked about her career: about the years she'd put in, about ambition and the loyalty they demanded. 'You know about that, God damn it; you were *part* of that.'

She told him about the house at Whiteleaf and the new house in London. She gave him a run-down on the three men: she mentioned the dogs, the phone-calls, the drugging of the boy. Yes, they had meant to kill Guerney. Yes, she was supposed to set him up again.

'I didn't know what I was going to do, Simon. Even when I arrived here, I still didn't know. That's the truth. For a while now I've been edgy about things – the people, the jobs, the lies and the dirt; the manipulation. The fact that it's treated as a game – some sort of governmental Dungeons and Dragons that they all make up as they go along. People like Jeffries and the people who run him. . . . I didn't know what I'd do; it's the truth. I know how it looks, but I'm telling you the truth.'

When she asked for them, Guerney fetched cigarettes and matches from her bag. 'What will they do with the boy now?' he asked.

'Kill him, I think. They haven't said it right out. It seems to me. . . .' She paused. 'I think they'd prefer to do it after they've killed you.'

'Yes,' he said, 'that would make sense. When is that to happen?'

Rachel dropped her eyes like a child who has been made

154

ashamed. 'They didn't tell me that.'

'Tonight?' he asked.

'Simon, truly, they didn't say.'

'They're here already.'

'Yes; this morning.'

'How many?'

'I'm not sure – that's the truth, too. I think they were recruiting one or two from Grosvenor Square. I can't be sure.' Tom would be among them, though, she was fairly certain of that. It would be much more to his liking than babysitting a freaky kid and doubling as dog-handler.

Guerney left the room, briefly, and returned with two handguns. One was a snub-nosed .38 that he'd taken from Rachel's bag earlier in the evening.

'How did you know?' she said. 'I don't understand how you could have known.' She was talking to herself: the words were barely audible.

'Get dressed.' He gestured towards the window and the blurred snow-flurries its light illuminated. 'I don't know whether they'll count this an advantage or not.'

'What would you do?' She shuffled into the bedroom with the duvet wrapped round her like a cloak and returned with her clothes.

'I'd use it,' he replied. 'It depends how good they are.'

She dropped the duvet and backed up to the fire, still shivering a little from time to time. 'I hadn't made a decision, Simon. It's true. I simply didn't know what I was going to do. Can you see? I didn't volunteer for this, damn it. I was *told*.'

'I understand,' he said. 'I know what you're saying.' While she dressed, he turned away his eyes.

At 2 a.m. the snowfall lessened. Before long it was little more than a few floating threads that mingled with twisters of white dust that the wind raised from the frozen surface of the hill.

Rachel and Guerney had gone through the motions of two people preparing for bed. They'd spent some time in the kitchen stacking dishes, put out the house-lights one by one, and spent time in the bathroom. Guerney had kissed her in full view of the bedroom window before drawing the curtains. He'd left the bedroom light on for twenty minutes before finally extinguishing that, too, then led her back to the main room and turned the armchairs to face the door. In the semi-darkness, with firelight scampering on the walls, they waited. Guerney checked the guns and put them on one arm of his chair. Rachel spoke softly, as he'd instructed. She told him what Jeffries had said during her briefing.

'The boy's psychic, did you know that?'

He nodded.

'They've been looking at that kind of thing for some time: psi, metal-bending, precognition, teleporting. . . . I guess you knew that, too. Not just us; the Soviets have a budget for it twice the size of ours. A lot of research has been done over the last twenty years. Controlled experiments under strict laboratory conditions. Very often people would volunteer themselves if they thought they had psi qualities. I suppose there might have been a certain amount of self-aggrandisement involved for some of the volunteers; still, a high proportion had *something*. Others were heard about via doctors or specialists of one sort or another. Most were children with confused and worried parents. That's how they learned about David Paschini, it seems. Tests were run which they filmed – he'd have been about twelve or thirteen at the time. It was discovered that he has a particularly strong ability for teleporting. Not just making things disappear into the ether. I mean, he can start vacuum cleaners and switch radios on, make lights go on and off; I don't understand much of this, really. Some years later – a couple of months ago – they wanted to use him for something. Several approaches were made. At first, I think they simply said that they wanted to run some more tests. He wasn't keen on the idea. I guess they'd made the mistake of forgetting that he's not a child any more.'

'They approached him directly – not through his mother?'

'Oh, sure. The idea was that he'd be working for them under conditions of secrecy – though they hadn't told him that. The fewer people who knew about it, the better. Anyway' – she lit a cigarette and tossed the match over her shoulder into the fire – 'they persevered with the business of "just a few more tests, research has progressed vastly over the last few years" – that kind of ploy – for a while and were rewarded with an increasingly cold shoulder. Their next move was to invoke Old Glory and "ask not what your country can do for you" – thereby showing rather more of their hand than they should've. The boy became wary. I suppose they could have butted-out at that stage. From what I can tell, David isn't the type who would have made life difficult for them. He keeps quiet about his abilities – always has, and almost certainly would have then. The likeliest thing is that he'd simply have wanted to forget the whole business. Anyway, that's the received opinion now that it's all too late.

'What happened next was entirely typical. I sometimes wonder just how some of the goons the CIA uses are recruited. Times without number they just crash in and do something without having the first fucking notion of what comes next. On this occasion, they gave the boy a rough outline of what they wanted him to do – not the whole thing, you understand, but enough. That's when they found out that he's a supporter of Greenpeace, the anti-nuclear movement and a whole clutch of other brown rice and rope sandal movements. No one had thought to check. They seemed to think that a couple of choruses of "My Country, 'Tis of Thee", and he'd fall into their arms. Fall into their arms-race.' She chuckled at the weak joke, then paused. 'It was cold out there, you know. I thought I was going to die. I've never felt cold like that.' For a brief second she was angry. 'I was *naked*, for God's sake!' He kept quiet. 'What I said was the truth: I hadn't decided to go along with them. I *didn't* know what I would do . . . was going to do.'

'You've said all that,' he replied. 'What was it they wanted him for?'

'Supposing I'd gone on denying it?' she wanted to know. 'What would you have done?'

'Kept you there. What was the boy's task to be?'

She sighed. 'I believe you. Son of a bitch. I'm not entirely sure. They didn't – Jeffries didn't – tell me the whole thing.' He looked at her. 'That's no lie, fuck it! He said two things: make of them what you will. One: that it was a matter of national security. Two: that it had to do with computers. He didn't say it straight out like that. I picked those two things up from a jumble of others.'

'Did he talk about David's father?'

'No.'

'His mother?'

'No.'

'What do those two facts mean to you?'

'Not mentioning the parents?'

'No. National security and computers.'

'Well, Jeffries seemed to me to have all the leeway of a bug about to hit a windshield; you know – it looked as if the last thing to go through his mind would be his ass. A heavy-duty type in a Brooks Brothers suit was sitting in on his meetings and generally sniffing around the department. I detected the sort of ominous distant rumble that usually means there's storm brewing above the Oval Office. It didn't strike me as the kind of gaffe that would rattle sabres – too domestic – but I did gather that it would be one hell of an embarrassment.'

'But you thought it had gone up to Presidential level?'

'Yeah, maybe. Except that most people think *down* to Presidential level would be a more appropriate notion these days.'

'Computers?'

'Your guess. Do I – as they say – know from computers? They're used for everything these days, aren't they? Given what I know about the boy's ability to switch things on and off, I guess they might have wanted him to activate a computer system they haven't got access to. Is that likely? It also occurred to me that a charge of electricity that could be produced as easily as directing a flashlight and sort of injected in some computer or another could be less than beneficial to the program. Maybe that's it. They want him to teleport a charge into a software system and screw it up. Yes?'

'Like you, I'm no computer engineer.'

'No, well, I'd imagine there are plenty of ways in which David could be useful to them. Switching on, screwing up. I don't know. And whose computers for what purpose?'

'That's all Jeffries said?'

'All. He didn't intend to say that much – didn't notice he was saying it, I guess. Came out as part of the briefing. Jeffries isn't bright, just powerful.'

'Why did they bring him to England?' Guerney asked. 'Why didn't they kill him?'

'Yes, I wondered about that. I don't really know. When I first asked I got a bunch of horseshit about the Brits paying their dues, that he was too hot for the States – nothing I believed. . . . Though I can see that, if they're going to kill him, they'd sooner have it on the front pages of someone else's tabloids if something goes wrong. After David realised they were trying to talk him into something more than a routine test or two – after they'd pretty much spelled it out for him, told him that he'd be a CIA operative second-class with woodsman's badge, or whatever – well, he got mad. For all I know, he was on the phone to the *Times* when they lifted him. Another dumb move, but it seems that Our Man in New England could think of little else to do. Once they'd got him, they couldn't manage to decide what to do with him. If he'd been a kid from an average home, he'd probably have wound up cold meat sooner rather than later. As it was, someone decided that might be risky. Moneyed connections always mean more power to those guys. Money makes them pause and go through a process that masquerades as thought. They must have known that they'd have to kill him eventually – after all, what else could they do? But if they made the parents believe it was a kidnap in pursuit of cold cash and nothing else, then his eventual death would seem the outcome of that. Enter Simon Guerney.' She sighed. 'How about a drink?'

He nodded towards the table and let her help herself. 'What do you think now? About the boy being in England,' he said.

'Not sure.' She took a pull at her brandy as she walked back to the chair. 'The Brits must have helped them to get him here. Military transport, I think. And it must have been the Brits who supplied the safe house in Buckinghamshire, because it's not one of ours. The London house is,' she added. 'Another thing: we left the place in Bucks pretty fast and did nothing to cover our tracks. Someone must have gone in to sweep up. Given all that, I don't see why your guys should bust ass to help, let alone get involved in something as messy as this unless it was necessary. They must realise the risk they run if David is killed while he's over here. Unless. . . .'

'They kill the parents and me before killing him,' Guerney said, finishing her thought. 'Enter Rachel Irving.'

She held up a hand. 'OK, fuck it. Do you imagine I didn't *think* about that? Do you?'

'I'll never be sure, Rachel. Will I?'

He stood up, taking the guns with him, and moved to the window that gave on to the steep rise behind the house. The curtains had been left a few inches apart. He walked a parabola, not to approach too directly, and stood a short way back to look out. He stood still for a few seconds, then turned towards Rachel. He said: 'Go and stand by the front door. If you make a move to open it, I'll shoot your spine away, OK?'

'Oh, shit,' said Rachel. 'Why didn't we go earlier?'

'Go where?' he replied. She stood by the door as he watched the three men descending the slope.

The end of a snowfall, when the wind drops, brings a certain kind of stillness. The air seems thinner than before, and natural objects, under their burdens of snow, somehow less solid. A single sound will span a valley: the bark of a fox, a bird's cry, a laden branch cracking.

Guerney wasn't sure what he'd heard. Probably not a voice, unless one of them had been stupid enough to yell as

160

he'd stumbled. It might have been the *clack* of metal against a tree trunk. They were moving in a reverse-arrow formation, one coming straight for the house, the other two angling out on either side, leaving deep furrows as they half-slid, half-ran down the high field.

He joined Rachel at the door and took two light, down-filled anoraks from a peg. 'We've got about three minutes,' he said. 'Directly opposite the door are three pines, closely grouped; that's where we're going. Call out or allow yourself to be seen, and you're dead.'

He opened the door and pushed her in the small of the back, and she began to run. He stayed level with her until they reached cover, then positioned her behind the left-hand tree, standing straight as he was but, unlike him, facing away from the house. The steps that led down to the car were about fifteen feet away.

Guerney leaned against the tree's bole so that the fraction of his profile that was to one side merged with the dark vertical. He held the gun pointing downwards, his arms extended so that the barrel just touched his knees. One man had taken a direct line on the house: he would find cover there and watch the bedroom window. The others would close in on the front, narrowing their pincer movement until they were either side of the door. What happened next would depend entirely on technique; it was pointless to try to second-guess them on that, Guerney thought: different tribes, different mores.

He waited, breathing shallowly, his hands firm but not tight on the gun's moulded grip. One errant thought struck him – *This is wrong* – and he remembered how the room at the Plaza, its chintz, the visits from room service, Caroline Rance's weakness and fear, had seemed part of a pattern that threatened to become random and uncontrollable. It had proliferated and brought him to this.

The rumple of footfalls on snow came from both left and right. A faint nimbus of firelight at the window gave better sight of the man on the side of Guerney's gun-hand, who crouched twelve feet from the door and braced his back against the wall. A dark shape, part-visible against the snow, matched his position on the other side. A cross-fire. It let Guerney know that the first move would come at the back of the house. He tried to judge from the silhouette what weapon the man on his left was carrying: it was a rifle, certainly; probably a .308. The red glow at the other window allowed him to see that the man crouched there was nursing a pump-action shotgun.

There was silence for another ten seconds. The heads of the two men were towards the door, and Guerney knew that for a short while – though not for long – their concentration would keep them from spotting the tracks that led away from it.

Two sounds followed instantly. The first was the light ring of breaking glass; on its heels, almost without interruption, came the violent percussive clap of a stun-grenade. *Shit*, thought Guerney. As the men rose and moved in on the door, he stepped from behind the tree, raised his gun and shot the man on his right before he could escape the backdrop of fire-light. Guerney assumed it wouldn't be a fatal hit, but didn't wait to check. He loosed off three more rounds in the general direction of the second man, then took Rachel by the arm and swung her towards the steps. They were a third of the way down before they came under fire.

The first two shots were high; the third clipped one of the posts carrying the grab-rope, a few inches in front of Guerney's hand. He went sideways, knocking Rachel off the steps and into the deep snow. Out of control, they rolled for twenty feet, hearing the solid crack of the rifle and expecting at any minute to be hit. A tree stopped them, winding Guerney who collided with it first. Rachel stood up at once, looking for a route to the road. Sucking breath, Guerney struck her at the back of the knees, bringing her down. In the same moment, the gunman fired again, hitting the tree on a level with her head. She screamed and whipped round as splinters took her in the face.

Guerney fired twice, rapid snap-shots, towards the top of the steps, then turned and began to snake down the hill.

162

Rachel followed, one hand pressed to her cheek, the other extended to brace her body as she skidded and slithered in his tracks. The rifle stopped, but there were two wild shots from higher up; then they could hear nothing but the crash and flurry of their own descent. They cannoned off trees and slid through clumps of scrub, raising clouds of snow-powder, cutting a zig-zag line and wholly out of control. Their pursuers would be using the steps and the grab-rope, threatening to overhaul their prey with every passing second. They would emerge near to the car.

Close to the bottom, Rachel lost her footing completely and went into a long slide that took her past Guerney and into the roadside ditch. She had got to her knees as Guerney reached her. At full tilt, he grabbed her arm, yanking her upright with his momentum and towing her across the road into the fringe of trees on the opposite side. Then he kicked her legs out from under her, falling simultaneously and switching position at once to look towards the steps.

The men were almost down; they had, perhaps, sixty feet yet to go. Guerney's gun lay somewhere on the slope – lost when they collided with the tree. He unzipped a pocket and took out Rachel's .38. There was no time for a careful shot. Once the men gained the road and the car, there wouldn't be a lot of hope left. He fired rapidly – four shots – and the men went sideways, seeking cover. Two of the rounds had been fired from a standing position. With the last, he'd started across the road, running in a diagonal for the car. Rachel hadn't expected that. She scrambled up and followed, a perfect target for the half-dozen seconds it took her to reach the passenger door.

Guerney was inside, stripping the key from beneath the driver's seat. He started the engine and put the car into gear while Rachel tugged at the locked door. She hit the window and screamed: 'Simon!' He was a dim shape behind the frosted-over glass. A shot was fired from the hillside, striking metal somewhere at the back of the car. '*Simon!*'

He flung out a hand and lifted the lock. As she opened the door and fell in, he gunned the engine, riding the clutch in an attempt to hold a straight line. The car fishtailed violently until it found traction on the crown of the road where the snow was thinnest.

The man with the rifle had time for two more shots. The first missed. The second entered Guerney's side-window with a shocking suddenness, then passed through the windscreen transforming the entire length of glass into a honeycomb of opaque crystals. Guerney punched at it, smashing a section away, but the car had already begun to drift. He corrected it, held the road for a brief moment, then lost contact again. He was heeling and toeing in an attempt to find a line out of the skid. The freezing wind drew streams of tears from his eyes.

For a while, he believed he would make it. Then he felt the wheels strike ice, as if he rode a cushion of air, and the car slewed violently to the right, striking a high bank and careering off it to make two complete pirouettes in the centre of the road. Guerney had only the dimmest impression of revolving and none at all of coming to rest. As the car hit the bank, he'd risen from his seat like a sprinter coming off the blocks and met the frame of the windscreen with his forehead. He was aware of a flood of red light suffused by black fissures; there was no pain. The motion of the car as it bounced back into the road slammed him against his seatback, then threw him sideways across Rachel's lap. He seemed to go on falling, and half-formed the thought that he'd been thrown clear and was travelling outwards, across the road and towards the trees on the verge.

He waited for the impact of landing, but the sensation never arrived.

11

David knew that he must be on a hill because during the hours of darkness the skylight, set low in the angle of the roof, would gloss with gold when it caught the lights of cars. He couldn't hear the engines and supposed that to mean that the room was soundproofed. The glass in the skylight was dimpled. Since he was sleeping less often now, David would often watch as a car ascended the hill, charting its approach by the way colour seeped unevenly over the rectangular surface, like honey filling cell after cell. Then there would come a moment when the car breasted the hill and the glow would be suddenly gone, leaving the pane dark apart from a puddle of light that sat always in the bottom right-hand corner; it was pink and resembled the ullage of some exotic drink. It must have been the reflection of a sodium street-lamp, he supposed.

He lay waiting for each unpredictable flooding of the glass as if by seeing it a certain number of times he might magic himself to freedom. Each time it happened he experienced a tiny irrational moment of hope: here's another one! The soundproofing cut him off from whatever was going on elsewhere in the house. They brought him food and drink; sometimes they offered him books and journals, which he accepted but didn't read. It was Harry who'd brought the meals yesterday and today. Each time he'd said: 'There you go, kid.'

For some reason, David felt a need to stay alert, though he knew he ought to be trying to contact the man who had almost reached him in the previous house. The drug-nightmares had been terrible: for an entire day, he'd been half-crazed by the images he'd retained; they had drawn him back into the realm of madness, though he'd fought against them – twelve waking hours during which he alternated between lucidity and terror. But that wasn't the reason for his wakefulness. Something new, something menacing, had entered the house. David felt like a sunbather, spread-eagled almost naked, his eyes closed, who is aware of a shadow blocking the sun for an instant and senses that someone has stopped at his side and is peering silently down.

Dick placed the telephone back on its cradle and reached for his drink. He carried it into the kitchen where Harry was taking a warmed plate from the oven. Harry's attention to domestic detail was meticulous; he'd have made someone a damn good wife.

'Why do you do that?' Dick asked him.

'Do what?' Harry turned, holding the plate with a dish-towel.

Dick gesticulated with his drink. 'Warm the platter. Put out a knife for the butter. Use a spoon and a serving-dish for the vegetables.' He took a drink. 'What about a single rose in a little vase – wouldn't that kinda set things off?'

Harry shrugged. 'My mother used to. That's the way we did it at home, y'know?' If he'd detected the mockery in Dick's voice, he'd chosen to ignore it. 'What did they say? Anything about the boy?'

Dick stared at the floor. 'Did you feed those damn dogs yet?' he asked.

'Sure.' Harry continued to look at him, waiting for an answer.

'It's coming apart,' Dick said, rubbing the bridge of his nose just at the point where the lines of his scar converged. 'They think it's time to tie off a few loose ends. We're holding one of them.'

'Jeffries?' Harry wanted to know.

'Yeah; and whoever's pulling *his* strings.'

'But it was Jeffries you spoke to?'

'Yeah. Sounds to me as if they're all hopping round like

fleas on a griddle. Ah, shit.' He finished his drink in one gulp and went to fetch another. When he returned, Harry had loaded the tray and was taking a can of Coke out of the fridge. He decanted it into a glass and set that next to the plate. Then he lifted the tray and looked at Dick.

'Shall I give the kid his dinner?'

'Sure.' Dick fingered the apex of his scar once more, then swept his hand backwards through his hair. 'Sure. Why the hell not?'

Caroline looked around the Plaza bar, squinting slightly when she tried to focus for distance. It was 1 a.m. and they'd been serving her Scotch since 9 o'clock – that was when the bottle in her room had become inexplicably empty. She shared the bar with two businessmen and six hookers. Earlier in the evening, one of the girls had told her that there was bad weather at Kennedy, which was why it was a slow night. They had sat at adjacent tables for a while, chatting while the hooker watched the door. Caroline hadn't known that the girl was a whore: it didn't occur to her. To make conversation, she'd asked what business the girl was in.

'I work the bars,' she'd replied and smiled without taking her eyes off the door. After a few more drinks, Caroline showed her a picture of David.

'He's my son,' she said.

The girl broke her vigil for an instant and glanced down at the photograph that was being held out to her. 'Oh, yeah?' she said. 'Nice kid.' Then Caroline told her that he was missing from home, and started to cry a little, and the hooker got up and moved to the bar.

Since then, she'd spoken to no one but the waiter. She would signal him, pointing at her glass. He'd come over and say, 'Scotch-rocks' – a statement. She would say, 'Yes, thank you,' knowing how superfluous that was in a New York bar. She wondered whether he might not notice her gratuitous politeness and stop for a moment to talk to her, but he'd simply pivot on a heel, putting her empty glass on his tray, and return in a matter of seconds with a fresh drink.

'Scotch-rocks,' he'd confirm as he set it down in front of her, along with the amended tab. Then he'd go to lodge against one of the stools near the kitchen and talk to the barman in rapid Spanish.

The two hookers with tricks in tow left within five minutes of each other. The girl who'd been shown the photo of David left, too. She didn't look at Caroline as she passed. A couple came in to get a nightcap, laughing as they arrived at the door, then falling silent when they realised they were almost alone in the bar. A few melting crumbs of snow lay on the shoulders of their coats.

Quite soon, thought Caroline, she would go to her suite and look at the photographs. She had deliberately ignored them all day in the hope of forgetting some. She drifted in and out of sleep, startling herself with bizarre images that occupied the edge of wakefulness and seemed to issue from somewhere at the back of the dim room, as if projected – suddenly, brilliantly – on to a screen.

She saw Cesare's face, disturbingly young, smiling at her. From what lay behind his shoulder, she thought they must be in the Borghese Gardens – in the fall, of course, their favourite time there. She saw her father sitting at one end of a rowing-boat and pulling on the oars. A bright sun clarified the water and ran across ripples left by the wake. She reasoned that her mother must be alongside her on the seat, but she could see only her father, his big hands extending and pulling, and sunflashes on the lake. She saw what, at first, she took to be a cougar, but then realised it was the cat David had been given for his sixth birthday. She saw David as he was in the photographs she'd pinned to her wall – each in turn, it seemed – and came back to wakefulness with a sense of having been cheated.

The waiter was hovering nearby. He glanced at his watch and looked over his shoulder at the bar and other tables. Caroline was the only person in there. Blearily, she dabbed a finger towards her glass. The waiter sighed noisily, and put it on his tray. 'Scotch-rocks,' he said.

*   *   *

The man with the beard suffered from a mild affliction; nothing visible – the thick growth on his face wasn't there to mask a deformity, or anything of that sort. In their youth, his parents had been addicted to the movies, often going three or four times a week. His mother had been better than eight months pregnant when her husband had taken her to see *Gone with the Wind*. She had loved it, from the first frame to the last. She might have become one of those record-setters who can lay claim to having seen a certain movie hundreds of times had her child not intervened by insisting on being born.

As it was, she managed to sit through it on twelve occasions and could pretty well take you through the script's better-known scenes without error. Though she knew, from moment to moment, what was coming next, she would still take pleasure in Scarlett's flirtatiousness, the grandeur of the Old South, the bravado of the young men. She would share the fear of those in Atlanta as it burned, shed a tear for the troop of Negroes marching to the front, agonise with Melanie as her child was born. She'd cry, too, when Bonnie died, and relish those famous lines – particularly Rhett's 'Frankly, my dear, I don't give a damn'.

Rhett Butler, she admitted it, was a dashing fellow; her real favourite, though, was Ashley Wilks. She dreamed secret dreams in which her husband waved to her from a troop-train window and, as she left the train station, her head bowed, the pains began and she fell amid the steam and the noise and the hurrying feet. Hands would lift her; a concerned face would peer into hers; the face would be Leslie Howard's.

In fact, her husband was declared 4F, the pains came one afternoon when she was drinking coffee with two friends, and no one remotely like Leslie Howard was ever to enter her life. Her concession to the dream was to name her new son Ashley. He didn't like the name – he never had; its syllables made him think of a damp rag, and after he'd watched the movie himself, at the age of fourteen, nothing he'd seen of his namesake had caused him to change his opinion. He hated the way his friends' parents would say:

'Oh, like in *Gone with the Wind*.' He struggled, in vain, to stop people shortening it to Ash, which was what Ed Jeffries had taken to doing.

They sat together in Ed's office and split a pint of vodka, which was Ed's regular drink. It was 2 a.m. in Washington and they had both been in meetings throughout the day. Jeffries put a fist into the ice-bucket, then tilted his glass as he tipped the cubes in so as not to cause a splash; he added more vodka and pushed the bottle across the desk.

They had discussed the situation from top to bottom. Jeffries owned that he didn't like any of it; it was a Christ-awful mess. He'd reported the events of the last few hours to Prentiss and to others – to the people Prentiss spoke to.

Someone had made a long phone-call to London. He'd gone into an outer office while those present at the meeting had continued to chew over what they'd been told. Forty-five minutes later he'd emerged, and forty-five seconds after that a decision had been taken. Ed had then made his own call to London, at the scheduled time, and issued some instructions of his own. This last, late-night meeting was for the same purpose.

Jeffries rattled the ice in his glass and made ring patterns on his blotter with the condensation. 'We've got one or two things going for us in this, Ash. She's been acting erratically. The staff at the Plaza have got her pegged as a crank. Photographs pinned to the wall, returning late helplessly crocked, tipping fifty-dollar bills. Room service deliver something, and she's sitting in a chair, crying. Showing photographs of the boy to the bell captain, the elevator attendant, the maids, anyone who'll give her some attention.' He paused. 'No one likes that bit. At present, she's just a flaky lady; but she's attracting attention. It's the right time. If it goes on much longer, she'll take the lid off, or go nuts, or both. She's a risk we can't afford to take.' He pushed a hank of hair off his brow. 'She's out on the streets late at night. She's taking risks. It shouldn't be too much of a problem.' He took a pull at his drink, speaking into the glass. 'Who will you use?'

Ashley shook his head. 'I'll think. It doesn't matter much, does it?'

'Just so long as there's no foul-up.'

'Give me a break.' Ashley smirked, then his expression changed to one of irritation. 'How in hell it ever got to this is a fucking mystery to me.'

'It's likely heads will roll,' Jeffries told him.

'No consolation. We're getting a reputation for this brand of shit, you know. When I think of some of the – '

'Sure.' Jeffries cut him off. 'It's not our fuck-up.' He jerked his head, indicating the floors above his office. 'They know that.'

'Terrific. That's great. But I'm the guy stuck with the pooper-scooper, right?'

'You're right, Ash.' Jeffries poured him a fresh slug of vodka. 'You're the guy stuck with the pooper-scooper. Try to keep your hands clean – OK?'

When Guerney opened his eyes he saw the same moon that had risen over the Thames on the night that he'd gone to Cheyne Walk: a richly gold, gravid disc that appeared to lodge just above the horizon as if trapped there by its own unnatural weight. Its thick deep light flooded his vision. A moon to hunt by.

The impression lasted for a couple of seconds, no more. Rapidly, he ran through the things he could detect. He was in bed in a large room. Nearby there were noises of other people shifting and stirring. Dimly, he heard the drone of a motorcycle. The moon was a flat night-light on the opposite wall. There was an unmistakable smell.

He half-sat up. At the top of the room, close to a pair of swing-doors, a nurse was making notes in a logbook. The effort of coming almost upright made him swoon, and he lay back heavily against the iron rails of the bed, closing his eyes. He felt himself sinking; his arms were shaky and barely supported his torso. In the few moments before he fell asleep, he thought back and remembered everything.

'The hell with it,' he whispered, and let himself go.

It was full day when he reawoke. Rachel was sitting on a chair close to his head. The bed behind her was empty. On Guerney's left was a very old man who lay flat on his back, eyes closed, and seemed to breathe once every ten seconds. A system of tubes and wires issued from his nose, from the partially open jacket of his pyjamas and from veins in his arms. A monitor screen at the foot of his bed blipped slowly.

'They said you would be all right.' Rachel smiled uncertainly and lifted a hand towards her own head as if by way of explanation. 'Are you?'

He'd followed the direction her fingers had taken and noticed the puffy cut on her cheek, an inch below her left eye; she'd taken two stitches in it. He remembered the splintering of the bark and the way she had grabbed at the place as she had been cut. 'You tell me,' he said. 'What have they found?'

'Concussion,' she said. 'No fractures, no other damage that they can detect. I think they want to run some more tests today – now that you're conscious.'

'What story did you give?'

'The car came off the road. It was icy – we skidded – roughly what happened. I knocked out the side-window – it had a bullet-hole in it. The rest pretty much fitted. I said I was cut by flying glass.'

'What *did* happen?'

She lowered her voice slightly. 'You fell on me after your head hit the roof. When the car stopped it was pointing the right way. I couldn't shift you but, then, I didn't try for long. I sat on top of you and drove for about five miles, as fast as I dared. The car did one or two spectacular things, but it stayed on the road. When I thought it was safe, I stopped and managed to heave you over. You fell into the space in front of the passenger seat, but it was the best I could do. I followed signposts and wound up here. Minehead. I don't know whether the goons knew anyone was hurt. They'd have seen the car skid, then drive off.'

'They might have read something into the skid. Thought that maybe they'd wounded one of us.'

'It's possible. Who knows?'

'Where's the car?'

'I drove it into a lane just outside the town, then ploughed through some bushes. It wasn't easy to take it that far.'

'If they thought one of us was badly hurt – shot – they'd expect to pick up our trail, sooner or later.' He was calculating time. 'They'll certainly come looking.'

'Simon' – Rachel regarded him directly – 'the shot that hit the tree – that gave me this – it was meant for me, don't you think?'

'If you mean that they could tell us apart and were aiming deliberately at you, no. If you mean that they were trying to kill us both, yes. How long was I out?'

'Unconscious, they say about twenty-five minutes. You came to, briefly, then slept for about seven hours. Why me, too?'

'That's easy enough. *Because* they couldn't tell which of us was which. I imagine they were told to kill me whatever it took. They wouldn't mind too much if that meant two bodies rather than none.'

Rachel fell silent. She thought she knew what was on Guerney's mind. It must seem that she had backed down in the face of the odds. If the attack on Druid's Combe had been successful – if she'd said nothing and Guerney had suspected nothing and she'd eased him into the trap – that would have left her with no options. Or if, during their escape, it had been only Guerney that their pursuers had tried to kill – well, then she would have had a decision to make, especially with Guerney lying prone and helpless in the car. But it hadn't happened that way; she could feel the new sutured scar on her cheek like a scorch.

No – somehow Guerney had known about her betrayal; and she had come under fire, too, during that hectic plunge down the hillside. There was nothing to do but stick with Guerney. Though why should he believe her to be a willing ally or trustworthy?

Now I have to trust *him*, she thought, and realised at once what a dangerous notion that was. She knew it would be pointless to try to tell him about the agonies of indecision she'd suffered. Even when she had got to Druid's Combe, she hadn't known what she would do.

Rachel's father had been a career soldier. She recalled how she'd once asked him what drill was for. 'Discipline,' he'd said. 'It's to ensure that they'll do exactly as they're told, no matter what the circumstances.' Rachel had been well drilled; she'd done what the job demanded and hadn't asked questions, even when better judgement had nagged at her a little. But, then, she'd never worked in the field before. Now she'd discovered the difference between just a name, and a name that had a face and a voice and a history . . . part of which was her own.

She believed – thought she believed – that she wouldn't have let the trap close on Guerney. The phone-call she'd made from London, her arrival at the train station, their drive through the thickening snow. . . . She'd felt as if the tension might kill her off. Somehow it had been possible to laugh, to chatter, to throw the snowball, to make love; but all the time she'd wanted to scream and roll on the floor and tear her hair. And then, by some means, he had taken the decision from her.

She wouldn't have let them take him. There was no way to tell him that. She'd have made her decision, and warned him, and let the next move – whatever it might have been – be his. Wouldn't she?

It made her desperate that the moment had passed, and still she didn't know.

A nurse passed the bed and smiled, then backtracked to take a look at the chart suspended from the bed-rail. She said, 'A doctor will be along to see you in about thirty minutes, Mr Leibowitz,' then hurried on down the ward.

Guerney raised an eyebrow at Rachel, who shrugged and said: 'My mother's maiden name. I wasn't feeling very inventive. You think they'll look here.' It was spoken flatly: a confirmation of what he'd reasoned earlier.

174

'Do you know where my clothes are?'

She pointed to a bundle wrapped in brown paper and tied with twine that lay alongside her chair.

'OK.' He threw back the bedclothes and swung his feet to the floor. 'Make it look as if you're helping me to the lavatories. Don't make too big a deal of it, or some nurse will get chippy. Just hold my arm. And talk.'

They left the ward and found a bathroom in the corridor, just before the doors that led into the public area. Rachel handed the package over and went to wait by the main exit, as Guerney had told her to. He arrived five minutes later and went past without looking at her. She counted to fifty, then followed him into the carpark. He was lounging up against a Porsche, in full view of anyone looking out from the adjacent administration block, and waved to attract her attention, though it was clear that she'd already seen him. When she reached the car, she saw that he'd broken the driver's side-window and lifted the lock.

'Get in,' he instructed.

She opened the door and shuffled across to the passenger seat while he pulled the bonnet-release lever. It took him a few seconds to hot-wire the car. He slipped in beside her and started to drive slowly across the carpark, making for the exit ramp, but when he reached it he swung the wheel and made another circuit. Rachel looked sideways towards him, but didn't speak.

'It's all right,' he told her. 'I'm not still concussed.'

After two more circuits, he saw someone approaching a car from the main doors of the hospital. Gunning the engine, Guerney drove another half-circuit, then pulled the wheel over to bring the nose of the Porsche between two rows of parked cars and waited until the figure was a few steps short of the alley. Rachel could see the white coat flapping in the cold breeze, then a face turned for a moment towards the Porsche. As the young man stepped from behind the last car, Guerney accelerated, roaring towards him. There was a vestige of a shout as the doctor leaped back, a glimpse of his shocked face, then they had covered the distance to the ramp, crossed it at speed, and turned on to the main road.

She didn't speak for a while. Finally, she said: 'I imagine you know what you're doing.'

'I know what I'm doing,' Guerney told her. 'Whether it's the right thing is another matter. Have you any money?'

She shook her head. 'Back at Druid's Combe.'

'Credit cards?'

'Same thing.'

'OK,' he said. 'Look around in the car.'

She rummaged in the glove compartment, removing maps, a pair of driving-gloves amd a fistful of tokens from filling stations before coming up with some crumpled banknotes. She counted them.

'How much have we got?' he asked.

'Forty-eight pounds.' He looked at her. 'Believe it,' she said. 'We're in a Porsche.'

He drove to Porlock and left the car blocking someone's driveway. In the town, they bought four blankets, a groundsheet, a water-canteen, some food that wouldn't perish, a Zippo and some thermal under-clothing. It took all but ten pounds of their money.

At the end of the main street, where signs warned motorists about the dangers of Porlock Hill, there was a saddlery. As they walked towards it, Guerney said: 'You're about to become a difficult customer. You want to buy a hard hat, for hunting – you understand?' She nodded. 'If you're asked, you hunt with the Exmoor. The Master's name is Ronnie Wallace. They hunt fox.' Rachel nodded again. 'You've got an odd-sized head; you often have trouble finding a hat that will fit. Take five minutes trying them on and rejecting them. You'll be doing that in a room out of sight of the main part of the store. Then come out and suggest that I shouldn't wait. Take another five minutes, say you can't find a good fit, and leave. There's a pub just a few steps up the hill to the left. I'll be in there.'

She performed very well, even thinking to say how disappointed she was that there should be snow and that she hoped it would melt in time for her to hunt before going back to the States. She remarked on how beautiful the country was, how likeable the people. The assistant unpacked every hunting-cap in her size, filling the small back room with boxes and tissue-paper, but Rachel had to admit that nothing felt comfortable. She thanked the assistant warmly. Five minutes earlier, she'd gone back to the main display-room and told Guerney that he might as well go on ahead. While she'd been trying on the first half-dozen hats, he had stolen a lock-knife, a hunting-slingshot, two sweaters, both of which he was wearing beneath his anorak, and a pair of walking-boots for Rachel which he'd put just outside the door.

It was early, so there were only three people in the pub apart from Guerney: a man and wife who were sitting at a table near the open fire and a beefy farmer who lounged at the bar next to the stool Guerney had occupied. She went over and asked: 'OK?' He nodded, handing her a small tankard of beer. She made an anecdote of the hats, to which he listened attentively. The one she'd really liked had covered her ears. It fitted everywhere else, but it covered her ears. Others were fine over the eyes and at the back of her head, but pinched at either side. Guerney said that he wondered whether it mattered much, since it was unlikely, with all the snow, that she'd manage to hunt before she went home. She remarked that she needed the hat anyway, because she would be riding just as soon as she got back and the hat she'd been wearing – for years now – was well past its best. He sympathized and said they'd try somewhere else. Then he bought them another drink and, in collecting his change, nudged his pint glass with his arm so that the beer cascaded over the farmer, who asked Guerney why the hell he couldn't be more careful. Guerney didn't reply. He simply passed his glass back to the landlord and asked for a refill.

'I'm talking to you, you clumsy sod.'

'I know,' said Guerney.

'You spilled your fucking beer all over me.'

'I know that, too.'

177

The landlord stood with Guerney's glass in hand, but made no move towards the beer-tap. He looked apprehensively from one man to the other.

The farmer swung Guerney round and indicated his soaked jacket and trousers. 'Look, you silly bastard. All over me.'

Guerney looked, as if to assess the damage, then turned back to the bar. 'It's a pint,' he said. 'Bitter.'

'Fuck you. Look at me.' The farmer pulled Guerney's arm and turned him round again.

On the turn, Guerney moved closer and hit the man, rapidly, three times, just below the heart. A stretched look appeared on the farmer's face and his eyes widened. He didn't speak, but made a faint gargling noise at the back of his throat, then sat down heavily in a nearby chair. His mouth was open and he appeared to be breathing in without also breathing out.

Guerney took Rachel's arm and led her out of the pub, turning right as they came out of the door and walking her briskly through the town. She trotted to stay level with him, their bags of purchases knocking at her side. They climbed up Dunster Steep and came out of the town on to a road bordered by fields.

'All for whose benefit?' Rachel asked. 'The police?'

'No,' he said. 'They'll return the car to its owner and make a report on the business in the pub. I doubt the things I stole from the saddlery will be noticed for a while but, even if they are, we'll simply be put down as a couple of light-fingered types, one of whom has a short temper. What can they do?'

'Wouldn't it be a good idea if you told me what you're planning? I mean, I might decide to pass.'

'Feel free,' he said. 'It would be easier without you.'

'All heart.' She hefted the bags. 'OK, it's your patch. I trust you. Where would I go, in any case?'

'I'm glad you trust me.' He was walking slightly ahead, looking off to the right at a wooded slope, beyond which rose the massive treeless escarpment of Dunkery Beacon.

'Oh, shit.' She lengthened her stride to catch him. 'I could have turned the goddam car around and delivered you to them cold, you know that?'

He stopped and gazed at her. If she hadn't been clutching the shopping-bags, she would have raised a hand to the cut with its two stitches that his eye was fixed on. 'No, you couldn't,' he said, and turned off the road into a lane signposted for West Luccombe.

They went half a mile before either spoke again. Without looking at her, still walking a pace or two ahead, Guerney remarked: 'We're heading for a place called Horner. We're going up into the woods there. We're going to wait. Eventually – soon rather than later, I'd think – they'll find us. I've left a trail a mile wide. I'm choosing my own terrain and conditions that favour me. It won't be comfortable.'

Rachel made no objection – a way of offering agreement. Instead she asked: 'How are you feeling?'

'Woozy. Light-headed. OK, more or less.'

'Really?'

'Really,' he assured her. 'I shouldn't have had the beer.'

At the foot of the hill where the woods began, on the only road that ran through Horner village, was a tea-shop that served scones and jam and thick cream to tourists throughout the summer. Guerney knocked at the door and asked the woman who answered if they could buy some milk. She explained that she had none spare: that they weren't open for business during the winter months. He thanked her politely and said it didn't matter. The woman was staring at the stitches on Rachel's cheek. Before she could close the door, Guerney put a hand to his head and sat down heavily on the path. The woman was concerned. Rachel showed concern as well. Guerney had fallen, she told the woman, and struck his head. Guerney got up looking recovered. It was nothing, he told them, just a moment's dizziness. Yes, he said, he certainly would see a doctor. He would go that very evening.

Three minutes later, he and Rachel were stamping through deep snow on the steeply rising path that led to the crest of the valley. They stopped for a breather only once on

179

their way to the top. There was something that Rachel had wanted to ask, and she asked it then. She was thinking about the room with the skylight and the boy sleeping as the effect of the drug receded. She was thinking about his face, which seemed to grow increasingly blank with each passing day, and of the way he would sit up sluggishly when she took him his food. On one occasion he had been dozing as she entered the room, and his expression had brightened as he turned; that had pleased her, but only for a second, because it became apparent at once that he wasn't properly awake and had believed himself to be somewhere else. Had believed Rachel to be someone else.

'Now it's out,' she said, 'now it's blown – what about David? I mean, what are his chances?' There was no reply. 'How long do you give him?' she asked. 'Do you think you can still get to him?'

Guerney had been asleep for seven hours in the hospital. He hadn't dreamed – or, if he had, the dream had faded on waking, as common-place dreams often do. There was no telling what effect the concussion might have had. He stared up at the track quilted with snow, the laden trees, the dull brittle shellac of the sky, and for a moment felt detached – distant – from London, from the boy, from the whole pattern of things.

'God knows.' He hefted the bags and began to trudge towards the summit. After a while, Rachel came alongside him. Without looking at her, Guerney said: 'I just don't know.'

Caroline was lost, and that was ridiculous. She knew the city as well as any New Yorker. Even so, she was lost. It *was* ridiculous, and she giggled at her own foolishness. She had been to a number of bars, though it was difficult to remember quite where or for how long. She had been walking for a while, but couldn't easily recall which direction she'd taken – or where from. She stood on the edge of the kerb, teetering slightly and looking for a taxi, but the streets were empty. She wondered what time it was.

She walked for a couple of hundred yards, looking back over her shoulder from time to time in the hope that a cab would appear, not knowing whether she was heading in the right direction. Uptown or downtown: she couldn't be sure. It was crazy. She chortled and waved an arm at a private car, losing her balance and staggering sideways into the road. The driver twitched the car round her and accelerated slightly, then ran a set of lights just as they turned red. Caroline chuckled as she watched the tail-lights retreating.

'Sorry, sorry,' she muttered, 'thought you were a cab. No cabs. No cabs tonight.'

She imagined one rounding the corner – maybe in the time it would take her to count to ten. She would see its yellow light and hail it. Getting in she'd say: 'The Plaza Hotel, please, Driver, as swiftly as you dare.' The idea made her laugh, and she spoke the words aloud. When she heard her own voice, she sobered a little and noticed how cold it was.

At the next junction, she stopped and looked around. Maybe she was on Broadway, north of the park. Nothing looked familiar. From beneath her feet came a faint rumbling, the sound seeming to issue from a nearby grating. *The subway*, she thought.

Near the crest, close to a place the local people called Weber's Post, were a number of trees the gale had upended. Their roots, and the earth packed round them, made a solid wedge, canted to the sky and frozen solid. Guerney chose the largest. It would provide a shelter and disguise. He cleared the declivity where the roots had been torn out – a five-foot circle – and laid the groundsheet on it, then unpacked the blankets and the other things they'd bought.

Rachel watched him. 'We're going to live in there?'

'Unless you'd sooner pitch a bright red tent and fly the Stars and Stripes from the pole – yes. It won't be too bad. I'll use snow to insulate it.'

Rachel turned and looked towards the other side of the valley. It was crowded with trees that must have been damaged during a big blow: each was stripped and skeletal and pale – not from a burden of snow, but because they had been dead for years. The entire hillside resembled a vast exposed nervous system, stark against the rufous bracken that showed through the carpet of white. As she watched, a pair of buzzards entered the neck of the valley, flying almost at eye-level, and gliding along the line of a river that creased the valley floor. Their *weep-weep-weep* was the loneliest sound she had ever heard.

She walked back to where Guerney crouched, preparing their living-space. He pushed the lock-knife under the elastic cuff of his anorak, then undid the zipper slightly and put the slingshot inside.

He lives closer than most to his instincts, Rachel reflected; like someone whose nerve-endings show above the skin. It was logical that he should be there, dug in on a hillside with a view of the bare tracery of dead branches, hearing the cries of the buzzards, choosing his own terrain for a fight. He was alive to what surrounded him and knew how best to use it; he was in tune. She worried, briefly, about the likelihood that she might prove to be the false note: their undoing. She felt at odds with it all – out of place, as a country girl would on Madison Avenue. It occurred to her to wonder why Guerney had brought her along. It was a dangerous thought, and she dismissed it.

He put the blankets at the back of the hide, close to the lofted tangle of roots and frozen earth, then motioned her to get in before walking around the site a few times, looking for any tell-tale signs. Satisfied, he wiped his tracks and backed in beside her. She shivered slightly and hauled a blanket round her shoulders.

'Give it a day,' he told her. 'Twenty-four hours. Not longer, I think.'

'They'll find us?'

'No,' he replied, 'they'll find the place. After that, we'll find them.'

On a different neck and shoulders, the head of Felipe Juan Maria Lopez might have seemed almost noble. His face was long and bony: a little lumpy about the jaw, perhaps, and the broken nose was pushed a fraction to one side, which spoiled its effect, but it was, none the less, a face that almost achieved good breeding. If you looked closely, you'd see that the lips were, perhaps, too full and too damply red; but it was the way in which the head was carried that really provided evidence of peasant stock. The young man's shoulders were rounded, his long neck thrust forward and drooping slightly as if the weight of that nobbly head were too much for it. The posture caused him to look doltish and rather brutal – and that was an altogether truer summary of Felipe Juan's nature.

The hunched shoulders, the extended neck and lumpish head had long ago earned him the nickname of Donk. 'The kid looks like a donkey,' Felipe Juan's father had once said. 'Hey – Donk.'

The name had stuck, though Felipe Juan's father had not. Twelve years before, he'd left his wife, together with their four sons and three daughters, to manage as best they could with two rooms, no money and no prospect of any money, in order to follow his star. The star in question was a much younger woman who hadn't then borne any children. Five years later that had changed, and Felipe Juan's father found a second star to follow.

The drunk lady had spent some time walking a few mazy paces up and down the subway platform; the tap and scrape of her high heels had echoed in the silence, then the effort of staying upright had seemed to become too much for her and she'd slumped back against the wall, propped there by her shoulders, her arms folded in front. It looked as though she'd closed her eyes. Donk wondered whether she knew he was there. He looked at her legs where the fur coat had fallen open; he looked at the bag lodged in the crook of one folded arm.

Drunk lady, he thought, *crazy lady*.

No cabs and now no damn trains, either. Caroline watched yellow irregular shapes as they floated beneath her closed lids and listened for the sound of the rail singing and a distant drumroll that would tell her a train was on the way. She felt more drunk than she had up on the street; she felt immensely tired.

She was almost too tired and too drunk to feel fear when she opened her eyes and saw Donk's big face swaying just in front of her own like a mask held out on a stick, the overripe lips stretched in a grin.

'Hey, lady,' he said.

Caroline levered her shoulders away from the wall. It was the wrong thing to do; the action brought her inside his body space, and he wrapped his arms around her and forced her into a little jigging dance, laughing before pushing her back against the tiled wall. He peered at her, then lifted a hand and moved it slowly towards her face, his index finger extended, and rested the finger on the bridge of her nose as if to hold her in position.

She transferred the bag to her left hand and lobbed it a few feet down the platform. He didn't go after it, though he did look, briefly, to mark its place. Instead, he let the finger move downwards, tracing her profile, then drew it into the hollow of her throat before reaching swiftly into the neck of her dress, grasping her breast on the right side and lifting it clear. The dress tore down the line of its buttons, and her breast fell into view, his hand still clasping it. He looked at her eyes.

'Hey, lady,' he said; the words seemed to stick in his throat for a moment as he spoke them.

They stood almost in tableau, while he mashed her breast against the ribcage with his palm. Caroline was panting with fear now; the tang of bile rose in her throat and nostrils. Donk increased the pressure, leaning on her so that her shoulders were hard up against the wall, then he ducked and brought his free hand up inside her dress, raising the material. Instinctively, she closed her thighs, but his fist was already between them, the fingers opening to clutch and tug at the crotch of her briefs. She struggled as best she could, moving her body, pointlessly, from side to side. He lifted her off the wall, then slammed her back again. Her limbs

184

loosened, letting him through, and she felt a finger go into her.

When that happened, Caroline froze. The muscles in her stomach contracted and contracted again. She took several breaths in through her open mouth. The tendons on her neck made a deep V, and her shoulders drew up, as if she was lowering herself into very cold water.

Donk worked the finger. 'Hey, lady,' he said, then released her breast and moved his free hand to his fly.

They both heard the train at the same time. Donk looked past his right shoulder towards the rumble and twang coming from the tunnel, then backed off and moved a pace or two away. Caroline moved in an arc to stay away from him and went to the platform's edge; she was shivering and rubbing the palms of her hands up and down against the side of her coat as if trying to clean them. She looked straight down the track at the black arch from which the train would appear.

The sight of her back turned on him produced a sudden rush of anger in Donk. He had started to move towards the bag, then stalled. The noise of the train was very loud now; it would come into the station in no more than a few seconds. Donk moved behind Caroline, two fast steps, and kicked her hard in the small of the back. She disappeared from the lip of the platform as if snatched by a line. He didn't wait to see her hit the live rail, or to see what the train would do to her. He picked up the bag and went to the exit stairs.

Out on the street, he ran a few blocks before stopping to empty the bag. It contained a wallet of credit cards and $150, which he pushed into a hip pocket. That was all, apart from a dozen or so photographs, all of the same person. Donk flipped through them, incuriously, then put them back and held the bag between the front flaps of his pea-jacket so that he could rub it clean. Next, he let it fall and drop-kicked it on to a waste lot.

'Crazy lady,' he said. Then he forgot her.

Ed Jeffries was in bed when the call came through. He lifted the phone and listened in the dark. 'Yeah, Ash,' he said.

'The mother's secure,' Ashley told him.

'Good. Any problems?'

'Far from it. We couldn't be cleaner.'

'How so?'

'You said she was taking risks. You were right. She got crocked and wound up on a subway in Spanish Harlem after midnight. Some Spic kid copped a feel, then kicked her ass in front of a train.'

'Christ.' Ed waited for more.

'She's a statistic. No question. We had a man on her. He watched it happen.'

'Is this good, Ash? There'll be an investigation. She'll be traced. Neighbours and like that. They'll want to contact the boy.'

'Are you serious? It's covered. I've got an anguished next of kin at the precinct right now. Relax.'

'What about the Spic?'

A shrug came across the wire. 'Who knows? Who cares?'

'What did he do?'

'I don't know. Took off.' There was a pause. 'What do you mean?'

'You said he copped a feel. What did he do?'

'Does it matter? Hell. . . .' Jeffries didn't answer. 'The report didn't say. Fooled around with her a little, I guess. He didn't get time to fuck her. The train came in. I don't know.'

'OK, Ash. You can handle this?'

'Sure, it's cool. Believe me. One of New York's victims.'

'Will they find the Spic?'

'Nah. I don't think so. If they do, so what?'

'Yeah, OK, Ash. Send me the report.'

Guerney had overestimated them. It was the morning of the third day, and no one had come to the woods. Their food had run out. Rachel was tired, bored, cold and apprehensive. They sat together in the hide, close to one another for warmth, and spoke in whispers like children taking part in a game of Hide-and-Seek.

'You said twenty-four hours.'

'I was guessing.' Guerney shrugged. 'They'll be here.'
He looked at his watch and saw that they'd been in the hide
for more than two hours. Yesterday and that morning had
been spent out on the wooded hillside looking for signs of
their pursuers. Soon, they'd have to leave the hide again; it
was dangerous to spend too long there.

'What'll we do for food?'

'Live off the wildlife. Rabbit, pigeon. It won't come to
that.'

'Are you sure?'

'Sure. They're around. They're just looking in the wrong
place at the moment. Come on.'

She followed him out of the hide, and a raw wind struck
her cheek.

'Couldn't I stay here?'

'Of course not.' He started to walk clear of the tree-line,
beginning the four-mile circuit that they'd already made
earlier in the day. It took them to a number of vantage-
points, each of which allowed a full view of both woods and
valley. Rachel tramped after him, her hands deep in the
pockets of her anorak. There had been a fresh fall of snow
during the night, but they made no attempt to wipe their
tracks. That was part of Guerney's invitation to the men
who sought them. The longest period of watching was fifteen or so minutes of observation prior to reoccupying the
hide.

They walked for more than a mile, then stopped to look
down the length of the valley to where the ocean seemed to
be held in the bowl formed by Selworthy Beacon on one side
and the steep wooded hills behind Porlock Weir on the
other.

The sky was a bright pearl – an almost luminous backdrop for the pair of buzzards that treated the valley as their
territory. The only other sign of life was a small herd of deer
on one of the slopes, a dozen or so hinds and an old stag, who
would scent the air from time to time before continuing to
browse patches of fern where the snow was thinner.

Rachel followed Guerney's gaze, then looked beyond the

herd to the sea. 'We could have taken the Porsche to London,' she said, 'gone underground.'

'Why didn't you?'

'Not alone.' She sat on her heels and drew a finger pattern in the snow. 'What are you going to do?'

Guerney crouched down and put his back to a tree-trunk. 'It's a more complicated game than before. David Paschini isn't their only concern. I've become unignorable. They have to kill me. And you, I imagine; that's why you're here. Everything has changed. I'm a target now; if they do what they plan to do, I'll be a victim. It's not the way I live my life. Hiding wouldn't solve anything – no one can hide for ever.'

Without looking at him, she said: 'You do know who you're taking on?'

'What are they going to do?' Guerney asked. 'Send in the marines? Nuke the county of Somerset?' He stood up. The deer had moved deeper into the valley, ambling towards the stream; now and then, one of the hinds would make a little darting run, a nimble haughty movement, then stand still as if posing for her portrait. Guerney crouched down again. 'It's the choice of no choice,' he said. 'At this stage there's nothing to do.' She nodded, but didn't speak. Guerney said: 'If there were, I probably wouldn't do it.'

'What happens if you're wrong – if they don't come here?' Rachel asked.

Before speaking, he put out a hand and laid it on her arm in order to counteract her instinct to rise. 'There are two of them,' he said. 'If they asked for reinforcements, it seems they were unlucky. They're traversing the hill just above the spot where the deer were grazing, going away from us towards the crest.'

'What do we do?' Though Guerney had prevented her from getting up, she stared fixedly in the direction of the valley's mouth.

'They're travelling away from the hide, but they'll find it eventually. We'll get back there before them.'

He turned and started back along the line of their tracks, keeping low for the first hundred feet. Rachel followed. She didn't feel cold any more, though her legs were trembling as if they wouldn't support her for more than a few steps, and there was a hardness in the pit of her stomach.

Guerney had taken a line that brought them two hundred yards beyond the hide and closer to their pursuers. He stood to listen for a moment. The woods were still. Rachel watched the feathery curlicues of his breath condensing on the air. She could hear the buzzards calling to each other as they quartered their killing-ground.

Guerney's voice was low. 'I'm going back to the hide,' he told her.

'You go that way' – he pointed – 'towards the main track that leads to the road. There's a fence and fields beyond it. Cross into the nearest field, but don't go into the open. You'll be pretty well screened by trees. Head for the road.'

There was fear in her voice. 'Split up?'

'They've got to be separated. You'll be ten or fifteen minutes ahead.'

'Suppose they don't separate.' She paused. 'Suppose they both follow me.'

'I don't think that'll happen.'

'Christ,' Rachel breathed. 'Remember the Little Big Horn? That's what Custer thought.' She started off between the trees, not looking back. Guerney took a couple of quick paces after her and caught her arm.

'It's likely that their car will be somewhere close. Probably by the mill just below the entrance to the wood. Do you remember seeing it?' She nodded, still looking ahead. 'Find it. Break a window, get in, release the bonnet but don't open it. OK?'

'Yes.'

'Then find some cover. Don't come out until you see me. If I call your name, stay hidden and look for a chance to get away later. Whatever happens – understand?'

'Yes.'

'If I say nothing, but just go and stand by the car, it'll be OK.'

'I understand,' she said. He released her arm and she moved away from him, leaving a set of clear prints on the unbroken surface.

When Guerney got back to the hide, he spent a few seconds putting a maze of footprints into the surrounding snow, then demolished a small section of the snow-wall that he'd built to form a windbreak. When he stood sideways to the gap and half-stooped, he could see the tangle of blankets against the lower part of the tree's circumference. Next, he stepped into the tracks he'd left on his way to the first vantage-point, continuing with them for about forty feet until he reached a low clump of gorse and bracken. He bent his knees and jumped sideways out of his own footprints, landing behind the gorse and clear of the path, then turned to face back towards the hide.

They would find the tracks pretty quickly, he reasoned, and once they had done that one or both of the men would appear within five minutes. One, he thought: it had better be one. There was some small risk that Rachel's fear would be justified – that they'd see from the size of the tracks that she had taken the downhill path, and decide to take out the easier target first. He thought it unlikely; they would be too worried that she might be a decoy, too concerned that they'd be leaving their backs exposed; but it was a risk, and one that Rachel would simply have to take. She was paying her dues.

He took the lock-knife from his cuff, opened it, and stabbed it gently into the crust of the snow before unzipping his anorak a little and extracting the hunting-slingshot. He'd collected some ammunition over the past couple of days – a dozen smooth pebbles, each about the size of a pigeon's egg, and roughly spherical. The slingshot was a black metal U-shape with a collapsible wrist-brace and a pistol-grip stem. Guerney slipped his hands between the struts of the brace so that the rubber pad lay across the narrowest part of his right forearm. In his left hand he held a pebble.

*　　*　　*

Tom read the tracks – Rachel's smaller prints heading out of the wood, Guerney's leading uphill. He didn't leave the man with him a choice. 'I'll take this one,' he said at once, and moved off without looking back.

Tom's companion was called Paul. His opinion of Tom was pretty much in line with that held by Dick and Harry. As it happened, Tom's judgement of Paul wasn't terribly high, either. He thought him a whiner and probably unreliable. Paul couldn't see why the Department couldn't clear up its own messes. He hadn't wanted to be recruited to help out. Sure it was his job. Sure he would do as ordered. No, he didn't care much that the other guy from Grosvenor Square had taken a bullet through the neck – hell, it was one of the chances you had to take from time to time. But why was he helping to shovel CIA shit under the carpet again? Why couldn't it have been done more neatly, and at some other time? And why had this son of a bitch left a trail that Helen Keller could follow? Like, he knew why the guy had left the trail: to be followed, so they'd have to be alive to that one; but his motive for doing it instead of simply going on the run – what was that? Was the guy a nut, or what?

Who cared? had been Tom's curt reply. Pretty soon he'd be a dead nut, so who cared?

Paul came into the open, past a grouping of three Scots pines, saw the trample of footprints round the hide, and went for cover straight away. He was carrying a silenced pistol, which he trained on the hide once he'd retreated to the pines. He waited for two minutes. Guerney saw that the man's gaze moved away from the site of the hide now and then to flicker round the whole area. Twice he looked directly at Guerney's clump of gorse, but seemed to find nothing there.

Paul came out from the trees in a rush, circling rapidly to reach the hide from the left but sufficiently far forward to be able to see what he was approaching. As he reached it, he held the gun to his right so that it pointed directly into the gap in the snow-wall, though his body was to the side. He fired four rounds in rapid succession, traversing the barrel from right to left, then looked in.

Guerney loaded the slingshot and rose to his feet. The man straightened up, preparing to turn, and for a moment presented his profile to Guerney. The pebble took him full on the temple. There was a sound like a glass rod snapping and he dropped. Guerney snatched up the knife and covered the distance at speed.

He lay face down in the snow and might well have been dead. Guerney didn't bother to check. He reached into the hide and snatched up one of the blankets, wrapped it round Paul's head and shoulders, then reached under its folds and cut the man's carotid artery. He flipped for a short while, like a landed fish, while Guerney held the blanket tightly round him and stood on the wrist of his gun hand. When the movements stopped, he took the gun and an ammunition-clip that he found in one of Paul's pockets. He didn't find the car-keys, though he searched every pocket in each piece of clothing. He hoped that Rachel had remembered to spring the bonnet on the car the men had come in. Supposing she'd found it. Supposing she'd got that far.

While he'd been covering the ground between the gorse and Paul's unconscious body, while he'd been killing him, while he'd gripped the blanket and held down the gun hand with his heel just in case, while he'd searched the man, Guerney had looked round continually, and listened, for any other approach. Now he pushed Paul's body into the hide and stood up, still looking, still listening. He closed the lock-knife and pocketed it. The slingshot went back into his anorak. The gun was held loosely in his hand. No one else came into view. There was no sound save for the slight soughing of the wind among high branches and the piercing call and reply, call and reply of the buzzards.

The mill was beautiful: all the more beautiful, somehow, for being derelict. The windows on each of the four floors were broken, and the planks just below the smashed panes bore a silt of snow amid the dust. A musty smell still lingered in the place, particularly in the room on the second storey where a grain-door opened directly on to thin air. Rachel had eased the door back a couple of inches in order to have a clear view of the car that was parked on the wide grass verge almost directly beneath.

She was frightened. Over the nutty odour of barley and rye, she could detect the thick wet smell of her own sweat. She rehearsed the moment when Guerney would come into view and walk silently to the car, letting her know that things were OK, that she could leave the mill and go into the open without fear and drive back down the road they'd walked three days before, past the tea-shop where they'd gone through the pretence about milk, then over a little bridge by a farm and back to the main road. She imagined the warmth of the car and Guerney's hands on the wheel. She pictured the snowscape as they passed through it, travelling towards the motorway. She heard Guerney telling her what had happened up in the woods and what they would do next.

She had so involved herself in the fantasy that when Tom came into view, rounding the bend that led down from the woodland gate, there was a brief moment when disappointment was stronger in her than fear – disappointment tinged with anger at Guerney for having let her down. Instinct made her take a step backwards from the door.

Tom went to the car and examined the broken window before going to the front and pressing down hard on the bonnet to lock it. Then he looked round. The road had been cleared of snow, so Rachel's footprints had petered out after she'd left the field that bordered the wood. The verge the car was parked on was largely clear, too; a tractor or jeep – or some heavy vehicle – turned there each day, and the broad tyre-tracks had churned the snow, leaving puddles and crusty furrows of slush. She'd been able to get to the mill by walking lightfootedly on the marks left by the treads.

She tried to anticipate Tom's train of thought. If she had been going for help. . . . No, they both knew she wouldn't have done that. But maybe he'd figure her intention was to get clear, leaving the car for Guerney, its bonnet open to save him time; or perhaps she'd holed up somewhere to wait.

The car, with its broken window and released bonnet, would let Tom know that he and his companion had been seen; he would know, now, why the tracks in the wood had diverged.

As if thinking that very thought, Tom looked back in the direction of the woodland path with a swift anxious snap of his head. He seemed about to move in that direction, but then looked further down the road. *Maybe her intention was to get clear*. . . . Next, he looked at the mill, his eyes travelling from bottom to top and back again. Rachel guessed at his reasoning. One option was to go back – maybe there was time to prevent Guerney from trying to even the odds, or perhaps he would be able to spring a surprise of his own. Another option was to assume that Rachel was ahead of him on the road and could be overtaken. There was a danger in letting her go whether or not Guerney took out the other man. Last, he could try the mill. If she were in there, she must be waiting for Guerney. Tom would have the advantage of killing her and using her hiding-place himself, to pick Guerney off when he arrived. If she wasn't in there, he'd have wasted time, lost her, and possibly have lost Guerney, too.

Tom stood still, his hand resting on the bonnet of the car. *I've gone ahead. Believe it. I've gone ahead.* Rachel projected the thought fiercely, the muscles in her neck and shoulders rigid with effort as if she might push the idea out across the cold air for Tom to take in. *I've gone ahead.*

He moved round the car; then, as if making up his mind, began to trot down the road. Rachel watched him out of sight. Without knowing it, she had been holding her breath and now she released it, like a swimmer coming up for air, taking fresh gulps and leaning for support against the rough wood of the door-beam. For a couple of beats, she closed her eyes, conjuring, beneath the lids, the sight of Guerney approaching, as if by imagining it she might will the vision to become real.

When she opened them again, Tom had returned and was standing by the car once more. He looked up at the mill as he had before. He was holding a gun in his right hand, tapping the barrel thoughtfully against his leg.

Five seconds passed, then he walked quickly across the verge, moving under Rachel's eye-line and into the building.

12

Tom would have preferred to have been able to take more time over it. He smiled at Rachel as he walked towards her, not bothering to bring the gun up until he got close. It would have been easy to shoot her from the doorway, but he could spare a few seconds, just a few, to watch her terror, to hear her plead, perhaps. He remembered her voice: 'I outrank you, you son of a bitch.' He remembered the softness of her breath and her look of contempt. 'Throw it to the dogs.' He smiled, watching the fear in her eyes and the way her mouth was ugly and loose, and knew that she was remembering, too.

He stopped just beyond arm's reach. His smile broadened. 'Well,' he said, watching her eyes, 'guess what's going to happen now.'

Rachel opened her mouth as if to speak, then closed it – not a gesture of resignation, but dumbness induced by shock. Tom stepped a little closer and, without needing to look down, kicked Rachel's feet out from under her. She fell heavily, her shoulder and hip crashing against the wall before she could put out a hand to brace herself, but her eyes stayed on his face. He stood over her, pointing the gun first to the left, then to the right; sometimes above her waist, sometimes below.

'What I'd really like to do,' he told her, 'is to shoot little bits off you for a while. A little bit here, a little bit there. . . . I'd enjoy that. Pity there isn't time.' He moved slightly to the side, and kicked her a couple of times, catching her ribs and her thigh. 'Bitch,' he said. 'You fucking bitch.' He brought the gun up towards her face.

Guerney didn't use words, he simply yelled to let Tom know that he was there – a harsh *yip* that echoed in the high ceiling.

Tom swung the barrel of his gun towards the door, saw there was no one there, and immediately grabbed Rachel, hauling her upright and jamming the gun against her temple. He dragged her torso in front of his own and peered past her shoulder at the empty doorway.

'Guerney!' There was no response. Tom called the name again. 'Guerney! I want to see your gun, if you've got one, then you. Throw it in at the door; follow it after a count of three.' His eyes were roving the room, looking for any other entrance or vantage-point. There was only the door. 'Do it, or I'll kill her.'

'I'm not coming in there,' Guerney called to him. 'I'm going to shoot you when you come out.'

'I'll kill her, Guerney.' Tom was trying to calculate how far from the door Guerney stood.

'Fine,' said Guerney, 'go ahead.'

'I mean it!'

'I believe you. Go ahead.'

There was a pause. Tom pushed the barrel tighter against Rachel's head as if prompting not her, but the unseen Guerney. 'I'll kill you both. Her first, then you. You haven't got a gun, you bastard.'

'OK,' said Guerney, 'do it.'

'You haven't got a gun!'

'That's right.' Guerney's tone was light with mock-reassurance.

Paul was dead. That had to be it. Tom edged back towards the grain-door and snatched a glance at the drop. Paul was dead; and of course the son of a bitch had a gun. Paul was dead, and Guerney was carrying a standard-issue Smith & Wesson .38 identical to the one Tom held at Rachel's temple. The drop looked to be about twenty-five feet. He could shoot Rachel and jump and try for the car if he didn't break an ankle. He could shoot Rachel and take the chance of out-manoeuvring Guerney. He could take a chance that Guerney was bluffing and shoot her to wound, then wait for Guerney to come in at the door. He could make her squeal like hell – take off a kneecap, an elbow. Would Guerney just wait there, outside, doing nothing? He looked again at the drop on to the icy ground. When he spoke again, there was a querulousness in his voice.

'You haven't got a gun.'

'That's right,' Guerney replied. 'So you can shoot her, can't you? Do it. I'm getting cold.'

Tom moved away from the grain-door and into a corner, dragging Rachel with him. 'Listen,' he called, 'what do you want? You want a deal? What?'

'No. Just hurry up and kill her if that's what you're going to do.'

'Look, I'll deal, OK?' Tom leaned over Rachel's shoulder to shout the words. 'We've both got a hold on this. There must be a deal, right?'

'Listen,' Guerney's voice was hard and precise. 'I'm staying here until you kill her. Understand? Kill her. Do it, for Christ's sake. Then I'm going to shoot the shit out of you. That's what's going to happen.'

'You bastard!' Tom screamed and dug the barrel into the loose skin above Rachel's cheekbone. 'Motherfucker! I'm killing her. I'm killing her now, you bastard.'

Nothing happened. There was no reply. Tom stared at the door, wide-eyed with fury and fear. '*Guerney*!' He screamed the name into the silence.

'Hand your gun to the girl,' Guerney instructed, 'then let her back up until she's in the doorway.'

Tom gripped Rachel's arm more tightly. 'Fuck you,' he said. 'What keeps me alive?'

'I want you to deliver a message.'

'That's the deal?'

'That's it.'

'What message? Who for?'

Again there was silence. Tom was breathing quickly, his eyes fastened on the doorway. He couldn't calculate where Guerney might be – to the left of the door, or to the right; he hadn't looked to see what lay in there. Were there beams, or a flight of stairs? Surely there must have been stairs to the next floor. Guerney could be above him, or lying flat on the stairs that led downwards. If he killed Rachel. . . . He rehearsed the idea for the second time, his mind hopping from that event to the next, from probability to probability. He'd shoot her. The drop from the grain-door was too great. Guerney could simply wait. Tom would have to go through the door. Sooner or later, he'd have to do that.

'What message?' Guerney stayed silent. Tom yelled again: 'Who's it for?'

After a full thirty seconds, Guerney said: 'Give her the gun.'

Tom's grip on Rachel's arm loosened, tightened convulsively for a moment, then was released. She turned and took the gun from him and backed towards the doorway, watching him all the time. When she felt Guerney's presence behind her, she stepped to one side to give him a clear eye-line to Tom. In the corner of her eye, she could see the gun, levelled at Tom, and Guerney's arms extended to brace the weapon and aim it.

'Crouch down,' Guerney said. Tom lowered himself on to his hams, cautiously, as if getting into a very hot bath. 'Now sit on your hands,' Guerney ordered. Tom obeyed. With his hands trapped under him, he felt how exposed his face was, and tried not to turn his head as Guerney approached him. Neither man spoke. The sound of Rachel's footsteps as she crossed the wooden floor was hollow, and seemed unnaturally loud.

She stopped beside Guerney and looked down at Tom, who held her stare for a second before switching his gaze to Guerney. 'What message?' he asked.

'The boy's OK?' Guerney's voice was calm – that of someone running through a checklist of items.

Tom shrugged. 'When I left him.'

'The parents? Where are they?'

'I don't know.' Tom seemed surprised by the question. When no response came, he added: 'I don't know . . . I mean, anything about them. I'm not running this show. I don't take the phone-calls – you know? I'm a mechanic – that's all.'

'How did you get him to England?'

'By plane. USAF. A regular transport flight.'

'Where did you land?'

'Brize Norton.'

'What did you want him for?'

Tom looked down at his knees and shook his head, slowly, as if expressing regret. 'You're wasting your time, Guerney. I mean, I just don't know, OK? They tell you what to do; they don't tell you why. Call Washington; someone there knows.'

Guerney leaned forward and hit the man across the mouth with his gun-barrel, a hard backhanded blow. Tom's whole torso went sideways, then he straightened. 'Forget it,' he said. Two lines of blood ran from his lips and across his chin; his teeth were awash with red; when he spoke tiny bubbles appeared, like thin foam, round his mouth. Rachel could see that a front tooth had been smashed back, almost out of the gum. 'Forget it. You can do that until your arm gets tired. I don't fucking know.'

Rachel said: 'It's likely he's telling the truth.' She was less anxious to save Tom a beating than to save Guerney the time.

'She's right.' Tom spat little runnels of blood with the words. He looked at Rachel with a kind of interest, as if a thought had just struck him. 'She'll know more than me. Much more.'

Guerney nodded. 'I believe you.'

Tom relaxed slightly, shifting back a couple of inches to take some of the weight off his hands. When he spoke he kept his voice low, but couldn't disguise the trace of relief it contained. He sounded like a salesman whose pitch has been successful and now, pencil poised, can start to discuss the size of the order. 'OK,' he said, 'what's the message? Who do I give it to?'

'There's no message,' Guerney said, and brought the

gun up and shot Tom in the forehead, precisely, twice. Rachel's yelp mingled with the dry cough of the muffled gun. When Guerney caught up with her, she was standing by the car, trembling, her head lowered. He touched her arm, and she rounded on him, eyes wide.

'You bastard!' She spat. 'He might have done it. He might have killed me. Did you think of that?'

He reached out and took Tom's gun from her, unlatching it gently from her fingers. 'Yes, I thought of it. I was pretty sure he wouldn't.'

'You were *what*?'

Guerney said nothing for a short while; then he asked: 'Why are you here, Rachel? What did you come to Somerset for?'

She turned her back to him and looked up the road towards the wood. 'I was frightened.' It sounded like an apology.

Guerney put the car-key that he'd found in Tom's pocket into her hand, tapping her fist to loosen it. She tightened her grip on the key, then faced him again. 'Open the boot,' he said, 'and keep an eye on the road. After I've put him in there, wait for fifteen minutes then drive up to the gate. Unlock the boot, but don't lift it. Just stand by the car.'

'The other one's dead?'

Guerney nodded. 'I have to clean up. Then we'll take them to Druid's Combe.'

It took him just that long. Rachel had driven to the gate and been standing next to the car for no more than three minutes when she saw Guerney appear on the track, Paul's body over one shoulder. He had used one of the blankets as a sling to carry everything from the hide. She turned her head as he loaded the corpse into the boot. One of the arms was rigid, and he had to break it in order to get the lid closed. She heard Guerney grunt as the bone gave.

Tiny jolts of shock were coursing through her, as if someone were dabbing a live filament at her nervous system. Her wrists tingled. She could feel her pulse tapping against the bruise on her temple where Tom had held the gun. Out there, in the snowbound countryside, she could scarcely make any of it real. A few hundred yards away, a small herd of cattle was browsing over some mounds of hay. Everything was still – the stillness of a winter afternoon – and the light had grown less sharp, blurring distances and making objects merge. There was a tang of woodsmoke in the air. She stood with the car and Guerney behind her, and for a moment was able to banish everything but what she could see.

When the lid of the boot slammed she began to cry, though her tears didn't fix her there, or sap her will. She walked to the passenger door in a businesslike way, climbed in, and slammed the door abruptly. Guerney joined her, glanced at her once, then began to manoeuvre the car off the stony approach to the gate where Rachel had parked it. She cried without ceasing until they reached the small road that led to Druid's Combe; she neither spoke to Guerney nor expected any words from him – of comfort or of recrimination. She looked directly ahead through the windscreen and cried, her hands resting motionless in her lap. The track was impassable still. Between them, Rachel and Guerney carried the bodies up to the house and beyond, to a spot under the hedge that bordered the pasture. She had stopped crying when she'd gripped Tom's ankles and swung his legs out of the boot.

The ground was hard; it would take some time to dig deeply enough. They had checked the house first. Rachel had been worried that the place might have been staked out, but when she'd mentioned it Guerney had simply said, 'No,' and shifted his grip on Tom's shoulders. He was right, she reasoned. No one would expect them to come back. Guerney hadn't said it for that reason, though. Three men had attacked the house; two had followed them to Horner. There had been plenty of time for others to come. If he'd had to go up against four men, or even three, in Horner Woods, things would have been very different. The men he'd killed that day were the only army that could be mustered.

Rachel stayed in the house while Guerney worked. The

broken window in the bedroom had made the place indes-cribably cold. Fragments of the grenade were scattered about and there was a scorch mark on the far wall. In the main room were the brandy-glasses and dead charred logs in the fireplace. The dog's slipleash lay on a table.

She gave herself a brandy and went to watch Guerney through the broken pane. He was using a pick to break the earth and a shovel to clear it. The bright nib of the pick rose behind his shoulder, and his back tensed each time he leaned against the blow. He seemed absorbed, working without pause and never once casting a look towards the two forms that lay in the lee of the hedge.

Rachel felt disorientated, as if she had woken in a strange room with no idea of how she came to be there. Images came to her, like markers on the road that had brought her to this particular place at this particular time. Guerney, at the Washington party where they'd first met, standing alone by the door as if for a quick getaway, holding a highball-glass by its rim, loosely, and allowing her to know that he was watching her. A beach in Maine, and Guerney poised on a lip of rock, about to dive. A Sunday, the pair of them in Central Park, both knowing that they had reached the end of things, weaving between the sightseers and pretzel-vendors and joggers. A time much later, when they'd met for dinner in the Village; Guerney was on a two-day trip to Manhattan; she'd been unaccountably nervous and had overdressed. Long Island, just a month ago, and the lights skittering on the water as she had leaned across the rail and felt his rhythm echoing the rhythm of the sea. Ed Jeffries, flanked by the other two, his fingers steepling over the folder that lay on the table before him. The boy. The cards strewn on the floor. The Dobermann pack running inside the chain-mesh fence. The hide. Buzzards floating above the valley. Tom's body driven back against the wall and the sudden shocking disfigurement of the bullet-holes on his brow.

There was the slightest gathering of dusk – a crepuscular thickening of the light between the boles of trees and in hollows along the hedge. She watched Guerney drop the forms into the grave and begin the work of closing it. Not until there were only a few shovelfuls left did she go outside to join him. He looked up as she approached, but didn't pause. When the earth was in, he reversed the shovel and scraped snow over the mound.

'It'll be found – if they check here, I mean.'

He shook his head. 'There's more snow coming. The hedge is to windward, you can see the way it's drifted already. There'll be a snow bank; that's all anyone will see. Beside which, why would they care? It will be assumed that they're dead. No one's going to want to dig them up.' He lofted the pick and shovel on to his shoulder.

'What about us?'

'I need to make a phone-call. Then we're going to drive to Taunton and get a train for London.'

'Are we?' There was a question in her tone that hadn't to do with what the next move might be.

'It's safer if you're with me. But it's your choice.'

'Safer for me?'

She had read him correctly. 'No; for me. I don't want you picked up. And I can use what you might know when it comes to a decision about whether to jump this way or that. Your choice, though.'

She looked beyond him to the field of snow above the house. A flock of crows was circling low over the blankness; then they landed, seeming, in the half-light, to be standing on air. As she watched, they formed a circle which two of them entered, strutting to and fro like advocates arguing their case.

'What are they doing?'

He followed her gaze and looked in silence for a short while. 'It's a crow's parliament. They fly in, gather in a ring that way; one or two will do what they're doing now – go into the middle and walk about. After a time they fly off – usually taking a new course.'

'It's as if they're judging something.'

'Or being judged; yes.'

'Why do they do it?'

He shrugged and turned away towards the house, the blades of the pick and shovel clanking gently. 'No one knows,' he said. 'It's a puzzle. There are theories, but no one really knows.'

She didn't follow. The circle of crows stood with their heads bowed in thought, while those they encircled paced in the ring, tense with the urgency of their plea. A light came on in the house, spreading a yellow patina over the nearby snow. Rachel waited until the birds flew, following them as they rose and wheeled, Bible-black against the field's flank; then she crossed the snow stained by lamplight and went into the house.

Guerney was putting the phone down. She looked at him, as if trying to find something she could recognise; finally, she raised a hand, palm uppermost, in a gesture of acceptance. 'OK,' she said; then: 'I can't think of what the hell else to do.'

The train was travelling through a fresh fall of snow that furled in the slipstream and hung in pale streamers outside each window. Rachel was asleep, the beer and sandwich Guerney had brought from the buffet untouched before her. Each time the train swayed her cheek-bone rapped the window-strut, though it wasn't enough to bring her awake.

Guerney looked at her sleeping face and wondered what he felt. Their affair, their friendship, the pleasure he had always gained from seeing her, the traces of her in the safe house, her betrayal, the ordeal of the last three days. He couldn't make an equation of it. If there was a pattern from which he might learn what had happened, then he couldn't gain a view of it yet.

He sifted through the options that faced him and realised they were scant. He'd formulated a loose plan for the next few days, but he was operating out of ignorance, and he knew that meant risk. It was all risk now. The thought worried him, and he tried to understand why. It had to do with a fear of being stopped before any kind of resolution had been reached. He needed, badly needed, to know why they had wanted David Paschini. He needed to know what he was fighting – how the boy's talent was to have been used. He realised that it also had to do with Rachel, though he couldn't detect how or why.

She came awake, briefly, as if his thought had disturbed her, and looked around blankly at the other passengers. Her gaze came to rest on him, then transferred to the beer and sandwich on the table between them. She seemed not to be able to identify anything. Guerney spoke, telling her how much longer they had to travel. Her reaction was to put her cheek back against the window and close her eyes. Within seconds she was breathing slowly and shallowly; beyond the glass, snow billowed about her sleeping head. Guerney looked at her and decided she must be left to chance.

Part Two

13

The girl turned full face to camera and delivered a wide smile that gradually faltered as she became increasingly self-conscious. She lowered her head and giggled. When she raised it again, the smile was a questioning one; she looked from side to side, at the people who were in the room with her but out of shot. The screen became white.

Prentiss walked to the door and rotated a dimmer switch to raise the lights, then he turned off the projector. 'That was '76,' he said. 'She was fourteen.'

Ed Jeffries lit a cigarette and turned in his seat to reach for an ashtray on a nearby table. 'It's weird,' he commented, 'all that stuff. I've never really seen it before.'

'Standard tests,' Prentiss told him. 'She and David Paschini were top of the class at that kind of thing.'

'Why did we go for Paschini as first choice?'

'Fewer connections.' Prentiss took a video-tape that was lying on top of a television console and thumbed it into the video-recorder. 'Paula Cole isn't exactly low-profile. I guess it made us wary.'

Numbers on the television screen ran backwards from six. There was a moment of blankness, then a blare of music and a voice that said: 'Ladies and Gentlemen: the Tony Cade Show.' A figure appeared descending a long staircase. Prentiss wound the tape on, keeping an eye on the revolving digits on the video-recorder's console. He said: 'This is what she's like now.'

You could see the girl in the woman, though the fourteen-year-old's chubby prettiness had been refined to something angular and intriguing. Paula Cole's was a beautiful face that bore none of the classic lines of beauty – the mouth a trace too wide, the forehead too broad, the planes of her cheeks a little too hollow to be perfect. It was the imperfection that made her beautiful.

She was sitting in a swivel-armchair close to the talk-show host, who held a wristwatch in his hand. His mouth was open in an exaggerated 'O' of surprise.

'That's fantastic. Amazing.' He turned to the studio audience, to register his astonishment with them, and held up the watch. 'It's stopped. It really has. Now, I've had this watch for over a year and it's never lost a minute.' He turned back to Paula. 'Truly fantastic. I wouldn't have believed it.' He paused for effect, then asked: 'You *can* make it start up again just as easily?' Paula gave him a coquettish look, experienced and well rehearsed – Cade's cue to offer a look of startled dismay first to the camera, then to the audience, who supplied the correct reaction by howling with glee.

'Now, wait just a minute,' Cade chuckled, holding the watch out to Paula, 'this isn't under guarantee.' The audience laughed more loudly; Paula smiled enigmatically; Cade held his pose to milk the audience reaction, and was fixed in it as Prentiss froze the frame.

'Yes, I'd heard of her,' Jeffries said. 'She's a looker.'

Prentiss looked at the screen. 'Yeah . . . well, she's scarcely known in Britain. Over there she'll be just another pretty girl. Listen, Ed, I want you to handle the liaison from the outset. There shouldn't be any screw-ups, but after last time. . . .' He closed his eyes briefly.

Jeffries absorbed the compliment. 'There's no question,' he asked, 'of this one getting leery of the project?'

'She knows what we want her to do. She's agreed to do it. It wasn't difficult. I think the idea intrigues her. It's a whole lot sexier than stopping watches or turning on the light.' He glanced at Paula's image on the screen again, then said: 'She's a strange lady, this one. It seemed to excite her.'

'So, she's doing it for – what? – kicks and the US of A?'

210

'Kicks, maybe. Also for a sizeable slice of the budget.'

'Like?'

Prentiss paused, then shrugged. Why shouldn't Jeffries know? It was the kind of barter he'd understand. It would probably give him confidence. 'Five hundred grand,' Prentiss said.

It was Jeffries' turn to look across at the television screen. 'Jesus,' he said, 'all for a little mental effort. Some negotiator.'

'Seller's market,' Prentiss observed. He picked up a hand-control and made the screen go blank. 'We can't delay. What's happening in England?'

Jeffries made an exaggerated show of exasperation. 'Who knows? Silence. No Guerney, no Rachel Irving, no sign of the guys who went after them.'

'There's no chance that Irving finked? You're sure?'

'Of course.' Jeffries shook his head vigorously, remembering the promise he'd made to Prentiss. 'I can't figure it. No one can. Christ knows how it could have happened, but it looks as though we'll have to consider them dead.'

'And Guerney?'

'We'll get to him somehow. He's only a danger if he decides to talk, but we've made provision for that anyway. The press, the police . . . that sort of thing. It might bring him into the open if he tries to make things public. Apart from that, he doesn't know whether it's Friday or breakfast-time. What could he know?' Jeffries gestured towards the blank screen. 'This stuff . . . he could guess for a hundred years without hitting the answer.' As he spoke, he was wondering about Rachel. *The hell with it,* he thought. *She doesn't know, either. She might think she does.*

Prentiss seemed to pick up on his thoughts. 'Irving set him up. That might have told him something.'

'Maybe. I don't know. Our guys knew she was expendable. If they killed her, Guerney would be sure of nothing.'

'And if they didn't?'

Jeffries looked confident, though he didn't feel it. 'Same thing. She's an old friend who got wound into Guerney's

211

trouble. She can act. And we've still got a line on Guerney.'

Prentiss sounded dubious. 'It's a mess, Ed. We've got to hold our schedule. I want it cleared up.' He got up and went to the door. 'You'll let me know.' His habitually soft tone of voice had an edge to it. He wasn't asking a question.

'Sure . . . uh . . .' Jeffries couldn't decide how to address the other man. 'Sure.' He raised a hand to reassure. 'Hell, maybe they're all dead.'

'I'd like to think so,' Prentiss said. Neither of them believed it could be true.

14

In London's larger parks, and on its heathland, the snow-scape looked much as it might have a century before, large areas remaining unbroken except for the tracks of animals. In the streets, it was quickly fouled as the city's dirt and fumes seeped in – first a noxious yellow tinge that seemed to lie just below the crust, then black grime eroding the surface like acid, until big, irregular blotches appeared making the fall look as if it were marbled by bruising.

George Buckroyd raised the blinds in the bow window of his first-floor flat in Maida Vale and looked out. The sky was low and coloured a dull pearl; there would be more snow that day. Tobogganing weather, he thought.

When he'd woken, three days earlier, and noticed the bright glow at the cracks of the curtains and detected the hush that seemed to lie over everything, he'd known at once what it was, and for the merest moment had experienced the same rush of delight that he'd felt as a child, knowing that snow had fallen during the night. He recalled the feeling now, as he peered down at the grimy pavements and the blackened piles heaped at the roadside. Strange how the memory of those childish delights still abided just below the surface of things, waiting to be evoked by a fragment of music, a smell, a particular light behind the curtain. He recalled something from his boyhood – little more than a series of sense impressions, really – which involved a sled clattering over smooth snow and the encouraging shouts of adults, cold air whistling at his ears and the quick hiss of the runners; then a warm hallway, his fingers tingling painfully, and his father laughing as he helped the boy off with his wellingtons.

Buckroyd sniggered at himself, a little embarrassed by his own tendency to sentimentalize. And then, he thought disparagingly, Nanny would have appeared on cue with a cup of hot cocoa. It occurred to him that she probably had, and he laughed louder, moving away from the window in the direction of the kitchen.

He filled a kettle for the coffee and put two slices of bread into the toaster. Next he laid a place for himself at the kitchen table: knife and plate, coffee-cup, marmalade in a dish with a little serving-spoon, milk in a jug, butter in an earthenware crock. Silly old sod, he thought, Nanny again. Nanny had possessed a stern sense of proprieties. 'A gentleman', she had once advised him, 'is someone who uses the butter-knife when he dines alone.' Some time later, during adolescence, he'd heard a different definition: a gentleman is someone who gets out of the bath to piss. He imagined how Nanny might have reacted to the later version, and chuckled.

Then he thought, *Daniel* – the thought he'd been holding at bay for three days, since the first snowfall – and his smile faded. He poured hot water over the coffee grounds, put the toast into a toast-rack and sat down to breakfast. His hands lay in his lap. He stared at the willow-patterned breakfast-plate, seeing only a smudge of blue. *Daniel*, he thought. *Oh, shit*. And knew there was no retreating from it.

They had been in Devonshire when Daniel had first seen snow, staying in a thatched pub that stood in the bowl of a deep valley. They were happy. Daniel seemed to take pleasure in everything about the place – its isolation, the hilly walk to a freezing sea, the bar crowded each evening with red-faced farmers and their overdressed wives, the novelty of overcoats and scarves and woolly gloves – and Buckroyd took pleasure in simply watching his enjoyment of these things. 'Not like St Lucia, George'; and Daniel would pull his cap down over his thicket of hair and grin delightedly.

The snow had begun as they'd sat at dinner: fat flakes

214

drifting past the windows . . . past Daniel's rapt gaze. After the bar had closed, they'd gone for a walk, leaning into the wind-driven billows and laughing like boys. They turned back before reaching the sea, sheltering for a short while in the lee of a tall hedge, and Daniel had gathered a double handful of fresh snow to taste, dipping his coffee-coloured face and lifting the cold crystals with his tongue. 'Not like St Lucia.' Then he'd kissed Buckroyd, taking the older man's warmth on to his numbed lips.

Did I really imagine it could go on for ever? Buckroyd thought. Did I? Why? Why should I have expected that?

He took a piece of toast from the rack and buttered it, then set it down on the plate. It had been three years ago, that Christmas they'd spent in Devon; and eleven months since Daniel had left him. When it happened, he'd wanted to die. He still didn't have much of an opinion one way or the other. I thought I was going to be happy, he reflected. What a fool. I retired from half a lifetime of shabbiness and deception and secrecy, playing those seedy games, signing memos that were as good as death warrants, and I somehow imagined that, because I wanted it so, everything could be new, a fresh beginning.

A life without stain – that's what he had once contemplated. As a young man, still at university, he had held to the idea of the priesthood. A contemplative life; a life filled with learning and ritual and the verities of obedience; a life given over to symbol and mystery. Then politics had become the issue and history the imperative. It had seemed a matter of when to invest his idealism. He smiled wryly as the word occurred to him. *Idealism. Ho-ho; that old thing.*

To check the train of thought, he got up and switched on the television. He thought breakfast-time television an abomination, but right now any distraction would do. *Daniel.*

The snow had marooned them, and they'd spent three days there, stomping through drifts, toasting themselves in front of the bar-room fire, being served drinks at any time of the day. An embattled community feeling had grown among those who were stranded in the places; guests who should have left on Boxing Day, people who had simply turned up on Christmas Eve for an evening's drinking or for dinner. Many of the women were wearing evening dresses and shawls and costume jewellery, their men dinner jackets with cummerbunds. None had any change of clothes. They slept in the bar like refugees, and everyone enjoyed the event enormously. In breaking the accepted order of things, the snow had also broken their reserve. They became a little enclave of souls, temporarily on holiday from their lives, all responsibility in abeyance. Buckroyd and Daniel were part of the group; no one seemed to think them strange or stop to wonder about who and what they were.

Buckroyd shook his head as if to clear it, and concentrated on the television. An announcer was offering gloomy prospects for the pound, backed up by a City pundit who wanted the government to take 'stern measures.' Then the programme switched to a report about a forthcoming peace rally. The organisers were predicting that it would be the biggest event of its kind ever staged: a march that would begin close to the site of a new Defence Ministry enclosure where Cruise and Pershing missiles would be housed, then proceed to London collecting protestors on the way. A massive gathering would take place in Hyde Park and would be addressed by Clive Holman.

At the mention of Holman's name, Buckroyd became attentive. He'd known the man at Cambridge, before Holman had embarked on a career in politics – a career that seemed more than promising. It was clear from the outset that the backbenches were to be no more than a transit camp for Holman. His instinct for the machinations of Westminster had been acute. He achieved the status of Junior Minister under Harold Macmillan, the tenor of the times perfectly suiting his particular brand of liberalism tempered by a keen sense of the practical. He had always spoken in favour of arms control, often for disarmament, but never unilateralism.

As the years progressed, though, his opinions held less

favour with those in power. He didn't adapt to prevailing opinion. As policy became less liberal, so his own position became less and less acceptable, and increasingly radical. He became a maverick – an irritation to his own party and, at times, a severe embarrassment. He never again came close to holding a senior post, of course, but he made sure his voice was loud enough to be heard. That served his purpose for a while. But Clive Holman wasn't the kind of person who was content to play a minor role. His need was to control, to organise; he saw little point in opinion if it was divorced from power.

When he accepted the position of chairman of the Peace Movement, resigning his seat in the Commons, the news had astounded everyone except those who knew him well enough to follow the logic of such a move. The effect was startling. Within a year, he had become a major public figure. His manipulation of the media was astonishingly deft, his reorganisation of the movement astonishingly effective. He had taken the post as chairman at a time when public sympathy for the unilateralist cause was growing by the day.

In under two years, Holman had doubled the membership figures, made unilateralism a credible choice and created a mood in the country which brought the Peace Movement real prominence and power. He was, in effect, leading an organisation which, under his guidance, had become an unignorable challenge to government policy. Peace Movement candidates would stand in the next election. The number of its members and sympathizers, together with the skilful persuasiveness of its case, would force any government, any political party, to take account of its policies and statements. The policies and statements of Clive Holman. He was back where he wanted to be.

Buckroyd watched as Holman's face appeared on the screen. He was being interviewed from a studio in Birmingham following a large rally there the previous evening. He managed, Buckroyd reflected, to combine in his appearance respectability, a touch of classlessness and a discernible air of fervent dedication – the look of a distinguished elderly don. His pepper and salt hair was tidy, but worn longer than would have been proper for an establishment figure. The lapels of his corduroy jacket had an almost imperceptible curl. His lean, hawk-like features bore the stamp of authority and dedication. He was perfect for the role; and, as a former Tory minister, the greatest coup the Peace Movement could have hoped for. Holman couldn't be dismissed as a loony or a well-meaning ignoramus either by the Movement's opponents or by the general public. His charisma and influence were undeniable – greater, Buckroyd mused, much greater than those of Bertrand Russell. Public opinion was working in his favour. He was a man who had found the right moment.

'This rally,' Holman was saying, 'due to be held in just over a fortnight, will be the most convincing demonstration yet of the mood of the country. It will be impossible for the government to dismiss it, or the groundswell of opinion it represents. It will prove, once and for all, that the ordinary people of these islands are calling for an end to Britain's involvement in the arms race. That they want to see American missiles cleared out of the country. That they expect the government that represents them to take a lead in de-escalation by declaring Britain a non-nuclear country.'

He paused, too clever and too experienced to try to make the interview a monologue. The interviewer took the opportunity.

'But do you think it likely, Mr Holman, that the government will be prepared to see the Peace Movement as an influence on the ballot-box, or its ideals as any real alternative to present policy? Isn't it true that your movement merely represents a vociferous minority? Why should government pay it much attention?'

Holman leaned forward slightly – not to crowd the camera, but enough to lend emphasis to what he was about to say. He looked relaxed, sincere and in possession of the facts; he knew how to do this sort of thing.

'To begin with,' he said, 'it isn't *my* movement. It's composed of the tens – hundreds – of thousands of ordinary people who are deeply concerned about the way in which this government, in concert with our American allies, has wilfully exacerbated the arms race and added to the terrifyingly large stockpile of nuclear weapons. Rather than seeking to lower the temperature internationally, they have caused it to rise to a point that many informed people – not merely myself – consider immensely dangerous. The expenditure on nuclear armaments, by our government alone, amounts to more than two thousand pounds every *minute*. At a time when our social services are falling apart at the seams, that might appear condemnation enough, apart from the unthinkable dangers involved in that kind of proliferation. You mentioned the ballot-box. It's clear to most observers that we're going to have a general election this year – possibly in the early autumn. The members of the movement I represent are voters. They understand the facts. They know where they stand. I think the government must be wondering whether it can afford to dismiss the likely effect on the outcome of that election caused by their current policies. No party can afford to ignore the Peace Movement now, or pretend that it's not a potent force in the political life of this country. Let the Prime Minister be warned.'

It was a nice note on which to end. The interviewer thanked Holman and swivelled back to camera in order to cue the weather report. Buckroyd poured himself a cup of coffee and watched with half an eye as more snow was forecast.

Impressive, he thought. Just the right combination of confidence and aggression. He wasn't surprised. From what he'd known of Holman, at university and later, he'd known that here was a man who would succeed no matter what role he chose to play. He would have brought the same skills, impartially, to the efficient running of a ministry, a brokerage firm, a cement works or a corner shop.

The odd thing is, Buckroyd thought, that despite knowing that I don't doubt his sincerity.

He smeared marmalade on his slice of toast and bit into it. He sighed. The diversion had worked for a while, but he had known that this day was going to be one of the bad days. There was no real defence. In fact he knew from experience that the only half-manageable way of coping was to indulge the feeling; to poke his fingers into the wounds; to court pain, rather than try to avoid it.

He spent two or three hours playing music, rereading letters he had never mailed, and leafing through photograph-albums. The sense of loss was crushing. He wondered, as he had wondered often over the last eleven months, why it hadn't killed him. He stared, dry-eyed, at the images trapped between the plastic sheets of the albums and watched the terrible scenes that played over and over in his head. He read the words on the stylish headed notepaper, and they appeared to him like the utterances of a dying man. I'm a ghost, he thought. I haunt myself. The phone rang and, though he was barely conscious of the noise, some Pavlovian reaction took him across the room towards it. He found himself talking without quite knowing how he'd got there.

It was his publisher, wanting to arrange a lunch-date for later that week in order to take charge of a new chapter. Buckroyd agreed to the date, knowing that he was falling behind with the work but hoping that by giving himself a deadline he would find enough energy to finish on time. He reheated some coffee and took it through to his study.

He had registered, almost without bothering to listen for it, an odd hollowness on the line during his conversation. It was good to know that the A-Branch troglodytes in Eccleston Street were still wasting time and tape. Maybe they'd got every church in Greater London staked out as possible meeting-places or dead-letter boxes. He smiled at the notion and in the same moment wondered where Guerney was, and how he was faring.

'St Mary-le-Grand,' he muttered to himself and sat down in front of the typewriter and tried to concentrate on marshalling facts about the church. 'Daniel. Oh, shit. *Shit*. St Mary-le-Grand.'

He took a piece of notepaper from the top drawer of his desk and began to write a letter that he would never send.

In the instant that she woke, Rachel imagined she was back in New York. She heard what she took to be the *whoop-whoop* of a siren and pictured the squad car barrelling down Fifth. The imagining lasted for no more than a second or two – just as long as it took for memory and perception to catch up with consciousness.

She swung out of bed and took a couple of paces to reach the window, prising apart two slats of the peach-coloured venetian blind. A tug was buffeting up-river, busy between the pleasure-cruisers and cargo-boats. Its whistle had woken her. She continued to look at the view for a while, even after she sensed that Guerney had come into the room.

'I've made some coffee.' She turned when he spoke. He had dressed, and was carrying a blue silk kimono robe which he tossed on to the bed.

'Thanks,' she said, but made no immediate move to put it on. 'What time is it?'

'Eleven-thirty. I slept until eleven. We were tired.'

'This is what the phone-call was about. The one you made from Druid's Combe.'

'That's right. It belongs to a friend. She's going to be away for a while – in Coeur Cheval.'

'I wish her snow and soft landings,' Rachel said. She looked back at the peach blinds, then to the neatly arrayed bottles and sprays and jars of cream atop the dressing-table, and beyond to a wall that bore about twenty black and white photographs in plain glass frames. 'Who is she?' Rachel asked. 'Where are we?'

Guerney indicated the robe. She put it on and followed him out of the bedroom into the only other room – or so it seemed – in the apartment. At one end, close to a window, stood a table where Guerney had placed the coffee-pot and two cups. Beyond the table was a kitchen area – sink, a pine table that served as a work-surface, a double oven and grill built into the wall. The window by the table was covered by

221

a light-blue Venetian blind, which Guerney had angled so that it all but obscured the glass.

'Just a friend,' he said. 'I mean, *only* a friend. She's a photographer. We're in an entire row of photographers' studios. They were warehouses once that served the river trade. Then they became derelict. Then they became fashionable, and serviceable. The studios are mostly on this level. Hers is downstairs, directly under us. She chose to live here, as well as work. It's a place called Wapping Wall.'

Rachel poured the coffee. 'That was the Tower of London we passed last night – just before we got here?'

Guerney nodded. 'We can operate from here for a while.'

'Operate?'

'Decide what to do next.'

'You don't know what to do next?' It was a genuine question. There was no trace of mockery in her voice.

'Not entirely. There's one thing.' He fell silent for a moment. 'I'm going out shortly. I'll try not to be long. In any case, don't worry for three or four hours. If I'm not back by six o'clock, you're on your own.'

'Simon . . .' She sounded alarmed.

'No, don't worry. It's just a precaution. While I'm out, I want you to make a phone-call.' He got up and fetched a piece of paper and a pen from the work-table at the far end of the room, wrote down the number and showed it to her.

'OK.' Rachel made to take the paper from him, but he drew it back and wrote something under the numerals.

'If it's an answering machine, hang up and try later. If a man's voice answers, say what's on the paper. If he seems puzzled, or doesn't respond, hang up. Otherwise listen to what he says, then get off the phone as quickly as possible.'

'I understand. Well, I don't, but – '

'It doesn't matter.' Guerney drank his coffee in three swift gulps and went towards the door. 'Lock this after I've gone. Put the security chain in position. I'll do this when I get back.' He knocked three times, paused, then knocked twice, paused again and knocked twice more.

'Don't worry,' she said. 'I was a member of the Black Hand Gang as a kid.'

'Fine,' said Guerney. 'If you get a different knock-pattern, throw yourself into the Thames from the bedroom window and strike out for Plymouth Rock.'

She locked the door behind him and put the chain into place, then collected her coffee-cup and wandered into the bedroom and spent ten minutes or so watching the river-traffic. Eventually, she left the window and amused herself by poking round the room. It spoke of someone who lived alone, but by choice; things were neat, but not neurotically so; there was an indelible air of femininity. A large perspex cube on the dressing-table trapped a dozen or so snapshots of *après-ski* tomfoolery. Rachel turned it this way and that, speculating on whether Guerney's friend featured in any of them, or was the eye behind the lens. Next, she opened the doors of the large fitted wardrobe and rifled through the clothes: Jap, Browns, St-Laurent, they were all expensive and, Rachel reflected, worth every cent. She delved among the drawers full of underclothes: little nylon pouches, cotton trimmed with lace, skimpy bras. Underneath a pile of care-fully folded handkerchiefs and scarves, she discovered a small cache of cocaine and a bundle of letters. She felt vaguely ashamed, but excited. It was like investigating the contents of another woman's handbag, or looking at some-one when she doesn't know she is being observed.

Finally, Rachel went to the wall of photographs and studied them. They were all landscapes taken at dawn or at dusk – brooding moorland or rough crags, a thickly wooded valley shot from above the tree canopy, a series of a beach taken from the foreshore at ebb tide. In each, the light was a principal feature – streaming from behind low cloud in multiple beams like searchlights turned on the earth, flooding the sky with a thin steely glow, or curdling on wet undulations of sand. They were unequivocally brilliant. Rachel looked at them for a long time. Then she helped herself to a couple of lines of the coke and retreated to the bed, lying so that she could keep the photographs in view.

No one would have thought Astley's an exclusive club. It occupied a basement in Greek Street. The floors directly above were divided into very small rooms, each of which had its own bell-push on the street-door, together with a card giving the occupant's name. Those who lived there seemed to be exclusively women. Some were known simply by their Christian names; others had more exotic titles. The house stood between an Armenian restaurant and an all-day theatre that offered 'non-stop nubile nudes live on stage'.

Not exclusive, though it was necessary to be a member in order to gain admittance. You could become a member by signing a scrap of paper and paying five pounds to a door-man whose jacket-sleeves creased under pressure from his biceps when he took your coat. Guerney paid the money and went through the inner door, passing from an ill-lit lobby to an even gloomier room that stretched the full length and width of the basement area. Light came from the small bar at the far end of the room, from the low canopies above two snooker-tables, and from the floor-lamps illuminating a poker game at a table close to a curtained window. The air was heavy with tobacco smoke. Guerney had already visited four rooms, elsewhere in Soho, each of them virtually indistinguishable from this. He'd also been to five pubs and two restaurants. He was relieved to see Colin Preston lean-ing across the baize and lining up for the pink.

He walked closer to the table and watched as Colin built his break, taking time over each shot, then walking round the table with the brisk confidence of someone who knows, before the cue-ball has come to rest, that he'll be properly set up for the next. The break stood at sixty-five before he slightly over-cued on a red ball into one of the baulk pockets and lost the angle on the blue. He played for a snooker and got it. Only the colours were left on the table.

'Enough's enough, Col.' His opponent snapped his cue

back into the rack, grinned ruefully and handed Preston a fifty-pound note.

Preston nodded and pushed the money into his hip pocket. Without looking at Guerney directly, he said: 'Fancy a game, Simon?' His accent was the real thing. Not the slovenly twang of south London, but a clear, sharp, energetic East End Cockney. He was a smallish man, maybe five feet eight, no more, but solid and sinewy. He'd spent most mornings of a recent three-stretch pumping iron, and he still worked out at the gym twice a week. Guerney didn't like the man particularly; Preston was a villain and always would be. But he was a little brighter than most, and a shade less crazy. He was one of a group of contacts that Guerney sometimes needed and sometimes paid.

'I don't think so, Colin. Buy you a drink?' Preston racked his cue and they walked to the bar. After Guerney had paid for their Scotches, they moved to a table. 'I realised you'd be out by now.'

'Yeah. Last May. Cheers.' Preston raised his glass, then took a swallow. 'Full remission. Nothin' out of order. Y'know. John and Frank came out at the same time. The rest of the firm are there or thereabouts.'

'What next?'

Preston sipped at his drink and shook his head. 'Fuck knows. In one sense it's a mug's game, really – piling into Barclays with a pair of the old woman's tights over your boat race and waving a shotgun at some poor cow. I'm yelling, she's pissing herself. It's as likely as not that I'll blow her tits off if she hiccups. The driver's outside watching for bloody traffic wardens. Someone else is terrorizing the punters. By the time we've had it away, we're all nervous wrecks. And all for a few grand. A week in the bookie's, a few of these' – he tapped his glass – 'and we're off again. Still, it's all tax-free.'

'You didn't get three years for armed robbery.'

Preston looked outraged. 'Do me a favour. I was stitched up. Warehouse job. I was nowhere near the fucking place.

225

Oddly enough, Old Bill managed to find a complete set of prints, a couple of handfuls of hair, a pint or two of blood and a small plastic bag filled with nail-clippings, and they all belonged to me. Just to be on the safe side, the DC on the case verballed me. Apparently I said something like "Strewth, guv'nor, you've got me bang to rights". They're a fucking joke, the filth. You'd think they'd try to be a bit more entertaining. I don't mind. We'd had a good run without getting nicked. I suppose they got frustrated. Well, Simon. What's the problem?'

'I need a gun,' Guerney told him.

'Do you, my son? Well, that shouldn't present no problems. When?'

'Now.'

Preston raised his eyebrows. 'That's a bit trickier, isn't it? It's not just a matter of popping out and getting you a shooter before the shops close.'

'You can do it, though.'

'Yes, I suppose I can. It'll cost a bit.' Guerney looked at him. 'Two hundred. Two-fifty. Depends on what you want.'

'I'll settle for what I can get, within reason. A handgun. Preferably a .38 special. There's another problem. You'll have to stake me for it.'

'Will I?' Preston laughed. 'You're in bother, aren't you?'

'I'll pay you five hundred for it when I'm clear.'

'That's more than handsome. The only problem being that it sounds as though you might not live to cough up.'

'Take the risk,' Guerney suggested.

There was a pause. Preston lit a cigarette and sipped again at his whisky. 'Yeah, all right,' he said. 'Fuck knows why. Finish your drink. There's a boozer up by Soho Square called the Pillars of Hercules.' Guerney nodded. 'Go in there and treat yourself to some of their shepherd's pie. It looks like bird-shit, but it's full of essential protein. Have a pint. Read the paper. I don't know how long I'll be. About an hour, I expect. Ignore me when I come in. After a bit, I'll go downstairs to the khazi. Count to fifty. I'll be gone by then – there's a side-door at the top of the stairs. First lav, on top of the cistern. All right?'

'Yes,' Guerney said. 'Thanks, Colin.'

Preston stubbed his cigarette out. 'How many rounds?'

'What's possible?'

'Not more than a clip. Say, ten if it's a revolver.'

'Do the best you can.'

Preston stood up. 'About an hour,' he said. 'Don't hang about in here too long after I've gone. I've got a reputation to keep up.'

Rachel had dozed for an hour or two. Hunger brought her fully awake, and she strolled into the main room to look for something to eat. Both the fridge and the cupboards above the sink were crammed with food. On the middle shelf in the fridge, propped up against a wedge of Stilton, was a piece of paper that simply said: *Enjoy!*

She made scrambled eggs, and took a beer from the fridge door. She felt neither threatened nor comfortably secure. It was limbo, this apartment with its aura of someone else, its tough femininity, its pleasant muddle of work and domesticity. The cocaine had sharpened her senses. She felt pleased enough to be there, among things she liked but didn't own, amid essence of Whoever-she-was: her view, her clothes, her photos, her secret letters.

She put her plate in the sink and took the beer to the telephone. It seemed to fit her feeling that she was about to phone a strange number and say something that was apparently meaningless to someone she didn't know. After two rings, he answered. Rachel consulted the paper Guerney had given her.

'Hello, Uncle George,' she said, 'it's Ermintrude. Are you free this evening at about eight o'clock? I thought we might meet for a drink?'

The man sounded genuinely pleased to hear her. He chuckled delightedly. 'Ermintrude, my dear; how nice to hear you. Let's meet in the pub by the park, shall we? I'll look forward to it.'

Rachel replaced the receiver. Who on earth was that? she wondered. She washed up her lunch-plate and switched on the radio, winding through stations until she found some music. She was having a hell of a time preventing herself from reading those letters.

It was a .38. There were only eight rounds, but the gun was clean and looked new. Before he'd gone to the pub, Guerney had made a small diversion and visited a supermarket where he'd bought some vegetables. Now he rearranged the contents of the store-bag so that the gun lay between the paper bags that held his purchases. He left by the same side-door that Colin had used and went directly back to Wapping Wall.

Rachel responded to his triple-double-double knock by calling: 'Who is it?' When she opened the door, they were both smiling.

'Very funny,' Guerney said. He put the store-bag down on the table and emptied its contents.

Rachel looked at the potatoes, carrots and turnips that spilled out of their paper bags. 'The fridge', she said, 'is full of smoked salmon, steaks and cheeses; the cupboards are crammed with cans of lobster bisque.' Guerney removed the gun from its wash-leather wrapping and put the shells alongside it. 'Ah, yes,' Rachel said, 'we are a little low on deadly weapons.'

Guerney checked the gun's action, then loaded it and dropped it into the side-pocket of his coat. 'You made the call?' he asked.

'He said the pub by the park. Does that let you know something crucial?'

'It lets me know that I'm to meet him in a pub by a park, yes. The Spaniard's Inn. It's in Hampstead. North.'

'I know where Hampstead is. Who's Uncle George?'

Guerney didn't reply. He put the vegetables back into their bag and dumped it by the sink. Rachel followed him. She was growing angry.

'Damn it, Simon, I'm going to meet the guy after all.' There was a pause. 'Aren't I?'

Guerney made to move towards a low sofa that stood beneath the window next to the dining-table – the apartment's concession to a drawing-room. Rachel took his arm, holding him back. 'Look!' She was annoyed enough to have to work at preventing her voice from becoming shrill. 'The point has been reached where you have to decide that you're going to trust me. If you imagine that I'm going to sit in this place while whatever is going to happen happens, then you're wrong. The role of little woman is not for me, chum. That aside, how in hell would I know whether my team was ahead? What happens if they get to you? What happens if they get some kind of lead on this place? At least Custer knew the fucking Indians were coming. Forget it, Simon.'

'Your team?' Guerney asked.

Rachel sighed heavily. 'They've already tried to kill me. I imagine that when those two guys failed to make it back from Somerset someone managed to deduce that their absence had more to it than bad traffic on the M5. It might have occurred to them that you and I have snatched the odd moment to discuss what I learned in Washington. OK, I set you up. I still don't know whether I'd have let it happen. I don't think so. You don't have to believe that. But you must see that, whatever my motives, I don't have a choice any more. I wish I did. If I had a choice, I could damn well prove something to you.' She walked away from him and sat in one of the dining-chairs.

Guerney looked at her in silence for a while. Finally he said: 'Uncle George is a man called George Buckroyd. He's a friend. Used to work for British intelligence. Now retired. He's been doing a little fishing for me among his former staff. I'm running low on ideas and I'm entirely without information. I'm going to ask him to take a risk.'

'Will he?'

'I don't know. Probably.'

'Why was I being childish on the telephone?'

'He thinks he's tapped. Staked out as well, for all we know.'

'Holy Christ. What if . . .?'

'I know.' Guerney's tone was sharp. 'It had occurred to me. We'll have to take the chance. I trust him to arrive unaccompanied. George used to be good.'

'He used to be young.' Rachel paused, then said: 'The call will let them know that we're in London. Active. Until now we were among the disappeared.'

'Yes,' Guerney agreed. 'We ought to assume that. I don't imagine that Ermintrude will have caused them much confusion. Worth a try, though. The guy on the tap might have a hangover, or be planning his next infidelity. They're only human. I expect James Bond farted in the bath.'

'Another illusion shattered.' Rachel smiled. She wasn't sure whether Guerney could become her friend again. She hoped it might be possible. Forgiveness had to be earned, she knew that much. 'Does he have a niece called Ermintrude – I mean, *Ermintrude?*'

'He doesn't have anyone,' Guerney replied. 'George used to work on the tenth floor. He'd spend most of his day alone; most nights, too. He told me once that he was lonely. We were having a drink to celebrate his fifty-eighth birthday. I went out and bought him a white rat. It used to live on top of his filing-cabinet in a rather extravagantly equipped cage.'

'I see,' said Rachel.

'Ermintrude,' Guerney told her.

'I'd guessed.'

His depression had lifted with Rachel's phone-call. He felt buoyant and energetic. It was good, apart from anything else, to know that Guerney was alive. He wondered who the girl might be. He wondered, too – or had earlier that day – about his motives for helping Guerney. What was he trying to atone for? What harm might he be doing, playing the role of gamekeeper turned poacher? He realised, after a moment or two of thought, that he didn't much care. He would, for the sake of whatever argument might later occur, assume Guerney to be on the side of the angels.

After years of skulduggery, he reflected, here was an

opportunity for derring-do. Why not think of it that way? The whole bloody business was played like international Cluedo. He remembered a time when an operative had been sent to Cyprus to kill Makarios – a piece of ill-temper and petulance on the part of a certain head of section. Nods and winks had been exchanged in a building close to Horse Guards Parade. The agent had arrived two days before the event, bought a case of the local booze and gone to ground in a brothel. A day later, the nods and winks became shakes and scowls: someone's mind had changed. The trouble was that the buffoon with the gun was incommunicado – tupping and tippling somewhere in the back streets of Nicosia. As time ran out, so things grew more frenetic. Virtually uncoded messages were whistling to and fro; panic-stricken rankers from military intelligence were running up and down alleyways like ferrets in a warren. All to no avail. As things turned out, the agent's hangover was so bad, and his hands shaking so violently, that he missed the shot. Buckroyd recalled a meeting at which they had all been filled in on the course of events – those senior enough to know. Everyone had laughed. The head of section telling the story had laughed. They'd laughed over every detail, until their stomachs ached from laughing. It was a bloody funny tale.

He didn't expect to see anyone. He worked on the assumption that someone would have been given the task of keeping an eye on him. He was pretty sure about the phone-tap. That could mean that Guerney was somewhere along the right track. If he was tapped, then it was just as likely he'd be watched. The business about Ermintrude on the phone meant that Guerney was taking it all rather seriously. Buckroyd was aware that he'd pushed a little too hard, leaned on old loyalties a little too much. Under those circumstances, the tap would be routine. But if Guerney's suspicions were even part-way accurate, then everyone was at risk.

He did what was simplest and most effective. Taking his own car, he drove sedately along the Edgware Road, regulating his speed so that he managed to be stopped by a traffic light with no other vehicle ahead of him. As he approached the next set of lights, he dawdled a little, waiting for them to go into sequence, just as those ahead would, and the set beyond that. As they switched to red, he accelerated, slapping his foot on the kickdown so that the automatic transmission slammed into a lower gear. He felt his back moulding the upholstery. He drove an elongated S between two other cars and reached a crossroads. The light had been red for a little over a second. He ran it, not bothering to look left or right. By the time he ran the third, it had been red for three seconds and he was doing close to seventy. There was nothing he could do to avoid the cross-traffic. It avoided him. He left behind a blare of horns, a minor crash and five terrified motorists. No following car had taken the same risks.

He left the car in a side-street just off Park Lane and hailed a taxi. The cabbie turned up South Audley Street and swung round Grosvenor Square before heading towards the Marylebone Road. He changed cabs at the junction with Baker Street, then again at Swiss Cottage. Guerney and Rachel were in the bar when he arrived at the Spaniard's Inn.

Guerney raised an untouched drink from the table and held it out. Buckroyd went over to their table and took the Scotch as he sat down. He smiled. 'Simon.'

Guerney gestured towards Rachel. 'George Buckroyd,' he said formally, 'Rachel Irving.' The smile had stayed on Buckroyd's face. Guerney raised an eyebrow. 'You look indecently pleased with yourself, George. I gather we're in no danger.'

'Don't think I'm taking all of this lightly, Simon. It's just that I was feeling horribly gloomy this morning. Now here I sit having committed unspeakable traffic violations in the Edgware Road before cloak-and-daggering my way across London. I'm in a good mood. Permit me to enjoy it; it won't last. What's happened?'

'Do you mind not knowing everything?' Guerney stopped

short of saying 'For your own good.' In any case, it wasn't just a protective instinct that made him want to give Buckroyd only a partial view. Instinct of another sort lay behind it: the fewer the links, the shorter the chain of knowledge. There was also the fact that Guerney's ability to explain stopped short at some points. A face reflected in a window-pane . . . a vision of Rachel entering a room . . . playing-cards scattered about the floor . . . a journey through a landscape . . . mad creatures whose shadows still sometimes flickered at the edge of sleep.

Buckroyd shrugged. 'Need-to-know basis.'

'Something like that.'

'No, Simon; I don't mind.' Buckroyd sipped his drink. 'I almost prefer it.'

'We know a few things for sure now,' Guerney announced. 'The boy was lifted by the CIA. He was brought here with the connivance of British intelligence – and with their help.'

Buckroyd restored his glass to the table. 'Well, well,' he said. 'You're sure?'

'Yes.'

'Why?'

Guerney shook his head. 'I don't know.'

Then he told Buckroyd a little more of what had happened in Somerset. He told him in more detail about what Rachel had learned at her briefing with Ed Jeffries, without saying where the knowledge had come from. The older man listened without a trace of evident scepticism.

'The New England technician,' he said, when Guerney had finished.

'That's right.'

'You've calculated the odds . . .' Buckroyd didn't bother to finish.

'I'm curious,' Guerney said. 'And angry.'

Buckroyd looked at him appraisingly. 'And vengeful,' he said. 'Ah, well; I understand that. Don't take against me, Simon, but shouldn't you cut your losses and go home?' He glanced at Rachel, as if eliciting her support, then addressed her directly. 'You can't be an innocent in all this, or why should you be here?' He turned back to Guerney. 'So you both know what your chances are. But, in case you don't, let me tell you. They're pretty much nonexistent.'

Rachel gave the answer. 'It's too late to pull out. I don't think we can.'

Buckroyd eyed the half-healed scar on her cheek. 'Is it?' he said. 'Yes, I see.' He looked thoughtful for a short while, then added: 'I'll help if I can.'

'I can't just walk away from this, George,' Guerney told him. 'Too much left unresolved.'

'It seems you won't be allowed to.'

No one spoke for a while. Guerney went to the bar and fetched more drinks. When he returned, Buckroyd repeated his offer. 'I'll help if I can.'

'I'll tell you what I want first,' Guerney said. 'Make your mind up after you've heard me out. I won't mind if you say no.'

Buckroyd smiled. 'Wouldn't expect you to.'

'I imagine nothing's been said to you yet. No approaches, no reprimands.'

'That's right.'

'You're sure about the phone-tap?'

'I think so. No one's ever really sure. A click here, an odd silence there, a *ping* or two – every phone behaves like that. In my case, they support a feeling.'

'I know. The likelihood makes those things evidence.'

'Exactly.'

'What about followers?'

'Who knows? Assume the one – assume the other.'

'Suppose they decided that the time had come to smack your hand. And ask some questions.'

'Well, I'd guess the tap went on after I'd been turning over the odd pebble or two. Questions about kidnaps, questions about New Hampshire. That would have connected you and me. I can't be sure about the time you called for the information about Whiteleaf Cross. I'm more certain about the time after that. I imagine you were thumbing your nose at them.'

234

'Something like that.'

'Yes, well, you can tell me about it some other time, if you've a mind to. They can't be sure we've communicated since then.'

'What about Ermintrude? To say nothing of your dramatic passage through west London tonight.'

Buckroyd shrugged. 'I suppose I'd go on the attack – say I object to being tapped and followed. Demand to know what's going on. Wait to be told to behave and mind my own business. It's not at all certain that I *was* followed.'

'No. OK. But, as things stand, there's nothing to prevent you having one more snoop?'

'Because I haven't been ordered not to, you mean?' Guerney nodded. 'In that sense, no. The order wouldn't be long in coming.'

'I won't be asking you to do it again.'

'I wouldn't listen if you did.'

'I need to know why they wanted the boy. Teleporting. Electrical impulses. Computers. It's all over the floor at the moment, and I haven't the first idea of how to put it together. The person who told you about the technician . . . you said he was simply handling the organisational side of it.'

'She,' said Buckroyd.

'And you trust her.' It was an assumption rather than a question.

'She joined the service as a secretary. Bright girl; very pretty. Before too long, she'd been offered a flat in Brussels, three times her salary and a rather jolly lifestyle. Attached to the embassy, of course. The occasional delivery; now and then a collection. She had a series of nicely stage-managed affairs with men who sometimes told her things they shouldn't have. Unfortunately, she fell in love. Even less fortunate, it was with a Russian. Nothing wicked happened – nothing Century House would care about, that is. As far as they were concerned, she was simply doing her job rather well. Something was likely to show eventually, though, because she loved the guy too much either to own up about

235

her real work or want to translate pillow-talk into state secrets. She told me. Or, rather, I deduced it, and she didn't deny. I liked her a lot. I found a way of getting her back and on to other duties.'

'Did she want to come back?' Rachel asked.

'No, of course not. She had some lunatic notion that she and the Russian might disappear; live in furtive bliss somewhere in the hinterland of Europe. Silly girl.'

'Silly girl,' echoed Rachel. 'What about the Russian?'

Buckroyd looked impatient. 'Street accident,' he said tersely. 'Hit and run. Tragic.'

'All this makes her grateful?'

'She recovered,' Buckroyd said. Suddenly, he looked less amused than when he'd first joined them. 'People do, I'm told. She was alive, she was free, her career was intact.'

'How much is there left in that,' Guerney queried, 'for old times' sake?'

'I can ask. I don't think she knew much more than she was telling me at the time, but . . .'

'But she works for someone who would?'

'Yes.'

'And there's probably some documentation?'

'Bound to be. "For your eyes only" stuff.'

'Unless I know more about how David Paschini was valuable to them, George, I'm in a blind alley. I've got one source to tap – someone of my own – but I don't know it'll come good.'

'All right, Simon.' Buckroyd finished his drink and stood up. 'I'll ask.'

'When?'

'Soon.' Buckroyd shrugged. 'Why not?'

'There's a pub called the Earl of Lonsdale in the Portobello Road. Can we meet there at twelve-thirty, four days from now?'

'You don't imagine they'll have every pub by every park staked out by then?'

Guerney grinned. 'Natural caution.'

'OK, Simon. Oh' – Buckroyd reached into his side-

236

pocket – 'I thought you might need this.' He handed Guerney a small package. 'Well,' he looked from one to the other. 'If I did have company when I left home, and they're feeling spiteful, they'll probably have asked the Met to clamp my car. You can't imagine how much that sort of thing amuses them. I expect it's the worst that can happen.' He raised a hand and weaved through the crowd of drinkers to the door.

Guerney put the package into his inside pocket without bothering to open it. He picked up his drink, but didn't raise the glass to his lips. After a while, Rachel said: 'Will he do it?'

'Yes.' Guerney nodded.

'She might not co-operate. The woman.'

'No. That's right.'

'You like him, don't you? I mean, a lot?' Guerney didn't reply. 'Oh, shit,' Rachel said. Then: 'What's in the package?'

Guerney drank off his whisky. 'Money,' he said.

15

She was feeling well. She was feeling purposeful. Last night's movie had been something she'd wanted to see; dinner had been excellent; she had slept soundly, stretched almost full-length in her first-class seat, and woken to a delicious breakfast served by solicitous stewards.

The flight had been largely uneventful; a little clear-air turbulence an hour or so out of Kennedy, but it hadn't troubled her. She felt exhilarated but secure, like a skilful driver at the wheel of a fast car.

The sky was a light icy blue. She leaned over to look down at the way sunlight was striking England's snowscape, the gleam appearing sometimes stark white, sometimes a soft shade of copper. Roads were dark scars. The surfaces of river flashed silver. With snow concealing most of its characteristics, the land had become geometric and simplified. She thought it a good omen.

A steward handed her a landing-card, and she removed her passport from her travelling-bag. It was her face; the rest was new. Suzanne Pollard. Birth date: 12 June 1962. Birthplace: Clearfield, Pennsylvania. She transferred the information and the passport number to the card. She had been intrigued by the way they'd done it – changing her hairstyle, using tiny plugs to fatten her cheeks just a fraction, so that she appeared just a little younger, then putting her in a summer dress to take the photograph. You could only see the neckline of the dress, but it completed that unmistakable look of a utilitarian studio shot taken one summer, maybe three years before.

The whole business excited her – the secrecy, the meetings, the purpose behind it all. As she thought of it her skin prickled, a little fizz of sensation that ran in her backbone and spread warmly to her shoulders. She shivered. As the plane made its final descent into Heathrow, she looked out of the window with renewed interest. England was new to her; London was new. She was looking forward to it.

Pete Ginsberg, on the other hand, knew London pretty well. He had been stationed at the embassy for more than a year – one of the reasons he'd been chosen for the job. No one knew how exposed Dick and Harry had become during the time they'd held David Paschini in England; everyone knew that things hadn't gone right for them. They had been recalled.

Pete heard that Tom hadn't made it. Tom's real name was Gerry Martin. Pete had known him slightly; had worked with him on a couple of routine jobs. Gerry had been a minor pain in the ass a lot of the time, and Pete couldn't honestly claim to be choked up about the man's death. Gerry was a statistic that happened to have a face. But he didn't much like the idea of wearing a dead man's shoes.

This time, there would be two of them: himself and a Brit. And this time it ought to be plain sailing. Pete hadn't been told everything about what had happened before. Enough to know that someone – maybe several someones – had fouled up. His job – his and the Brit's – was easy enough. All they had to do was keep an eye on the girl for a while and produce her on time. Babysitting. And maybe a little more. He'd been briefed on Guerney. A freelance with a grudge. That had puzzled him a little when he'd heard it. The motive puzzled him. Guerney had nothing to gain – or nothing that Pete could get a line on. He wasn't under instruction. The kidnap pretence had broken down. So why not pull out? Why point a pop-gun at a tank? Why go on spending *money*?

The thought struck him again as he stood by the Terminal 3 barrier waiting for Paula Cole to appear. He dismissed it finally. Who cares? he reflected. If he turns up, he'll get dead. Fuck him. An appearance by Guerney, he reflected, might even provide an interesting diversion in what promised to be a dull job. Easy, but dull. His confidence gave rise to a slight irritability. It would be good to get this over with; the next one, he figured, would have to be a little more – well, *active*.

When Paula Cole emerged from the Customs hall, he recognised her at once. Her hair was a touch blonder than in the photo he'd been given; and she was taller than he'd imagined. He stopped her a few feet past the barrier by putting a hand on her arm. 'I'm Pete Ginsberg,' he said.

Anyone watching the encounter might have been surprised that they didn't embrace. They looked like candidates for one another: both tall, both young, both good-looking. Paula glanced down at the restraining hand, then at Ginsberg's face. 'OK,' she said. 'Good.' There was the merest arrogance in her tone. It was there to counter the expression on Ginsberg's face.

They left the arrivals gate and walked towards the lift that would take them to the short-stay carpark. Ginsberg walked with his hands in his pockets – an air of mild indifference. Paula carried her suitcase herself.

He said: 'I've been told to look after you – see that you get what you want, go where you want to go, that kind of thing.' He grinned with mock-deference. 'Make sure your stay is a happy one, like any good courier. Show you the sights . . . you know.' He lowered his voice as if bored by the notion, and glanced at the pretty girl walking the other way. 'Just say the word.'

Paula put down her case and leaned against the wall as they waited for the lift to arrive and appraised him coolly. 'You could be pretty busy, Ginsberg. I haven't been on vacation in almost a year. I intend to have a good time.'

They rode up in the lift in silence. Paula was amused by the little conflict that had appeared so quickly, so spontaneously, and tried to identify its cause. Sex? Yes, something

240

of that. Power – that, too; and the fact that he was anxious for her to know that the role of 'courier' wasn't one he cared for. But there was something else, something to do with her talent. He found it ridiculous – that they were using her; thought it laughable, perhaps. That was most likely to be it – he was doing as he'd been told. But he couldn't take Paula seriously.

'You know what I'm in England to do?' she asked him.

'Sure.' He nodded, slouched against the side of the lift, his eyes fixed idly on the numerals.

'You know how I'm going to do it?'

The laugh-lines at the corners of his mouth deepened just a trace. Again he said: 'Sure.'

Paula felt a thread of anger rise in her, like mercury demonstrating the temperature. So, she thought, I'm right. Patronizing bastard.

When the lift doors opened, he stepped out first – preparing to lead the way to his car. Paula laid a hand on his arm – the same abrupt gesture that he'd used at the barrier. 'Stand still,' she ordered.

'What?' Half-amused, half-annoyed.

Paula turned slightly to look at him full-on. For about three seconds she said nothing; then she repeated the instruction, separating the words as if she were talking to someone simple-minded. 'Stand still.'

Chugging towards them, on a track between the parking-bays, was a small battery-driven float, towing a chain of wire-mesh containers. The driver was perched on his seat like a kid in a toy train. Every now and then he stopped to onload some of the luggage-trolleys people had abandoned.

Paula looked fixedly at the float. Nothing changed immediately. Then the float gave a kick and started to gather speed. The driver looked puzzled, then anxious, then frightened. He stamped his foot on and off the accelerator. The line of containers began to weave and rattle.

Ginsberg and Paula were standing close to the lift, pro-tected by a triple row of cars. Others were more exposed.

The float was unstable, travelling faster and faster as it approached the right-angle bend and the next set of bays. The driver was fighting to stabilise the vehicle, but it swayed alarmingly, moving snake-like and much too quickly.

A man loading suitcases into the boot of his car was struck, his legs crushed for a moment against the bumper, then sent reeling to the side. His bellow of pain and shock was barely audible over the din made by the mesh containers. The driver yanked at the controls. The float yawed across the aisle towards a car descending the central ramp. There was a shriek of locked tyres on concrete, but the car-driver was always going to be too late. The float whacked into him, smashing headlights and stoving in the radiator grille.

By the time he hit the bend, the driver was slack-mouthed with fear. He tried to hold the turn, but it was a lost cause. The float over-steered, bouncing against a pillar, then clouting the front ends of three parked cars. The conga-line of containers flew out like a whiplash, first crashing into the vehicles directly behind then becoming airborne, clattering over bonnets, smashing into windscreens. When Paula looked away, the float stopped dead.

The driver came out over the front, hitting the concrete floor and tumbling along the aisle, like a downhill skier taking a bad fall. A pillar stopped him and he lay still. People began to run towards him. There was glass everywhere. The sounds were of people's feet crunching it as they ran, and the cries of the man who had been struck by the float.

Ginsberg looked at the scene, then at Paula. He was trembling very slightly: anger and shock. She nodded slightly, as if to say, 'OK?' For some reason, when he spoke it was to offer a flat contradiction of what he knew to be true.

'You didn't do that.'

It was Paula's turn to be wry. 'Sure.'

She gave him back the little smile she'd received in the lift, then led him between the lines of battered cars, stepping delicately over the bright crystals of glass. 'I hope we're

242

parked on the far side of the down-ramp,' she told him. 'I'd hate to be stuck here while they sweep all this shit away.'

They drove to the house in silence. Paula looked out of her window, showing little interest in the view until they came off the dual carriageway. Then she studied the stores and the lunchtime crowds as if she were anxious to get a measure of the foreignness of things. From time to time, she turned in her seat, wanting a longer look at a hairstyle or a window-display. She seemed intrigued and a little excited – a tour-ist. It was as if she had forgotten the chaos in the Terminal 3 carpark.

Ginsberg found a space close to the house, backed into it and cut the engine. 'We're here,' he said.

'Fine.' Paula waited. Ginsberg had made no move to get out of the car.

'I know you've been briefed,' he told her. 'They asked me to add a couple of things – and repeat a couple.'

Paula raised a hand and half-extended it in his direction: the floor is yours, it said.

'You'll be with two of us. The other guy's a Brit. His name's Alan. You can't go out on your own. Apart from that, we can do pretty much anything you like. You know – movies, theatre, sightseeing, that kind of stuff. You can be with me or with Alan when you go out. It makes no difference. One of us stays there to cover – until we all move out, of course. On that day we'll both be with you. No one knows you, no one know us. Nothing can foul up so long as we keep a low profile.' He was going to say more – mention what had happened at the airport – but he decided his best plan was to look for a truce. He didn't mention Guerney, either. No one in Washington could see any percentage in telling her about David Paschini, or the fake kidnap, or the rest of the shambles. She'd been hired to do a job. As far as she knew, the operation had begun in Washington three weeks before.

Ginsberg continued. 'That's the house.' He pointed to a roof, just visible from their low angle, behind a tall wooden

243

fence. The place stood on its own, separated from the other houses by a main road on one side and waste ground on the other. 'There are some dogs. They're in a run just behind the fence. They can't be seen and they don't bark, so no one gets curious. What they do is they kill people. If you like dogs, don't get tempted. You don't like *these* dogs. There's a way of getting in and out, but you'll be with one of us, so you don't need to know. Anything you want brought in that you can't buy yourself, just ask. Except dope. They told us you like to smoke now and then. Don't we all? There won't be any on this trip.' He reached into a pocket and took out some banknotes in a money-clip. 'That's five hundred. You want more, you'll get it. That's about all.' He shrugged. 'Anything you need to ask me?'

Paula ran her thumb over the edge of the notes. 'Never mind about the dope, Ginsberg. There are other ways to get high.' She pushed the money into her bag. 'Did they tell you that I like to gamble?'

Ginsberg shook his head. 'I don't think so.'

'I like to gamble. Do you think you can find me a poker game?'

'I don't see why not.' He looked at her with curiosity. 'Are you good?'

She grinned; and for the first time he saw how beautiful she was. 'Fucking dynamite,' she said.

Guerney had deliberately arrived fifteen minutes late. He stood by the door of the Members' dining-room and scanned the tables that were arranged alongside the far windows. Arthur Meadows had chosen one at the angle of the room. He was peering out at the Thames, chin on hand, his face almost completely averted, like some coy celebrity. Guerney crossed the room and sat in the vacant chair.

Meadows swivelled his eyes, but he didn't alter his position. He looked nervous. A slight sweat had made his forehead clammy. 'Sadism,' he asked, 'or an impulse to suicide?'

Guerney picked up the embossed leather-clad menu and

244

studied it until Meadows turned to look him full in the face. Then he said: 'Sorry, Arthur; I'm not with you.'

Meadows was suddenly seized by a paroxysm of fear-filled rage. He spoke from behind gritted teeth, and his voice trembled slightly. 'There's a price on your head, do you know that?' It wasn't a question that required an answer. 'Yes, of course you do. You also know damn well what would happen to me if I were found in your company. We could have met anywhere . . . *anywhere.*'

Guerney looked round the room. 'I didn't want to take you away from your work, Arthur. I know how busy you must be. In any case, I like eating here. The food's good. The House of Commons wine is better than passable. The view's pleasant. One gains a sense of the importance of it all. A seat of power. Law in the making. The cut and thrust of debate.' He paused. 'The indelible smells of piss and wind.' Another pause. 'Thank you for coming.' Meadows glared at him. Guerney smiled. 'It's quite the safest place for both of us,' he said. 'I'll have the minestrone and then steak and kidney pudding.'

Meadows summoned a waitress and ordered their meal. After the wine had arrived, he sat back in his chair and abandoned himself to the risk he was taking. He said: 'This is the last time, Guerney – be advised.' His accent was the slow strangulated distortion that afflicts some members of the English upper class.

Guerney reacted to the remark with sudden sharp annoyance. 'There was only one other time so far as I recall, Arthur. And it cost you nothing. *You* be advised.' He lifted his knife an inch from the table and advanced it by half its length so that it lay like a pointer on the stiff white tablecloth – both threatening and accusative. 'I emptied a cesspit for you. The smell was pretty bad. So far as I remember, you were nowhere near at the time.'

Meadows tried to hold Guerney's stare, but his eyes flickered away and he looked out again at the slow grey Thames.

Some years before, he'd taken up with a girl he'd met at a party. Like many other MPs, he tended to stay in London during the working week, travelling up to Suffolk to be with his wife and children only at weekends. It was generally accepted that those who felt inclined might keep a doxy in town. Arthur's type would have said 'doxy'.

Things were fine for a while. Then Julia had started to become a little over-demanding. He was too careless to see the danger signals. She started to spread clues. Phone-calls to his home early on Sunday morning – before church, his wife lifting the phone with a white-gloved hand; notes left among the parliamentary papers he would take home on Friday evenings; gifts of ties and sweaters, handed over as he was about to catch the train. It irritated him slightly, but he was arrogant enough to put it down to a belief that the girl was hopelessly in love with him.

The fact that his wife found out about the affair wasn't the worst thing to happen. She didn't threaten to ruin him, or ask for a divorce. She was someone who couldn't have easily survived on her own. She relied on him for money and stability, for home and position. He felt it posssible to maintain the outward show of a contented marriage, believing that his wife would settle for what she'd got. He was concerned that she was hitting the bottle a little hard, and would lecture her about it from time to time. Neither of them referred to the fact that his affair was patently continuing.

Meadows's wife got crankier and crankier, but most of the time he wasn't around to see it happen. Her crack-up, when it came, was pretty spectacular. She vanished. For years, she'd felt as insubstantial, as insignificant, as a fallen leaf. She wanted to turn her husband's attention towards herself, to be the centre of things for him. She wanted to be unignorable.

She had made a good enough job of it to terrify Meadows. She left a note filled with such vehement bitterness that he couldn't doubt her threats of suicide and other – more damaging – rashness. She claimed to have written letters, filled with documentary evidence about his affair, which she planned to send to newspapers, television companies, the Prime Minister, Meadow's agent, anyone whose ill-will

Meadows might fear. She had taken his clothes out of the wardrobe, hacked them to shreds with a pair of pinking-shears and pitched the remains on to the lawn. She had left a two-thirds-empty bottle of gin on the kitchen table alongside the note. She had become unignorable.

Meadows hired Guerney on a short-fuse contract: fifteen thousand against seven days to complete the job. He calculated that a week was as long as he could comfortably conceal the fact that something was wrong. Guerney detected at once that Felicity Meadows was someone who was pacing the length of her tether, but hadn't, by any means, reached the end of it. He found her within three days, holed up in a £300-a-night suite at the Dorchester. She had laughed a lot and shared a bottle of champagne with him. Then she'd cried. Guerney had liked her. She'd been a bit crazy and a bit drunk, and he'd liked her a good deal.

Some time later, he'd torn Meadow's cheque in half and handed it back to him. 'I'll take it in kind,' he'd said, 'some day.' It had amused him to think of Meadows having to worry about that. It would keep him on his toes. It gave Felicity an edge that Guerney wanted her to have – one she couldn't gain on her own.

Guerney's soup arrived. Meadows was having avocado vinaigrette. He picked up his spoon and dug criss-cross patterns into the soft yellow flesh. 'What do you want, Guerney?' When there was no reply, he sighed laboriously and began to eat. Guerney went on with his soup, pausing from time to time to look out at the vessels on the river.

Meadows ate the avocado swiftly, as if he were ravenous. He said: 'There are some things I simply can't tell you. Can't.'

'Yes,' Guerney said. 'Let's hear what you can tell.'

The waitress came to their table and cleared the dishes. Meadows waited until she was clear. 'It wasn't our idea,' he said. 'The bloody Yanks. The PM still isn't happy about it.'

'We can forget the PM's sleepless nights,' Guerney advised him. 'Tell me about David Paschini.'

'Boffins,' said Meadows. 'Shrinks. Bloody trick-cyclists.

247

I don't know what you'd call them. Special advisers. Do you know . . . that crew at Bletchley, during the war, actually came up with a scheme that involved chipping a slab off the polar ice-cap, towing it into mid-Channel, and flying bombers off it to give them greater range. The idea was that, when it was bombed, you poured water into the crater which would then freeze over, leaving the surface as it was before. They're all as mad as hatters.'

Guerney advanced his knife another four inches. 'Don't fuck about, Arthur.'

Meadows helped himself to more wine, filling Guerney's glass as an afterthought. 'You know that . . .' He glanced up as the waitress approached with their entrée. While she arranged the plates before them and set down dishes of vegetables, both men gazed wordlessly at the river. Finally, Meadows lifted his knife and fork and sliced into a lamb cutlet. 'You know that both the Russians and the Americans have been interested in psychical research for years now. They have pretty sizeable budgets for that sort of thing. Bizarre though it might seem to some, they take it very seriously.'

'You're right. I do know that.'

Meadows looked across the table sorrowfully. 'Don't be impatient with me, Guerney. I'm trusting you with the remains of my workng life, to say nothing of my freedom.'

A picture came to Guerney of Felicity Meadow's encampment at the Dorchester – the sad patterns she'd established. Then his mind went to Caroline Paschini and the track she had walked from bottle to window, window to bottle. 'I'm deeply moved,' he said. 'Go on.'

'It seems they've all been interested in teleporting for a long time – before Geller and the other showmen. In America, particularly, kids with an . . . aptitude . . . for that sort of thing were put through tests, if the parents were willing: filmed, studied under laboratory conditions and so forth. Records were maintained, then and later. There was a system for keeping track of the subjects – what they were doing, where they were living. Not day-to-day, or anything like that. But someone would check now and again.'

'Why kids?' Guerney wanted to know.

'No – well, it wasn't. I think that, if adults came forward in some way or another, they were asked to take part in experiments, or whatever. The fact is, though, that most of the subjects were known about because confused parents had consulted a doctor, who might then refer them to a shrink or someone like that. They had set up a department which was known for the study of pyschic phenomena, psi, what-have-you, which existed under the aegis of some university or another. The department itself was in Manhattan, I think. There were no visible ties to the government.'

Guerney interrupted. 'To the CIA.'

'If you like.' Meadows took more potatoes. He seemed to be eating a lot. 'Anyway, I expect the department made itself known. Worried parents might have been in touch directly, or the kids might have been sent there – as I've said – by unsceptical medics.'

'And David Paschini was such a child.'

'Yes.' The word came slowly. It was as if – by mentioning the boy's name – Guerney had made the conversation riskier.

'What happened?'

'I imagine you've worked that out for yourself . . . with a little help from Miss Irving.'

'I'd like to hear about it from you.' Guerney's expression gave nothing away.

'It was a monstrous cock-up, really. Our lot were told that the boy was going to take part in some important tests. Not the usual stuff; something of military significance. Highly classified. The PM knew, one or two of us in the Ministry knew, and, of course, the mob at Century House knew. We were invited to send an observer.'

He put down his knife and drank some wine. 'Someone must have known that the kid was a bit of a leftie; it ought to have shown up somewhere in the file they'd been keeping on him. I don't know. Anyway, it all got a bit hairy. They said too much; the boy *threatened* to say too much; they had to

249

take him out of circulation.' He aligned his knife and fork tidily on his empty plate. 'You *do* know the rest.'

'Why bring him to England?'

'Two reasons. They didn't know what to do next. You had been employed by the parents. If – *when*, I suppose – the kidnap theory broke down, it would be safer for everyone if it wasn't a local mystery. Fewer direct questions. Also, they thought we might be more likely to have some success with you. Official Secrets Act, ex-diplomat and all that. I think they rather saw you as our responsibility; felt we might be able to trade off old loyalties.'

'Did they?'

Meadows smiled grimly. 'Well, they were entitled to *think* that.'

'What about those direct questions?' Guerney asked.

'What?'

'Schoolfriends of David; teachers, neighbours. And David's parents. To all intents and purposes, I've disappeared from the face of the earth. Their son is still missing. There's been no news, no developments. Why hasn't the whole issue gone sky-high?'

'Friends, neighbours, that sort of person . . . they believe that David has gone to Italy for an extended stay with his father.'

'And the father?'

'No one has the faintest idea. Just upped and went. His businesses seem to be working efficiently in his absence.'

'The mother,' Guerney wanted to know.

'The story is that, with David away, she has decided to travel – that she went with him to Italy, stayed for a short while, then moved on. A rich woman's whim, et cetera, et cetera. . . .' Meadows' voice petered out. Guerney looked at him and waited, a coldness growing in his chest. The other man fidgeted with his dessert-spoon, angling the bowl to take light from the window, and studying the inverted reflection of himself. 'Well,' he said finally, 'you know that's not so. She's dead, Guerney.'

As he spoke the words, Meadows flinched slightly,

anticipating Guerney's response. There was none; or none that he could detect. His gaze fluttered away, then back again, as if in defiance. When Guerney spoke, his tone was sinister in its evenness.

'So it's a little safer to you now, isn't it? I imagine that the father's disappearance is causing severe heartburn to some.'

'They're keen to find him.'

'I'll bet they are.' Guerney's fist lay on the table, bunched.

'It wasn't. . . .' Meadows almost said 'us'. 'It wasn't what you might think. She'd been acting crazily, it seems. Wandering round all sorts of unsavoury parts of New York. She got mugged on a subway platform. Hit by a train.' The last word emerged along with a little nervous hiccup. 'It's not even certain that the mugger pushed her under, if you see what I. . . .' Guerney's hand flexed and became a fist again. 'It had to be hushed up, obviously.'

There was a long silence. Eventually, Guerney said: 'The purpose. What was the purpose?' He wasn't talking about Caroline Rance's death, Meadows knew that.

'Guerney, I can't. I can't tell you that.'

'Yes, you can. You're going to. It's not just a matter, any more, of an old scandal that would put you out of politics for a while, is it? Not just a matter of paying your dues. We've met, you and I. I've listened while you talked. You've already realised what's at risk for you. Try asking for leniency on the grounds that there were some things you *didn't* say.'

Meadows reached under the lapel of his jacket and scratched, his fingers crabbing back to his armpit where the itch was worst. 'No more than twenty people know this stuff, Guerney. It's . . . Christ, it's *saleable*.'

'That's something you're going to have to worry about.'

Meadows gave a tiny shudder. Under his breath, he said: 'God help me.' Guerney waited. 'I don't know all of it.' He raised a hand to quell any disbelief. 'Whether you accept that or not, it's the truth. You might want to know things

251

that I just don't have the answer to. Please don't shop me because of that. I can tell you what I got at my briefing.'

Guerney smiled. 'We'll have to trust one another, won't we?'

Meadows was silent for a long time. He wore the expression of a man counting his steps to the gallows. His elbows rested on the arms of his chair and he stared down into his lap as if afraid to meet Guerney's eyes. Eventually, he spoke, but without looking up.

'There's a system called the Hot Line. No doubt you've heard of it. Most people seem to think it consists of a couple of telephones, one in the White House, one in the Kremlin. There's a fanciful notion that as the world's fate hangs in the balance two old men will chat on the phone and jolly each other out of Armageddon. It's nothing like that. It's a means of exchanging information.'

Meadows leaned back in his chair slightly and switched his gaze to the river-traffic; it was as if, by not looking at Guerney, he could pretend that he was talking to himself.

'Many strategists believe that a full-scale nuclear war would be likely to grow out of a limited war in Europe. Sabres rattle, shots get fired, borders are crossed, then someone starts to lose his advantage and lobs in a tactical weapon. The other side retaliates. After that, it's a quick sprint downhill. That's not news to you.'

His head snapped up and he looked Guerney full in the face, like someone grasping a nettle.

'No,' Guerney said. Then: 'The Hot Line's a fail-safe, isn't it?'

'The idea is that both sides trade information – keep each other informed. In that way, a balance is maintained. It sounds a military nonsense, really, but the theory is that both sides are seen to have their hands on the table and nothing up their sleeves. Well' – he raised a hand as if about to state the obvious – 'there are some hawky types in the Pentagon who don't care for the idea. In their terms, it's a bit like showing the other man your cards but continuing to bet. They've been trying to come up with a way of giving

252

themselves an edge, but without seeming to. They knew they couldn't get the Hot Line system scrapped. Apart from the outcry it would cause, it would seem to the Russians like a positive act of aggression. No, they wanted to find a way of having an advantage at the time – if a war in Europe really did break out. It was important to them to be able to steal a march; but without anyone knowing that's what was happening. Do you see that? The people involved in operating the Hot Line would have to believe that they were playing the game according to the rules.'

'In order to convince the other side,' Guerney suggested.

'Exactly. It wouldn't be much of an advantage if it seemed that someone had simply switched off. The rules would change. I'm having a brandy. Do you want one?'

Meadows waved at the waitress for a short while. When she came to the table, he ordered two Remy Martins.

'They wanted to find a method for knocking the system out,' Guerney said, 'and have it look like a malfunction.'

Meadows nodded. 'It used to be a pretty primitive set-up, all in all. I mean, ridiculously crude given its supposed importance. Two teletype machines, one in Washington, one in Moscow – standard lines – just a couple of guys typing things on to the keyboard. Now they've tarted it up a bit. Computers have replaced the teletype: the operatives have VDUs, of course; the information goes via satellite. Even so, it's still very basic.'

'And therefore vulnerable,' Guerney said.

'Yes. I mean, the weapons systems themselves are unbroachable. The back-up is phenomenal – computers stretching away to infinity, each ready to take over if another is affected in some way. There's no second-guessing it, really, except for the business of atmospheric explosions. They can have a pretty radical effect. One of the American atmospheric tests blacked out Hawaii, did you know that? So far as I understand it, a couple of strategically placed bangs of that sort would bugger up the automatic control systems over a very large area, no matter how deeply they were buried.

'Anyway, the Hot Line is a Meccano set compared to all that. But it's likely to have a hell of a lot to do with whether there's a full-scale nuclear exchange or not; and with who gets in first. That's why they wanted –'

The waitress returned with the brandies, and Meadows paused while she set them down. He gathered his glass at once, and took a large sip.

'That's why they wanted the boy. Or someone like him. Someone with his abilities.' He stopped again. Guerney was pushing his brandy-glass around an invisible square on the tablecloth.

'Yes, Arthur, I see. Go on.'

Meadows sighed. 'The idea was to run a series of tests in a simulated Hot Line centre. The same conditions, same equipment – everything. They wanted to see if the boy could close the computer down just by being in the same room and doing whatever the hell it is he does. If that worked, they'd do it again but with a computer link – more like the real thing. There had even been talk of trying it out *on* the real thing – a sort of dry run. I don't know if they'd have got that far.' He finished his brandy and signalled to the waitress for another.

'What would they gain?' Guerney asked.

'Well, they'd know it could be done. I don't suppose for a minute they'd thought of using the boy after that. I imagine they'd try to recruit someone with his talent who would eventually find himself operating a VDU.'

'Yes,' Guerney said, 'I didn't mean that. What would they gain if it ever happened for real?'

'Time,' Meadows told him. 'Time to manoeuvre.' He looked flushed, and his words were arriving in the staccato fashion of someone beginning to have to control his drunkenness. 'It works like this. The most sensitive part of any computer is the silicon chips. OK? The Hot Line computer would be protected against a sudden pulse of current – a lightning strike, say; a system of trips would prevent the pulse from entering. So it would take a very sharp electrical field to screw things up. But if the chip were affected by some sort of electro-magnetic pulse. . . .' He stopped for a moment, thinking hard. His briefing had been meticulous. 'There would be a cascade of electrical disruption. Things would go decidedly wonky.'

'Could David do that? Or someone like him?'

'Yes, it seems so. At least, they thought so. The experiments would have been to make sure. Some of the tests they'd done on him as a child – and others they'd performed with other children since – made them think that he could. It seems he could direct the charge very accurately – like someone using a scalpel – and it was very concentrated and so, in turn, very powerful. That's what made him special. I've said: the computer's protected against random disruption.'

Meadows' second brandy arrived. This time he didn't bother to stop talking when the waitress handed it to him.

'What happens next is that a chip or two is destroyed – maybe four or five. Some are left intact, though, so the computer continues to process input. But the way it's processsed results in gobbledegook. It would be like working a calculator that didn't have a number one. In theory the computer ought to know when it's making an error; as a standard operation it would report it. But, with all those chips knocked out, the error-checking code is likely to be up the creek, too. So the computer continues to function, but produces gibberish. That's the whole virtue of the ''scalpel'' approach – you could do all this without killing the computer off completely, and without affecting the power supply.'

'And next?' Guerney asked. 'The operator would know that something was wrong.'

'Naturally. It's time they're after – time to move a few chesspieces around in the dark. This is where they start to gain it. One side's getting garbage from what looks like an innocent malfunction on the other side. The operator – blameless, so therefore convincing – checks his VDU. It would have some primitive intelligence, so he'd have to make sure that the terminals were OK. They are. What then?

'Well, they'd check the software, though that would have been thoroughly tested and they'd be pretty sure it wasn't that. Then they'd check the firmware. There are functions called ROMs – Read Only Memories – that contain bits of the system: some of the basic instructions. Anyway, that'd all be all right. Then the hardware. So they'd call in a hardware engineer, who would, sooner or later, investigate the boards, isolate the burned-out chips and replace them. By the time things are functioning properly again, the side that was prepared for all this to happen, and set to make use of it, will have gained its advantage.'

'Who briefed you?'

Meadows looked for the waitress again, but Guerney slid his own glass across the table and Meadows grasped it. 'One of our boffins. He'd been over to New England when they were talking about this. He'd seen some of the films they'd made. By and large, he was as pleased as a pig in shit; thought it a wonderful idea. The combination of computer architecture and parapsychology seemed to make his little world complete.'

'And who do you report to?'

Meadows gulped the brandy. 'Who does anyone in the MoD report to? It's run by the civil servants, of course; you know that. I sat in on meetings: I advised; I came up with an idea or two. Mostly I made sure the trains were running on time.'

'Yes, Arthur,' Guerney smiled without humour, 'I'm sure that's the sort of thing you'd be good at.'

'What?' Meadows seemed to lose touch for a minute. He looked flushed and bleary. He downed the last of Guerney's brandy and set the glass down, too heavily, on the table.

'Why now?' Guerney wanted to know.

'I don't follow.'

'Why did they decide they had to run these tests now?'

Meadows looked thoughtful. Finally, he said: 'I suppose the idea hadn't occurred to them before.'

'Why should it have occurred to them now?'

'Bloody hell, Guerney, I don't know.' His voice was too loud – amplified by the booze – and he turned a couple of heads. His flush deepened. He said: 'Unless they're planning on having a war.'

'Yes,' Guerney said. 'That would have made them think of it, I suppose – Hot Lines and how to cross them.'

'Yes.' Meadows half-smiled, then the smile faded. 'Yes, it would.'

The waitress came to the table with the bill and put it down between them. Meadows asked her for another brandy, and she took the bill away to amend it, then brought it straight back with the drink. Neither man spoke. Meadows took a pull at his glass. He looked both resentful and ashamed, as if he'd been caught out in some meanness.

'What else?' Guerney wanted to know. 'What else? What haven't you told me?'

'There's nothing. The boy wouldn't co-operate. The scheme's in abeyance.'

'Is it?'

'As far as I know. Look, Guerney' – the words came in a rush – 'you've had all there is.' For a moment, it seemed that Meadows might be on the brink of tears.

'Why now?' Guerney pressed him. 'Why *now*?'

'I don't know. I've told you.' Meadows hissed the words. 'I don't bloody know.'

'Are they going to have war, Arthur? Is that it? Have they got a little war planned for the near future?'

Meadows looked as if he might cry out. His mouth opened and the brandy-bloom in his face darkened. After a short while, he simply said, 'I don't know,' speaking on an exhaled breath so that the words seemed to flutter from his lips.

The Brit – Alan – had taken Paula up to her room. He'd given her a short tour of the upper floor, then left her to unpack.

The room was small, quaint in its way. The skylight built into the slope of the roof cast a rectangle of brightness on to the counterpane. She hung some clothes in the wardrobe, then became bored with the business of unpacking and pushed her suitcase against the wall. The hell with that, she thought.

The patch of sunlight attracted her, and she lay on the bed so that her face took the glow. She wondered whether Ginsberg was telling about what happened at Heathrow. She hoped so. It was good that they should understand who had the clout in all this. She'd come to London to do a job; she was also going to have a *time*. Those guys might have to jump through a hoop or two.

She smiled, facing the skylight with closed eyes to make patterns of white and red cruise beneath the lids. Then the smile faded and she put her fingers to one temple, as if afflicted by a sudden headache. Her body stiffened slightly – attentiveness, not alarm – and the expression on her face became one of curiosity. 'What?' she said.

When she went downstairs some fifteen minutes later, the two men were in the kitchen. Alan was chopping raw meat into chunks and throwing them into a couple of large metal bowls. Pete sat on the kitchen table, a can of beer in one hand.

When Paula appeared, he swung his feet back to the floor and went towards the fridge. 'Beer?' he asked.

'Why not?' Paula took the can and pulled the tab, waving away the proffered glass.

'Listen.' Pete sounded pleased with himself. 'We've found you a game. Alan knows a place.'

'That's good.'

Pete raised the beer, as if toasting the discovery and grinned. He seemed a little uneasy. So he has told Alan about the luggage-truck, Paula thought. Now they don't know quite how to behave.

Alan rinsed his hands under the tap to remove the blood. 'Room OK?' he asked.

'Fine,' Paula told him. She swallowed some beer, then said: 'The boy who was kept in there. Tell me about him.'

It was as if they were playing a game of statues and Paula had just stopped the music. Pete was the first to recover. He set his beer down on the table. 'Who told you about that?' He tried to keep his voice even, but the anger was evident. God damn them, he thought. How in hell am I supposed to operate if I don't know what she knows?

Paula watched as anger replaced surprise on Ginsberg's face. She said: 'He did.'

The anger changed direction. Ginsberg rounded on the other man, who had stopped, shocked, in the act of drying his hands. 'You *asshole*.'

Alan started to speak. 'Christ, I didn't say – '

'Not him,' Paula interrupted. 'The boy. David – isn't that his name?'

16

'They never come, do they?'

'Sorry?' Buckroyd was making a pretence of reading *The Times*. He looked up.

'They never come.' The woman was Irish, about sixty.

'They do seem rather erratic,' he said and dropped his eyes to the newspaper.

'I'm waiting for a fifty-two.' Having lost Buckroyd's attention, she spoke round him to the man standing at his back. There were five of them in the bus queue: the Irish woman at the head, Buckroyd, an elderly man in a check cap, and two young women.

Not the man, Buckroyd was sure of that. He was too old, too frail, and had about him a down-at-heel look that would have been impossible to fake. It wasn't the appearance, it was the smell: a thin seepage composed of poor food, cold rooms and ill-luck. Not the Irish woman, either: no one could have invented her. The young women . . . Buckroyd had eavesdropped as best as he could on their conversation. They had talked about films, about each other's clothes and, briefly, about someone called Mark whom one of them was involved with. They seemed at ease with one another; the rhythms of their speech sounded authentic, switching naturally from this topic to that – the serendipity of lives lived much the same way.

It seemed unlikely, but he wasn't sure.

A bus arrived, and everyone boarded it except the Irish woman. She chuckled sourly and spoke to one of the young women passing her to step on to the platform: 'I'm waiting for a fifty-two. They never come.'

Buckroyd sat down on one of the cross-seats close to the back of the bus and watched people in the streets flick by like the pages of a hastily thumbed book.

Nothing's what it seems, he thought: the Irish woman is a character-actress getting the feel for a part; the old man is an eccentric millionaire; the girls secretly loathe one another. I'm a retired bank-manager on his way to visit a married daughter whose children call me Gramps.

Buckroyd left the bus two stops later; the old man and the girls were still aboard. He watched the bus out of sight, but no one came to the platform to look back or hop off nimbly when the bus was slowed by traffic. He had watched carefully through the back window of the bus, looking for likely cars, but had spotted nothing that seemed a contender. To be sure, he'd taken the bus to Shepherd's Bush and now walked briskly along the north side of the Green, staying alert for any vehicle that looked familiar. Nothing did. Finally, he took the Tube to White City, then travelled back again, eastwards, for three stops. Before he emerged at Notting Hill Gate, he removed his mackintosh and wore it draped across his shoulders, unbelted. A small enough thing, but it changed his shape.

'I'm getting too old for this sort of malarky,' he considered. 'It's tiring and faintly ridiculous.'

Despite the cold and the black porridge of slush underfoot, the Portobello Road was thick with shoppers, many of them tourists. The antique-shops were doing brisk business. Stallholders sat behind their displays, warmed by the cash they were taking. Buckroyd threaded a zig-zig path between the browsers until he reached the vegetable market and came clear of the crowd. The Earl of Lonsdale stood on a corner, the pavement alongside its door littered with boxes and the tattered outside leaves of cabbages. As he entered the pub, he heard the roar of a crowd overlaid by the excited jabber of a commentator.

He went to the bar and had to lean across and raise his voice in order to defeat the noise from the television. The screen was gigantic. A larger-than-life-sized head advised viewers of which football matches and race meetings had been snowed off. He looked around and spotted Guerney and Rachel at a table close to a flight of stairs that led, apparently, to a 'games room'. The rest of the clientele looked rough or tough, or both. It resembled a dockside pub. The men looked as if some deep grudge against the world in general was becoming more apparent to them with every drink. Most of the women wore lipstick so thick that it threatened to fall off when they spoke.

Guerney took his coat from a third chair, and Buckroyd sat down, still glancing round at the room. He smiled at Rachel, then said: 'Who are these people, Simon?'

Guerney raised his eyebrows. 'Stockbrokers. A smattering of accountants. Housewives.'

'Weekenders, I imagine.'

'Many of them spend Monday to Friday living in converted oast-houses in Surrey,' Guerney agreed.

They grinned at one another. Rachel detected the outline of a routine that had once helped shape a friendship. It occurred to her that there were all sorts of things she didn't know about Guerney.

'Well' – Buckroyd took a pull at his drink – 'I hope I haven't done more harm than good.'

'Is it likely?'

'It's possible. I'm sorry.'

Guerney shook his head as if to refuse the apology. He knew that if harm had been caused, then Buckroyd was likely to be damaged as much as anyone. He simply asked: 'How bad?'

Buckroyd chose to misunderstand him; he was alive to where Guerney's concern lay. 'You'll have to weigh the information I got – which isn't much – against the cost of getting it.' He paused and raked his fingers through a silver wing of hair that the wind had dislodged. He felt tired, and suspected that it showed. 'I thought it safest to drop Catherine a note – the woman I mentioned to you. It was usual for us to meet now and then – a little gossip, a little scandal, a little nostalgia. We'd phone each other from time to time. I don't think we ever wrote, so to send a letter was likely to make it a bit of an issue. I couldn't see a way around that. A phone-call wouldn't have broken our pattern, but I imagine nothing's going unnoticed now. Someone would have tagged along. Of course, in trying not to alert the Eccleston Street buggers, I was bound to alert her. I was relying on the idea that I was still owed something for old times' sake.'

'Were you?' It was Rachel who asked the question. She had given some thought to Buckroyd's story about this lady's affair – the way feeling had overtaken duty, the Russian lover dead in a staged street-accident. How wide is the gulf, she wondered, between betrayal and inaction?

'Yes and no. She'd learned one or two things since we'd last met. Apparently, her boss has been putting in a lot of unpaid overtime. She's a confidential secretary – even within the confines of Century House. Her role isn't exclusively secretarial, of course. She has a tiny area of operations to herself. It's not that her boss used her as a confidante, or anything as lax as that. But he didn't pull his coat over his ears, either. Bits and pieces came her way in the normal course of events.'

'Who's the boss?' Guerney wanted to know.

'William Prior.'

'Ah, yes.' Guerney drank some Scotch. 'They say he's good.'

'He is.' Buckroyd hesitated. 'He worked for me at one time. He's pretty much of a bastard.'

Guerney smiled. 'I believe you.'

'Catherine was edgy when we met – didn't want to be there. It made me edgy, too, and a trifle guilty. She made it plain that I'd begun to ask favours that came above and beyond the call of friendship. In fact, there's little chance of my seeing her again.'

'I won't ask you to. I've said that.' As soon as he'd spoken, Guerney realised that Buckroyd's remark hadn't to do with risk, but with loss. There was an embarrassed pause before he said: 'I'm sorry, George.'

The older man smiled wryly. 'You've every right to be

singleminded at the moment. Don't worry about it. I don't feel cheated. In any event . . . she was willing to give me the bits and pieces that had come her way recently. Or maybe she gave me what she could afford to give. But there was no question of anything beyond that. No peeps into ''For Your Eyes Only'' documents; no quick flicks through the attaché case; no rifling the wastepaper-baskets, to use an old metaphor.'

'You weren't being led on?' Guerney suggested. 'She's still straight?'

'Oh, yes.' Buckroyd didn't hesitate. Lifting his glass, he drained it and stood up. 'I'll get some more.'

As he walked towards the bar, Rachel looked at Guerney, though neither of them spoke.

Guerney was presented with a picture, in his mind, of the lethal fragments of a Claymore mine, travelling outwards in slow motion from the impact of a footstep. He struggled to decide who might have been held responsible for having taken the first destructive step. The man in Washington – Jeffries? David Paschini, when he'd started to threaten? The father? Guerney himself, in continuing to pursue what seemed already lost? Rachel? Perhaps it was already impossible to know.

Buckroyd returned and set fresh drinks down on the table. 'You're right', he said, 'about the boy being an embarrassment. So far as I can gather from the feel of what Catherine told me, our lot are less than happy to be caught up in this business. God knows why they wanted him at all – I got no closer to that – but I think it was always seen as something the CIA had started up – and had made a mess of. I suspect that there's some gloating being done in Waterloo, but it's outweighed by irritation and there are certain Cabinet members who feel the same way. I think our involvement wasn't supposed to go much beyond sending the boffin to New England – whatever that signified.'

He turned to Rachel. 'I think there was a time when they half-believed you were still working for them. I don't know the ins and outs of what's happened, and there's no need that I should. It seems, though, that for safety's sake they're assuming the opposite. I'm in the dark about all this. Just telling you what came through from Catherine.' To Guerney he said: 'If I learned anything interesting, it was this: at first, no one could quite understand why you didn't act the pragmatist and pull out. What happened in Somerset – well, that could be explained as conditioned reflex. But' – he glanced at Rachel – 'when you didn't return to the fold they might well have made other assumptions.'

'They made it difficult on themselves,' she retorted. 'They tried to kill me.'

'I can see how that complicated the issue,' replied Buckroyd drily. 'Still, you might *both* have decided simply to disappear. As it is, you've let them know otherwise – mostly via me. The phone-call from Ermintrude, incidents in the Edgware Road – that sort of thing. . . .' There was a question in his voice.

'You weren't a lure, George, if that's what you're thinking. Nothing could have happened if I'd stayed underground for ever. They'd have felt my presence sooner or later. I wish it had been later.' Guerney frowned. '*Mostly* via you?'

'We all swim in the same ocean, Simon, you know that. There are bits of Soho that resemble the staff canteen. You bought a gun.' Guerney didn't reply. 'One way and another they know you're still on the case. Here's what might be useful: my intuition is that, although they're still surprised by that, they're also worried. My hard information is that the CIA operation over here hasn't been dismantled yet. Ergo. . . .'

Guerney finished the thought: '. . . whatever they wanted David for hasn't been affected by his refusal to help.'

'That,' Buckroyd agreed, 'or they're busking – looking for a way to solve the problem.' He heard a voice he recognised, and looked up. Clive Holman's face was filling the television screen, though few of the drinkers at the bar were paying him much attention. There followed a shot of Holman at an informal reception. The newsreader set the scene – a four-day meeting of representatives from European branches of the Peace Movement. A young man,

265

darkly good-looking, stepped forward to shake Holman's hand, keeping the gesture going in response to persistent photographers.

Rachel followed Buckroyd's gaze. 'Sylvio Ortiz,' she offered. 'Spanish. Disarmament's El Cordobes. Militant, but non-violent.' She might have been reciting the details from a file. 'You didn't get any idea of what the problem they're trying to solve might be?'

Buckroyd took his eyes from the television. 'No,' he said. 'She didn't know. I'm sure of that.' He smiled at Rachel's expression. 'I asked her. Drew a blank. Had she known but not been prepared to tell me, she'd've said so. Not everyone behaves as if the truth were a killer disease.'

He glanced back towards the bar. Ortiz was leaning towards two or three microphones held out by pressmen. 'We mus' haff piss in the worl',' he was saying. 'All people wan' piss.'

Buckroyd chortled and picked up his glass. 'He's absolutely right, you know.' He was aware that his merriment bore some measure of rashness.

'What does it signify, George?' A man and a woman passed behind Guerney and headed up the stairs. Guerney lowered his voice a little and leaned forward. 'What do you think it means?'

Buckroyd shook his head. 'Not sure. Some sort of test – experiment, demonstration, call it what you will, and David Paschini the star turn. Something to do with computers; something using his strange ability.' He caught a reaction in Guerney. 'Did you learn any more about that?'

Guerney shrugged. 'I can't say for certain.' Rachel opened her mouth to speak, then changed her mind. She couldn't see why Guerney should be so defensive – unless, perhaps, he believed that Buckroyd might come under pressure at some stage.

'Then their star refuses his role,' Buckroyd continued. 'In theory, they're non-operational, aren't they?'

'In theory.'

'You'll have considered the likeliest answer.'

'An understudy. Yes. Any hint of that?'

'If there was, I didn't pick it up.' Buckroyd pondered, as if checking through his conversation with Catherine, then shook his head. 'No.'

They were all silent for a while. There was only one thing left to be said. It was Guerney who gave the lead. 'And the harm, George,' he prompted gently.

Buckroyd sighed and pushed again at the stray hank of hair. 'Catherine and I had a regular place to meet: an Italian restaurant we both like – in Chelsea. I couldn't decide whether or not to tell her to be careful: I didn't think the note would be read by anyone but herself – why would they check her mail? – but I didn't want to alarm her, either – frighten her off, maybe. In the end, I compromised; said something to the effect that I wanted to talk to her about something very confidential. For all I know, she thought I needed an agony aunt. It wouldn't have been the first time that I'd bared a bit of my soul to her. In any case, she was never skilled in the field.'

'She had someone in tow,' Guerney stated.

'I'm almost certain, yes.'

'And she'll be asked questions.'

'For sure.'

'What will she do?'

'I've thought about that. I'm positive that no one actually came into the restaurant: they're not stupid enough for that. If I'm right, then she was picked up as she left – having been followed there, presumably. The noise in the restaurant would have ruled out any long-range listening devices. They know that she and I met there, but they can't know what was said. Catherine's no fool. She won't try to pretend that it was no more than one of our occasional gossips. Her best bet would be to say that I'd made a few delicately staged attempts to gain information, which attempts she had delicately foiled. It's enough of the truth to get by, with the minimum damage to both of us.'

'And if you're right?'

'They'll leave me alone in order to give us rope – you and

me – on the grounds that I'm their best lead at present. Or they'll leave me alone because not to might cause more fuss than they want. Or they'll haul me in to see what they can get.'

'If it's that?'

Buckroyd smiled. 'I expect they'll start by being dramatic about the way I've let the side down. It's startling how many people in that place still talk as though the espionage war was subject to rules laid down by the MCC. I'll be surprised and a little indignant. So far as I know, you're involved in a kidnap case that had moved inexplicably from America to England. It had gone off the rails – you felt yourself losing touch with it. You wondered whether you hadn't, perhaps, missed the point. Maybe the American authorities – and now the British – *did* know something about it but had their own reasons for keeping matters quiet; virtuous reasons. Perhaps C Branch were involved.'

'The anti-terrorist squad?' asked Rachel.

'That's right,' confirmed Buckroyd. 'It's reasonable that you might have thought the wild card to have been the IRA, or the Red Brigades given the father's nationality and his wealth. There would have been reasons for security, maybe; and you might well have asked me to try to dig a little. Not quite cricket, in their terms; but not a mortal sin, either. They'll be aware that you know more now – what happened in Somerset and so forth. But you needn't have told me about that. Come to think of it, your purpose would be better served by letting me continue to believe the terrorist theory. I'd continue to poke around for you without feeling that I might be doing something dreadfully wrong. They might try section two of the Official Secrets Act. I'd enjoy that – opportunity for a prolonged sneer. It ought to work. There's bluff on both sides. They couldn't be sure whether I'd be lying or not. If I were telling the truth, and they pressed too hard, they'd be running a needless risk. I'd know that something more sinister is afoot. They can't even ask me for a lead on you without arousing my suspicion. They might have to play along in some way: ask me to tell you to leave well alone. I'd be warned to do the same, of course.'

'What about your evasion tactics? It's possible you've been running their men all over London.'

'Well,' Buckroyd smiled, 'I didn't say the story was free of flaws. It just requires them to be unsure.' He shrugged. 'I might affect to have no idea what they're talking about. Or I could be vastly annoyed and tell them how much I object to being used in that way – as a pointer to you. Perhaps I'll be aggressive and ask them why they did it at all. Why not simply tell me what's going on? If they admit they tailed me, you see, they're admitting all sorts of other things, too. I'm gambling that they won't mention it for just that reason.'

Guerney stared into his glass. 'Christ, George, I'm sorry.'

'Don't worry. It's not waterproof, but there's enough room for doubt. And I know these sods. I'll quite enjoy the cut and thrust.' Buckroyd raised both hands, as if to declare the topic closed. 'I'd better go. You're on your own now.' He touched Rachel lightly on the shoulder as he stood up, as if to bestow something – luck, perhaps – and then walked away.

'What do you think?' Rachel tried to read something from Guerney's expression.

'Who can tell?' He shook his head, then extended a finger and pushed his whisky-glass back and forth on the table – a random pattern of tiny broken movements.

'You had a bad night.' She had been woken by him on two occasions. Each time, he'd remained asleep, though his moaning had filled the room – a low eerie sound like that of an animal puzzled by pain – and his body had been slick with sweat.

'Bad dreams.' He looked thoughtful for a second, then was all action: draining his glass, rising, snatching his coat from the back of the chair. Rachel followed him to the door. As they emerged into the street from the gloom and thick heat of the pub, she felt the brilliance of the day fall on her like a spotlight, and the sharp wind made a rawness of the scar on her cheek.

* * *

269

Just as before, he had returned to Druid's Combe – crossing the slope of pastureland, then descending to the house. The sky was azure and tight as a drumskin. He could feel frost in the air; it pricked his temples and cheekbones.

As before, David Paschini was standing by the kitchen window, looking in; though on this occasion his presence seemed less surprising. He was an actor, taking up his mark for another run-through. It was as if the set had been lit, David settled in position and the cameras made ready. On cue, Guerney had started to trek between the snowy furrows.

He came up behind the boy. The reflection in the window-pane was impassive for a short time. Then followed the terrible inchoate mouthings.

A wind sprang up, growing steadily in strength until its power was so great that Guerney had to fight for balance. Trees surrounding the house bent inwards, trailing their uppermost branches, roaring, converging on the house to make it the centre of a dark vortex.

David Paschini's hair streamed in the wind, mimicking the flailing tips of the trees. It issued a thin sound, like distant singing. His cheeks belled. The gale began to pluck at the flesh on his face, dislodging it in scraps at first, then in strips that peeled and fluttered and were whipped away.

Guerney stared horror-stricken at the image in the window, at the balding dome, at the back of the boy's head, as the wind flayed it ribbon by ribbon, until there was only the bright bone glistening in the cold light. It became a superstructure – a hard white lattice-work that gathered a phosphorescent aura, indelible on the eye.

Just before he'd woken, the boy had turned. For the first time, he had turned. Through the trellis of the brow, Guerney could see David's brain. It palpitated like a small living creature. And the lipless mouth had spoken his name.

'Guerney. Guerney. Guerney.'

17

It was necessary for the Saudi to invent rules of his own, because all games of chance, extended far enough, will submit to the laws of average. On average, a flipped coin will as often come up heads as tails. A pair of dice will show seven or better as often as six or worse. A man wagering on black, or on even numbers, will have as much good fortune as another whose money goes on red, or on uneven numbers. Play poker for long enough and, no matter how much you might lose, the wheel will eventually turn and restore your losses to you. Given time, everyone comes out even.

The excitement lies in knowing that this isn't possible. Luck is a partial application of the laws of average. They go this way, they go that. Their pattern is never completed. There are times when you join the pattern and feel its ineluctable rightness. You win. The trick is in detecting a change and pulling out at the right time. There are players who aren't sensitive to the change. They go broke. On other occasions, you know at once that the pattern is working against you. There are people who intuit that, but don't want to believe it. They go broke. In order for none of this to matter – in order to continue regardless of the pattern's alterations – you would have to be almost unimaginably rich.

The Saudi was almost unimaginably rich, and so he made his own rules. They enabled him to lose, and thus put chance back into his game. He preferred to win, though, so the rules gave him something of an edge. Why not? They were his rules, after all. He would assume a five-hour evening – from ten till three, perhaps – and roughly twenty-five hands. There would be breaks now and then, and sometimes he'd ask to be dealt out for a short while. Twenty-five was about right. He'd multiply the first pot by that number to arrive at his cash limit for the evening. This time, his ceiling was twelve and a half thousand pounds – the house had taken five hundred to open the game some three hours earlier.

The ploy restricted him; but few people had that much to lose in a night, which meant that he could usually extend the pattern of chance a little further than most. He expected to wind up better than even. In fact, he was down eight grand.

There's another law: those who have more to lose lose for longer.

The club occupied two upper floors of a house in Ennismore Gardens, near the south-west corner of the quiet square. The place was sufficiently close to Knightsbridge to impress rich punters, but far enough from the centre of things to remain discreet – the sort of address that would have sounded suitable for a poor country's trade delegation or a psycho-analyst's consulting-rooms.

Paula Cole and Peter Ginsberg had arrived at 10.30. Alan Mountjoy had elected to stay at the house. Before she'd left he'd given Paula a few pointers.

'The Malts run it – Maltese. Mostly they stay in Soho, but they're moving up-market. The games are more or less straight. The house gets a little help in craps and roulette; I expect they straighten their luck in other games if the odds go against them for too long, but for most of the time they're happy with the pro-house average. The square mile's one thing: they own it and they expect it to pay. Elsewhere, they're respectable – it attracts a different class of punter.'

'Don't worry,' she'd told him, 'I won't make waves.'

Later, as she'd climbed out of the car, she had linked her arm through Pete's and said: 'Watch closely, Ginsberg. You'll enjoy this.'

He'd played some roulette, allowing himself a hundred-pound loss. It wasn't his money, so he didn't mind; and he wasn't a gambler, so he didn't go after it. He descended a flight of thickly carpeted stairs into the lower room and perched on a bar-stool to observe the play.

She'd made her five hundred into twelve thousand and gained a small reputation that was spreading to the rest of the room. It was five-card stud. As he watched, she flipped her hole card to show jacks over eights. The house made aces and tens – the aces showing. Paula smiled and sat back in her chair.

There were seven at the table. She was the only woman. He watched the way the men watched her. He could see curiosity and desire and something else: a muted violence that seemed not so much aimed at Paula as drawn by her. She courted it. Ginsberg had been aware of that, too. There was something lacking in her beauty; something it needed to be complete. He realised what was missing and felt a sudden excitement rise in him, thrilling and sick. Pain. Her beauty wanted pain.

He fumbled for his drink, looking away for a moment as if to avoid her eyes. All at once, things had gone out of kilter. He recalled standing by the arrivals barrier that morning, glancing now and then at the information board – *Landed, Baggage in hall* – and feeling little more than mild impatience at the role he'd been given. He remembered the tidal wave of noise as the baggage-truck had hurled its train of containers against the parked cars, and Paula stepping coolly over the flotsam of smashed glass.

He told me. The boy. David – isn't that his name? She hadn't explained, and they hadn't asked her to. Mountjoy had made a phone-call and reported it. Like Ginsberg, he'd felt safer making no mention of what had occurred at Heathrow. They'd been told to be sure that she kept a low profile.

Mountjoy had listened as the voice had asked: 'What? She said *what?*' He'd been made to run through the circumstances again.

When he'd returned to the room where Ginsberg and Paula still sat, she sipping her beer in silence, he had shaken his head: *No. She hadn't been told. No!*

Because it was inexplicable, Ginsberg had tried to put it

273

from his mind, but fear kept bringing it back. Now he looked at her again as she leaned, forward to place a bet. Beauty and desirability and that other dark exhilarating need; they were all there; and so was . . .

By the nature of his job, Ginsberg stood apart from most men. His reactions were not like theirs; his apprehension of the world was different. Something in him had become blunted. He had to struggle to identify what he felt.

He stared at Paula's face, and the sense of it came clear. It was the awe and unreality, the morbid kinship, the disbelief people were said to experience if they met, face to face, someone who had committed an appalling crime.

She laughed as she took the pot. The Saudi muttered something to her and offered a neat little bow as they both rose from the table. Paula went to the bar. She had a lithe, light walk: smooth, almost feline. Under the heavy dark-blue silk of her blouse, her small breasts moved just perceptibly, making oxbows of reflected light flow on the material.

'Gin and tonic,' she told the barman, then: 'How're you doing, Ginsberg?'

'Good.' He raised his glass to her. 'So are you.'

'We're ahead, we're ahead.' She seemed elated, full of nervous energy. 'I'm fizzing. Jet-lag, I guess. Neat place. Thanks.' This last to the barman as he slid her drink over. She took a sizeable gulp. 'Maybe we'll do another couple of hands. Three. Then split. It's cocktail hour for me.' She checked her watch, still on New York time. 'Six-thirty.'

'Sure. OK. What's going on?'

'Well' – she glanced back at the table – 'they're mostly average. The guy in the green shirt, blond hair?' Ginsberg nodded. 'He's varying his bets quite nicely. Shows too much reluctance to play back at me when he's got a high pair back to back, though. Predictable for that. The white tux, curly hair – knows when to go for the throat. I thought maybe they'd put a collector at the table to help the deal, but he started to chill after going down on the last three hands, so he's getting close to his limit, which means he's no stooge. The Arab plays mechanical poker, win or lose. I think he's the Tooth Fairy. The rest can hold their own.' She grinned. 'The house is giving itself an edge. Not much. Enough to put back what I'm taking out.'

'Keep it easy,' Ginsberg advised.

'Sure. Depends on him.' She nodded towards the Saudi, who had rejoined the table, then gulped at her drink again and set it down on the bar. Ginsberg watched her walk back – slim-hipped, her body balanced. Two of the men rose courteously as she sat down.

She played not three hands, but ten. After four, the Saudi rose from the table, a little sour smile on his lips. He bowed as he had before, but didn't drop his eyes. Paula's gaze met his. There was a question, which she answered. *No.* His place was taken by a bulky man in a dark business-suit.

As Ginsberg watched, Paula took the next two hands against the deal. She was going for the house. Throughout the evening, she had won the right hands and lost those that didn't matter. In doing so, she'd turned fifteen grand. The pleasure she took in it was on her face, plain for all to see. You could feel it, too. Something electric gathered in the air. People began to drift over to watch, drawn – like all gamblers – by the possibility of a big hit.

Of the next five hands, she won two – both of them light pots, though it seemed that she'd made a misjudgement on the second, failing to draw bets to a high flush. Someone called for a fresh deck. When the dealer broke the seal, Paula said: 'This will have to be my last hand, gentlemen. I'm on New York time.' It was poker etiquette.

The house showed a pair of kings at the fall of the fourth card – one atop the other. Paula took a six to match another above her hole card. No one bettered the kings. The dealer moved chips into the pot. Paula checked, but didn't bet back against the kings. The house hadn't been able to check in case Paula made the third six on a free card. On the next turn, the house gained the eight of clubs, Paula the ten of hearts. Two other players stayed in – one with a pair of aces

275

showing, another looking at a possible straight. After two
rounds of betting, the straight folded. The aces stayed for
another round – that was as far as he'd go. When her
chance came, Paula played back at the house, raising five
hundred against the kings.

Ginsberg wasn't a poker-player, but he could see what
was going on. As things stood, a pair of kings was playing a
pair of sixes. Paula hadn't shown too much enthusiasm
until she'd been dealt the ten. The house player had
watched her riding the two sixes, then come back at him.
She had a ten in the hole. Two pairs – tens and sixes. He
showed no sign of taking fright.

Ginsberg looked at the man – at the crisp white shirt
under the satin lapels, at his sleek dark hair, at the half-smile
on his face. He had the confidence of someone who knew
what would happen next. *He's matched another card*, thought
Ginsberg. *Possibly the eight.* When the eight had fallen,
Ginsberg had noticed how the man shifted slightly in his
seat.

Now he looked across at Paula and loaded more chips into
the pot. The look said: 'Try. Try to make me believe you.
The more you try, the deeper you get. I've matched my
kings. You're holding a pair of sixes. Your next best card is
a jack – no good; but you loosened up when you got the ten.
You're tens and sixes. Every time you want to make me
believe otherwise, it's going to hurt.'

Paula checked and raised two thousand. It was what the
dealer wanted: she'd decided to bluff. He worked the pot up
in five-hundred-pound bids, hoping to continue to draw her
rather than face her down with a single gigantic wager. She
had taken the Saudi for a further four thousand; others had
contributed, too, bringing her stake to nineteen. Then
she'd lost three and gained one over the remaining hands.
No one knew that she'd been carrying only the five hundred
she'd sat down with. She let two more rounds of bidding
follow, chasing the dealer's five hundred each time. Finally,
he decided to go for the kill. He smiled briefly, and bet three
thousand.

In following his leads, Paula had bet three thousand. Her earlier bet of two, together with the initial play, had cost three and a half, leaving her eight thousand five hundred. She checked the three thousand and raised five. It left her what she'd arrived with.

The dealer looked at her fingers as she pushed the chips into the pot. Then he looked at her face. He had watched her playing all night and he'd watched her win. He seemed puzzled for an instant: *She must know;* then frightened: *What if . . . .?* Then the smile came back: *She's a high roller – what else could she do?*

Swiftly, he matched the raise and said: 'See you.' The tone meant: *Got you.*

The smile was still on his face as Paula brought the third six out of the hole. Some laughter among those watching – a release of tension – helped distract from the ugly quiver about his mouth as he adapted the smile to a wry grimace. Paula collected her chips. When she stood up, Ginsberg was behind her and she handed them to him. She thanked the other players. 'I'm sorry – I really do have to go.'

The cheque had already been written by the time Ginsberg returned from the lobby with their coats. He had unloaded the chips on to the teller's desk while Paula ambled across to watch the play at a couple of other tables. A small dapper man in a dark blue tuxedo was standing at her elbow. As Ginsberg came close, the man took Paula's coat from him and helped her into it, then accompanied them to the inner door. They paused and he produced the cheque. It was for a little more than forty thousand pounds. 'I hope', he said, 'you give us another chance. Yes?' His voice was thin and precise, lightly accented.

She scrutinised the cheque, folded it and put it into her coat pocket. 'I'm prepared to give us both another chance,' she said. 'Thank you.'

Ginsberg had parked the car in a mews behind the square – an elementary precaution, but it didn't make any difference. He and Paula had rounded the corner and taken only a few steps on the polished cobbles when he saw the man approaching from the far end of the mews. Ginsberg checked his stride, then continued. In that moment, Paula also saw the man.

'What?' She was asking for instructions.

'Keep going. Try to stay out of the way.'

There was a good deal of light. A clear sky and half-moon. Frost glittered on the raised cobblestones. One in front, he thought, one behind. The usual set-up. He was listening for the sudden rush, like something falling, that would come at his back.

When he heard it, he shoved Paula to one side, hard, then swivelled and kicked in one movement, not waiting to judge the target. His attacker had run at him from about ten feet away. The kick took him high on the abdomen and neatly between the ribs. He made a noise like a macaw.

Ginsberg dropped and rolled sideways, letting the man's momentum carry him past. A street-light's pillar took the teetering body full on. He sat down, then pitched on to his face, back humped, his arms wrapped round his body.

When Ginsberg had rolled, the second man had been almost up to him. The roll had gained him six feet of space and taken him under the man's weapon. He rose and moved to the left, like a boxer, circling away from a right-handed blow. There was a pause. Ginsberg looked for an opening. The man was holding a sap – tape-wrapped metal – hefting it at shoulder height and off to the side to try to draw Ginsberg's eyes. He lunged, and Ginsberg moved towards the action, going for the hand. The sap took him on the collarbone before he could check it, then he got a grip and stepped in, doubling the man's arm, his thumbs laid along the back of the hand. He bore down sharply, twisting hard away from the man's body, and heard the wristbone go with a loud pop. They both fell, Ginsberg putting his shoulder into the form beneath him, but still gripping the hand. He knelt up quickly. The man's face was stretched in agony.

Ginsberg straightened the arm and laid it gently on the cobbled surface, palm down. He stepped back. He could hear the other attacker whooping like an asthmatic. Raising his foot, he brought the heel down on the fingers of the hand he'd placed so carefully on the cobbles. The man bucked and rolled away.

Without looking round, Ginsberg said: 'You drive. My shoulder's going numb.'

They didn't speak on the way back. From time to time, Paula glanced at him and laughed delightedly as if he'd made some witty remark. He looked straight ahead. It wasn't until they got into the house that he said: 'You didn't have to clean them out.'

'No?' She went into the kitchen and reappeared with two glasses. 'Drink?'

He pointed at a sideboard and she took a brandy-bottle from the stock, broke the seal and poured.

' ''I won't make waves'' – remember that? You could have surfed on those mothers.'

'I'm sorry, Ginsberg.' She handed him a glass. 'Am I making life awkward for you?'

'Just a tad.'

She moved to a couch, sitting at the far end and regarding him over the rim of her glass. Then she smiled. 'It's the fall of the cards, Ginsberg. . . .'

He look exasperated. Then, when her smile broadened, he found he was smiling back and went to join her on the couch. The smiles meant nothing. He felt angry; outwitted. He wasn't sure why. After all, she might have lost that last hand. He heard himself say it out loud – a concession.

'I guess you could have lost.'

'Oh, sure,' Paula said. Then: 'No.'

Ginsberg unbuttoned his jacket and felt for the bruise along his collarbone. 'Of course you could.' There was irritation in his voice.

Paula drank some brandy and put the glass down on a nearby table. 'Do you play much poker, Ginsberg?'

The habit she'd fallen into of using only his last name riled him. He knew what she was up to. 'Some. It's not a religion.'

'You watched the last hand.'

'Yes.'

'Do you have a cigarette?'

'I don't use them.'

'Neither do I, really. Just now and then.' She swallowed some more brandy instead, then kicked her shoes off. 'Listen,' she said, 'by the time the fifth cards were dealt, he was showing two kings, right? I had a pair of sixes – clubs and diamonds. I also had a six in the hole. I didn't play back at him when I turned the third six, but I stayed in when I got the ten. He matched the eight, to give him kings over eights. I was showing a jack, but he knew a jack in the hole couldn't help me. I thought he'd found a pair with the last eight.'

'His hole card could have been a king,' Ginsberg observed.

'And mine a six. He didn't think so, but he'd have looked at the odds. I did the same. Three players folded – one after three cards, two after four. The rest stayed in. That's twenty-four cards showing – and his were the only kings. What I couldn't see were six hole cards and twenty-two in the pack. Take his hole card out of it, allow the fact that there are two hidden kings, and you've got better than thirteen to one against his having trips.'

'Your odds were worse,' Ginsberg said.

'Sure. Double. Green Shirt was showing the six of hearts; but I knew I'd got 'em. He might have worried a little when I bet the two grand, but he had to make it sixes and tens. He eased me up in five hundreds after that, trying to increase my commitment. If I'd played back at him when I turned the second six, he might have got scared. I could have been bluffing, of course – but he'd have to think about it. As it was, he believed he was looking at two pairs and a gambler. What he was really looking at was the odds against both of us having trips.'

'Long odds?'

'Pretty long. It's tough enough for *one* player to luck out that way.'

'It can happen, though.'

'Sure.'

'People do lose that way, don't they? Despite the odds?'

She hesitated, then picked up her drink. 'Not in my game.' Ginsberg laughed. She put the glass down without drinking. 'The play was just as I described it to you. The odds were the odds – for the house, anyway. You're forgetting something about me, Ginsberg.' He looked at her uncertainly.

'Think of a word,' she said, 'and a place, and a name. Concentrate on them.' She turned away, facing the wall. After a few seconds, she said: 'Hot. Santa Fe. Susan.' She turned back. 'Which does "hot" apply to?'

'Jesus,' he said softly. 'Jesus Christ.'

'Don't misunderstand me. I like poker-play. I like to calculate the odds. I'm intrigued by how the other guy might be figuring it. But there's no question of losing. I can't tell, minute by minute, what people are thinking. Thought's too random, too fast. But one image – one important image – held firmly in the mind couldn't be simpler. He thought of his hole card. Of course he did; anyone would. He thought of it very hard. Each time, it was like getting a wide-screen view of the eight of clubs.'

The room gathered a silence. It was as if she were giving him time to accept what he already knew – what he'd known since that moment of violence and shock at the airport.

'So you see, Ginsberg,' Paula said quietly. 'I *didn't* have to clean them out. Sorry.'

He made no reply. The shoulder was worrying him, so he slipped out of his coat, unbuttoned his shirt, and slid it down on the right side. A bruise lay along the bone, dark red and slightly swollen. He fingered it lightly.

'How is that?' She drew closer and replaced his hand with her own, tracing the length of the narrow discoloration. Her fingers were cool.

'Painful. It doesn't matter. I think he caught a nerve – it was numb. I lost sensation in my upper arm. It's fine now; nothing.'

Paula shifted back to her end of the couch as if to regard

281

him better. 'I think they took the worst of it. You can fight, Ginsberg. Do they teach you that stuff?'

'Everyone. It's basic.'

'You really hurt them.' There was something in her voice. 'You broke that guy's wrist.'

Ginsberg recalled the moment when he and Paula had started towards the car. The two men were down. She had been standing to one side and a few feet back. He had said: 'You drive. . . .' He'd walked a few steps along the mews, hearing her footsteps behind him. Then they'd stopped and he had turned, hand in pocket, feeling for the car-keys.

Paula had been standing still, her feet close by the head of the man with the damaged hand, and staring at him with what seemed intense curiosity. She'd been looking for something. Although she'd been motionless, Ginsberg had felt as if he were watching a search – watching someone being frisked. Before she'd left the man's side, she'd put a toecap under the limp arm – moving her foot with care, like forceps – and shifted the limb slightly. He'd thought the action had about it the fascinated repugnance people show when moving a cat corpse into the gutter.

When he didn't reply, she said: 'You broke his fingers too.' He noticed that her hand was inside her blouse, resting on the upper part of her breast.

He knew what she meant. It hadn't been necessary. A grace note.

He made to lift his shirt back across his shoulder, but she leaned towards him and checked his hand. Lowering her head, she bit softly into the bruise. She got up and regarded him seriously.

'Come with me, Ginsberg. My evening isn't over yet.'

In the small room with its dark skylight, Paula stood before him and undressed, letting the blue silk run backwards from her torso like a water-flow to puddle on the floor. He removed his shirt and unbuckled his belt. She stepped forward, naked, and he moved to embrace her, but she held up a hand.

'Not yet.'

She grasped the buckle and pulled his belt through its

282

loops. Then she handed it to him. 'You know,' she said. 'You know what I want.' And, of course, it was true.

He said: 'Up against the wall.' There was a catch in his throat as he spoke.

Meekly, she did as she was bidden, raising her hands, flattening her palms against the white plaster, spreadeagling herself like a hoodlum pulled from a car.

Not giving himself time to think, Ginsberg flung out his arm, and the belt snaked between them, taking her hard across the buttocks. He waited. A tongue of red lay across her skin, shocking for its suddenness.

She had gasped when the blow landed. Now she brought her hands down and felt for the place, not looking, but moving her fingertips there like a reader of braille. Finally she raised her hands once more, then sighed and laid her cheek against the wall. He saw her eyes close. She spread her feet slightly, and bent her back, as if her lofted arms were about to support some great weight.

Her voice sounded druggy. 'If I say stop,' she said, 'don't stop.'

Guerney lay awake and watched the water-lights dancing just below the ceiling. It was dawn, and he hadn't slept that night. *It's high tide,* he thought. *High tide in this room. I'm submerged.* He thought about George Buckroyd and the way in which the friendship had taken the older man out on a limb.

'You feel you've simply used him,' Rachel had said earlier. 'That it wasn't fair.' She was wrong. He felt concerned; he felt powerless; knew that what Buckroyd had said – *You're on your own* – applied to all of them. But he'd do it the same way, given a second chance, using whoever and whatever he could. Fair. What was *that*?

He was afflicted by the need for movement, for action of some kind. As things stood, he could make little sense of what had happened. He realised that what Arthur had told him was dynamite. He tried not to think about the wider implications of holding those secrets. They were a part of his

283

armoury. He'd needed to know – had put the bite on Meadows and sent Buckroyd into uncharted territory – because understanding how the boy's talent was to have been used was a means of guessing what might happen next and where his adversaries would be most vulnerable. He had to know what they *needed*. To know someone's need was to know his weakness. And knowing that provided a target.

He thought it through. There were still too many blanks. Cesare Paschini's disappearance, for example. Guerney thought it likely that he'd been killed, like Caroline, because his existence was too great a threat. But there was no knowing for sure. Guerney sensed that it wasn't just his own aggression that now linked event to event. Other energies – some continuing purpose – was there. The understudy that he and Buckroyd had theorised about.

It was a sense of urgency that Guerney still detected. It chilled him. The things he'd learned from Meadows . . . and a sense of *urgency*. How long could his private battle remain private? What were the real stakes? It seemed possible that Meadows hadn't given him anything like the full story – either because he didn't know it himself, or because he didn't dare.

He understood something of their weakness, Guerney reasoned, but he didn't know enough to guess what their next moves would be. *He* would have to act: that was what his disquiet was telling him; it would be necessary to draw them, to take chances. That's why he'd bought the gun.

He registered a change in the pattern of Rachel's breathing, and knew that she had woken. They lay in silence for a while. She had become aware of the growing restlessness in him. As if reading his thoughts, she asked: 'What next, Simon?'

'You could find the house again – the house with the dogs?'

'We're going after them,' she said. Then: 'Sure, I can find it.' There was a pause. 'What are we into?' she asked quietly. 'I mean, that Meadows guy. . . . You believed that? It's dynamite.' He smiled that she should have chosen

284

his own word. 'You believe it?' she asked again, and yawned.

'I don't know enough to disbelieve it. What I do know is that I walked away from Meadows unscathed. It wasn't a set-up. And he was scared shitless. What he told me gels with what we know about David Paschini – and with the bits and pieces you learned in Washington. What else is there to believe?' He sighed. Perversely, Rachel's wakefulness had made him suddenly weary.

'It's odd,' she said and stroked his calf with her foot. 'It's all strange. You and me here – what's happened between us. What's happened.' He remained silent. 'Try to sleep, Simon.' She turned away from him, taking her body-warmth with her.

He looked at the lines of light moving across each other, then separating, shifting as the tide shifted. They were hypnotic. He felt his limbs slackening towards sleep. In that moment of vacuousness, a memory of the dream washed through him. He had resolved one affliction – the fear of immobility. Another remained. The fear of what sleep might bring.

'OK, OK.' Ed Jeffries held up both hands. 'It was our idea. I'm not arguing with that. But it was their goddam problem.' He looked round the table, seeking allies.

'No one cares any more, Ed.' Howard Prentiss' tone was sharp. 'It's not important. What does matter is that there are some strong voices in favour of calling it off. We're in great danger of pissing on our shoes here.'

'Suits me,' Jeffries replied. 'I just wish they'd make up their goddam minds.'

'They can't. That's why we're here.'

Jeffries overemphasized his exasperation: it was good to have someone else to blame. 'Sure. Sure. Some of those guys wouldn't know what to do with a hard-on in a whore-house.'

It didn't fool Prentiss. Speaking quietly, he said: 'So we've lost Irving.'

Jeffries almost winced. 'Looks that way. There's been no visual contact, but – '

'You mean no one's seen her?'

'What?' Jeffries looked up.

Prentiss put an edge on his tone. 'No one's seen her?'

'That's what I just said – right – but we're assuming – '

'Sure.' Prentiss cut him off again. 'And Paula Cole?'

Sitting on Jeffries' left was the man with the heavy moustache who had been present at Rachel Irving's first briefing. He said: 'She's there – uh, they'll have taken her to the north London house. The Brits are sharing the load: one of their men, one of ours. Uh' – he shrugged – 'what's there to tell?'

Prentiss said nothing of the report that had come through a few hours before. There were things that Jeffries' department didn't have to know; didn't have to worry over. What would it have meant to them, anyway? He remembered something Jeffries had said to him – before they had watched the video of Paula Cole's appearance on the talk-show: 'Do they believe it can work, this stuff? I mean, it's spooky and like that . . . but, hell – '

'But what?' Prentiss had asked.

'We're mixed up with a bunch of *crazies*, here.'

Prentiss gathered up the pages of his brief. Across the table, the moustache was giving some more details about the schedule for Paula Cole. Maybe, he thought. Crazies – maybe. Somehow, she knew about David Paschini. Said she'd spoken to him, or some such stuff. What the hell did that mean? And did it matter? Ben Ascher had been brought back from New York; he was supposed to know about this brand of crap.

'OK.' Prentiss pushed his chair back and stood up. 'I'll need daily reports. Anything comes from left field, I want to know immediately. Right now, we're going ahead. If that changes, you'll hear about it.' He looked at Jeffries. 'It's your show, Ed.'

The other man smiled. 'Sure; you bet.'

Everyone round the table heard it the same way. *It's your ass.*

William Prior rarely arrived at his desk later than 8 a.m. He took it to be a virtue. His mother had been a Presbyterian Scot and he'd learned, at an early age, the lessons of diligence and self-discipline. Later, he had discovered in himself that most heady of human attributes – ambition. It was this, rather than maternal example, that prompted his early mornings. He remembered his mother with something less than affection. In fact, when he thought of her at all it was to reflect that she had been a sour-faced old cow with a voice like a gimlet boring through rock.

He was making a phone-call. As he spoke, he slowly rotated the regimental dagger that he used as a letter-opener, letting the tip make a tiny precise hole in the centre of the untouched blotter on his desk.

'. . . I'll be speaking to them shortly,' he said. 'I'll be intrigued to hear what theories they offer.' He listened for a while, then responded with a smile to something that had been said. 'Deep water; yes. No one seems to know what it might mean. Our chaps are talking to their chaps. "Psychic residue" is a phrase I've heard bandied about. The question is does it matter that she seems to have . . . what? . . . picked up something from the ether?'

He listened again, occasionally saying, 'Yes . . . yes . . .,' and twirling the knife absentmindedly. A question was asked. 'Annoying but not dangerous, I think. He's tapped, of course; and followed – when possible.' He added this last remark wryly. 'We're of the same mind as the Americans; it's a bit of a bloody nuisance, but it can't really affect matters at all.'

Another question. 'No,' Prior answered. 'Of Simon Guerney and the Irving woman, nothing. Our feeling is that, eventually, he'll come to us. We're looking, naturally.'

The voice on the phone sharpened, but Prior's expression didn't change. He continued to roll the shaft of the knife idly between his fingers. He looked completely relaxed.

When the voice ceased, he said: 'Yes, of course.' His tone was soothing, as if he were quietening a fractious child. 'Of course, Minister; yes. If you would prefer it that way.' He hung up, but didn't alter his position. His eyes were fixed on the turning blade. He liked its symmetry.

'Wait, damn you.'

Pete Ginsberg stalled over Paula's body, at the very edge of his climax. His face bore a rictus of painful pleasure. He stayed very still, trying to push the sensation backwards by fixing on an image of water flowing uphill.

Paula arched her back to bring her pubic bone hard against his, and began to work her hips in a quick rhythmic circle, letting go a series of tiny grunts as she produced flicker after flicker of sensation. Her eyes were half-closed, and she looked past him at the skylight glowing as it took the early-morning sun. The feeling grew in her; she built it, wave upon wave, her legs forked, her shoulders driven hard against the bed.

From time to time she grasped the backs of Ginsberg's thighs, pressing him more firmly against the jut of her pelvis; then she'd ease off, wanting to let the promise of her orgasm fade a little. Ginsberg remained motionless, wondering if she had forgotten he was there.

Her voice grew louder, each outward breath a long *Aaah* of pure pleasure. She worked at it, skilful with her hips, letting the moment arrive and retreat, arrive and retreat. It was flooding her body like the light from the high window that washed her retina with eddies of red and white.

Finally she let go, ramming against him, her fingers biting into his thighs. A yell of delight built in her. As the first quake of orgasm came, she switched her hands to her own breasts, twisting the nipples hard; her mouth gaped; she looked past Ginsberg – seeming to stare at the skylight as if transfixed by some wild vision there. She spoke – shouted something – but her voice was distorted by the moment's greed.

288

'Wait!' she said again. The backwash ran through her, ebbing, returning, ebbing, like remnants of her dream.

David had been there. David, whose presence still clouded this room; who had lain on the bed she lay on now and watched the changing light that suffused the high window. His eyes. . . . She seemed to look at the rectangle of glass with his eyes, just as she had seen, with his eyes, a man crossing a snowy pasture, his figure reflected in a window which held images of bright sky, white field, the figure descending, and David's own terrified face.

The man had been tall and dark; curly-haired, his features strong. A dog walked at his side.

'Who is he?' Paula had demanded to know.

She had felt David's resistance – a palpable thing, like a shove – and she had shoved back, expecting to be the stronger. David had turned his face from her but – when she forced it – began to move in fractions towards her as if a movie were being progressed frame by frame.

'Who is he?' As their eyes met, she'd borne down on the boy, seeking control.

'Guerney,' she'd heard him say. 'Guerney. Guerney. Guerney.'

Suddenly, against her will, the scene had switched. She'd heard the angry voices, a man's and a woman's, just as she'd heard them a hundred times before. The man's voice said: 'It's over. This time it's over.' Then the garden – a view of the tall hedge, and the amplified roar of machinery that seemed to blot out all other sounds. It never changed. Terror and rage had possessed her. She had fought, just as she always fought, to alter things, to stave off what the dream would do to her next. It was impossible.

She'd watched the blades of the hedge-trimmer shuttling back and forth in a bright blur of sharpened steel, and had experienced the jolt of her own power, black and ecstatic.

'No one will know,' the voice inside her had said. 'No one will ever know.'

But this time there had been a difference about the dream. This time someone had been watching. It was his presence that she'd wanted to obliterate in passion. How had he followed her? How had he known where she was most weak?

She turned her head from the gleaming glass and caught a glimpse of Ginsberg's head and shoulders above her, though the light that still fogged her eyes made his face a dark featureless blob. Patterns ran on the white wall.

'All right, Ginsberg,' she said. 'Now you can hump me.'

'Guerney. Guerney. Guerney.'

In the dream, David Paschini was speaking his name, then pointing at the window-pane as if it were an oracle. A flurry of angry voices hard on his ear: a man's and a woman's. Then a picture of the garden, the drone of the hedge-trimmer the man wielded, using the noise and the mindlesss task to cover his sorrow. Guerney concentrated on the figure of the little girl watching, the pain and anger that made her stand stiff-limbed in the centre of the lawn, a sprinkler behind her cutting the sunlight to form a rainbow waterfall. The way her body suddenly rocked. He could feel the bolt of power as it left her. The hedge-trimmer reared like a striking snake, its blades chattering.

In the horror that followed, he heard the child cry out; he heard the word distorted by the force of her orgasm as she stared at the sun-shot glass. The girl's cry, and the woman's.

'Daddy,' Paula had screamed. '*Daddy!*'

18

Rachel half-lay on the bed, propped up by pillows, her eyes closed as Guerney had instructed. She heard his voice – a low monotone. He went slowly, taking her body piece by piece.

'Your feet are becoming numb,' he told her, 'becoming weightless. Now your calves . . . now your thighs. . . .' She moved with him, letting her torso, her arms, her upper back lose substance and grow light, until she could see only a ribcage and a slowed heart lying below a disembodied head.

As he talked, she lost touch even with that. The fatness of her tongue dissolved, and the weight of her jaw. The superstructure of ribs became a soft wattle, then melted. Her heart was a distant throb that lay outside herself. She was pure thought, pure recollection.

'You're standing outside the house,' Guerney told her. 'Where are you?'

He watched her lick her lips reflexively. Her answer took a while. She was building the picture. 'Near the heath.'

'Where?' he persisted.

'Hampstead Heath.'

'What's the name of the street you're in?'

'It's a hill.' She struggled. Her vision of the place shifted. She took herself to the corner and walked past, looking for the plate that would bear a street-name. It was white with black raised lettering. She passed and repassed it, striving to concentrate. Finally she said: 'Windmill Hill.'

'Where is the house?'

'Top of the hill. There's a blank, then a road. Other side. Nothing this side. Just an open space.'

'Walk up to the house,' Guerney commanded. 'What do you see?'

This part she knew well enough. The mild hypnosis was merely to sharpen her senses. 'The fence,' she told him. 'Dogs on the other side.'

'OK. How do you get in?'

'Press a bell. Someone in the house works two partitions in the dogs' run. They come down to form a walkway. There's a gate in the wire mesh of the run. Go through the wooden street-gate, close it, along the tunnel . . . walkway . . . open the mesh gate, close it. Then the partitions are raised again.'

'The man who works the partitions – does he watch you come in?'

There was a long pause. Then: 'Think so.'

'Go up to the house – how far is it from the mesh gate?'

'About thirty yards.'

'You're at the front door. Now what happens?'

'Gerry let us in.'

'Who?'

'Gerry Martin. The man you shot.'

'OK. You don't knock?'

'No. He just opens the door.'

'So he must have watched you coming through the walkway.'

'I guess so.'

'Is it day-time or night-time?'

'Day-time.'

'Go back to the street-gate.'

'OK.'

'It's night-time.'

'OK.'

'You go through the gate into the walkway.' He paused. 'Is it dark?'

'No. Spotlight; low on the ground, shining up.'

'In your eyes.'

'Yes.'

'All right. It's day-time again, and you're back at the

door. You've been let in. The door has closed behind you. OK?'

'Yes.'

'OK. Take yourself round the house. Tell me about it.'

'I'm in the hallway. Walk forward. Door to the right. Like a den. The phone's in there. Wasn't used for anything else. Walk a little further, there's a room on the left. The drawing-room. Window looks out at the gate. We mostly lived in here. Double door at the back of the drawing-room leads through to the dining-room. Door off that into the kitchen.'

'You're in the kitchen now?'

'Yes. I walked from the drawing-room into the dining-room, and from the dining-room into the kitchen. But there are doors to the dining-room and the kitchen off the hallway.'

'Where are the stairs?' Guerney had a piece of paper by him. He was sketching quickly as Rachel talked.

'Back down the hallway. Next to the study. They lead off to the right, then bend to the left.'

'Go upstairs,' he said. 'How many flights?'

'Three, turning left all the time.'

'Windows?'

'On each landing.'

'You're at the top of the stairs.'

'OK. . . . A corridor. Three rooms, one to the right: my room. Two to the left.'

'Both looking out on the street-gate and the place where the walkway comes down.'

'Yes.'

'Go into your room.' He waited. 'Are you in there?'

'Yes.'

'What can you see from the window?'

'Garden. A small orchard. The dogs' run. Another house, way off to the side. The road. The heath.'

'Could someone in the other house see you?'

'No. There's a high wall around it. We've got a fence. I can just see its roof . . . the wall. . . .'

'Move back into the corridor.'

'Yes. OK.'

'Turn away from the stairs. What's there?'

'A door with a latch.'

'What's behind it?'

Rachel hesitated. She wasn't confused: she knew well what was there. It saddened her. 'More stairs. They lead to David's room.'

'How many stairs?'

She took them, carefully, trying to count. 'Not sure. Twelve . . . fifteen?'

'They go straight up?'

'Sort of. The bottom two twist round to the right. Then you go straight.'

'To a door?'

'Yes. A small landing, then the door.'

'Go through the door.'

She sighed. 'Yes.'

'What do you see?'

'Just walls. There's a window high up in the roof. Sloping roof. It's padlocked shut. Table. Chair. A bed.'

'That's all?'

Rachel nodded. She had begun to cry, silently, because the light trance she was in made everything so vivid.

'That's all?' Guerney asked again.

'Yes.' Her voice was oddly placid. It wasn't all, of course. David Paschini lay on the bed, looking up as she held the tray of food, his expression slack from the drug. He had the look of an infant waking from a deep sleep in a strange place. As Guerney talked her back, restoring to her her torso and arms and legs, the boy's face stayed before her and she cried freely, making no effort to stifle her tears, but now knowing who she cried for.

She thought of David again, that afternoon, while she waited for Guerney to return with the hired car – safer, he'd decided, than hot-wiring something that the police would then be looking for. She wanted the boy safe. She remembered how his drugged head had flopped and rolled against the car's upholstery as they'd driven away from

Whiteleaf; he seemed infinitely vulnerable – constantly at risk, as if it were a piece of delicate glassware the men were casually hefting from place to place. Rachel realised, now, that part of the agonised conflict she'd felt at Druid's Combe had to do with David. She felt for him a tenderness that was new to her – an emotion that had nothing to do with desire or gain or the need to get something back. She wanted to trust the feeling just as, now, she wanted to trust Guerney. What else could she hold to? Knowing him at all had brought her here. Her presence in the strange flat with its river view, with its trappings of another woman's life, had lain in her future from that first moment when she'd seen Guerney at the embassy reception, lounging near the door, dangling his highball-glass by its rim.

If I'd never known him. She dismissed the thought. People filled their lives with such speculation. *If I'd never gone to that movie, rented that apartment, taken that vacation, been on that train, overheard that remark.* It was worthless.

He arrived as if on cue, knocking at the door as before. She released the security chain and let him in. 'OK?'

He nodded and threw his coat over a chair. 'You can drive with a manual change?' he asked.

'A what?'

'Gear-shift. Not automatic.'

'Sure.'

'Good. There wasn't a lot of choice.' He shook his head when she held up a whisky-bottle she'd found in one of the liberally stocked cupboards. 'No. And, if you're having one, make it small.'

She recapped the bottle without having poured herself a drink. 'What do you expect to find?'

'I don't know. Maybe nothing.' He went to the kitchen area and started to make some coffee. 'It's a place to start.'

'Not David?'

'No.'

'But you're expecting someone to be there.'

'Yes.'

'Because of what Buckroyd said – about them being still active.'

'Mostly.'

'OK,' she reasoned, 'they don't know about us – what happened, where we are. Whether or not we're together. They can make guesses, but they don't know.'

'They know I'm in London. They don't necessarily know about you.'

'All right; so one of the guesses will be that we *are* together – I could be with you out of choice, or not. They'd assume out of choice, wouldn't they?'

'Guessing that way – yes.'

Her voice grew quiet. 'Because I'd be too much trouble any other way. You'd have probably killed me.'

He spooned some ground coffee into a filter bag. 'Yes.'

'So they'd also assume – '

He cut her off. 'That you'd told me about the house. Sure.' He lifted the boiling water and poured. 'It works a number of ways. One: they might not have thought of it. They haven't won too many prizes for intelligence so far. Two: they might have thought of it and so not be there. Three: they might have thought of it and still be there.'

'Expecting us.'

'That's right.'

'Which do you figure?'

'Well, at the moment they can't find me, but they can't exactly ignore me, either.' Guerney poured coffee into two mugs. 'If I were in their position, I'd stake the place out. What have they got to lose?'

Rachel took her coffee from his outstretched hand. 'Terrific,' she said sourly, then held up a hand as if to ward off his rejoinder. 'No, OK, I can't think of another idea.'

Guerney smiled. 'Even if you could, I'd do this.' Rachel looked at him for an explanation. 'If they've thought of it, then the place won't be empty – someone *will* be there. I'd sooner find them before they find me. Nothing's happening. I need to make contact – my terms, my timing.' He seemed to be about to say something else.

'You're thinking you'd sooner be doing it alone.'

'Of course.'

'We've had this discussion, Simon.'

'It's OK.' He drank some coffee. 'Just do as I tell you – don't do more, don't do less.' It wasn't a concession. If he'd intended to go alone, he would have – simply not returning after he'd picked up the car. He wasn't content to leave her behind, though. It would make everything more difficult, everything riskier. At some other time, he might decide to abandon her. Right now, that was too chancy. She knew things about him; and knew things that he knew – damaging things. Right now she was cash in the bank.

Rachel took their cups to the sink. She thought she felt hungry, then realised that the hollowness was fear. They'll be waiting, she reasoned. Guerney's guessed it right.

He'd guessed wrong. It would have been logical to suppose that he'd learn about the house from Rachel – would turn up there sooner or later. The right move would have been to stash Paula Cole somewhere else, use the house as bait. But Guerney had hit the truth with one of the options he'd rejected. No one had thought of it.

19

The file on Guerney was surprisingly slim. Its details were concise and accurate up to the point when he'd left the civil service; after that, they became decidedly sketchy. The nature of his activities was known, but little specific detail had been gathered – apart, William Prior noticed, from that silly business of Arthur Meadows' neurotic wife. Briefly, he read through the notes on that, and wondered whether it mightn't be a good idea to have Meadows watched for a while.

The home-based stuff had yielded rather more fruit, but most of Guerney's operations had taken place outside the country. Something was known, at any rate, of his regular contacts. A Mr McGregor at Tennyson's, the gunsmiths in Hobb's Lane; and Mr Dawson at Bostock & Wombwell, a firm of security specialists in Bond Street who prided themselves on being able to supply pretty much everything from an armoured car to a voice-activated tape-recorder the size of a fingernail.

It was also known that Guerney had some contacts less respectable than Messrs McGregor and Dawson. The trade-offs with London's villains was day-to-day barter in some quarters – a market-place where most things carried a price-tag of some sort.

Prior sat back in his leather swivel-chair and pushed Guerney's file away from him. Then he picked up the regimental dagger and turned the point, gently, on the ball of one finger. He was waiting, with relative good patience, for another phone-call.

*   *   *

Colin Preston's patience had long since run out – replaced by the fear that had lain behind it from the start. For the third time in ten minutes, he lit a fresh cigarette, got up from the wooden chair that faced the bare wooden table and walked to the window of the interview room. He couldn't see out – the window was frosted glass sandwiching a layer of chicken-wire – but it provided a focal point for his little walks, and the walks helped shed some of his tension. The uniformed constable in the room with him stood close to the door, impassive, his arms folded. He'd seen this kind of edginess a hundred times and it bored him.

The instruction had been to get a result as soon as possible, so Pat Thomas had decided to let Preston stew for only thirty minutes. Like most good coppers, DI Thomas knew that timing was important. He knew that the rhythm of an interview – the way it was stage-managed – could count for a lot. You had to know your villain, too. Thomas, like all detectives, had met some who didn't break. The hard men. They gave nothing; they went the tough route, on the streets or in the nick. They took no prisoners. The punishment-block regulars – you got nothing, whether you threatened, offered, cajoled or kicked them round their cells. They wouldn't cross the street to piss on you if you were on fire.

Preston wasn't one of them. Even so, Thomas would have preferred to wind him up a bit more – leave him alone for another hour, say.

He paused a moment outside the door of the interview room, then went in fast, as if in a hurry to get matters over with. Preston turned, but didn't speak: none of the usual 'What's this about?' bluster; he knew damn fine why he was there.

Thomas looked at the uniformed man, who nodded and left, closing the door as he went. Thomas sat down in the second chair and produced a packet of cigarettes, holding it out wordlessly. Preston took one and sat down opposite. Thomas struck a match.

'It took us a while to find you, Col. That was naughty, wasn't it?'

Preston rolled the tip of his cigarette in a tin ashtray – the table's only ornament. He kept his eyes down and his voice more or less even. 'You can't have been looking very hard.'

'Bollocks,' Thomas said. 'The idea was you'd come to me. Did you forget that, Col?' There was a silence. 'Never mind, Colin. Let's see what we've got. You sold him a gun – what was it, by the way?'

Preston said nothing. He drew on his cigarette. It was too early, yet, to know what he was bargaining for.

Thomas sighed. 'All right, Colin, let me mark your card.' The accent was as thick as Preston's. Same patch, same culture, same methods a lot of the time. . . . In a war, the foot-soldiers are indistinguishable.

'We don't give a toss about the shooter – all right? We told you that he might be in touch. We told you what to do if he was, right? One way if he was alone, another way if he was with a woman. Didn't we? Either way, it was down to you to give me a bell. Now, we know you saw him, my son; there's no confusion about that.' Thomas crushed his cigarette stub in the ashtray. 'You want to know how you stand. That's reasonable. I'll tell you. I've got you nicely fitted up for a post-office blag – '

'You bastard!' Preston spoke quietly, without moving or raising his head.

'It's been hanging about a bit, and my guv'nor would be well pleased with a result.' Thomas continued as if there had been no interruption. 'Now, since you've only been out of the nick for – what is it? – ten months? – I can see you going down for a good while. I mean, you walk into a defenceless sub-post office in Hendon, waving a shotgun about and shouting at the top of your voice. Knock shit-skittles out of the poor old duck behind the counter. Have it away with two hundred quid, assorted postal orders and a fistful of registered letters – '

Preston slammed his hand down on the table. 'You can't have this one!' He got up and crossed to the window. 'Fuck it! You can't fit me up twice in a row.'

' 'Course I can, son. You're a bloody villain, Col. I can

do what I fucking like, can't I?' Thomas lit another cigarette. His voice took on a tone of mild reasonableness. 'Last
time I looked, there were five down to you and friends – all
still on the books. One of them was a wages snatch. A
security guard decided to have a bit of a go, I remember.
Every Friday, he wheels himself down the road to collect his
unemployment benefit. Now, what did you get for the
Briggs Warehouse blag? Three, was it? What are you
whining about, my son?'

'I wouldn't do a fucking sub-post office, Mr Thomas, you
know that. Only cowboys and kids – that sort of thing. Two
hundred quid?' He sounded affronted. 'It's totally out of
order, this.'

'Well, you might be right, Col. We know it's not your
style exactly – you and me. It's even possible that you'll
convince your brief of that, though with half your firm in
nick he might be inclined to think you'd fancied a bit of
freelance. But judges don't make a habit of studying form,
Colin, juries even less. I'd imagine they'll be more
impressed by the positive ID and the fact that we found the
registered letters at your gaff. Wouldn't you?'

Preston returned to the table and took a cigarette from
Thomas' packet.

'You sold him a gun,' Thomas stated.

'A .38 – Colt. Eight rounds.'

'Very good, Colin my son.' Thomas offered encourage-
ment.

'He paid well over the odds for it. Promised to, anyway,
so he wanted it badly enough.' Preston paused. He'd
known it was trouble when he'd first been approached by
Guerney. The man was an oddball. He paid well for bits
and pieces of information, and none of it too close to home.
Guerney had never been interested in street crime, or asked
for any names. Now and then, he'd wanted a whisper on
the Irish, or to get a lead on some new faces – people passing through. Preston had been able to help him out with
information about some laundered Deutschmarks on one
occasion. There were one or two like him – specialists,

301

often ex-SAS and always with connections that you could guess at but didn't want to know about. Dealing with the filth – you could trade. Jacks like Pat Thomas – he'd grown up with them, gone to the same schools. Guerney's kind of action was something different.

'He was alone,' Thomas said.

'Yeah.'

'What happened?'

'I left it in a boozer for him. On top of one of the lavs. He collected it from there.'

'I should have heard about all this, Col. Instead of which, you did a runner.' Thomas flicked the packet of cigarettes towards the other man and brushed back a lock of dark wavy hair. There was a daintiness about Thomas' hands that Preston hadn't noticed before – a soft, well-manicured look.

'I didn't like the sound of it.' Preston shrugged. 'We're not talking about common or garden villainy, are we? I mean, being slipped a few quid for marking his card about some Spic minder, that's one thing. . . .'

'He collected the shooter,' Thomas continued blandly.

'That's right.'

'And you did as you were told.'

'Jesus Christ.' Preston went to the window once more, and leaned against the wall, hands in pockets, staring at the chicken-wire diamonds trapped in the dirty glass.

'Sit down, my son.' Thomas sounded amused. 'You're up and down like a whore's knickers.' He paused. 'She was sixty – the old dear in the post office; the one you smacked. No reason for it, Colin. She wasn't putting up a fight or anything like that. Very nasty. Gratuitous. Concussion, broken ribs, shock.' He shook his head. 'No one liked it.'

'Yes,' Preston said at length.

'Yes, what, my son?'

'Yes, I did what you asked me to do.' Thomas waited. 'Wapping Wall,' Preston told him. 'A row of warehouses. Photographers' studios. They haven't got numbers. It's a blue door.'

302

'The only blue door?'

'Yes.'

Thomas left the interview room and motioned the uniformed man to go back inside. Then he went to his office and made a telephone-call. As a result of his call, two more were made. He sat at his desk for a few minutes, smoking and trying out one or two theories.

Christ knows, he thought finally. I'm as much in the dark as that daft sod in the interview room. I do what I'm told; he does what he's told. It wasn't the first time Pat Thomas had heard the Official Secrets Act quoted, but he resented it none the less. It made him feel he was out of his class.

His sergeant came in with two cups of tea and handed one over. 'Is that toe-rag Preston still in the interview room?' he wanted to know.

Thomas nodded. 'I'll let him sweat for a bit, then go down and warn him off. He'll keep shut. He's looking at robbery with violence, GBH, and a few more.'

'You get what you want?'

'Oh, yeah.' The tea was scalding. Thomas took a cautious sip.

'Why did he have it away in the first place?'

'He was frightened.' Thomas left his tea to cool and lit a cigarette. 'It wasn't his league.'

'Why didn't he just stay clear, then?'

'He was down as a possible contact for this Guerney. That's why I went to see him. He was under instruction. And he was frightened of me, too. I don't think he wants to see the inside of another nick for a good while.'

'He was a bit stuck, then, wasn't he?'

'Just a bit.'

The sergeant looked up, suddenly struck by an idea. 'We couldn't do him for the post-office job anyway? Just for old times' sake?'

'No chance. Sorry. I've had the word. I wag my finger under his nose, then he walks. He's getting an honest deal. Sickening, isn't it?'

The idea seemed to fill the sergeant with genuine delight. 'Colin Preston', he observed, 'wouldn't recognise an honest deal if it knelt down and gave him a blow job.'

'Now?' Rachel asked.

Guerney confirmed it. 'Why not?'

'I don't know. I thought we'd go much later.' She smiled. 'I'm a newcomer to this kind of stuff – remember?'

'If there's anyone there,' he told her, 'they'll be mob-handed.' She looked puzzled. 'Several of them,' he explained. 'And at this time of the evening it's likely that they'll all be in one place. I don't particularly want to have to tiptoe from bedroom to bedroom like Santa Claus. If they switch on an alarm, or post a guard – if they're really expecting us to show – then they'd probably do that later. Right now they'll be eating, playing cards – whatever. Occupied in some way.'

He remembered the shepherds in Sardinia. He had waited until they were occupied. Concern touched him, and at the same time a flash of annoyance. His tone sharpened. 'You know what to do?'

'Yes.'

'If I'm not back in fifteen minutes, drive away. Don't get out of the car, don't go near the house. Come back here. If I haven't phoned within an hour of your return, clear out.'

'I know.' She followed him to the door. 'Try not to fuck up, won't you? I haven't figured out the currency and the subway system yet.'

There were two cars, a Jag and a Rover. They had come up to a red light soon after Tower Hill, and that had delayed them for thirty seconds – about the time it had taken for Guerney and Rachel to cross from the door of the studio and get into the hired car. At one end of the narrow street was a ramp, an iron bridge and then a dead end. Guerney had parked so that his car was pointing towards the junction that would take him to the main road.

He saw them at once: the Jag coming slowly down the

street, the Rover waiting by the junction and partially blocking it. For a fraction of a second, he considered letting the men in the Jag go into the studio before making his move, but reasoned that they'd almost certainly check the parked cars – possibly block the street, too. It would be foolhardy to let them manoeuvre.

'Oh, shit.' Rachel watched the slow progress of the lead car. Gurney took the .38 from his pocket, thumbed off the safety and handed it to her. He'd wait until they reached the blue door of the studio. In that moment, they'd be distracted, tense.

He released the handbrake, put the car into second, held the clutch out and took a grip on the ignition-key. 'Wind your window down,' he told Rachel. 'As we start to move, fire at the windscreen. Same with the other car as we approach it. Don't try to aim, just point and fire.' She eased her window down, never taking her eyes from the approaching Jag. The gun felt heavy and cold.

The men had seen the door. They continued to drive slowly to keep the engine noise down. As they drew level with it, Guerney switched on, revved his engine and let the clutch in with a bang, driving directly at the other car before anyone inside had a chance to get a door open. Rachel got off two shots, one of them spangling the windscreen, then ducked back as they side-swiped the Jag and were past, heading towards the junction.

'Keep firing,' Guerney yelled at her. She leaned out of the window again, clutching the gun two-handed.

The back door of the Rover began to open as Guerney drove towards it. In the same moment the car lurched backwards. The driver had decided to try to block the intersection. There was a shout from the man who was climbing out. When the driver hit the brake, the door cannoned open, then back taking the passenger on the legs. He fell into the road and tried to scramble upright. Rachel fired twice, shattering the Rover's side-window. The man lying in the street rolled towards the front of the car, seeking cover. She had time for one more shot before Guerney found the gap and swung the car right, heading towards east Smithfield.

They'll have to turn, he reasoned. *One car's had its windscreen shot out. Maybe we've got thirty seconds on them.*

Rachel had turned to look through the rear window. As he swung the car right, Guerney asked: 'Anything?'

'No.' There was a shake in her voice. She held the .38 loosely in her right hand.

'Put the gun back in my pocket,' he told her. 'Keep looking.'

They were threading through a jigsaw of small streets, heading for Whitechapel. After a while Guerney turned back in the direction of the river, driving a mazy route towards Southwark Bridge. They crossed the Thames and kept heading south.

'We've lost them,' Rachel said.

'For the time being. We can't just drive around all night. They'll be searching.'

'Will they?'

He nodded. 'They've flushed us; we're in the open. It's no time to abandon the hunt. They learned a lesson in Somerset. Two cars, seven men – they've decided to take us seriously. This car's a target. We'll have to leave it.'

Seven. Rachel wondered how he'd had time to register that. She remembered only the noise and the recoil of the gun, the deafening percussion of each shot. She asked: 'Did I hit anyone?'

Guerney smiled. 'I doubt it.'

'What will they do?'

'Not sure. Use police patrols, I expect. Have them report sightings, but issue instructions that we're not to be stopped or challenged. That way, they'd run us to earth without the embarrassment of some overzealous copper getting involved.'

He was taking side-roads where possible, driving fast but snatching a brief glance to left and right if they paused for a junction.

'What are we looking for?'

'A pub,' Guerney replied. 'They'll check cars parked at the roadside.'

After they had driven for another five minutes, neither speaking, Rachel said: 'How?'

Guerney simply shook his head.

'Buckroyd?' she asked.

'No.' His voice was too soft for her to catch the inflection. She wondered whether the single word had been a denial or a protest.

He found what he was searching for by taking the risk of driving along a main road for a few minutes. The pub was called the Friend at Hand. Neither of them missed the irony. He stopped on the far side of the carpark and left the keys in the ignition. If they got really lucky, someone would steal it.

'What now?' Rachel followed him back into the street. He was heading for a small arcade of shops, all of them closed except a general store. He bought a two-litre bottle of red wine, choosing one with a screw cap.

When they emerged, he took her arm, steering her into another warren of side-streets. They walked past rows of dull little houses, each with a lit window. Unreasonably, Rachel felt excluded. There seemed to be something smug about the closed doors and tightly drawn curtains. She wanted to be inside – wanted a wall to put her back against.

The waste ground covered about half an acre. On one side was a highway: four lanes of swiftly moving traffic. The space was a rubble of bricks, old mattresses, shattered furniture. Three houses were still standing, one without an outer wall at the gable end. A staircase rose nakedly through wrecked rooms.

Some attempt had been made to board up the plot, but the fence was gap-toothed where planks had been torn out for firewood. Rachel could see a blaze on the far side and, as they got closer, people sitting round the fire, their faces lit by the glow.

Guerney had seen them during his early-morning run

that first day he'd spent at the Connaught. Sprawled by the doorways and gratings of the West End, they were foragers in the territory of the rich. Here, they were on their own terrain, like outlaws back from a raid. Rachel and Guerney were travelling in the badlands. Such places were everywhere in the city and easy to find. Most people simply didn't see them. They didn't want to.

There were two women and four men, though it was difficult to tell that at first. It wasn't just that the bulk of tatty greatcoats and wrappings of scarves and stringy hanks of hair made them indistinguishable; more that gender had become meaningless. Their bodies signalled nothing but their plight. They thought about booze and shelter, sometimes about food. Life had brought them low, and unsexed them.

As Guerney and Rachel advanced, all the faces but one turned towards them. The face that didn't turn belonged to an old man. His bush of beard and filthy hair disappeared into the upturned collar of a ragged coat. He stared at the fire, sipping from a small bottle that he brought to his lips in a measured way, as if allowing a precise count between drinks.

Guerney sat down, pressing Rachel's arm so that she would follow suit. He uncapped the wine and took a drink, then passed it to the person nearest him – a man of about forty, who took it anxiously and drank until another pair of hands prised his loose.

Rachel expected Guerney to say something. Neither of them, she reflected, was exactly dressed for the part. Maybe he would offer some sort of reassurance – 'Bit of trouble with the police' – something to provide status. Then she looked at the faces round the fire and saw nothing in the eyes of suspicion, or even of curiosity. It didn't matter to them who these strangers were. The down-and-outs couldn't be robbed or threatened; they didn't wonder what Rachel and Guerney might have done; they didn't fear them any more than a leper might fear a visitor to the colony. They were glad of the wine and took it without caring how or why it had arrived. There wasn't much left that life could do to them.

The wine came back to Rachel. She took it from the woman who was sitting next to her and passed it on without drinking. The woman's eyes followed the bottle. Rachel looked at her, trying to guess her age. She might have been thirty, or fifty. Her face was like a bruised fruit.

They stayed for half an hour or so – long enough, Guerney reasoned, to establish their rights. The bottle had long since been emptied. He got up and led the way towards one of the derelict houses. Rachel followed, stumbling over debris. In some of the downstairs rooms there were tangles of ancient blankets and sacking, with newspapers underneath for insulation. Rudimentary beds. They looked like rats' nests. Guerney tested the stairs, using his toecap on the support to each step before trusting it. They found a bedroom that gave them a view over the waste ground – away from the highway. The floor was littered with trash, but there was no bedding in there. The windows were mostly broken. The whole room smelt acrid and stale.

Rachel looked out at the group still gathered round the fire. She could see the silhouette of the old man with the beard. He hadn't moved. Even his hand was still, now, because he'd finished whatever had been in the small bottle.

'Why do we always visit *your* friends?' It was an old joke. She said it without a trace of a smile, and Guerney didn't laugh. She turned away from the window and started to kick a space out of the rubble on the floor.

'We've joined a community,' he said. 'It's the last thing anyone would expect. But, better than that, it's a community that no one really sees. Those people out there are almost invisible; they're no different from the trash they live among. Someone looking across from the street would just see enough to convince him that there's nothing here.' Rachel squatted in the area that she'd cleared and leaned back against the wall. 'It gives us time,' Guerney continued.

'For what?'

'I'm looking for an edge. That's why we were going to the safe house. I need some sort of advantage.'

'What?' she asked again.

'I'll know when I see it.'

Rachel raised her knees and wrapped her arms round her shins. She was cold. From below, she could hear sounds of people coming in from the fire, shuffling and coughing.

'You don't know what to do next,' she said. The thought had only just occurred to her.

Guerney's narrow face was impassive. 'Wrong,' he asserted. 'Nothing's changed – except that we're a lot less comfortable than we were. It's possible that we're better-hidden. We'll stay invisible for a few days. They'll find the car, look around, draw a blank. Then we'll try the house in Windmill Hill again. Nothing's changed. If anything, the odds have shifted in our favour. Earlier, they had a lead on us; now they don't.'

There was more coughing from downstairs and, for a moment, the sound of voices raised in anger. 'What about them?' Rachel asked.

'They want to be left alone. As things stand, they can live here. They just need to scrounge enough for a bottle. They won't go near any sign of officialdom. They live outside that. Police, the Social Security system, welfare offiers – they know just enough about authority to stay away from it. We'll keep them in booze for a while. They won't want anything to interfere with that.'

'You have some money left?'

'A little. Enough for now. We'll need to get more eventually.'

Rachel was concerned. 'They'll guess we have money.'

Guerney laughed. 'Did you get a close look at them?' he asked her. 'Don't worry.'

When her expression didn't change, Guerney walked to the door and pushed it almost closed. The underside stuck against warped floorboards. He found a half-brick among the rubbish they'd kicked into a pile and balanced it atop the door. Anyone shoving it would have to dislodge the brick.

'You sleep,' he said. 'I'll stay awake for a while.'

He kept his vigil for two hours, trying to empty his mind. Errant images crept in. The garden. The girl. David's flayed face. He strove against them, wanting the blankness that running brought – mindlessness. He remembered the run he'd taken after returning from Paris, and the buzzards wheeling in and out of the sun. He concentrated on the metronomic rhythms of the discipline – saw his legs crossing and recrossing, until the image became strobe-like, hypnotic, and he slept.

An hour later, at 2 a.m., Rachel woke, remembering at once where she was. The room was lit by a faint sodium glow. She could hear snoring from one of the rooms below and the occasional noise of vehicles on the highways. She could hear an intermittent scrabbling in the walls and ceiling, quick and light and full of menace. There was another noise that she couldn't, at first, identify: a low sound and close at hand, fluctuating as the wind does when it splits on the angle of a wall.

She strained to listen. It was Guerney, she realised finally; he was talking in his sleep, the words breathy and incoherent. The sound chilled her. It was lilting and intimate, like someone praying or whispering to a lover.

To begin with, only David had been there – in the room with the skylight. Guerney knew it from Rachel's description. David was hunched over something that he held on his lap, as if protecting it, and when he raised his head it was clear to see that he was pale with effort, his features stretched like someone engaged in a feat of strength.

Slowly, he extended his clenched hands, though not willingly; some force was manipulating him. His arms and wrists trembled as he fought until, finally, the power he wrestled against broke him, and his fists unfastened and let drop what he'd been holding. It was a mask, rubberised and flaccid, the kind of thing kids wear at Hallowe'en. David's hands had been so tight round it that it was stuck in gruesome folds, the lips peeled back, the nose flattened, the jowls twisted. Slowly it found its real shape. Guerney saw that it was his own face.

David looked at him bleakly, his arms still extended as if in supplication. Then he was gone, and someone else was there, in the shadows, breathing softly. A step forward, and a face came into the wan glow cast from the skylight.

She had sought him out. Like someone scanning film clips for a scene or face, she had sought him out in dream.

Because it amused her, Paula came to him as a succubus, naked and lithe, smelling of sex as a stoker smells of sweat. She wanted power.

Guerney fought her and lost. Even in his conscious mind, he didn't know why this should happen or what made it possible. It was a dream, but not a dream. It was something shared, something controllable.

She didn't know who he was or why the boy had retained his image. She sensed that he was important and was part of the things that had been kept secret from her. At some stage, perhaps, she would want to know about him – about the house in the country and what David had seen through the window. But first she wanted power.

She broke him down, response by response, until only instinct was left and he came to her, drawn like dog to bitch. 'Yes,' she coaxed, 'you do, don't you? You do. You want that. You want that, don't you?' He mounted her, seeing plainly the smooth escarpment of her back, the outcrop of a shoulderblade. 'You do. Ahhh, you do.' And she reached under her own body to cup his balls.

He grunted as he worked at her. She willed his hands to her throat, letting them tighten. With each drive forward his loins slapped at her buttocks.

'Ahhh, you do.' Her voice was a choke. A great headiness grew in her, excitement like drunkenness, as she choreographed the dream. He would ride her all night. She'd drown him, draw him into her caul. She'd have him secure.

The sense of power toppled her. In striving to envelop him she felt her orgasm building. At first she toyed with it, letting it ebb and flow, but finally it found its own impetus, like a breaker that's been running under the surface of the sea, and exploded over her in a deluge of unalloyed sensation, washing her mind clear of everything but the rush of pleasure.

The moment was Guerney's too. He sensed a hunger in her, something spawned of power but also of guilt. It was dark and lay in her deepest places and needed to be fed. It had taken his hands to her throat.

As she climaxed, he took the dream from her. She arched her back, letting him throttle her softly as she clutched and clutched, spasm after spasm. He saw the garden again, the child, the broken rainbow. Power flowed out of her. '*Daddy*,' she cried. Guerney felt the machine buck in his hands, flailing and out of control.

No one will know. No one will ever know.

For three days, they scarcely moved from the room. Guerney left on one occasion to fetch food and bottled water and more wine. At night they would go out on to the waste ground and sit by the fire, letting a couple of the bottles he'd bought go from hand to hand until they were empty.

Now, more than at any other time, Guerney wished he were alone. It would have been possible for him to sink into himself, letting the necessary time pass without logging it or feeling it weigh upon him. Lacking the possibility of action, he would have inhabited the limbo that made a virtue of passivity. As it was, he grew increasingly aware of Rachel's mood. At first she was edgy. But then she began to pick up the despair and wretchedness in the place. She watched the down-and-outs and saw how close to death they were and how little they cared. They looked for oblivion as a scavenger looks for carrion – a constant search – and found it in whatever would shut their senses down. They drank anything, from the wine Guerney brought to neat meths and metal polish. Rachel had watched one of the women return with a bottle of milk she'd stolen from a doorstep and force gas through it from a still-working pipe in the derelict house.

More than anything she was depressed by the isolation of these people – one from another. They were locked up inside themselves. It seemed that they almost never spoke. They moved past and around one another – past and around

Guerney and herself – like ghosts who haunted only themselves. Her abiding image was of the fire at night; the circle of stupefied faces; the sudden eerie animation of hands plucking at the bottle.

Sharing that south London gulag with them, she felt their dead rhythms soaking in. Her limbs ached from sleeping rough in the junk-cluttered room. Boredom and lack of purpose made her feel marooned. She was perpetually cold.

On the third night, after the fire had died, she sat in the spot underneath the window that had become her territory and listened to the patterings in the ceiling. They had ceased to worry her.

'Do you know how they make gas and milk?'

'Yes.' Guerney knew from her dulled tone that it would be necessary to leave; too soon, perhaps, but necessary. 'It's not very potent. You have to drink a lot of it.'

'Sometimes it's the best they can do.'

'I know.'

'I'm sorry. I sound like a fucking social worker.'

Guerney shrugged. 'You've seen them before – Eighth Avenue, Union Square, the Bowery. Every city has them. They're one of the species.'

'They never had identities before.'

He laughed. 'Did you imagine that they'd always been like this?' She didn't answer. 'We need money,' he said, 'and somewhere else to be. We'll be considered lost by now. It's safe to go. Tomorrow's a good day to make a move.'

'Why?' she asked.

'Because it's a Thursday.'

314

20

They were boxed in by a crowd and by the slowly moving line of cars that filtered through tall gates. To their left was a stadium: a large curving structure, slab-built and dowdy. The throng inched towards it, stopping and starting as those at the front went through the bottleneck of the turnstiles. On Thursdays and Saturdays, Wimbledon Stadium was given over to greyhound racing.

Once inside, Rachel made to follow those who were ascending the double staircase that led to the viewing-area above the track, but Guerney took her arm and steered her through a set of glass doors to a tiny paddock where the dogs that would run in the first race were being displayed.

'It's all a fix, isn't it?'

He was staring at the dogs and seemed not to have heard her. Finally, he said: 'So rumour would have it. Not always.'

'How much have we got?'

'A little over twenty pounds.'

'That's not much stake-money, is it? How lucky do you expect to be?' Again, he didn't reply at once. She followed his gaze. 'They are beautiful,' she added.

'Pure essence of dog.' He said it quickly, as if the need to speak were an annoyance. After a moment his concentration broke. 'No,' he said, 'I'm just indulging myself by coming to the paddock. I can't take my eyes off them.' He pointed to a fawn-coloured dog in the middle of the ring. 'You're looking at something with the most ancient lineage of its species. Apart from one or two minor modifications, nothing's altered since the pharaohs. No cross-breeding, no genetic engineering.' He stopped himself, and answered her question. 'No, I couldn't count on getting lucky. Someone else will get lucky for us.'

They went upstairs to the enclosure. Eight tiers of enclosed wooden tables, like the desks in a lecture-hall, ascended to the bar and rows of betting-windows. Guerney and Rachel found an unoccupied table and sat down. He handed her a race-card and a five-pound note.

'Place some bets if you want to. The easiest thing to do is bet a forecast – which dog will win, which will come second. If you like the look of both, do a reverse bet: that'll give you a combination of the two in first and second place.'

'Am I supposed to win?'

'It doesn't matter much. I thought you might like to know what you're doing.'

'OK. What will you be doing?'

'There are ten races. The last takes place at ten o'clock. As soon as they've passed the post, go up to the bar. You'll find me there.'

The lights in the stadium dimmed so that the track illuminations seemed brighter than before. The handlers had walked their dogs to the traps and put them in. The hare started along the rim, gathering speed until it rocketed past the traps and they opened automatically. The dogs appeared to emerge at full sprint, coming down the straight at astonishing speed. The fawn dog was leading. He was baulked on the first bend and ran wide, but gained ground on the back straight.

'He's going to win.' Without waiting for the finish, Guerney rose and climbed the steps to the bar. He bought himself a beer and took it to a small circular table close to the window where people would collect their winnings on five-pound bets or larger. Over the next five races he kept watch, looking for a face that would become familiar.

The face was chubby and friendly and very pleased. A German, on holiday with his wife and gleeful at having found a small diversion from the well-worn tourist path. It

316

was clear that he'd decided to follow one of the press tipsters, since a folded newspaper was pushed into the side-pocket of his sports coat. The tipster was paying off. On his fourth trip to the pay-out window, his wife accompanied him. She was beaming with excitement.

'Wenn wir so weiter gewinnen, könnten wir noch 'ne Woche bleiben.'

The man laughed, his plump face shiny under the neon. He waved some banknotes under her nose. 'Ein Monat – und zwar ein besseres Hotel.'

'Vorsicht, Arnolf; sonst verlieren wir das alles wieder!' Her voice was suddenly stern as she followed her husband to the betting-window.

'No,' Guerney thought, 'pay attention to the good frau; don't be rash. Percentage betting will do from here on.'

He stood up and checked rapidly the altering numbers on the illuminated board beyond the winning-post. Only two dogs had accumulated better than fifteen hundred bets. Looking down at his card he found the name Lady Jane. His mind flashed up an image of the sinuous muscled form swerving to intercept her prey; of her narrow head close to his knee as they walked back to Druid's Combe in the half-light. Since the bet was of no matter, he decided to put his money there. When there was nothing much to lose, he reasoned, instinct and chance might well coincide.

He stood behind the German in the queue and watched the fat fingers pluck banknotes from a full wallet. Guerney placed his bet, then retreated to his seat opposite the pay-window. The German had paused to check the odds on the closed-circuit television. He was betting the second favourite at 7-4. As he waddled back to his viewing station above the track, he lifted the flap of his jacket and pushed the wallet into a hip pocket.

Rachel was making a small wager on each race, using the method Guerney had given her. She did it only to keep in touch with him. She felt isolated and nervy. Once, as a child, she had gone with her mother to a large department store and had looked round from some distraction to find her mother gone. There had been a maze of counters, a thousand strange faces, and an awesome sense of loss. The world her mother had controlled with her presence had suddenly become a foreign place. It was the same feeling. Guerney didn't once look towards her when she walked past him on the way to the betting-window, but it was enough for her to touch base.

After the dogs passed the post in the tenth race she climbed the steps and crossed to the bar. Guerney was at the far end, propped up by an elbow, watching for her. As she reached him he handed her a beer. There was a lot of noise; people were crowding the bar trying to buy a last drink. Even so, he kept his voice low, and she had to stand close to hear him.

'In a couple of minutes a guy will go to the nearest window – just behind me – to collect his winnings. He's a German. Short, over-weight, about fifty-five. He's wearing a grey sports jacket. His wife will probably be with him – a bottle-blonde in a fur jacket.'

'I gather he's had a good night.'

'Until now. Get on the far side of him – he'll be walking back towards the stairs. You're going to have an accident. Walk into him. Fall over. Drop the glass, but try not to spill beer over him; I want you to be the focus of attention. OK?'

'OK.'

'You'll see me go past. After that, take off as fast as you reasonably can.' He nodded towards the table where he'd been sitting. 'Go and stand over there. I don't want to call attention to the fact that we're together. I'll meet you by the entrance-gate.'

She had only a couple of minutes to wait before the German arrived, his wife in tow. They were chuckling. The man in particular seemed childishly pleased. From time to time, his wife would ask: 'Wieviel hast du, Arnolf?' But her husband was too animated to listen, standing on tiptoe to look towards the head of the queue or examining his tickets, as if fate might conspire to alter the numbers on them.

318

Rachel concluded that his final bet had been a large one, and recalled that the winning dog had been returned at 8-1. She watched the pudgy figure peering up the line as if to hasten it, and the fat face concertina'd with glee. For a moment she felt a stab of remorse for what was about to happen. Then the man gazed again at his winning tickets, and her thoughts echoed the blonde wife's question: 'Is it much?'

In less than a minute, he'd reached the window. He stared at the cashier's hand as she counted his money, then scooped it up and took a couple of paces to the right, pausing to check the amount himself, his lips moving as if he were translating the sum into Deutschmarks.

Rachel lifted her beer-glass from the table. She waited until he had stuffed the notes into his wallet and walked well clear of the window before starting towards him. They met a few paces from the stairs that led to the exit. She looked over her shoulder as if seeking someone, and walked straight into the man, falling backwards with a shriek and letting her beer fly from her hand. The glass shattered. She lay on the floor as if stunned.

The German stepped back, then instinctively forward to help her up. 'Es tut mir herzlich leid,' he said. Then, again, 'Es tut mir herzlich leid,' half-turning as Guerney cannoned into him from behind, making it seem that the man's sudden halt had caused the collision.

Guerney said, 'It's OK,' and walked on, leaving the apologetic German to hoist Rachel to her feet. People had stopped to stare.

'Sind Sie OK, junge Dame?' The man's plump fingers lay on Rachel's arm. Separating the words carefully, he repeated the question in English: 'Are you all right?'

She nodded, doing her best to look dazed. 'I think so. Sorry.' She stepped back, freeing her arm. Someone started to kick the shards of glass into a pile. The onlookers continued towards the exit-doors. The hubbub of voices grew. The incident was over in less than thirty seconds. Rachel smiled reassuringly at the German, then turned and went to the steps, trying not to quicken her pace as she descended.

Guerney was standing just outside the gate. When Rachel was in sight of him, he turned and walked on, letting her follow but making it evident that he wanted to keep a distance between them. He let her catch up at Tooting Broadway tube station. He'd bought two tickets.

They changed trains once, as anonymous as any of those going home from their evenings out. Rachel felt lightheaded, her system loaded with adrenalin. She sat apart from Guerney as he'd instructed. Eventually, the German would think to check his wallet; then he'd remember the girl bumping into him. Even if he didn't know enough about pickpockets' methods to make a connection, the police certainly would.

She saw Guerney get up and go to the door of the train. When it stopped she got up, too, staying behind him until they had gained the street and crossed a few intersections, when he stopped and allowed her to catch up. They were walking south on the Gloucester Road. Guerney hadn't spoken to her since they'd stood at the stadium bar. He took her arm and they circled back along Clareville Street.

'We're booked in at the Royal Gloucester Hotel,' he told her. 'I made a call earlier. Mr and Mrs Leibowitz.' She smiled briefly. 'Our luggage has already arrived.'

'It has?'

Guerney had been gone for an hour earlier that day, leaving Rachel in the derelict house. He'd spent some of their remaining money on a large cheap suitcase and one or two other items. A cab-driver had quoted him a price for making the delivery. Then he'd phoned the hotel from a call-box, saying that he and his wife wanted to spend the day sightseeing.

When they checked in, the receptionist smiled brightly at him. 'Your luggage has been taken to your room, Mr Leibowitz.' She handed him a key. 'Four-oh-nine.'

They took the lift, Rachel leaning heavily against the mirrored wall. She said: 'It might have occurred to him – the German.' Guerney stayed silent. 'Maybe he'd've seen it in the movies. Maybe he'd had his pocket picked before. He might have checked his wallet right away.' She was staring at the carpeted floor of the lift; her tone was weary with understanding. 'I could have been stopped right there and then. Yes?' Rachel looked up for a moment, then away. 'Which is why you didn't tell me about this hotel – what you'd planned.' They reached their floor and he steered her towards the room. 'Thanks.' Her voice was barely audible.

Guerney unlocked the door of 409 and ushered her in. Rachel went first to the window, then into the bathroom. When she emerged, she said, 'I'm going to take a bath,' and pulled her clothes off in front of him, as if he wasn't there. Guerney read it for what it was: a tiny gesture of contempt.

She emerged half an hour later, wrapped in the hotel's towels. The suitcase had contained mostly ballast – a pile of newspapers that he'd foraged, cans of cheap food to give weight; but there was also a razor and shaving cream, a comb, shampoo, toothpaste and two tooth-brushes. Guerney was lounging on one of the beds, his eyes half-closed. Rachel lay on the other. The hot bath had sapped her. She looked at the little pile of toiletries he'd arranged on the table between their beds.

'Look, Simon, it doesn't matter.' He turned, and they regarded one another for a moment, as if accepting, for the first time, that the issue between them might not be capable of resolution. 'I won't suggest that we're quits, because I know it doesn't work that way.'

'You're right.' There was no aggression in his tone. 'We're both taking risks. No one can make it fair.'

She lay back, briefly, and closed her eyes; then she gathered the towels round her and walked to a table on the far side of the room where she'd left her coat. Delving into the pocket she came up with a few crumpled banknotes. 'I won,' she told him, and laughed. 'Just a few pounds. Did you?'

He shook his head, then took the German's wallet from his pocket and lobbed it on to the bed. 'In a manner of speaking.' He'd counted the money while she was taking her bath.

'How much?'

He anticipated her. 'Enough', he said, 'for a few days of good living – and a moderate clothes allowance.'

She curtsied, hoisting the hem of the towel a couple of inches and making him grin. It was a little truce.

21

The boy was wearing a blue satin posing-pouch. His body was slender, but muscled, and coated in a thin sheen of oil. He stood on a platform midway between floor and ceiling, ringed by golden bars. When the music began, pulsing and heavy, he began to dance, his buttocks clenching, his skin taut across the neat lattice of ribs. They were playing coloured lights on him, and the hard flat surface of his abdomen caught glistening pools of red and green as he flexed.

This particular Thursday, Buckroyd reflected, had possessed a bizarre symmetry. He had woken early and detected in himself the kind of mild depression that was almost indistinguishable from anger. A bad bout of misery would immobilize him; this type seemed to require movement – a sort of pointless bustle. He knew the mood well enough to understand that it often preceded some foolishness or another.

He had gone to mass, though whether out of a desire simply to *do* something, or in an effort to wipe clean an overcrowded slate, he wasn't sure. Not then, at least. Later, when he recalled what day of the week it was, he had a better idea. Since Daniel had left, many of his Thursday evenings had been spent at Elysium. The club was full and noisy as usual. Couples packed the dance-floor, lit by flickering colour like the boy above their heads. In the semi-darkness, it seemed he floated there, the product of some ingenious illusion. Buckroyd sipped his drink and watched like a window-shopper.

Rituals, he thought. The priest had taken the wafer and delivered it to Buckroyd's outstretched tongue: *The Body of*

Christ. His voice had been a conspiratorial whisper. Buckroyd had gone back to his pew and knelt there for a while, then risen from his knees to sit and watch the rest of the congregation leave. A silence descended. The statue of the Virgin had worn a frozen, endlessly merciful expression.

Blessed are the meek, Buckroyd thought, for they shall inherit whatever's left of the earth.

He signalled for another drink and allowed his eyes to meet those of the man who had been watching him for the last fifteen minutes. They smiled at one another. Buckroyd asked the barman to give the man a drink and watched the dancers for a few seconds. When he looked back, a glass was being raised to him; the smile had broadened. Soon there would be the exchange of names, some casual conversation.

Rituals.

'Peter,' the man had said. He'd been telling the truth.

In the taxi, Buckroyd had said little. He had been conscious of feeling tired and a little drunk and something else – desperate, perhaps. As he led the way from the lift to the door of his flat, the mood lifted. It wasn't the first time – this foolishness; there had been other pick-ups, other half-anonymous lovers. They didn't pierce his solitude, but neither did they make him feel regret. He thought of them as small consolations: passing pleasures that he allowed himself because there wasn't, now, anyone else to please.

'Peter,' Buckroyd said, and laid a hand on the man's arm. 'What would you like?'

Peter was young and good-looking and was aware of that. Blond hair, expensively highlighted, flopped over his brow. He had a broad open face; his skin was smooth in an almost babyish way; the smile stopped just short of being coquettish.

'Vodka,' he said. 'I think vodka would be nice. Just on the rocks. Nothing with it.' The over-emphasis was delivered gently, as if he were worried that Buckroyd might not get it right but didn't want to make a fuss.

'On its own.' Buckroyd smiled inwardly. 'No mixer.'

'That's right.' The same softness in his tone, almost a simper.

A flare of irritation touched Buckroyd as he walked towards the drinks-table, then was gone. For him there was no sharing to be had in these moments. He took, but gave nothing back. Peter's girlishness could only have mattered to him if he'd wanted to make the man real. He wasn't real. He was a concoction.

Buckroyd put ice into a glass and uncapped the vodka. He wasn't surprised to feel Peter's hand on his shoulder. The first movements between strangers, that odd pavane, were something he'd grown accustomed to.

He had a second in which to register his own name on Peter's lips: 'George' – a childish whisper; then the hand moved to his mouth and clutched, turning his head sideways and lifting it. He thought nothing. There was a brightness descending out of the lamplight, then pain and panic and shock as the glittering thing passed across his throat. Finally, there was only a terrible loosening, a drubbing blackness. He wasn't aware of the awful quaking that filled his body, of his knees rattling the drinks-table, of bottles falling. He didn't hear the sound he made – a cawing that strove in his throat and died as he died. He didn't feel the blood that soaked his chest and saturated the sleeves and shoulders of Peter's jacket.

He fell fraction by fraction, his hands extended backwards and clutching at the person who stood there. Peter crouched, letting the weight of Buckroyd's body fall on to his thighs, then supporting the arched back and rigid legs, his hand still fastened across Buckroyd's mouth. He leaned forward, enveloping the torso as it heaved and shook, and waited patiently, his eyes fixed on the gleam from one of the fallen bottles. The razor was still gripped lightly between the thumb and first two fingers of his right hand. When all movement had ceased he lowered the corpse to the floor and stood up.

'George,' he said, and shook his head. Then he went to the telephone and dialled a number.

22

Pete Ginsberg watched Paula as she watched the wolf. The enclosure was on the outer edge of the zoo, next to the green acres of Regent's Park. Strollers went to and fro; young mothers wheeled their children in baby-buggies; groups of young men played football, yelling instructions to one another. The wolf looked through them towards the horizon.

'People used to think that they never kill their own kind.' She spoke without turning her head. 'But they do, sometimes.'

'Yeah?' Ginsberg was edgy, though he couldn't have quite said why. It had something to do with power – Paula's power. She was her own weapon; he felt as if he were walking alongside something loaded and primed. And there was the way she drew him sexually. He couldn't withstand it, and the knowledge weakened him. There was something dark in her, he knew that, and it eclipsed him.

The wolf lay down and seemed to sigh. Paula turned away, leaning against the bars of the outer enclosure with her elbows, then pushing off and walking away from Ginsberg without a backward glance. He followed as if he were being led. Now and then, she paused to peer into a cage. An eagle flapped from one perch to the next, barely finding room to spread its wings.

Something was troubling her, though he had no idea what. Not boredom, nor irritation – nothing as trivial as that; something deep that she couldn't displace. He remembered her body spread against the wall of her room – the beginning of their ritual of pain. She beckoned him with it, this desire to be punished. He pictured the way she would duck her head and push her haunches out, then give a little throaty sigh as she waited for the first blow, and a rush of lust coursed in him like an electric charge. Her need made him the weaker because he couldn't exploit it, merely feed it. On the one occasion when she had allowed him to sleep beside her all night, he'd been constantly disturbed by the black choppy rhythms of her sleep: nightmares, mutterings, sharp sudden movements.

She had grown brash and withdrawn by turns. There had been no more talk of David Paschini.

'What's the next move?' he asked.

Paula shook her head as if she were too preoccupied to consider the question. The plan had been to have a hell of a good time in London, do the job and go home to a much fatter bank balance. Things hadn't worked out that way at all. Her discovery about David had unlocked a cage – just as if someone had slipped the catch of the wolf-enclosure. The creature inside was sniffing at the open gate, unsure of what freedom might mean. For years it had been confined and fed. It hadn't hunted, hadn't killed; but a wildness was gathering in its eyes as it looked towards the horizon.

Guerney was a presence to her, nothing more, but she wanted to dominate him, just as she wanted to dominate all men. But something was different this time. He matched her strength. In the dream, he had read her sexuality and used it against her. There was something in him that compelled her, and it felt like love. Only one man had roused that in her before. In her imaginings, sometimes, her father wore Guerney's face.

Ginsberg asked her a question, though she barely heard it. They were approaching the main gate of the zoo, but she didn't want to leave yet. Where else was there to go? Outings, sightseeing – one place seemed as pointless as the next. She walked through the swing-doors of the reptile-house into the blue near-darkness and went from window to window. Each tiny cubicle was dressed and lit like a miniature stage. Mostly the actors were sleeping or had gone to ground. The faces of the audience glowed as they came close to the light and peered in. When they withdrew from the glow they became shadows, voices, disembodied laughter. An invisible child ran down the centre of one gallery, a clatter of footsteps and shrieks.

Ginsberg tracked her from one window to the next until they both came to rest for a moment, watching a python shift its slow weight across the coils of its own body, thick as a man's thigh.

In there, Ginsberg thought, *that's where I am; suffocating in the dark intestine.* He allowed himself a wry smile. *Paula the python.*

He looked up, conscious of the fact that she had moved away a second or so before. Keeping the same direction round the gallery, he went after her, looking for the light-coloured linen jacket she was wearing. Bodies swam towards him out of the twilight. He experienced a moment's panic, then checked it and scanned each window in turn, carefully, along the gallery's length, knowing that she would be standing at one of them. Or at a window on the other side. Or between windows, and not visible for a moment or two.

In truth, he had known at once that she had lost him; he just hadn't owned up to the knowledge yet.

23

They would only see each other on one other occasion, though neither Guerney nor Paula could have known that.

After leaving the zoo, she'd found a taxi in Prince Albert Road and driven from there to Covent Garden where she'd watched the street performers. Afterwards, she'd wandered into Leicester Square and gone to the early showing of a film. She hadn't tried to find cover, nor had she been watching her back. It mattered little to her whether she was found or not.

Just after eight o'clock she left the cinema and began to wander, heading west but without any idea of a destination. Her mind was full of dreams. They plagued her, like urgent, unwelcome, inescapable tasks. She knew that things were being kept from her: the role of the boy; Guerney's role. They hadn't told her that she had an opponent. They hadn't told her that he could fight on her terms. Somehow he had unlocked the old dream, the dream she feared most, and had become part of it. She knew nothing of him except that they couldn't escape one another.

She walked for an hour or so until she began to feel hungry and went into a Tex-Mex restaurant with a big wooden Indian on the doorstep, surprised and pleased to find such a place. A television over the bar was playing clips from old Western movies. It was a floorboards-and-booths arrangement, the room as big as a barn and noisy with piped Country and Western music. She traversed two aisles, walking directly to a booth opposite to the one Guerney and Rachel were occupying, and sat down.

It hadn't surprised her. She'd half-known all along why she had dropped Ginsberg and what she'd been looking for. To have found him came as no shock. Most people used words like 'coincidence' and 'chance' to describe events they thought of as extraordinary – things that they only noticed in moments of crisis or of heightened sensibility – in times of illness, breakdown or bereavement. Such things happen because we make them happen; for a moment we step sideways into another world where those mysteries are commonplace. Paula Cole lived in that world most of the time. She watched Guerney's face until he felt her gaze and looked up.

Rachel sensed rather than saw his reaction. It was as if something had leaped in him, then checked. By the time she had registered this he was looking into his drink, eyes fixed on the frosted beer-glass. She knew he had turned his head from something or someone, and glanced round the restaurant for clues.

'What?' she asked.

Guerney leaned forward and spoke softly, so that his voice would lie under the music. 'It doesn't matter now. Don't worry; nothing dangerous. Don't speak for a bit.'

He turned to face Paula, who was still regarding him. Her eyes were bright, and she seemed not to blink. So there you are, Guerney, the look said. So that's who you are.

Although he was watching her face – and she his – there was no competition to find who would look away first. They appeared absorbed in one another, like secret lovers who meet, by accident, in a public place and find disguise impossible. Each knew something of the other's power, but not its purpose.

Paula lit a cigarette. When her eyes met Guerney's again she was smiling almost imperceptibly. A battle, she thought. And it's never an even match. Even people in love find that one of them is the stronger. She smoked and didn't drop her gaze. He is my enemy – that's for sure. And like all enemies he wants something of me. And his want binds us.

Guerney watched her hand rise and fall with the cigarette. Paula, he thought. The name filled his mind. Her look acknowledged the word as if he spoke it aloud. She glanced down to stub out her cigarette, then rose from the booth, her head turned from him, and walked out of the restaurant.

Rachel watched her out of the door, then faced Guerney. 'Who was she?'

'Their weapon,' he replied levelly. 'Whatever they wanted David Paschini to do – she's going to do it.'

'She is? She?' Rachel's head snapped round as if she were expecting to find Paula still at the door. 'What do you mean? How do you know that?'

'I've seen her before,' Guerney said. It was the only explanation he would give.

'We can't leave it any longer.' Alan Mountjoy's face was fierce with worry. He kept putting his whisky-glass down on the mantelpiece, then snatching it up again like an alcoholic on the brink of defeat.

Ginsberg sat motionless in one of the armchairs. 'Yes, we can. We can leave it until she comes back, or someone finds out. Why be a Boy Scout?'

'*Will* she come back?'

'How the fuck should I know? Listen, she's in a strange mood. She likes throwing a scare into people. Where the hell else would she go?'

'We ought to do something.'

'Name it.'

Mountjoy took up his drink and put it down again, untouched. 'Look for her.'

'Gimme a break.'

'I don't like any of this.'

'Is that right?'

'It's freaky. *She's* freaky.' Mountjoy collared his glass again, sipping at it this time. A silence settled in the room. 'You're screwing her, aren't you?'

Ginsberg's head snapped up. 'What're you? House-mother?'

Mountjoy gestured loosely with the glass. 'No. No. I just. . . .' He sat down in the chair opposite to Ginsberg's. 'Do *you* believe any of this stuff?'

The American shrugged. 'We'll find out, I guess. . . .' *If we find her; if she comes back.* He left that part unsaid.

An hour later, the phone rang. It was Paula. 'Fence off the dogs,' she said. 'Send Alan out to the gate. I'll be there in five minutes.' She sounded tired.

So that's who you are. She lay and tracked the patterns of light as cars climbed the hill – each, for an instant, flooding the skylight with white. His presence seemed strong, as if her memories of him consisted of more than the brief contact in the restaurant.

She had smiled at Ginsberg when he'd asked where she had been. 'Walking,' she'd said. 'And I went to a movie.'

He had pointed a finger at her. 'Never. Never again.'

Paula had continued to smile, as if listening to a boastful child. Then, as a consolation, had offered: 'The man Guerney. He'll be coming here. Tomorrow night, I think.' She'd paused, as one recollecting a stray remark. 'Yes, tomorrow; I'm almost sure.'

Ginsberg hadn't asked how she knew. She grinned and watched white light spill across the dark glass. *Never an even match.* Her father's voice said: 'Paula.' A strong hawky face hovering above her bed. She recalled how, sometimes, he used to bring her a glass of milk. His nose, his eyes; and sometimes those of Guerney, the curly hair, a gypsy's dark looks.

Even people in love. . . .

24

'Do we believe it?' For the tenth time Howard Prentiss scanned the half-page of notes compiled from Pete Ginsberg's telephone report. His question was to Ben Ascher.

There was a short silence. Ed Jeffries said: 'Sure. Why not?' He pushed his own copy of the report to one side. 'Get Cole out of the place, let Guerney jump through a few hoops to make it convincing, then' – he clapped his hands together as if trapping an insect in mid-air – 'gotcha! What's to lose?'

The silence persisted, as if he hadn't spoken. Finally Ascher said: 'You mean, if it's true, how does she know?'

Prentiss nodded. 'What is all this "psychic residue" stuff? I mean, there are other ways of people getting to know things.'

'What?' Jeffries sounded startled.

Prentiss lit a cigarette. 'She wasn't told about David Paschini – right?' Jeffries nodded. 'And she wasn't told about Guerney. She was told about the job: what she had to do, how it would be set up. She smiled, she took the money, she flew to London. OK?' Again Jeffries nodded. 'Suddenly she knows' – Prentiss held up a finger – 'about the boy' – another finger – 'Guerney' – a third finger – 'and can even tell us that Guerney plans to go to the safe house tomorrow night.'

'What are you saying?'

Prentiss made a fist of the fingers and let it fall on to the table. 'I'm asking how she knows. I'm saying that, if there

333

wasn't this psychic stuff, we'd be pretty damn worried about how she came by all that information.'

'But there is,' Ascher said. Prentiss looked at him. 'All this psychic stuff.' He reached over and worked a cigarette out of Prentiss' pack. 'Think about this, too. Would she be likely to let us know that she knew?'

'Sure – of course. Double bluff. If she *is* conning us, then the con involves letting us know; she'd be trading off her – whatever – powers.'

'Motive,' Ascher said.

Prentiss shook his head. 'Christ knows. She performs a trick, she gets rich, she comes home. You tell me.'

Ascher lit the pilfered cigarette. 'There's a place in Wisconsin called New Oxford. A boy named Billy Kappel lived there. He went to a special school because he'd suffered brain damage at birth. Billy couldn't do much. If you gave him a pan full of water and an empty pan, and asked him to fill the empty pan from the full one, he could just about handle that. If you asked him to go into the kitchen and fill the empty pan from the faucet – well, he couldn't handle that. The mechanics of it would confuse him. He couldn't read or write – that goes without saying. His apprehension of the world at large – our world – was very limited. People – teachers, parents, other kids, you know – sort of moved around Billy, looking after him, trying to help him develop a few basic skills, but knowing that he really inhabited a kind of world where few things made any real impression. It was clear that he'd spend the rest of his life that way – having to be looked after, kind of hitching a ride through the world. He was – oh – twelve at this time.

'A year before, one of the teachers at Billy's school had given her daughter a special birthday present: a car.' Ascher leaned forward and crushed out the cigarette. 'A used car. She must have mentioned it to someone at the school – another teacher, whoever. Why not? It was a big deal. A year later to the day, she was working with Billy and some other kids. Billy said to her: "It's just a year since Maisie got her car." I don't know: whatever the daughter's name was. The teacher couldn't believe it. She fetched the principal. They asked the kid some more questions. When had the teacher joined the school? She'd been there four years, but he knew the exact date. He also knew when the teacher's birthday was: on such and such a date, and that she'd be – who knows? – forty-two next birthday. Then they asked what year had she been born. Billy told them.

'They went on testing him over the next couple of days – not making an issue of it, just asking them, now and then, if he knew some fact or another. He knew the dates of all the teachers' birthdays. He knew that it was the first Sunday in March of the previous year that someone's dog had died. He knew lots of things.'

Ed Jeffries couldn't see where all this was leading, but he offered an opinion anyway. 'The kid had been faking,' he suggested.

Ascher looked at him. 'Are you listening? He was brain-damaged. In any case, that's not the point.'

'How did he know,' Prentiss said. It was a statement.

'Exactly. The teacher couldn't recall having told Billy about the car. Why would she have told him? Maybe he overheard her telling someone else – maybe – but why would it mean anything to him? Maybe he'd been around when each of the teachers had been told "Happy Birthday" by someone. Maybe he'd been fond of the dog. But even if all that was true – and no one believed it was – then the kid either has a phenomenal memory, which in theory he can't have, or he's psychic.'

'What happened?' Prentiss asked.

'Interesting. They asked questions for a couple more days. The kid's response was to close down. Not at first, but after a while. It was as if he realised that the questions were loaded. That he was being tested. He stopped answering. He went back to being brain-damaged.' Ascher paused. 'Whatever that means.'

'OK.' Prentiss waited for the connection.

'It's one example. There are lots. We've been working

with this kind of thing for a long time. It's not the world you live in, but it exists.'

'And Paula Cole inhabits it.'

'Like most psychics, she lives in both places. The difference is that when you fetch things from the icebox, and realise you've forgotten to close the door, you go back to do it. She looks at it, and it closes. No big deal – not to her, at least. You think we've sent her over there without being sure about whether or not she can do the job? No. She can do the job. Believe it.'

'And she knows about Guerney and the rest of it . . .?'

Ascher nodded. 'The way Billy knew stuff.'

'Probably.'

'Almost certainly,' Ascher told him. 'The odds are for it. It's much the likelier thing.'

Prentiss sighed. 'OK,' he said, 'we'll ship Cole out and let Guerney in. Let's hope Irving's with him.'

Ed Jeffries grinned. 'Terrific.' He stood up, as if to close the meeting. 'That's what I said all along.' Prentiss looked again at the notes of Mountjoy's phone-call and said nothing. 'Isn't that what I said we should do?' Jeffries asked.

25

Guerney had drawn a rough map of the house's floor-plan from Rachel's description. He studied it as she drove.

'I don't know whether there's an alarm,' she'd told him earlier. 'Do you suppose there is?'

'At the gate, maybe; in case of pedlars, hawkers, Jehovah's Witnesses. A warning, if it's there at all, not a trap. I won't be going in that way. If there was anything more elaborate, they'd run the risk of the dogs triggering it.'

'What about the dogs?'

'Depends who trained them.'

'Who . . .?' She'd been puzzled.

'Sometimes they're schooled to restrain, sometimes to attack. If there isn't going to be a handler around – if the dogs work on their own – it's usually attack.'

'These are on their own,' Rachel had said.

'I know.'

She stopped the car, as he'd told her to, by Hampstead Pond.

'OK.' He took her arm and drew it towards him so that he could see the face of her wristwatch. 'Remember, wait for twenty minutes – until eight-fifty.' Guerney was using the technique he'd planned on before they'd left Wapping Wall: an unlikely time, a time when people normally ate, or watched television, the innocent beginning of the evening. 'Make sure the revs don't start to die away,' he instructed. 'If the engine stops, I've got to hot wire it again.' Rachel nodded. 'If I don't show by eight-fifty, go. But not back to the hotel.'

'We've been through this, Simon.' She hadn't the first idea where she'd head for – or even whether she'd drive north or south. 'Be careful.'

He left, pressing the car door closed.

There was a raw wind blowing. Guerney came to the top of Windmill Hill, took a fix on the house, then circled until he found the fence. The heath was behind him. There was a road some thirty feet from the bank that the fence was built on. He knew, from Rachel's memory of it, that the dog-run was immediately beyond the high wooden slats. He also knew that the fence was too tall, too sturdy, to be damaged, otherwise he would have torn part of it away and simply waited for the dogs to find the gap. Tough on the inhabitants of Hampstead, perhaps, to find a pack of lethal Dobermanns roaming the streets, but an easy solution to the problem. As things stood, there was little else to do but take them on.

Guerney unzipped his jacket and took out the rudimentary grapple he'd made from a butcher's hook and a length of nylon rope. He secured it on the first throw, wrapped the rope around his left forearm – the anchor arm – and walked flat-footed up the fence, gripping the rope behind his left fist each time he made an advance, then reaching up with the left before grabbing, again, with the right. If he wanted to pause, he could double the rope just above his left elbow and take the strain one-armed.

At the top, he straddled the fence and looked down on either side. There was no one in the road to see him there. The dogs were nowhere in sight – presumably on the far side of the run. He unfixed the hook, pulled it free of the knot, let the rope fall into the run and followed it down, going at once into a crouch – knees to chin, head lowered, arms wrapped around his shins. He was still gripping the meat-hook, the larger of the curved ends pointing upwards, the hook itself tucked out of sight between his calves.

The dogs arrived almost at once. He'd known they would: that's why he hadn't yet tried to scale the mesh that enclosed the inner perimeter of the run.

The first two were so eager that they cannoned into him, winding up a sprawl of legs before righting themselves and turning. Guerney stayed still, his face pressed up against his knees. There were four in all. They circled him, backs stiff, dewlaps drawn up to show the gum, a fan of hackles hoisted across each thick set of neck muscles.

Guerney breathed slowly, a count of four on the in-breath, a count of six on the out. His eyes were closed. He dismissed the dogs as if brushing aside the image he had of them. He thought, instead, of the slow circles the buzzards had made under the sun that morning at Druid's Combe, of watching as white light coated the underside of a wing, the tips of the broad pinion feathers streaming a glow like a luminous slipstream. He saw the great birds turning and turning as if they walked on the wind, and held the picture until the movement became hypnotic, stately curves of the wide wings repeating and repeating the same track. The dogs plucked at him from time to time or rushed in to nip and worry at his arms and shoulders. Then they would back off, walking past and round one another, as if to take a look from another angle.

It wasn't so much the immobility, though that was important because the dogs would target anything that moved. It was the indifference. Guerney behaved as if they weren't there. He ought to have been man-shaped, but he wasn't; and though he smelt like a man there wasn't the acid taint of fear on him. But mostly it was his refusal to acknowledge the dogs that confused them. There wasn't the bargain that fear usually made with violence. They retreated a little way down the run. One of them sat down. For a full two minutes, they continued to watch him, seeming to expect him to do something. Then, with one accord, they turned and loped away.

Guerney sensed them go. He uncoiled at once, taking a run at the mesh and leaping to grab it as high as possible before drawing his knees up and taking a toehold in the diamond-shaped holes. He was over in a few seconds. The back of the house was in darkness. He didn't wait to study

339

it. He knew he hadn't been seen or heard. He began to walk towards the tall french windows that opened on to the orchard. It was eight minutes since he'd left the car.

Only one downstairs room was lit. Red curtains were drawn across the french windows, but someone had tugged them a little too hard, leaving a gap at one side, and a thin shaft of light fell on to the grass. Guerney ran through the scant orchard, taking a curving line that would end close to the house-wall and alongside the rod of lamplight. He moved low and stayed low, looking into the room at a point well below eye-level.

Two men were sitting at a table, playing backgammon. The night was so still, the back of the house so far from the road, that Guerney could hear the whirr of dice in the cup and the clatter as they were thrown on to the board. One of the men gave a small shout of glee and moved his counters with a swiftness born of long practice. Their heads were bowed; it was clear that the game engrossed them.

Guerney took a pace back from the french windows, at the same time reaching into his pocket for the gun. The movement brought him into contact with something that must have been there almost as soon as he'd first looked into the room. It bored into the back of his neck, unyielding and cold. A shock of adrenalin poured into his limbs, sending a sick tingle along his forearms and into his finger-ends. Three thoughts whipped through his mind almost without registering: *Oblong – an automatic*, and *The gap in the curtain – a beacon*, and then *Stupid! You stupid bastard!*

A voice said: 'Finger and thumb, Guerney: then let it drop. Don't think clever thoughts. It's shit to me whether you live or die.' The words seemed amplified by the cold air. Inside the house, the players lifted their eyes from the board; one of them, half-facing the french window, looked towards the gap in the curtain and began to laugh.

Rachel's first instinct, as the passenger-door opened, was to put the car into gear. Her second was to open her own door and run. What happened was that her foot came off the clutch and the engine stalled.

The man had gripped her high on the upper arm. Even though she was wearing a thick coat, his fingers bit into her bicep. He waited for her gasps of fear – a series of stuttering indrawn breaths – to subside. Her body was upright and rigid, head tilted backwards, chin jutting. She looked like someone who had just gone waist deep in very cold water. Gradually, her shoulders unlocked and her breathing, though it still came in little sobs, levelled. The man's grip didn't slacken – his fingertips and thumb nipping beneath the muscle. Rachel turned to look at him.

The man smiled. 'Now, then,' he said, tapping one side of his pea-jacket, 'in this pocket I've got a gun. It's got a silencer on it, so there wouldn't be a lot of noise. Something like a bottle of wine being uncorked. No one would notice.' He paused, and Rachel turned her face away from him to look through the windscreen. 'I've been told to kill you if it's necessary, and I think you ought to know that I'd quite like to. So don't look for it, because it's right here next to you. OK?' The fingers clenched, sending a rod of pain through her arm. 'OK?'

She nodded.

'Fine. What we're going to do is to get out of my side of the car. I'm going to be holding your arm, just like this . . . just like your sweetheart would. We're going to walk a little way down East Heath Road to a car and we're going to get into it. Then I'm going to handcuff you to the seat; then we're going for a short drive. I'm telling you all this so that nothing will come as a surprise and you won't make any sudden movements, or not know what to do next. OK?'

She said yes; the word was barely audible.

'Fine,' he said soothingly. 'Now – here we go.'

The wind had grown colder, or so it seemed to Rachel; colder and stronger. The river was in spate. They had driven for no more than twenty minutes, but it was as if, during that short time, winter had set in again. As she got out of the car, she reflected that a wind that strong was rare in the city. A light sharp rain had begun.

Rachel remembered passing this address on to Guerney, remembered how Ed Jeffries had given her the instructions.

'Tell him this address' – and he'd given the number in Cheyne Walk. 'Tell him it's a classy whorehouse: which it is. You can tell him about the dope, too; let him know that Paschini isn't necessarily Mr Clean. OK?'

'What's this for, Ed?' Rachel had sounded edgy. She had started out to do a little discreet digging for a friend and wound up with her shovel in an anthill. 'Am I setting him up?'

'Nah – pointing him in the wrong direction, that's all.'

She hadn't believed it, but she'd said: 'All right. Then what?'

'Then we'd like you to come down to Washington – in a few days. Nothing heavy – you know. There are some things to talk through.'

The two men holding Guerney had arrived first. The man with Rachel stopped the car close to the house, but didn't make a move to get out. He pointed to a dark-coloured Citroën parked directly in front. 'Your friend's already here. Well, well.' Rachel recognised the accent now: the soft lilt, the rolling vowels of southern Ireland. 'I think we'll just wait a wee while, shall we?' He leaned over and unlocked the handcuff that was fixed to a seat-stanchion and wrapped it round his own wrist. Then he took Rachel's hand, twining his fingers with hers, so that it appeared to be the only attachment between them.

For five minutes or so they sat there holding hands as the car grew chillier, like clandestine lovers reluctant to allow their evening to end. Then someone came out of the house and walked over to the car. A woman, tall and slender, wearing a full skirt and boots and what was clearly a very expensive sweater. A fall of blonde hair swung heavily forward as she leaned to the window, looked through at the driver, and nodded before turning on her heel and walking quickly back to the rhombus of light left by the half-open door. She wrapped her arms round her upper torso as she walked, rubbing briskly to defeat the cold.

'Now we can go.' They walked towards the house, still holding hands. The woman was standing just inside the door. She was smiling, the way a hostess might smile as guests arrived for supper, and she looked round the man to peer at Rachel in polite curiosity. As they began to walk down the hallway towards a flight of stairs, she said: 'Hello. My name's Stella.' When Rachel didn't respond, the woman quickened her pace a little, getting in front to lead the way. Upstairs there was a gallery, and a corridor, then another corridor ending in a blank wall. There were three doors to their left. Stella opened the middle one. In the room was a long sofa. Guerney was sitting at one end of it.

The Irishman unlocked the cuffs and ushered Rachel into the room, then he left. Stella remained at the door. She was smiling again.

'I'll come back with some food soon,' she said. Then, gesturing towards Guerney: 'He'll tell you what to do.' She closed the door. Rachel listened, but there was no sound of a key turning.

Guerney was looking at her, but hadn't got up. Finally, he said: 'Sorry.'

'What happened?' she asked.

'We were expected,' he said simply.

'How?'

Guerney shook his head. *Paula*, he thought, but kept it to himself. Rachel sat at the opposite end of the sofa.

'What will happen?'

Guerney had been guessing at that himself. 'They might want some information from us. We – I – have been a thorn in their side for a while. They suspect I killed a couple of their men. I knew some things I shouldn't have known. They'll ask about George and wonder whether anyone else knows what I know. They might wonder why you screwed up on the stake-out at Druid's Combe . . . your side of the story since then. It's possible they'll want to set the record straight. If so, they'll ask us questions.'

Rachel read the tone of his voice. 'You don't think they'll be too polite?'

He shrugged. 'No.'

'Then, we tell them – at least, I shall. What difference could it make?'

Guerney saw the fear in her eyes. He said: 'None. Of course.'

He knew that she could tell everything – everything that she was aware of – tell it truly, tell it to the last detail, but it wouldn't save her. No matter how convinced the questioners might be that she was giving them all she knew, they would want to be sure. They would listen to the story she told, then they would see if it held up under pain. However eager she was to help, however anxious to please, they would want to try each sentence under pain, as steel is tested with flame. They would know how to do that. Too much, and she would change her story, confess to a lie even if what she'd been telling them was all true – anything to make it stop. Too little, and she might sense them backing away from causing her real hurt. They'd look for a line somewhere between, feeling for it along her flesh, along her nerve endings; sensing it in the darkness of what they did to her.

As if catching something of his thought, she said: 'There are things I don't know' – a tremor in her voice. 'Like: Druid's Combe – the set-up; how you were so sure.'

'Instinct,' Guerney said.

'That sounds like a two-fingernail reply.' She half-smiled, but lost it.

Without looking at her, he said: 'It's the best I can do.'

There was silence. Rachel got up and walked to the window. There was a mirror set into the opposite wall and she avoided her own reflection. The window was heavily barred.

'And after the questions? If they bother with questions?'

The silence extended. Finally Guerney said: 'They'll either kill us here or take us somewhere else and kill us there. Whichever's easier.'

Rachel looked through the bars. Beyond, and two floors

344

down, there was a garden. A plane-tree was being punished by the wind.

'There's no chance you've got that wrong?'

'I suppose it's just possible that they'll demote you and ask you to take a cut in salary.'

'Yes,' she said. 'OK. What do we do?' Then, as an afterthought, she asked: 'Why haven't they' – she hunted for a word; everything sounded bad – 'started?'

'I don't know.' To the earlier question, he replied: 'There are at least three men here – my two and the man who brought you. There's a girl, Stella. Beyond that, who knows? The bars you're looking at are an impossibility. The only route out is through the door and turn right. I imagine they know that. They probably have a gun or two between them. Right now, there's little that we *can* do.'

She turned from the window, and he registered the panic. Her face was pinched. She couldn't decide what to do with her hands. Fear came off her like a leakage. She looked around the room as if judging its size and scale, and he knew what she was feeling. *This is here – not another place, but here. This house. This room. If it were another place, I wouldn't be going to die.* Her eyes travelled the walls and ceiling as if enough looking could make what she saw into another place.

Guerney watched her as she walked to and fro. Then he hoisted his feet on to the sofa and went to sleep.

26

He registered the sound of the door opening and was instantly awake. There was a movement behind him as Rachel also turned towards the noise.

A man came into the room and stopped, looking first at Guerney, then over Guerney's shoulder at Rachel. There was a smile on his lips – rueful, almost apologetic.

Because Guerney recognised him, he looked beyond to the door, expecting – for the briefest moment – to see whoever might have brought the newcomer to the room. Then he realised what the smile said, and knew that the man had come alone.

'Mr Guerney,' he inclined his head, before stepping forward and extending a hand to Rachel. 'And Miss Irving.'

Guerney recalled the light brisk tone, the careful enunciation. *Of course*, he thought. Then he spoke the words: 'Of course.'

'Ah, yes, Mr Guerney; of course. But, then, why should you think such a thing?'

Rachel was looking from one man to the other. Her eyes lit upon Guerney's and she said: 'David's father.' Then she became quiet and sat on one arm of the sofa and thought to herself: *Of course*.

Cesare Paschini smiled at Rachel and continued to look at her for a while, even after she had lowered her eyes to stare at the floor. His face grew thoughtful; then he gave a tiny start, as if bringing his thoughts back to the matter in hand. 'Well,' he said, and spread his arms in a gesture that seemed to say: 'Here we are; isn't this pleasant?' He was wearing dark elegant trousers and two sweaters in pastel colours, the outer one thrown skilfully across his shoulders, the sleeves loosely knotted. He looked lithe and vaguely sporty.

'Well,' he repeated, 'there might not be a chance for us to meet later. Somehow – I don't know why – I couldn't manage to leave this unresolved. It's a form of curiosity, I suppose. So much has happened since we met, Mr Guerney.'

Guerney remembered the urbanity from their meeting in Rome, the meticulous choice of phrase. On that occasion, Guerney had put it down to emotion held in check. Now he could hear the amusement behind it. Paschini took out a cigarette-case and offered it first to Rachel. She accepted and he lit her cigarette with courteous care. When Guerney didn't respond, Paschini turned back to Rachel. 'Perhaps you have none of your own,' he said, and left the case on a nearby coffee-table.

There was a pause while he lit his own cigarette and selected a chair. He crossed his legs, resting his right ankle on his left knee.

'My wife is dead.' He said this to Guerney. 'Also my son.' He smiled when Guerney made no response. 'I wonder whether you knew that. I can't say that I am sorry. Not that I'm glad, you understand. Just that I find it difficult to connect sorrow with such events. Much less remorse. Caroline was acting stupidly – drunk, confiding in bell-boys, growing increasingly' – he stopped to select a word – 'rash. I had not known her for such a long time, really. We met occasionally, of course, when David stayed with me. We had spoken on the telephone. When I learned of her death I had to concentrate before I could recall her face. She was a stranger. Strangers die all the time, really, don't they? Entire plane-loads of them.' He looked at Guerney for a comment, but none came.

'David – well, that is different. To some extent, I confess, I blame myself. I was weak. When Caroline and I divorced, she wanted the boy. I permitted it. Foolishly. As a result he received what some call a liberal education.

347

Indeed, he *became* liberal. Unilateralism, conservation, pacifism, racial equality. The young are such romantics, don't you think so?'

He was looking directly at Rachel as he asked the question. She said: 'You knew David was going to be approached.'

'I suggested it. Or, rather, my advice was asked and I thought it a good idea. He seemed ideal for the task that was being proposed. I was glad to help. David, it seems, was not.'

'You knew about his . . . abilities? You knew why they were asking you?'

'Of course. Yes. I am his father. I didn't divorce until he was ten.'

'And you realised that he was going to be taken – when he threatened them with exposure?'

Paschini lifted a hand, palm up. 'It was inevitable.'

'You didn't know. . . .'

'I knew that, like all young people, he listened to trivial strident music and dressed extravagantly. I wasn't aware that he'd become weak-willed, or learned to dislike money – to the point of refusing a great deal of it in return for a small undertaking, that is.'

'And now he's dead.' Rachel took another cigarette from Paschini's case and walked across to where he sat, holding her hand out for the lighter. She couldn't guess at Guerney's reaction to the knowledge. *My wife is dead. Also my son.* When the words had been spoken, she'd experienced a jolt of shock and had known that some of it must have been visible in her face, but wasn't sure quite how. It was akin to a sudden movement of physical pain: impossible to say, afterwards, what her expression might have betrayed. The boy's face came back to her; she saw his eyes, foggy with drugs, turning to watch as she entered the room with his tray. *How,* she wondered, and *who?* In the room? Somewhere else? An overdose? A bullet? Speculation sickened her but, like a lover who discovers infidelity in the loved one, she felt a terrible compulsion to know everything,

every detail, unless the imagined possibilities became endless and could torture her for ever. Then she remembered
that she didn't have for ever.

Paschini's fingers touched her palm, briefly, as he gave
her the lighter. They were cool and dry. Rachel asked only
one question: 'When? When did they kill David?'

'There was a day when you left London, I think, to join
Mr Guerney at his home. In the West Country, is it not?'
There was a pause. Paschini looked from one to the other, as
if expecting some contribution. 'In Somerset, yes. Many
things happened there; a man was killed.' Again, a short
silence. 'Well . . . I am not sure exactly when. On that day.'

'Did someone *ask* you?' Rachel spat the question.
Paschini looked at her, one eyebrow raised, as if she had
offended against etiquette.

'It was not necessary,' he said. 'I understood that David
was. . . .' He paused, as if seeking the right term, then
half-raised a hand, apologetically, to demonstrate that he
couldn't find it. '. . . not viable.'

'Do you feel anything?' Rachel lit the cigarette, and
Paschini waved a hand to let her know that she could keep
the lighter.

'A sense of waste perhaps. Annoyance at having realised
too late that I should have had the bringing-up of him
myself.'

'Why did they come to you – our people?'

'They had tested David as a child. They knew – '

'No,' Rachel interrupted. 'How did they know they could
trust you?'

'Well,' Paschini smiled thoughtfully, 'perhaps they could
not be entirely sure. But their intelligence was good. They
knew of me that I had certain friends in Italy. Few people
knew of that.'

'Fascists,' Rachel said.

Paschini looked irritated. 'Labels. Easy definitions to
permit easy responses.' He smiled and lowered his voice
slightly, as if about to divulge a secret. 'I suspect that your
former colleagues think me a little mad. They just wanted

my advice and my complicity. Now, it seems' – he spread his arms – 'they require my help. I am glad to give it. Their cause is not my cause – not quite – but in this matter we agree; and, of course, I am involved because of David – I feel some responsibility.'

'What? Because he let the team down?' Rachel's voice was sharp with anger.

'That is a silly way of putting it.'

'But no responsibility to David?' she asked waspishly.

Paschini looked at her as if she were simple-minded. 'To David? No. He is dead.'

Rachel held his eyes for a while, then looked away. He walked to the door and laid a hand on the knob. 'Well, really. I came to say this: tomorrow you will be moved. It is not terribly convenient for you to be here. In the meantime you may not leave this room.' He sighed like a bored hotelier running through the house rules for two new guests. 'There are a number of men in the house, they all have guns, they will kill you if you do not stay here. I would sooner that did not happen – there are some questions to be asked of you; but if it must happen it will.' He opened the door. 'I think we will see one another again, but not, perhaps, with an opportunity to chat.' He paused in the doorway, briefly, then smiled and shrugged and said, 'Well . . .,' in a reflective, almost whimsical manner, then closed the door very softly, as someone might who was attempting not to disturb a sleeping child.

Rachel regarded Guerney quizzically, then retreated to the barred window and looked out at the blackness. There was a garden and a tree at the end of it; beyond that the dim glow from other windows. She watched a plane go past, low, its signal-lights blinking. After a minute or two, she said: 'You didn't have a hell of a lot to say.'

'That's right.'

'What was his motive?'

'I think he was just digging a little. Trying to gauge what we know – how much, how crucial, that sort of thing.'

Neither of them mentioned David Paschini's death,

though it lay between them like a burden that neither could yet pick up. Guerney was dizzied by it. He knew that it was unfathomable to him, but knew, also, how dangerous it would be – here, now – to let its implications warp his concentration. Fleetingly, he saw the boy's face reflected in reflected blue, the mouth working, wind stripping flesh from the bone. He saw the face again, racked by exertion, the extended arms, the limp mask bearing Guerney's own features falling from his fingers. He heard the voice speaking directly to him, calling his name. *Guerney, Guerney, Guerney.*

You were dead, he thought. Dead, dead, dead.

Rachel was speaking. 'What about the National Socialist shit?'

Guerney shrugged. 'Oh, I'm sure he believes it. There's a logic to be found – new money made by diligence and a few carefully forged contacts. There's a point at which all financial opinions are political opinions to some extent. New money tends to go hand in hand with contempt. So does power – same thing. A desire for discipline, efficiency, societies run like machines . . . you know the stuff.' He sounded impatient with his own theories. 'The real point of it all was to try to find out whether or not we knew that Caroline and David were dead, what David was supposed to be here for – that kind of thing.'

'Why? I mean. . . .' She raised a hand – an almost supplicatory gesture – because she didn't want to say what was in her mind.

He said: 'I expect Paschini's antennae are pretty sensitive. It's one method of gaining information – deduction.'

It wasn't quite true, and Guerney knew it. Paschini had been trying to fix on one item of truth – any single fact – that Guerney and Rachel knew about but weren't openly admitting. But his purpose was not simply to discover that. In itself, it would be unimportant. He needed some yardstick for others that they would – oh, certainly would – tell him; wanted to know how and where to apply pressure in order to get back the truth. Guerney knew what

Paschini had meant when he'd said that they would meet again, though not for a chat. He wondered how soon the moment would arrive.

They went for some time without speaking. Guerney stretched his legs out before him, folded his arms on his chest and closed his eyes. Rachel knew that he wasn't sleeping. She watched the tree rolling in the wind, a dark shape on a dark background, and tried to imagine the noise it would be making. After she had been standing there for five minutes or so, one of the house-lights, far beyond, went out. The event seemed to dismiss her, and she returned to the sofa, taking one of Paschini's cigarettes. She exhaled smoke and picked at a loose flake of skin alongside the quick of her left thumb, concentrating on the operation closely, slitting one eye against the column of smoke from the cigarette.

'Do you see any way out?' she asked.

Guerney looked across at her. He just said, 'No,' and she nodded, tweezering the fragment of skin with her nails.

The phone-call on the priority line had come at ten minutes past nine. William Prior had taken it – not speaking, apart from one phrase, and listening for only a few seconds – then returned to his dinner guests.

The table-talk had been of a production of *Ariadne auf Naxos* which everyone had seen and no one had liked. Prior rejoined the table and listened to the opinions going back and forth. He took pleasure in his fortnightly dinner-parties. By turning up, his guests acknowledged their debts to him. Over there was an art dealer who knew he must phone Prior if a Poussin came into his possession. Further to Prior's right sat a gossip columnist who was always happy to push some career or another up to the brink and watch it topple over. Prior knew who to cultivate and how to control them. He considered it a marvellous bonus that among them were some whose company he enjoyed. It made the transactions so much more civilised.

He saw them settled in the drawing-room with coffee and brandy before excusing himself once more and going to his study. In a faintly malicious moment, he hoped that dinner was being eaten somewhat later at the Wiltshire number he was about to dial. Politicians were bloody amateurs – he'd always thought so. Sometimes he'd even been heard to say it out loud. It would be better if civil servants could be allowed to manage matters unimpeded – even if their masters happened to be of the correct persuasion. There wouldn't be so many messes. There would be consistency.

The ringing tone sounded fifteen times before the receiver was lifted. Prior smiled, though his voice bore no trace of it. 'Good evening, Minister,' he said. 'There's some rather pleasant news.'

Prior had taken his brandy with him to the phone. He sipped it from time to time, when the other man spoke.

Her real name was Janet, though almost nobody knew that. She had re-christened herself Stella a long time ago. It had been her play-name as a little girl: '. . . and I'll be Stella. . . .' The Stella she had imagined was beautiful. Her long blonde hair fell across her face in a fragile veil, and she wore perfect clothes. People worshipped her.

In her teens the dreams had begun to come true. It seemed that she grew lovelier by the month. To some people, she was the centre of the world; she realised it and loved it. When she was fifteen, she made love with a boy four years older. She lay on her parents' bed and felt what was happening to her, and wanted to go on feeling it for ever. But even as she discovered that, she was discovering something better – the look of ungovernable desire on the boy's face, and the look of gratitude; his weakness, her strength; his enslavement, her gain. It had made her rich.

She walked upstairs and balanced the tray against the door-frame with her hip so that she could turn the handle. When she went in, they were sitting on the sofa side by side. Guerney with his eyes closed, Rachel smoking and gazing into space. Like tired travellers, Stella thought, with just one stage of the journey left to go.

Guerney opened his eyes, but didn't move. Rachel

353

watched her cross the room and set the tray down on a table to the left of the sofa. She gestured at the food as if to say: *Help yourselves*. There was smoked salmon, a salad, fruit, a bottle of champagne and three glasses. Stella smiled.

'We thought you might like to eat something,' she said. Then, as if a formality had been dispensed with: 'Hello, Simon.' Her voice was warm and bore a trace of pleasant laughter.

Rachel looked at Guerney, a question in her gaze. He got up and walked across to the tray, took a segment of lemon, squeezed it on to a strip of smoked salmon, put brown bread on either side to make a sandwich and took a large bite. Without looking at either of the women he began to open the champagne. Through a mouthful of food he said: 'This is Stella. When she's not working as a kitchen maid she fucks men for money.'

Stella smiled. When she turned towards him her eyes seemed to convey curiosity and a genuine fondness. He passed in front of her to take a glass of champagne to Rachel, who asked: 'Do you?'

The women looked at one another appraisingly. 'For money,' Stella said eventually, 'for favours, for information, for gifts, for barter – for many reasons.' Her timing was excellent. 'Often for pleasure.'

Rachel nodded. 'I see.' There was something between them that only Stella properly understood. 'Well, why not?' Rachel drank some champagne. 'This is a brothel after all.'

Stella laughed. Her amusement appeared genuine – as if she were demonstrating that she wouldn't allow herself to be made angry. 'Yes. Other things happen here. Business deals. Gambling. Sweet dreams.' She pointed towards the tray. 'Good food.'

Rachel went to the tray and folded some of the plump pink fish into a slice of bread. She was surprised to find that she had an appetite. The third glass stood empty on the tray, its purpose obvious. Rachel poured champagne and held it out to Stella.

'Thank you. I have eaten, but I must wait until you have

finished and take the tray back.' She gestured. 'The bottle
. . . you know. I thought you wouldn't mind if I drank a
glass of champagne with you. It's very good.' She took a sip
as if to confirm this.

'What's it like?' Rachel uttered the question in an offhand
way. Her eyes slid across to where Guerney sat on the sofa.

Stella giggled. 'You mean you've never done it?'

'Not for money.'

'It's more or less the same as when you do it for fun.'

'Is it?'

'More or less.'

'Suppose you do it for love?'

Stella's face clouded over, as if Rachel had broken the
rules in some way, though she didn't seem distressed by the
idea – annoyed perhaps. Rachel didn't trade off the taunt.
She asked: 'Do you usually come?'

'It depends.' Stella's tone became friendly and informa-
tive – the specialist fielding questions on her subject.

'On what?'

'On whether I can concentrate on myself or not.' Rachel
remained silent. 'You know what I mean,' Stella said. She
raised her glass and sipped. 'It doesn't always involve
screwing, of course. I mean, often not. Some of them can't.'

'What do they want?' Rachel asked. She was conscious of
just how bizzare the conversation was, but to have it at all
seemed some kind of defence. It made the room another
place.

Stella's eyes widened. 'Sex. It's not necessarily a matter
of' – she spoke the word in a hollow voice, like someone
passing sentence – 'copulation. I've got a rather aged mer-
chant banker who likes me to take my clothes off and sit at a
dressing-table combing my hair while he throws cream
éclairs at my back. Mr Duncan,' she added unnecessarily,
'nice man. He always loses at poker, but I don't think he
minds. Lots of them are like that.' She laughed girlishly and
put her fingers briefly across her mouth.

Rachel suddenly became frightened – was reminded of
her fear. Stella's preoccupation was so clearly with herself

355

that it forced Rachel to think of what might happen soon, to her and to Guerney. The other woman's indifference was eerie. She turned away to hide her distress and caught Guerney's eye. He nodded, very slightly, and raised his eyebrows. The expression meant: *Don't stop.*

What does he want? she wondered.

He wanted Stella distracted. He wanted some time.

He reasoned that the girl had come to the room pretty much on her own account. Paschini wouldn't have objected – probably would have scarcely noticed. She wasn't there to gain information or for any purpose of that sort. Her reasons were her own. There was something of the narcissist in her, and something of the sadist. She liked herself; she liked power; but, for all that, she was small fry. She went with the house: cards, coke, girls. He remembered her slight pique – almost puzzlement – when he'd turned her down that time. What could have brought her here with her picnic of delicacies but curiosity and exhibitionism?

He'd thought it through. He'd been thinking it through since they had brought him to Cheyne Walk. Two men with him, one with Rachel. And Paschini. Possibly others. The room they were in was discreetly foolproof. Outside the room, to the left, a blank wall; to the right a corridor that led to stairs. One man at the end of the corridor, perhaps, and one – maybe more – at the foot of the stairs. Impossible. It was like being in the furthest of a series of locked boxes. Their only way clear was to enlist someone. And the only person available was Stella.

He put together what he knew of her – the indifference that went with self-love, the amorality. He glanced at her as she poured more champagne and saw the expensive clothes that her figure held to a perfect line, the immaculately tousled hair that fell across her cheek as she stooped to grasp the bottle. He heard her voice saying: *The saddest thing in my life is that I can't make love to me.*

Not bribery; and in any case he had nothing to bribe her with. Not the promise of gain; he had nothing she wanted.

356

Certainly not guilt; there was nothing in her to respond to that. Fear, he reasoned. And fear proceeds from knowledge.

The women were sitting close to one another, Rachel with her head slightly inclined, like a confidante. The pose was deceptive. Guerney could see the tension in her neck and shoulders, the way she held herself almost flexed against a desire to tremble. At that moment, it was Rachel who owned the fear.

'. . . why . . .,' he heard Rachel say; and '. . . how did you . . .?'

'. . . who would think . . . only someone . . .' Fragments of Stella's reply. '. . . there's nothing they can't ask for. . . .'

He got up and went past them to the table. Stella's back was to him; she was sitting on the sofa's arm like a hostess pausing for a while before moving on to another set of guests.

Guerney was wearing a sweater under the blouson jacket, part of what they'd acquired with the fat German's winnings. Once he was fully behind Stella, he slipped his champagne-flute under the two garments, stooped so that the material wrapped the glass, then squeezed sharply with his free hand. The glass broke silently. When he removed it, he saw that the line of weakness had run from just above the stem to a point halfway up the bowl. He was left with a two-edged dagger of glass protruding from the base.

Turning, he wound a hand into Stella's hair and dragged her head back so that she could see the weapon. Something between a gasp and a yell started in her throat. He said, 'No noise,' speaking quickly and sharply; then he laid the cutting edge of glass against her face.

There was a long silence. Rachel got up from the sofa and backed off as if she were releasing her touch, very delicately, from a structure that threatened to topple. Her eyes were on Stella, who was breathing rapidly and staring straight up at the ceiling. Guerney held the broken glass very still, his knuckles braced on the girl's cheek.

When she spoke it was a whisper – 'Don't cut me' – and Guerney knew he had got it right.

He allowed another pause, as if he couldn't quite decide what to do. Finally he said: 'You don't know why we're here.'

She started to shake her head and felt the glass. 'No.' Again, a whisper.

'A boy was kidnapped. Did you know that? Paschini's son. His name was David.'

'No.'

'He's dead now. They killed him because he wouldn't help them with something. Do you know what it was?'

'No.'

Guerney slackened his grip, letting her lower her head. He kept his fingers knotted into the hair on her nape and turned her face to his so that she looked straight into his eyes, but could also see the extended arm that held the shard of glass.

Then he told her. About Caroline, about David, about their deaths. He told her who had made those things happen. He told her about Arthur Meadows and, particularly, told her everything that Meadows had said. He told her that someone else, a young woman, had been imported to do what David had refused to do. He made her understand that it wasn't so much his – and Rachel's – nuisance value that made them dangerous; they were going to be killed because they knew the things that he had just told her. Telling her all this took about five minutes. As he was speaking he wondered how long she was supposed to be away, or whether anyone was bothering to notice.

'You understand why I've told you this?'

The remark caused her to understand. Fear sprang into her face like a blush.

'Please,' she said. 'I can't. Don't make me.'

'You must. There's no alternative.'

She struggled with the idea, her mind turning this way and that as she sought a way out. 'If they tell me that you've told them I know. . . .' She stopped because it had begun to sound like a riddle. 'Why should they think you have told me? What for?'

'For this. To make you help us. That's what I'll tell them.'

'I'll say no.'

'They'll believe me, not you.'

'Why? Why should they?'

Stella and Guerney faced one another, their voices low, their expressions solemn, response following response as if they were exchanging marriage vows.

Guerney sighed. 'Before they kill me, they'll ask me questions. Then they'll want to be sure that the answers I give are true. So they'll probably torture me. If I tell them that you know what you know, then eventually they'll believe me.' He paused. 'And, if they weren't sure, they could always find out from you in the same way. And even if they were still in doubt after that – well, the doubt alone would be enough to make them kill you. They can't leave anything to chance, you see; and I really don't think you would be that much of a loss.' Again he paused. 'Would you?'

Rachel watched the other woman and saw how the elegance had been destroyed by fear. The flow of limb into limb, the calmness that beauty possesses, the poise, had been rendered awkward. There was something slack and uncontrolled there, something raw. It was embarrassing.

'How many in the house?' Guerney asked.

Stella didn't reply. She looked at him for a time. His expression seemed almost gentle. 'Five.'

'Where?'

'One in the corridor – at the head of the stairs.'

'In sight of this room?'

'Yes.'

'And?'

'Two at the foot of the stairs, just to the left, by the banister. Paschini and another in the lounge.'

'The room you took me to?'

'Yes.'

'What happens in there?'

359

'People talk business, usually. They're using the phone sometimes, I think. Paschini and the other man.'

'The card rooms?'

'Two. They're both downstairs.'

'How many rooms upstairs?'

'Five bedrooms. A sitting-room.'

'Three of the bedrooms are in this corridor?'

'Yes.'

'Next to one another?'

'Yes.'

Guerney got up, still holding Stella's hair, the glass still to her cheek, and led her to the mirror opposite the window. The woman looked at herself blankly, as if failing to recognise what she saw.

'Is that a two-way mirror?'

'Yes.'

He'd been certain that it was – a risk he'd had to take. 'Who was watching us?'

'Paschini – just before he came in here.'

Guerney's reflection stood behind hers. 'Where's the one that allows people in this room to see the next?'

She held one arm out behind her and pointed. They both looked into the mirror, following her extended finger to the image of the thing she was pointing at. Then they turned and watched while Rachel lifted one corner of a reproduction Matisse. The mirror lay beneath.

'I can't see anything,' Rachel said.

'It's a matter of where the light is,' Stella was still whispering. 'If the light's on in there and off in here, it works.'

Guerney walked her back to the sofa and sat down next to her. 'Now,' he said. 'I'm going to tell you what to do next.' She didn't move her head or look towards him. He took the glass away from her face and leaned close.

'Listen,' he said, 'listen,' and put his mouth next to her ear, speaking softly, like someone who adored her.

There was a thin triangle of light on the polished oak of the sideboard where the drinks were kept. Paula thought, *I'd like a drink*, but she stared at the sliver of light and made no move to rise.

Pete Ginsberg was sitting near to her; Alan Mountjoy was at the dining-table dealing a hand of patience. Mountjoy spoke, then Ginsberg.

'They made the call. We won't have to.'

'To Jeffries?'

'Yeah.'

'Will he call us?'

'It's possible. Just to check things out.' Mountjoy looked at his watch. 'Soon, if he does.'

She couldn't find the source, but thought it might be the tall standard lamp in the far corner of the room. *If I had a drink*, she thought, *I'd have a whisky*.

Mountjoy laid his cards out; he was whistling, reedily, through his teeth.

Ginsberg got up and peered over Mountjoy's shoulder for a moment, watching the fall of the cards. 'What did they say?'

'Nothing much. The girl was in a car not far away. Guerney came in the tradesman's entrance and wound up with a gun in his ear.' Mountjoy laughed. 'Surprise.'

The sound on the restaurant's television had been switched down. Hunkered behind a rock, two good guys had fired silent bullets at the bad guys. A Tanya Tucker number had been on the PA system. She had traversed two aisles and found him at once. Of course she had. His dark curly hair and hard profile; like a gypsy. It hadn't been chance. She knew that sort of thing was never chance. She remembered his face in the dream, his hands on her throat.

'What happens next?' Mountjoy swapped the position of two cards.

Ginsberg drew a finger across his throat. 'Eventually.'

'Just three days,' Mountjoy observed.

'Guerney,' David had told her. His flayed head glistened; the image in the window had trembled as the glass flexed in the fierce wind. 'Guerney. Guerney. Guerney.'

'Three days,' Ginsberg confirmed. He'd be glad when

the whole damn business was over. Then he could get back to the States and forget things. Except that he knew there were things he wouldn't easily forget. Things that Paula had started up in him. Things he didn't like and couldn't easily resist.

A tiny rainbow from the lawn sprinkler. The hedge-trimmer lashing like an enraged snake.

Paula felt the beginning of a headache, the pain nibbling at her, just above the eye.

Mountjoy got up. 'Anyone want a drink?' he asked. As he crossed to the sideboard, the triangle of light disappeared.

Three days, she remembered and put her fingertips to her brow.

'Whisky?' Mountjoy held up the bottle like someone in a commercial.

For about an hour, Rachel faked sleep as Guerney had told her to; then she fell asleep, as if some alchemy in her body had converted tension and fear into a thick sugary drug.

Guerney stayed awake. The light in the room was on a dimmer switch, and he'd turned it low to give the impression that, perhaps, he and Rachel had decided to try to get some rest, but also to make the view through the two-way mirror a dim one.

His eyes were lightly closed so that his facial muscles didn't twitch. He half-lay with the small of his back supported by the edge of the sofa's cushion, and listened carefully. At the same time he ran through the action again, bringing into his mind everything he could of the layout of the house in order to rehearse what he'd planned. He occupied the event as a sleeper occupies his dream. He heard the voices, sensed the anger, saw the small sudden movement, felt the cold night air strike his face. He projected his thought to the moment. It was his way of getting the drop on reality.

He didn't know it would happen. Not exactly. 'When it seems safe,' he'd told Stella. In truth, he didn't know *whether* it would happen. At the edge of his listening, he could hear Rachel's low steady breathing. Their options had narrowed, now, to a single possibility.

'So. Three days, right?' Ed Jeffries checked the date on his wristwatch. He didn't need reminding.

Prentiss said: 'Who phoned?'

'Paschini.'

'And they're secure.' Prentiss' voice sounded thoughtful; he wasn't really asking a question.

'You bet.' Jeffries grinned, but the grin kept threatening to fall away. 'Secure. Tight. No problem.' He tweaked a cigarette from Prentiss' pack, as if the familiarity might afford him some protection. Then he said, 'I would never have believed it,' and laughed and shook his head, trying for a casual shrug in the way he spoke.

'You said she wouldn't turn.' Prentiss stretched out an arm and put the pack out of reach. Jeffries hadn't got a match. He sat a couple of places from Prentiss at the meeting-room table, and held the unlit cigarette cupped in his hand. 'I had your guarantee.'

Jeffries sighed. 'If you'd told me, I would never have believed it.'

'You believe it now, don't you?'

Jeffries spotted some book-matches on a small table by the wall and fetched them, lighting his cigarette with a fast snap-tear-flourish.

'Who could know for certain?' He raised his eyebrows and widened his eyes; his shoulders lifted to amplify the gesture. 'Huh? Tell me. For *certain*.' There was a pause. 'No one. Not until she was there in the car blasting away like Annie fucking Oakley.'

Jeffries drew on the cigarette and shook his head, letting smoke out of his lungs in a swathe that went left and right with the motion. 'Hell, I'm not psychic.' He thought about what he'd said and began to laugh.

'In any case,' Prentiss said, 'we're not in any doubt now.'

'I guess not.' The laugh was still on Jeffries' lips. 'I guess not.'

'You said she wouldn't turn.' Prentiss' face was like stone. 'Didn't you?'

A door opened and closed with immense softness. Guerney heard nothing else for a short while. Then he caught the faint low timbre of a man's voice.

He got up and went over to where Rachel sat on the other end of the sofa, her head tilted onto her cocked fist, and put a hand over her mouth. Her eyes opened. She looked up at him, then across to the picture on the wall. Guerney nodded.

While he lifted down the picture, Rachel turned the dimmer switch so that the light shrank. Stella was standing quite close to the mirror and almost facing it. The man was a little to one side. He was looking at Stella. She had kicked off her shoes and unzipped her skirt, letting it fall to the floor. She was stepping out of the crumple of material as Guerney looked through. The sweater was long and heavy, falling to just below her hip-bones. She turned to flick the skirt away with one foot. The man's eyes went to the neat under-curve of her buttocks, just visible beneath the sweater's ribbing, plump where they met her thighs, divided by a tiny vee of peach-coloured satin. Her legs were long and tanned and perfectly slender. She turned back, presenting those naked legs, the rest of her body hidden beneath the sweater.

The man stepped forward. She put an arm out to restrain him – flat-handed against his chest – then got close enough to undo his zipper. His back was to the mirror, but Guerney saw her shoulder and upper arm moving like someone locating an object underwater.

As the man lifted his arms to hold her she broke the pose, smiling at him, and slipped his jacket off, easing it over his shoulders and on to the floor. Then she said something, and smiled, and lowered herself in front of him.

After he had taken the broken glass away from her face and told her what she had to do she had smiled. Not that there had been any mirth in her face. Then he'd aked her a few questions to make sure she'd taken it all in.

364

'When do you do it?'

'When it's safe.'

'Why do you go into that room, not the one you can see us from?'

'Paschini's got the key to the other room.' Then she'd added: 'He won't ask why.'

'What's essential?'

'That you see where the gun is – shoulder holster, belt, wherever.'

'How will you make him do it?' A different kind of question.

'Don't worry,' she'd said. 'You don't have to worry on that score. I'd better go. I've been here too long.'

She stood up and stepped back, stripping the sweater in a single fluent motion, her breasts springing free as the ribbing passed over them. Then she turned and walked to the bed in the centre of the room and stood straight-legged to free herself of the peach-coloured briefs. She flicked them over her shoulder, but kept her back to the man. Her blonde hair hung like a screen.

He took his clothes off rapidly, unclipping the holstered gun from the back of his belt, and left them where they fell. The gun he tossed on to the bed. Stella's head turned the merest fraction as it bounced on the coverlet.

The man looked foolish as he crossed the room. He was tall, but heavy in the waist, and waddled slightly; his shoulders and upper arms were flecked with hair. He embraced Stella from behind – one hand reaching for a breast, the other descending – then turned her towards him so that they stood in profile. The fat bulb of his belly with the arching erection beneath it looked gross.

Rachel peered through the mirror like someone observing an operation. Guerney had to tap her arm and point before she went to the door. He watched as she turned the handle slowly, eased the door open a fraction, then closed it again without releasing the spring. She gripped the handle with both hands to make sure that it didn't slip.

Guerney looked back into the other room. The man lay between Stella's splayed legs, his hips thumping. She had her hand at the back of his head, holding his face into the angle of her shoulder and neck. She was speaking.

Guerney remembered the Sardinian shepherds, their savage distraction. He'd learned that lesson. All the time he'd been talking to Stella earlier, coaching and threatening, he'd had in his mind the picture of the diplomat's wife slammed across the table in the tiny lamp-lit hut and the rapt attention of the three bandits. Stella's weakness came out of fear. And his – this man who banged and slapped at her with his quivering hips – his weakness came from appetite. Guerney could trade off weakness.

He turned and walked rapidly to the door. Rachel pulled it open, her silent arrangement of the handle allowing him the precise moment. She closed it behind him.

He made no noise as he entered the next room. Stella saw him. Her legs closed on the man's back at the base of his spine. Guerney thumbed back the trigger strap and flicked his wrist, sending the holster across the room. Stella looked up at him. Her face was a blank. The man whacked at her, oblivious to anything but sensation. He groaned. The groan became a soft crowing.

Guerney grabbed the man's hair and jerked his head back hard, ramming the gunbarrel into his open mouth. The man's head was lifted and turned so that he could see Guerney and the extended arm that held the gun; his body was still locked with Stella's and spasming with his climax. An odd grinding sound came from his throat, like something mechanical.

Guerney had taken two teeth out with the gun, and the man was spouting blood over his chin, putting red splash marks on Stella's breasts and ribs. She levered herself up on her elbows and pulled away leaving him beached. As Guerney turned the man, a last gush of semen dabbed on to his naked thigh.

'Keep quiet.'

The man was watching Guerney's eyes. He nodded. Guerney took the gun from his mouth and turned him on to his stomach again, then handed the gun to Stella.

'If you make a noise or try to get up, she'll have to shoot you.' His mouth was close to the man's head, his voice barely audible to Stella. Again the man nodded. When Guerney touched his forearms, he lifted them as a child will lift its arms for the arms of a coat held ready. He was expecting to be tied up.

Guerney crossed the arms, as you would to tie them, but knelt on them instead. He leaned forward, winding his own arms in a lock on the man's throat and the back of his head, then yanked back, twisting and pulling to the side with enormous violence, but still bearing down with his knee. The neck broke.

Guerney got off the naked body and took the gun from Stella. 'Put your clothes on,' he instructed.

While she did that, he looked into the mirror, staring Rachel out, expressionless.

The men at the foot of the stairs had been joined by a third – the Irishman. They were sitting at a table that had been set up in the broad corridor and placed alongside the staircase. Beer-cans were grouped neatly at the table's centre. The men were talking together, sometimes laughing softly. They looked easy in their work. A gun with a silencer attachment lay close to the beer-cans.

Guerney sent Stella down. His bird's-eye view told him that he would need to descend at least half the staircase to control things.

As she rounded the banister, she spoke. The Irishman had glanced up as she'd started to descend the stairs; now he smiled, looking her up and down.

'OK?' he asked.

'Fine.' Stella returned the smile. Then her gaze fixed on a point just behind the man's ear, but a little lower than the lobe – as if at his shirt collar close to the side of his neck. She put out a hand and took a step towards him, saying: 'Keep still.'

There are two moments that will fix a man. The first mindless outrush of piss as he stands spraddle-legged and relaxes, and the instruction *Keep still* as someone advances to pick something – an insect, something – away from his collar or hair.

Stella moved to him, her index finger and thumb almost touching his face. He froze. The others watched. People always watch, in the same way that they will follow someone else's skyward stare. Their companion looked ahead, fixedly, like someone having his bow-tie adjusted.

When Guerney's arm came over the banister, directly level with their heads, they started, but didn't get out of their chairs. They knew enough to avoid doing that.

'Sit on your hands.'

Guerney waited until they had done it, then inclined his head, telling Stella to pick up the gun. She lifted it by the silencer, but didn't make the mistake of trying to pass it to him over the banister. She circled the table and handed it to him as he came down the last three stairs. Rachel arrived behind him, and he passed the gun he'd been holding to her. She moved to be a little way off from the group at the table, backing across the corridor until she felt her shoulders touch the wall, then held the gun two-handed and stiff-armed to put all three men in her arc of fire. Stella walked to where the corridor turned and led off to the left. Guerney went with her, but stopped just short of the corner. Stella looked at him, and he nodded. She walked away out of sight.

A few minutes later they heard Paschini's voice: 'What else did she say?'

Then Stella's: 'Nothing. Just that she wants to talk to you.'

Guerney, Rachel, the three men – the whole tableau stiffened, as if a noose of tension circled them and had suddenly drawn tighter. Rachel shifted her feet slightly and flexed her arms – it was like a nudge, a reminder. The men seemed to stare more intently at the table, each with his head half-bent. A violence lay in their stillness like the violence of a sprinter about to come off his blocks. Guerney brought his gun up to face-level, the barrel pointing at the ceiling.

'About?' Paschini sounded brisk and a little irritated.

'She wouldn't tell me.'

Paschini said, 'All right, all right,' and rounded the corner.

Guerney swung his arms, bringing the gun out so that it rapped Paschini across the eyes as he stepped into view; then he took a forward step to counter Paschini's natural instinct to hop backwards. The gun stayed an inch from the Italian's face.

He said, 'Ah!' very sharply, like someone who has inadvertently touched a hot plate. Then his shoulders dropped. 'I should have known better.'

Guerney walked behind him and quickly felt for a weapon. Then he moved closer and slid his free hand under the man's hair, upwards from the nape, taking a tight grip. Paschini felt the skin by his eyes draw back. Guerney slid past the table, putting himself and his captive closer to the street-door. 'Car-keys,' he said.

One of the men dropped a set on to the table, and Stella collected them.

'Make sure,' Guerney told her. She returned within a minute and nodded at him. He looked towards Rachel who crabbed across to where he stood, still keeping the men at the table under the barrel of her gun. She and Guerney would make a switch – her gun going to the back of Paschini's head, his swinging out to cover the table. As they began it, Paschini dropped like a stunned steer.

The men had been waiting for that, or for something like it. The Irishman rose swiftly, reaching to his belt and back again as his arm extended in a fast backhanded swipe. There came a rapid double click as the blade shook out, and he punched upward. The other two were on the move.

Guerney swayed backwards and fired – a snap shot that took the Irishman's cheekbone away. His head snapped back, and the second bullet smashed his thorax. Guerney

369

traversed the gun, firing in a line across the others' approach. A lucky shot found the bridge of one man's nose, hurling him sideways across the table as half his face caved in. The other had stayed back to draw his gun. It was clear of the holster. Guerney aimed at the broadest target, but took the man left of the abdomen, somewhere around the hip. He pitched forward towards the table but grabbed the rail of a chair to right himself and tried to raise his gun again. Guerney fired rapidly, three times, grouping two just below the sternum, the third a little higher. The man went back to the wall, taking the chair with him, then fell forward over it, face to the floor, legs hoisted on its back, like a diver frozen in flight.

Paschini was sitting on the floor. Rachel stood above him, the barrel of her gun pressed to the crown of his head. As Guerney walked towards her, she saw the knife protruding from his left arm, halfway between elbow and shoulder. It was angled downwards following the direction of the man's strike.

He said, 'See if it's all right,' and nodded towards the door. Paschini sat patiently, staring at Guerney's gun hand.

Rachel came back. 'Nothing,' she said. 'A few people, a few cars.'

Directly behind Guerney there was carnage. Two faces wrecked and pulpy; the diver checked in space; blood splashed around like paint. Rachel coughed, almost a sob. 'She's standing by the car. She ran out when things started. She doesn't seem able to move, but I've taken the key anyway.'

'There's a cupboard near the door.' Guerney's eyes didn't leave Paschini. 'There might be a coat or something.'

She looked and came back with a wide-skirted raincoat.

'Put it over my shoulders.'

She hung it there, arranging the left side carefully.

'Walk ahead of me,' he said. 'If you move too fast, I'll kill you.'

'I know,' said Paschini, and got to his feet.

*   *   *

370

They sat in the back seat together. Rachel drove with Stella beside her. She'd had pretty much to kick the blonde girl into the passenger-seat. Guerney had said, 'Her, too,' but Stella had been rigid, her knees and hips locked.

Odd, Rachel thought. Why that moment? She plays hostess to a condemned couple, screws an ape, watches Guerney kill him, distracts the guards with a nicely done charade, lures Paschini into the open, then finally goes into shock when someone gets shot. She imagined what it must have cost the girl to keep going – the weight of terror dammed up in her while she did her striptease, felt the man inside her, walked downstairs, summoned Paschini. The bullets that had opened the terrible wounds in those men had also breached the dam.

Stella stared through the windscreen. Her hands quivered in her lap.

27

The residents of Ash Road had stopped campaigning long ago. So had the people who lived in Elm Road, Beech Road, Hawthorn Road, Hornbeam Avenue and Lime Crescent. They had discovered that the little man never wins; and they had discovered that they were very little men. Those who could afford to sold their homes, even taking the risk of moving to a new address and leaving the estate agents to get the best price. The rest endured. Sometimes the empty houses were occupied by squatters, though even they found conditions in Ash Road not to their liking. It was directly under the Heathrow flight-path and close to the airport. Very close. Hell, it was virtually at the end of the runway. When a plane went over, it sounded like the end of the world and houses shook. A plane went over about every two minutes.

It hadn't always been like that. Heathrow hadn't always been the busiest airport in the world. There hadn't always been that many planes. It used to be a nuisance. Now there were seven houses in Ash Road standing empty. The estate agents' For Sale signs were a cruel joke.

Guerney picked the middle house. There was no problem. The four of them went to the back door, and Guerney knocked a hole in its glass panel, laying the skirt of his raincoat on it to muffle the sound and tapping briskly with the gun. The key was still in the lock.

They went into a bare room that looked out on to the garden. A faint orange light swamped the floorboards – seepage from the sodium lamps that lined the next street, backing on to each garden fence.

'Sit over there.' Guerney waved Paschini into a corner, then he tilted his left shoulder to free it, and shrugged the coat on to the floor. To Rachel, he said: 'Take this.' She took the gun and sat down by the wall, ten feet away from Paschini, holding the weapon two-handed as before and resting her wrists on her drawn-up knees. To Stella, he said: 'Come over to the window.'

The girl saw the glint from the knife-handle, steel and pearl; she saw the way it hung from his arm. When she opened her mouth to speak nothing happened, so she shook her head.

Guerney went towards her. Within arm's length, he swung at her with his palm laid flat, a hard blow that connected perfectly and sounded like a handclap, then he grabbed her fast, before she could react, and held her tightly with the unwounded arm, talking softly to her. The tone of someone gentling an animal.

She began to cry after a while, and he held her until she had finished. Then he stepped back and said: 'Come to the window.' They went there together, and he turned so that she could get a grip on the knife.

'Ease upwards,' he told her, 'to lift the cutting edge. Don't jerk, don't pause. Just take it out.' She did it exactly as he'd instructed; he watched as the blade slid out, his face stretched. She helped him off with his blouson. The material of his shirt was gummed to the wound with blood. He simply yanked it.

It had gone in between his biceps and triceps to a depth of about two inches. The angle and length of the wound had held the blade. Now it was out, and the shirt-sleeve pulled away, blood began to flow, welling up along the lips of the incision and running in beads towards his wrist. He made Paschini take his shirt off. Stella tore strips from it and bound the cut.

'It needs stitching,' she told Guerney.

He nodded. His eyes were on Paschini. A plane went over and the roar seemed to balloon the whole house. The four people in the room paused for it, like musicians watching

373

the conductor's baton for the first beat.

Guerney spoke to Rachel. 'Take Stella into another room. Give me the gun.'

She handed it over and took the blonde girl by the arm. She seemed reluctant to go. Rachel gave her a little push.

A plane went over. The women huddled in the noise. It was all they could hear. They drew it round them like a blanket.

It was the fourth plane. The slow build from whine to enveloping boom was part of the rhythm Paschini had to follow. Gradations of colour formed in his mind – grey whine, black boom. The black noise lasted for fifteen seconds. Eternity. In the time between they spoke to one another, he and Guerney.

From time to time Stella looked at the wall separating the two rooms. 'What will happen next?' she asked.

There was a murmur from the other room – two voices, interleaved, one even and persistent, the other lilting, like an animal whimpering or a man singing to himself.

Rachel shook her head to say she didn't know.

A plane went over.

It was important to know why David Paschini had died. It was important to know why Paula Cole had replaced him. It was important to know what task she was to perform – the one that David had refused; something that one person couldn't and another would. It was important to know when and where. Guerney's muscles were aching with effort. His wound throbbed abominably.

'He refused me,' Stella said.

'What?'

'Ten minutes' worth on the house. He was making a joke of it. I've thought about it since. No one had ever not wanted me before. He sounded indifferent. You know?' She looked downcast. She wanted to hear something that would reassure her. 'What's he like?'

'I don't know,' Rachel told her. She thought Stella meant Paschini.

It was impossible that it should go on, but it did go on, a continuous thing like a coat with no seam, or the note of a yogi's flute when breath is drawn in through the nostrils and out through the mouth with no interruption, or a serpent that swallows its own tail then disgorges itself in perpetual overhaulings, or a man who goes hand over hand up a rope that is moving downwards at his rate of climb, fixing him in one place for ever, it went on, as the sun loses energy, as the seasons turn, as a number is infinite. Then it stopped.

Through the cold darkness Paschini heard Guerney's voice. Asking, asking.

The women waited. They sat squaw-like, knees drawn up, shoulders hunched, and waited for the business to be over. For the work to be done.

An idea struck Rachel. She looked at Stella curiously. 'How?' she asked. 'The man in the room – when we watched you. What makes it possible?'

Stella regarded her blankly.

'You know we were watching.' Rachel paused. 'How many men?' she asked. 'How many altogether?'

'That have fucked me?'

'Yes.'

'I don't know.' She hadn't considered it before.

'Hundreds?'

Stella seemed to give it some thought. 'Must be,' she said. 'Men usually ask these questions.'

Rachel persisted. 'What makes it possible?'

There was a silence. Stella said: 'You have to love flesh.' Then she frowned, as if she had already half-forgotten what she'd meant.

A plane went over.

Guerney leaned against the wall. He looked tired. He looked like someone who had run a race, or expended a terrible rage.

Paschini said: 'What do you know? What is true? What they told me . . . what I've told you . . . I do not know.' He lay on the bare boards shaking spastically – arms scissoring in front of his body, legs twitching and leaping. Speaking was difficult. He had bitten off the end of his tongue. The words were smeared.

Halfway along one wall was a fireplace – a simple cast-iron frame with a narrow mantelpiece. Above it was a rectangle of wall lighter than the rest, where a picture had hung. Some screws and part of a light-fitting lay on the mantel. You couldn't tell what colour the room was because of the street-lamps' sodium monochrome. If you looked through the window, you could see a clutter of shrubs and an overgrown patch of grass. On the window-sill was a small dirty glass vase that someone had abandoned.

A plane went over.

Suddenly Rachel felt the fear come back. She didn't feel safe. It was easy to imagine that Guerney was miles away.

A plane went over, and the vibration seemed to run in her backbone. She tried to guess what the time was. The light from outside wasn't enough to allow her to see the dial of her watch unless she walked to the window, and that was too risky a thing to do.

Stella said: 'What will happen next?' She asked the question now and then, as if Rachel might eventually come up with the answer.

'For Christ's sake,' Rachel breathed. Then: 'I can't tell you. I don't know.'

'He killed those four men.' Stella toyed with her hair, winding it between forefinger and thumb.

'Yes.'

'What he told me – about the boy they kidnapped. It's all true, isn't it?'

'Yes,' Rachel told her.

Then they stopped talking because a plane went over.

'We're leaving now.'

Guerney appeared in the doorway, and the two women got to their feet. He led them to the back of the house. Neither of them looked at the door of the room Guerney had just left.

Before they reached the road, he asked Rachel for the car-keys. She was holding them in her hand, in order to be ready. He extended an arm without looking at her, and she dropped them on to his palm.

He put Stella in the back seat and Rachel in front. It was all very normal, Rachel thought; just like three people going for a drive.

Guerney took some money from his hip pocket. It was more than half of what he had left. Turning, he gave it to Stella.

She looked at the notes in her hand. 'No,' she said. 'Please.'

'There's no alternative.'

'No.' She tried to give it back.

'What did you expect would happen?'

'I don't know.' Stella began to sob. 'I don't know.'

'We'll drive to Heathrow. Get a shuttle to Glasgow. Go north from there. Stay in bed-and-breakfast places. No one'll come up there. You're nothing to them, anyway. They don't know you know.'

'How long?'

'Make it a week,' Guerney told her.

'And after that?'

'I don't know,' he said. 'It's up to you.'

Stella turned to Rachel, holding the money out as if to show it to her, then folding it into her hands. 'The men,' she explained, 'the four men at Cheyne Walk . . . they were strangers. I didn't know them. They were brought in because of you. Usually, it was Tony . . . Tony and Franco; they had some others there, but they ran the house. Do you see? They looked after me – and the other girls.'

'Yes,' Rachel said. 'I see.'

'There's always been someone. . . .'

As Guerney started the car, a plane went over, obliterating

the engine noise. He drove to the end of Ash Road and turned into Beech Road.

Stella looked down at her fist of banknotes.

'. . . to look after me.'

None of them had noticed the street-number of the house they'd been in. It had no significance. As it happened, the number was 48. It had been under offer three times, and on each occasion the offer had been withdrawn. The estate agent hadn't received an enquiry about the place for a long time.

Cesare Paschini lay quite tidily facing upwards, his arms by his side, one knee slightly raised and turned towards the other. Guerney had punched the knife hard into the side of the man's throat, taking the carotid artery and the windpipe.

A plane went over, rattling the windows.

28

After they left the airport, Guerney drove east towards central London for a few miles, then turned south.

They travelled in silence. Rachel was thinking of the way she and Stella had waited, knowing what other, inaudible, sounds lay underneath the aircraft noise. As each plane passed, they had avoided one another's eyes, like relatives in a hospital anteroom.

She had appeared strangely childlike, clutching the money Guerney had given her. The expensive clothes, the flawless make-up, the fast cars and high rollers – these were things that love or money had always been able to provide.

Now something had broken the sequence. She'd walked towards the terminal building with awkward, worried, staccato steps and turned in the light to regard them where they sat in the car, before going through the sliding doors. She looked lost, like a child in a strange part of town.

Rachel remembered all the men who had lain on top of Stella. Hundreds of men. It was either sad, she thought, or meaningless.

'She wasn't part of it,' Rachel said.

'No. There was no other way.'

'What do we know?' She asked it casually, as if not really wanting to own her share of the knowledge Guerney had acquired from Paschini.

'He may have seemed like a general to you. He wasn't. More like an officer in the catering corps. I don't think they would have been too impressed by his politics or by his wealth. They needed his son and the use of his London operation. They needed him for a few odd jobs. In that sense he was an ally. They flattered him with a little information. Also, he was bound to be around when a few things leaked. It probably excited him. I've no doubt that the business seemed to fit in with his private war against pinko liberalism.'

'What business?'

'He couldn't tell me much about that.'

'But he did tell you something.'

'He confirmed a substitute – a person who will do for them whatever it was David wouldn't.'

'The girl in the restaurant.'

'That's right.'

'You said you'd seen her before.' Guerney made no answer. 'How? Where had you seen her?' A pause. 'Why were you sure she was the replacement?' The silence grew. Rachel sighed. 'Is it what Meadows talked about? An experiment – fouling up the Hot Line?'

'Yes. It seemed so. Paschini knew less. He talked about it differently – approximately.'

'You mean he was lying.'

'Oh, no. He was telling me what he knew – what he'd been told; a few things he'd picked up. I believed him. But what he was saying didn't sound true.'

'Why not?'

'Because there was something else that he'd learned. There's a deadline.'

'He told you that?'

'Yes.'

'Something to do with conditions? Maybe they can only run the test at certain times. A thing like that would have to be pretty sensitive. A lot of setting up – pre-planning, organizing fail-safes. Unless they *want* to run the risk of the world going up in flames. It would figure.'

'Perhaps.'

'When is it – the deadline?'

'In three days.' Guerney glanced at his watch. 'Two.'

'Holy Christ.' She thought about it. 'That's why you told Stella to stay away for a week.'

'Another thing he'd heard – something about the election.'

'What?' Rachel was puzzled.

'There's a general election due in this country; it'll almost certainly be the autumn.'

'I know. I know that. I meant what's that got to do with David Paschini, or this girl you say they've brought in?'

'Paula Cole.'

'He told you that?'

Guerney nodded. 'I don't know. Paschini didn't know. He'd heard it mentioned.'

'It's months off. You said two days.'

'Yes. It's all I could get.' He paused. 'It's all there was.'

She felt drowsy – the aftermath of fear and shock and tension acting like a narcotic. For ten minutes or so, she drifted in and out of sleep, coming-to each time with a little twitch of the shoulders. Finally, she said: 'Will we have to find a hospital?'

'No. We'll find a chemist in the morning.' Surgical spirit, some tape, two or three small bulldog clips if the wound wouldn't stay closed. Rachel could forage for all that.

She had started to doze again, when she heard him say: 'George Buckroyd is dead.'

After a minute or two she said: 'He told you that, too?'

'He told me that, too.'

She looked at his face, and continued to look as he drove. There was nothing in it of sorrow and regret. Or nothing she could find.

29

Christ on a crutch, thought Howard Prentiss, he looks like the goddam president of some goddam bank.

The man opposite to him was sitting on a straight-backed chair that he had moved slightly from its position in front of a walnut bureau. He was wearing a dark grey suit, a crisp blue shirt and a discreet maroon tie. His shoes were highly polished Oxfords. His brown hair was neatly trimmed to just above the collar. His hands lay lightly folded in his lap, and he regarded Prentiss coolly. They were at the Hilton where the man had been booked into a small suite.

He was scheduled to leave later that same day. He was briefed. Then Ginsberg's phone-call come through. Prentiss had taken it on the direct line.

He'd said: 'I don't believe this shit.' Then 'Tell me,' his voice weighty with anger.

'We put four guys in there. Three were shot. One had his neck broken. Paschini's gone. This Guerney's good, you know? He's good.'

'Never mind that crap. Tell me how. Paschini?'

'Impossible.'

Prentiss had sighed. 'I guess so.'

'The guy with the busted neck – he was in a bedroom upstairs, bare-assed. He'd been screwing. One of the hookers has gone missing. The one they used to put Guerney on ice the first time. They were using her as gofer. Also figured she might pick up a thing or two from Irving – maybe even from Guerney: a slip of the tongue, whatever. You know – before they got leaned on.'

'She didn't know anything . . .?'

'No. She just had to report anything that was said to give Paschini an idea or two about how much Guerney and Irving had really discovered. . . . You know the technique.'

'Sure.' A yardstick to measure truth with, because people in pain will agree to anything.

'OK. She's gone, anyway. Stella something. It wasn't her real name.'

'Willingly?'

'Who knows? She decides to treat this guy to a party. Guerney arrives on the scene while she's getting humped. Our man's got a wet dick, a mouthful of tit and not much else on his mind. Guerney offs him. Easy.'

'It sounds like a set-up.'

'Yeah.'

'What do you think?'

'Guerney would do?' Prentiss had imagined Ginsberg's shrug. 'Offload the hooker; sweat Paschini.'

'Yeah. Christ. How would he stand up to that?'

'I don't know. He's into all this Nazi shit, you know? I guarantee he could dish it out. Doesn't mean he could take it.'

'Christ.' Prentiss had sounded weary. 'They should've blown his ass off right away. Irving, too.'

'We take instructions from you guys.'

Jeffries, Prentiss had thought. 'What's happening?'

'Well, we're looking. The Brits are. Unspecific APB, like before. I wouldn't count on it. This guy's good.'

'You said that.'

'You asked me what I thought.'

'OK. OK.' There had been a long pause, then both men had started to speak at once. 'What?' Prentiss had asked.

'Is it still on?'

'What about Cole?'

'She's ready. She's fine. That's all fine.' Ginsberg had kept his voice even.

'Stay by a phone,' Prentiss had told him. Then: 'It's still on.'

*   *   *

The man who looked like a banker said: 'I saw a man called Jeffries. Ed Jeffries.'

After speaking to Ginsberg, Prentiss had made two phone-calls, one of them to this man. Then he'd checked the file briefly. The man's name was given as Cauldwell – at any rate, it was the name they knew him by. He spoke with a trace of accent. The file said he was Belgian, not a US resident, reachable via a Swiss phone-number. He'd been used a number of times before.

'Not now. Now you see me.'

Cauldwell nodded. He sat completely still. 'There's a problem?'

'No. No problem.' Prentiss took a photograph from his pocket and walked over to the bureau. 'This man might show at some time – he might be there.' He removed another photo. 'He might be with this woman.'

Cauldwell turned his head slightly to look at the photos.

'It's not likely,' Prentiss continued. 'The odds are against it. He doesn't know what's going on. And there's no way he could have a line on you. No one does.'

'A few,' Cauldwell waited until Prentiss had gone back to his chair. 'You. Jeffries. A couple of others, I imagine.'

'Three,' Prentiss assured him. 'Jeffries; me; one other.'

Cauldwell gestured towards the bureau. 'The man. What is his name?'

'Simon Guerney.'

'How is he connected? Don't give me the details.'

'He might be tracking Cole.' *Though Christ knows how,* Prentiss thought. He was working off Ben Ascher's theories. 'Just consider him the opposition, OK? The less you know. . . .' He paused. 'We had him; now we've lost him. We think he'll go to ground. But still. . . .'

'Yes. All right.' Cauldwell raised an eyebrow. 'Careless to lose him,' he said, not expecting a response. 'The girl?'

'One of ours.'

'But not now.'

'Not now.'

'Yes, I see.' Without looking, Cauldwell stretched out a

384

hand and retrieved the photos. He stared at them for a moment, then tossed them aside. 'He's a specialist.'

'Yes.' Prentiss told him. 'OK?'

'If they show. . . .' Cauldwell waited for confirmation.

'Kill them if you can. Don't make waves. Everything else must go smoothly. We don't want any questions asked after this. But if you get the chance. . . .'

'I understand,' Cauldwell said.

'The priority remains the same. To kill Paula Cole. That's all you need to know. Nothing's changed there. We want Cole dead.'

'Yes,' Cauldwell said again. 'I understand.'

30

Finally, Rachel had slept. It wasn't until the comfort of the
engine noise and a sense of movement stopped that she woke
up. There were hard white lights and, nearby, a low
building.

'Where are we?'

'About two-thirds of the way to Brighton.' Guerney
eased his arm out of the raincoat's sleeve, unzipped his
blouson and unbuttoned his shirt one-handed. 'It's a pull-
in; truckers use it.' He turned towards her, getting his arm
into the light. 'Is that bleeding?'

She looked. 'A little, I think.'

'Check the sleeve of my jacket – and the coat.'

She held them to the light like a housewife. 'Nothing,' she
told him.

'OK.' He started to button his shirt.

'Why are we here?'

'Why not? I don't know how long it would take them to
find out we'd gone. It depends on how frequently Paschini
was expected to check in. Probably when he moved us.
Maybe he was planning to do that about now – three
o'clock. Certainly in the small hours. But it could have been
sooner. It could have been almost at once. We couldn't take
the car back into the city, just in case. We couldn't walk. It
seemed best to get clear. But it's time to dump the car. We'll
hitch a ride from here.'

'Into Brighton?'

'And get the train back. There's no reason that they'd
think of that. I imagine they'll put out another alert for us.

We won't go all the way on the train. Do you want coffee?'

While she drank her second cup, Guerney found them a lift.

The trucker was talkative. He organised Rachel next to him on the bench seat of the cab and told her about the girls he sometimes picked up and how they would pay for the ride. Guerney stayed awake, but didn't do any talking himself. The driver swung the big wheel and stamped on the clutch, now and then leaning over to pat Rachel's knee under the pretence of emphasizing a remark.

As they drove past the Royal Pavilion, Guerney said: 'Anywhere here is fine.' He helped Rachel to clamber down and threw the cab door closed; then they walked down to the promenade. The sea was grey under a grey dawn sky; the waves broke on the shingle in placid opaque folds.

'That guy had three hands: one for steering, one for shifting gear, one for me.'

'I noticed.'

They came to an expanse of grass with a few benches facing the ocean and sat down. Thirty or so gulls were feeding on offal just above the tideline, rising and dropping, fighting for ownership, and all the time putting up their raucous, unearthly cries.

Rachel fixed on them for a few minutes. She said: 'First, we go back.'

'Most of the way. We'll take the tube from one of the south London stations.'

'Then?'

'The hotel. We've only been away for a night. They probably didn't even notice.'

'And then?'

A dawn breeze had begun to blow, lifting the whitecaps further out to sea and putting some muscle into the breakers. Guerney shifted position to favour his injured arm. 'It might be time for you to bale out, Rachel.'

She made no reply.

'Whatever's happening is happening tomorrow. I don't

have too many choices. One way or another, I have to get close to the girl – to Paula Cole.'

'You're going to use yourself as bait.'

'Not quite. Break cover, though. Try to make it cat and mouse.'

'You'll likely die.'

He stared at the waves. The wind was taking a feather of spray from their backs. 'Give me another idea.'

'Forget it. Just leave it alone. I mean, what in hell do you gain? You're not a crusader.' He didn't answer. 'Look,' she continued, 'you know how it works. They make their own laws. No one's aware of it. Does Joe Public understand what's going on? So you threw them a couple of curve balls this time. So what? Nothing's going to change. It's their game – their rules. Maybe we should both bale out.'

She turned to look at him. 'Simon?' His eyes didn't move from the line of white foam on the shingle. 'No,' she said. 'OK.'

Later, as they walked through the town towards the station, she said: 'I'll hang in, I think. For tomorrow, at least, I'll stay in the hotel; it won't cramp your style. Who knows? There might be something. . . .'

'Who knows?' Guerney said.

They found a chemist, and she bought bandages and antiseptic lotion. On the train she stayed awake so that he could sleep.

Paula had woken early. The skylight was opalescent in the dawn light. She lay still and gazed straight up at it, unfocused, so that its edges fudged and shapes swam on the glass. She drifted back into sleep, taking the mottled images with her. Trees birds, drifting on the wind. . . .

Both the person and the place were familiar, but Guerney couldn't take a fix on either. There were birds overhead calling like the gulls on the beach. His companion stood next to him, but wouldn't come far enough forward to be identifiable; Guerney was aware, only, of a presence like a shadow at his elbow. He tried to turn and look at the face, but they were among a vast crush of people and he was boxed in.

Raised above the crowd was a gigantic television, its colours brilliant, almost hallucinatory. Everyone was gazing upward. George Buckroyd appeared on the screen, holding a drink. He waved to Guerney, then began to speak, though it was impossible to hear him for the noise made by the crowd. He seemed to be introducing someone.

Though he hadn't seen her, Guerney became suddenly aware that the person next to him was Paula Cole. She was watching the screen intently. Guerney watched, too, seeming to view things along her eyeline. The broadcast was coming from the pub in Portobello where he and George had last met. Some men were drinking at one of the tables, and Buckroyd was pointing to one of them as he spoke. Behind the table, pinned to the wall, was a flag which bore a large simplified image of a tree with a bird flying from its branches.

The other man rose from the table and came close to the camera, replacing Buckroyd. Guerney felt Paula's concentration intensify, as if a dynamo, somewhere deep in her head, had begun to rise in pitch, cranking up from a low hum to a steady whine. He struggled to marry his vision to hers, like looking along someone else's sightline, and felt her resistance. She started, as if suddenly aware of his presence, then the face on the screen grew foggy; she was deliberately blurring the features. Fighting to reassemble them, he heard her voice, a harsh whisper: *Guerney*.

As a memory hovers near recollection, as a word lies on the tip of the tongue . . . The lines and planes of the face began to reassemble, then half-dissolved again. Guerney felt the effort of concentration as a physical thing. He wrestled with the image, pulling it back into focus. Piece by piece it came clear. He looked at the man's face. It was Martin Luther King.

The crowd began to whoop and moan.

King leaned towards a bank of microphones. 'I have a dream!' He seemed almost to sing the words.

The crowd responded. 'O Lord,' the voices came back. 'Yes, Lord.'

Paula had braced herself. She was drawing on a hunting-bow; it curved back from her fist and from the long barb at the arrow's tip. In the corner of his eye Guerney could see the nocked shaft and the smooth flights lying close to Paula's cheek.

'I have a dream!' Martin Luther King crooned the refrain. The crowd was a forest of lifted hands. Guerney felt the *whoosh* of the release as a draught on his face. He seemed to follow the arrow's flight as it turned imperceptibly, seeking its victim like a heat-homing missile. He seemed to ride its back. When the impact came he was too close to know what had happened.

Then he was among the crowds again and watched the screen. Paula was next to him. He wanted to turn and look at her, but the dream wouldn't permit that. They stood shoulder to shoulder as places and faces poured across the screen like video-tape on fast forward. Guerney knew that among them was something Paula wanted to hide. He thought: *Still; stay still;* the rush of images became a slow slide. Beside him, Paula began to tremble; she gave a small sharp cry, as if she'd been struck, and a picture locked on the screen – a black limousine, open-topped, the people in it arrested in freeze-frame. Then the car took off at speed, swerving out of the motorcade. A woman scrambled backwards from the rear seat, as if trying to catch something. Security men jumped on to the sides of the car as the camera zoomed in for a closer look at Kennedy's clenched face, at the sprawl of his body, at the blood-splashes on his jacket and the car's upholstery and his wife's pink suit.

Paula lowered her rifle. George Buckroyd came on screen holding a placard which read: *President Kennedy Assassinated.* When he removed the placard, Guerney saw his own face appear on the television. He was scanning the crowd, trying to get a fix on Paula. He found her and went to stand by her once more while they both regarded his larger-than-life-size face, until gradually the features began to blur and change,

390

the nose growing a little shorter, the hair darker, the face broader.

Paula's whole frame leaped; it was as if she'd been touched by a live wire; her panic was palpable, and with it came a new strength. She scrambled the features, working frenetically to make them an unreadable jigsaw of teeth, eyes, jawline. Guerney tried to reassemble them: chin, nose, forehead, putting piece upon piece. He half-built the face and, for a moment, thought he would recognise it, then Paula's frantic energy bore down on the picture and the sections flew apart.

Guerney stopped trying: he stopped looking at the screen. Instead, he turned all his attention to Paula in a single rush of the imagination. It was like an ambush. At once he could see her full-face, eyes wide, face drawn with effort. He wanted to drag a name from her – a name that would fit the half-formed face. He pushed her mind with his and, for the briefest of moments, almost had it. Then he heard her say *Guerney,* and his own name blotted out the other.

He turned back to the screen, and his face was there as before. He wiped it, and another scene appeared. He knew that Paula saw it, too; he heard her whisper. Her strength had kept from him the face he wanted, but Guerney could tell that she was weak now, like a spent runner, and couldn't disrupt what would happen next.

The camera tracked back. A man was trimming his hedge in a suburban garden, his young face drawn with tension. Paula reached down, and Guerney saw that she was lifting the flex that fed the hedge-trimmer. It altered in her hand, becoming a snake, hissing and writhing as she clutched it. Her arm went back, and she hurled it at the screen. It flew to the man, bucking and twisting in his grip as he caught it, the fangs glinting at his face and neck as it struck and struck and struck.

31

The man who looked like a banker woke at 8 a.m. He
showered and shaved and selected his clothes for the day.
Then he phoned the Pan Am office to check his reservation.
He was told that, yes, indeed, Mr Nathan Cauldwell's
reservation was confirmed on flight 106 leaving Dulles Airport at 1815 hours.

It irritated him slightly – having been brought to Washington, installed in a hotel and left with a full day to kill.
He'd missed a concert at Carnegie Hall and dinner at the
Four Seasons. He'd missed the girl who was going to share
those things with him. Prentiss had wanted to speak to him
personally – and, of course, he wouldn't risk talking on an
open line; probably, Cauldwell reflected, for fear of some of
his own people picking up on the matter. As he understood
it, this one was being operated from behind tightly closed
doors.

He wondered briefly about Jeffries. He didn't like the
guy much; but he'd put a few jobs Cauldwell's way. This
Prentiss was in a different league somehow. He'd upped the
ante: that was one consolation for passing up a great piece of
ass and spending a dull day.

Cauldwell sighed and picked up the photos of Rachel and
Guerney. A specialist, he thought. Well, that makes things
interesting. He continued to study the shots while lifting the
phone and ordering juice, coffee and toast from room service. Then he slipped the photos into his walk-on bag and
switched on the television.

*　　*　　*

Rachel stood under the shower for a long time as if she might sluice away more than just the grime of the last twenty-four hours. Finally she emerged and towelled her hair briskly for several minutes, bending slightly from the waist and slapping at her nape and scalp. She wrapped a fresh towel round herself and tucked the loose end in under her armpit. Then she stood still. A thought made her shudder.

When she left the bathroom, she found Guerney lying on the bed and staring into space. He hadn't moved in an hour. She let the towel drop on the floor and began to hunt for clothes.

'You'd better look at this arm.'

She finished dressing while he picked at the knots Stella had tied in the strips from Paschini's shirt. The material was glued to the wound. He took off the rest of his clothes and went through to the shower, coming back five minutes later with his arm bared and the cut seeping blood. It had closed a little towards the elbow and looked like a thin mouth wearing a lopsided grin.

'How is it?' she asked.

'Stiff. Not too bad.'

Rachel washed it with the antiseptic and applied the bandage, trying to close the wound further without pulling too tightly. He stood still, staring at the wall, docile, like a horse being shod. 'It's not enough,' she told him.

'No. It'll have to do.'

She tore the bandage and tied it off. 'What are you going to do?'

The dream plucked at him. It was still vivid, its colours startling, its sound effects loud on his inner ear. He saw the slow oscillation of the arrow as it flew and heard the whirr of wind in the flights. He saw the snake, curving and flexing in space, and then its fangs, like steel barbs, scoring flesh. He concentrated on it, trying to make the codes come clear. Martin Luther King. Kennedy. The young man sullenly gardening. And Paula among the throng, using the press of people as cover, like an assassin.

393

Rachel repeated her question. 'They'll have the house in Cheyne Walk blanket-covered, won't they? And the Hampstead place.'

Guerney wondered what story the police would be operating on. A gangland killing, maybe. They'd be kept clear of Windmill Hill if Cole was still there. They would also be working hard to keep the press away. Gunplay in east London; four men dead in Chelsea. It just took one concerned citizen, one eager police patrolman. He checked his watch and flicked on the television.

'If I'm going to draw them,' he said finally, 'it'll have to be Hampstead. You're right. They can put police patrols in Cheyne Walk and round about. They can't put anyone too close to Cole. They wouldn't even want the place known about.'

'You think she's still there?'

'Maybe not. Probably not. It depends on how well organised they are. There'll be other safe houses. They could put her in a hotel – minders and all – though that's less secure.'

'Is it?'

'We saw her once, remember? I don't imagine she was supposed to be out on her own.'

'I don't understand any of that part.' Rachel paused. 'And you're not going to tell me, are you? It's OK' – she held up a hand – 'I've come this far knowing that you were keeping some things under wraps. Maybe I earned it. Maybe you're right – I shouldn't be here. You don't have to trust me. Just don't let me walk under any trucks – OK?' He made no reply. 'Simon?' she asked. 'OK?'

He half-raised a hand to quieten her. His eyes were fixed on the television. A man was talking. Close to the camera, Guerney could see the head of the interviewer, nodding as his most recent question was answered. Then the talker. And beyond him, as in the dream, the image of a tree with a bird flying from the branches.

Rachel followed his gaze.

Clive Holman was saying: '. . . and so tomorrow, in Hyde Park, we expect to witness the most conclusive evidence yet of the revulsion most ordinary people in this country feel for the government's nuclear policy. People from all walks of life, from all political parties and of all persuasions will be there to say to government – in effect – we've had enough. We don't want these weapons. We don't want American bases. We want a change of policy. And, most of all, we want a peaceful world.'

The director cut to the studio. A newscaster said: 'Tomorrow's rally, likely to be attended by upwards of half a million people if estimates are correct, is causing concern in government and police circles. The Home Secretary has warned of a danger to public order . . .'

Guerney watched the rest of the bulletin without stirring. Then he switched the television off and stood for a moment looking at the blank screen. A chin, a nose, the line of a jaw . . . piece upon piece. Holman's face seemed still to lie on his vision; behind it was the peace symbol; like a crude inverted image of a tree, the way a child might draw it; and then the dove in flight, a white silhouette against the dark background.

They were burning in Paula's mind – of course they were – the tree and the bird, both indelible as she stood among the crowds of people. As she watched the man rise and come forward to speak. As she readied herself, like an assassin.

Rachel was puzzled. 'It was Holman. Isn't that his name?' She remembered the television broadcast in the pub in the Portobello Road. For a moment, George Buckroyd's face came back to her, grinning as he raised his whisky-glass.

Guerney sat down. 'I know what it is,' he said, 'but I don't know how.'

Paula Cole sat very still. It was a bright day, but there were still patches of frost on the lawn in sheltered places. Where it had melted, the grass glistened. Two thrushes were hunting in the wet, close to the verge alongside a long gravelled driveway. They would bounce a little way, then stab.

Bounce and stab. She watched the bright eyes and needle beaks. When they rocked forward in a tight arc, stabbing, the whole body was a weapon.

The house they had brought her to was large and set well back from the road. Tall cypresses grew next to the wall at the bottom of the driveway, so it was virtually impossible to see the house until you rounded the curve that led away from the double gates. When they had arrived, Mountjoy had unlocked these to let the car enter, then locked them again before climbing back into the passenger-seat. She knew that something had happened and that Guerney was involved in whatever it was. He was safe, though; had to be – she expected to see him tomorrow. Safe. She didn't know whether to be sorry or glad. He knew everything. Nobody else knew except Guerney and Paula herself. She sat very still watching the thrushes and, although it was sunny, the sun carried no heat, so she was wearing a thick coat and gloves.

I killed him, she thought. *I killed my father, and now someone else knows that.* It made her love him and hate him.

One of the thrushes snatched a worm and drew it from the earth; it knotted and unknotted itself furiously. She wondered about the faces in her dream: the famous dead people, and she felt again the recoil of the gun, the lightness as the arrow left the bow. Who did that? Was it Guerney, or her? The thick dry body of the snake in her grasp. *Daddy!* His face dissolved in a welter of red as the fangs struck, as the steel nibs of the machine struck, out of control, the flex standing up like a cobra's length, and she said *Daddy* under her breath. *Guerney.*

When she had first sat down on the garden bench, it had been in the sun; now shade had inched along, dividing the lawn with a slanting line that crept millimetre by millimetre towards the house. The thrushes paraded along it like tightrope-walkers.

Pete Ginsberg came out of the house. He'd been watching her from the window and hadn't taken his eyes off her for a second. He looked irritated and nervy.

'Why not come inside?' he asked her. 'Aren't you cold? For Christ's sake. . . .' When he got no response, he ambled once round the lawn, returning to the bench and standing over her. 'Don't you want to come into the house?'

Paula didn't look at him. She sat very still and looked at the thrushes.

'Why?' Rachel asked.

'Think about it,' Guerney replied. 'You know about this kind of stuff, don't you?'

'The election?'

'The Peace Movement is putting up a hefty number of candidates. That couldn't have happened five years ago. Holman took over the leadership five years ago. The guy's got enormous influence. He's made protest respectable. He came along at the right time, made the right moves – all that. No one could pretend it was just a bunch of freaks and vegetarians any more. The man next door was joining, and the man next door to him. Holman's charismatic. He's also very far from being a red.'

'He's also very ambitious, or so I hear.'

'Probably.'

'And a pain in the ass so far as your people are concerned – sure, I see that.'

'More. He's dangerous. The right man, the right mood. There's no one like him.'

'He controls votes.'

'Must do. The membership of the Peace Movement in this country has grown to the point where they *could* elect candidates to Parliament; or at least engage in some clever manoeuvring using a tactical vote. For years, they've been under surveillance – that's nothing new. Phone-taps, mail-intercepts. It's not enough any more. You've seen this kind of thing happen before.'

'You mean some nuisance or another quietly put to sleep.' Guerney nodded. 'Oh, yes,' she said, 'not seen – I know it's been done, though. A car loses its brakes, someone

397

drowns; it's happened, of course.' She remembered something she'd once learned. 'Insulin injected into the anal artery – foolproof; no traces, no marks. I don't imagine that's an option, though – not if you're sure about it happening at the rally.' She laughed humourlessly.

'Yes,' he said, 'pretty sure.'

'Not the Hot Line. Not an experiment. Nothing to do with all that.'

'I believe that Meadows believed it.'

'But Paschini didn't.' Rachel searched his face. She knew he must have got it from Paschini – or, at least, enough of it to make the television broadcast a clincher. What she couldn't figure out was why he'd decided to trust her with it now. 'Paschini,' she said again. 'He told you.'

Guerney looked through her. 'An accident,' he said. 'Something that would use the kind of power that David possessed.'

'Holman has that much clout? That killing him would turn things around?'

'Of course. I've told you. He did things no one else could have done. Why does anyone get taken out? It's just another political hit-job.'

'Except for the method,' Rachel observed. She remembered the deck of cards fanning out in mid-air and David Paschini's face, drugged on the pillow, as she entered the room with his food. 'Whatever that might be.' A thought struck her. 'He's not coming in by helicopter . . . I mean, something like that?'

Guerney shrugged. 'I don't know what it is,' he said. 'I don't know what the hell it could be.'

'It was Paschini, wasn't it?' Rachel wanted to know. 'You were going to keep it to yourself – that's why you suggested I cut out. So what is it now? You need my help? What?'

'No,' he said.

'Then how did you know?'

Guerney lifted a hand, as if explaining the obvious. 'I dreamed it.'

'Sure,' Rachel said. 'You're full of shit.' She sounded angry – angry and impatient like a wife who knows that she's being lied to.

Cauldwell flipped through the channels, found nothing he liked and pointed the remote control at the screen. 'Zap,' he said softly, and the screen went dark. He took an apple from a bowl on top of the bureau and ate it while he walked around the room, then threw the core underarm, scarcely bothering to look, and put it cleanly into the waste-bin. *Zap*.

He took the phone to the bed and dialled a number. A voice answered, and he smiled. 'I'm sorry about the concert. I'm sorry about dinner. I'm even sorrier about after dinner.'

'Your lousy business,' she chided. 'I hope you fall on your ass.'

'No, you don't.'

'I hope you close the deal and make a million.'

'I know it. Maybe we'll buy you something. Would you like that? Something nice.'

'When will you be back?'

'A couple of days.'

'Where are you?'

'Chicago; you know that.'

'I mean *where*.'

'A hotel – in the room.'

'You know where I am?'

'Tell me.'

'In bed. You know what I'm wearing?'

'Tell me.'

'Nothing. I'm lying on top of the bed with nothing on. You know where my hand is?'

'Tell me.'

'Mmmmm, it feels good. *Aaaah*, that feels so *good*.'

Cauldwell cupped the phone under his chin. 'Tell me,' he said. 'Tell me.'

Clouds were scudding up out of the west, big cumulonimbus formations, dark and heavy, their undersides flat

399

like an anvil. The windows at the back of the house had large inner sills like seats, with fat soft cushions. Paula sat huddled in, close to the window-panes, her back propped by the cushions, and watched the clouds sailing past. Her knees were drawn up, her head tilted to one side and lodged against the window-frame. The place was like a little hideaway.

She stayed there as the sky cleared and grew a deeper, darker blue; flights of birds went over, heading for home. A broad band of aquamarine spread across the horizon after the sun had gone, and the first stars hung above it glimmering like liquid. As the night grew blacker the stars multiplied until they filled the sky, seeming to crackle with their brilliance, as the frost-covered land crackled.

Alan Mountjoy came to tell her that some food had been prepared. She didn't reply or acknowledge him. He leaned over, studying her face. 'Enough of this,' he said. 'Come and eat. What's the matter with you?'

Paula turned her head. 'Fuck off, cocksucker,' she said, and laughed delightedly like a child astonished by its own impudence. Then she looked back at the stars, humming a tune to herself.

They had checked news broadcasts throughout the day. Rachel had phoned the Peace Movement headquarters announcing herself as a journalist. They knew that the rally would begin at two o'clock and that Holman would speak at about three. He wasn't arriving by helicopter. A car was taking him there at 2.30.

'Something with the car,' Rachel suggested.

'Who knows? I wouldn't have thought so.' Guerney poured some drinks. 'There's no certainty in it.' He handed Rachel a glass.

'You don't have to be there.'

'I know.' She sipped. 'I might as well be; I've come this far.'

It didn't surprise her that Guerney was able to sleep. There was something animal-like about his ability to find refuge that way. Rachel lay awake, listening to the even rhythm of his breathing and trying to isolate her feelings. She was fearful and puzzled and excited; and there was something else, something that had to do with Guerney's easy rest and her wakefulness. She felt fretful and oddly protective. I care about him, she thought, God help me.

She dozed, on and off, through the night. When Guerney woke the next morning, she was in a light sleep, mouth slightly open, her forehead puckered by a tiny frown. She had left the bedside light on as if for reassurance, and he could see his wristwatch on the nearby cabinet: 6.40. Briefly, Guerney closed his eyes. There was nothing to remember. He hadn't dreamed. Or, if he had, couldn't bring the dream to mind.

Pan Am 106 had touched down on time at 6.25. Cauldwell presented his passport and waited for it to be stamped.

'Business,' he said, smiling. 'Just a couple of days.'

Paula Cole sat by her window, wide-eyed, and watched the slow spread of light into the dawn sky.

32

The hotel was a tower block directly opposite the park. Cauldwell took some clothes from his bag – a windcheater, a sweater, some blue jeans, a pair of sneakers – and laid them on the bed before going to the window and pulling aside the curtain. The park looked busy. In the middle distance, he could see some workmen building a stage from bright yellow and blue scaffolding poles.

Logistically, this was an easy one. His last trip to London had been for a consortium of diamond merchants who had discovered that one of their London handlers was slicing a little off the side. Since their shipments often arrived in the country concealed in the bulkhead panels of a small private cabin-cruiser, they hadn't felt inclined to notify the police of their colleague's dishonesty.

They had paid well, but the job had turned messy. Cauldwell had taken the mark at his home, expecting him to be alone. As it turned out, the man was cheating on his wife as well as on his business partners, and Cauldwell had walked in on a candlelit dinner for two. He'd killed them both, but with no chance of refinements. In her fear, the girl had walked backwards through a glass door. Cauldwell had shot her to silence her screams.

On that occasion, he'd flown first to Amsterdam, using an American passport, then travelled back to Switzerland via Paris on an English passport that had been waiting for him at his hotel. The police had been looking for a professional, and Cauldwell knew how to be wary.

He knew that Cole was here on department business. The

two guys looking after her didn't know what was coming, but it was sure that they wouldn't holler *cop*. Immigration might get jumpy eventually, but Cole hadn't entered the country under her own name, and Cauldwell would be long gone by then anyway.

Briefly, he wondered what Cole's purpose had been – what they wanted her for and why there should be this tangle with Simon Guerney and the other woman. He shrugged. There were always complications he knew nothing about. He didn't want to. Ignorance kept him alive. It was his job to unravel the tangles, to solve the complications, by simply cutting the knot. It was odd how often a death would make everything come right.

Mountjoy poured coffee into three cups. Ginsberg brought some toast to the table, and a dish of butter, then went away and came back with some marmalade. Paula raised the cup to her lip, and the two men watched her like anxious parents. Ginsberg bit into his toast, then dropped it on the plate.

'I'll go and check the car,' he said. As he walked towards the outer door, he thought: Christ, I've had enough of this. Something was going on, but he didn't know what. She sat around like some kind of dummy. He and Mountjoy had taken turns to be with her that night.

Mountjoy had wanted to phone in – to report it. 'She's acting weird,' he'd said. 'She's acting crazy. Shouldn't they know about that?'

'She *is* weird. That's the whole goddam point.' Ginsberg didn't want things postponed or changed. He wanted the job over and himself on a plane back to the States. He didn't want freaks in white coats asking questions. They might get to some of the nights he'd spent in the small room with the skylight. He wished to God none of that had ever happened.

Outside, he hoisted the door on the garage, then got into the car and reversed it into the driveway. A few hours, he thought, just a few hours. In the car, with the engine ticking over, he felt a little less jumpy.

*   *   *

'He fucked me, did you know that?'

Mountjoy looked at her over his cup, startled. 'Yes, I did know that.'

'He tried to kill me. He put his hands round my throat.'

'What?'

'He wanted to leave me.'

'Who? Who are you talking about?'

'If I kill him, he can't leave me, can he?'

'What?' said Mountjoy again. 'Who? Who tried to kill you?'

'David,' she told him. 'Did you know David?'

Mountjoy put his cup down and looked towards the phone. He reached out and grasped Paula's wrist and jerked it slightly. 'What are you talking about? Who do you mean? Paula!' He tugged on her wrist again.

She sat still until he let go, then picked up a piece of toast and began to butter it. 'It was a dream,' she said. 'Don't worry. It was something from a dream.'

Mountjoy stared at her. 'Jesus Christ,' he said.

Ginsberg came into the room. 'The car's fine,' he told Mountjoy. 'Everything's OK with the car.'

33

There were flags and banners and an enormous number of
people, and overhead the constant clatter of a police helicopter. It was a bright cold day. A V formation of ducks flew
just above the trees. Marchers were still entering the park,
chanting slogans.

Rachel and Guerney were close to the raised stage. They
had been looking for about half an hour.

'I want to find her,' Guerney had said, 'and then just try
to keep on her tail but without being seen. I don't know
what's going to happen, so the only chance is to stay with
her.'

'How do we find her?'

He had shaken his head. 'If you think of something
clever, let me know.'

'Presumably she'll be somewhere near the speech-area.
Won't she?'

'If I knew what was going to happen, I'd know the answer
to that. Possibly. We'll look there. Do you remember her
face?'

'I think so,' Rachel had said. She had been eating as they
spoke, and had paused with her fork lifted, trying to picture
the girl. 'Yes, I remember.' Now she stopped and surveyed
the acres of heads, the figures sitting on groundsheets and
raincoats, the sheer press of bodies. 'We could look all day,
Simon; it's hopeless.'

Guerney took her arm and walked with her until they
reached a large chestnut-tree near one of the pathways.
'We're west of the stage,' he said, 'and about eighty metres

off. This tree's our marker. We'll split up and meet back here in fifteen minutes. Even if you find her, don't try to look for me somewhere else, OK? Here – in fifteen minutes.'

They went in opposite directions, working outwards from the stage.

Cauldwell zipped the windcheater to cover the harness strap. The harness was custom-made – on one side a silenced .38 fixed to a spring release, on the other a honed knife, no broader than a kebab-skewer, in a metal scabbard. The gun was just for insurance.

He crossed the street and went into the park, weaving between the crowds and making directly for the stage. The speeches had begun; he could hear the tinny boom of the PA system and recalled the briefing he'd had, first from Ed Jeffries, then again from Prentiss.

'She's going to a peace rally that day. There'll be speeches. Here are the details.' Jeffries had put an envelope into Cauldwell's hand. 'Read them and burn them. There's a photograph in there – also of the guys with her. They'll be close to the speakers. A man called Holman will be making a speech. While he's speaking there'll be a diversion. Take her any time after that. OK? But not if Holman's still speaking, you understand? If he's still on his feet, you wait. He's last to speak. Get the timing right. There's a number in the envelope. Call it that morning. Say your name. You'll be told if anything has changed.'

Cauldwell had called the number, and nothing had changed. He'd been told three o'clock, directly in front of the speech-area. He pushed through the crowds. That was good, he thought: crowds were added cover. No one was looking for him. No one knew he was there or what he looked like. He wondered what the diversion would be. A bomb, perhaps. Hell, that would ginger things up.

A girl knocked into him and apologised. Cauldwell turned to watch her go, stepping hurriedly between the groups of people who had spread themselves on the grass.

Well, well, he thought. Well, well. Then: That comes later.

Rachel circled and headed back towards the meeting-point. She felt nervy and exposed, just as she'd felt when she'd played stalking games as a child. As you looked, so you were being looked for. How could she count on seeing without being seen?

She stopped a moment and scanned the nearby faces, then people further away; some were walking towards the stage. A man and woman close to her were talking about maybe getting closer – they couldn't hear too well. Most of all, they wanted to hear Holman speak. They talked about the man, telling each other how fine he was, how principled, how full of energy.

The woman told the man something he hadn't known.

'Really?' the man said. 'Really? I didn't know that.'

Rachel felt as if she had been punched in the back. Her finger-ends tingled.

'Oh, yes,' the woman said. 'Didn't you know that?'

Rachel began to move through the crowd as fast as she was able. Oh Christ, she thought. Oh Christ, oh Christ, oh Christ, oh Christ.

It was as if someone had spoken his name. Guerney looked up like a creature catching a scent and thought: She's in the park. He didn't question how he knew. He worked towards her as a hound follows spoor. Here it was stronger; here weaker; now stronger again. Whether he tracked her, or she drew him, scarcely mattered. He was feeling his way along the thread of whatever bound them. He hadn't counted on this – hadn't thought of it. But now he knew how to find her.

Rachel got to the tree and looked around. She was over-due. Guerney had gone. He can't have, she thought. He can't have.

There was no sign of him. She looked towards the stage and, for the first time, saw Holman, sitting among a line of

407

other speakers and waiting his turn. She waited for three minutes until her nerve broke and she began to push through the thicker crowds circling the stage.

Within a minute or two of looking, she found him.

The people closest to the stage were sitting down – orderly, attentive, listening to the speeches; many of them had children; they'd brought food along with them. They sat quietly while the speakers told them horror stories. They drank coffee from flasks or hugged their children against the cold.

Directly in front of the stage, Ginsberg had been told, and about thirty metres back from the barrier. It was easy enough to position himself, Mountjoy and Paula there. It was easy, too, for Cauldwell to find them. He stood just behind Paula, almost close enough to have reached out and touched her. They were on the edge of a huge semi-circle of people, some sitting, some standing under banners or flags. Behind them, the crowd thickened.

It had been like tracking a fox in snow: the clear markings, the sharp hot stink. In his mind he had pictured the signs that way. Neither the press of bodies nor the tens of thousands of conflicting signals they issued made any difference. Her spoor had led him between and around them, strong and unmistakable. *Paula.*

He stood some twenty feet behind her, and she acknowledged him without turning, or even glancing round. There was a man on either side of her, but neither of them could detect, as Guerney somehow could, the bubble of manic laughter that ached in her chest, as if she were a little girl in class, lips pressed tight, trying not to catch her friend's eye for fear that the bubble would burst and spoil some practical joke.

'You wait.' He almost heard the words aloud. 'You wait and see.'

He didn't realise, immediately, that Rachel had come alongside him. The PA system whistled and boomed as a new speaker adjusted the mike. He was there to introduce

Holman. People began to clap. Some of those who had been sitting clambered up for a better view.

Rachel caught Guerney's arm and turned him, putting her arms about him and her forehead against his as if they were lovers resting gently on one another.

'Listen . . . listen. . . .' She was breathless. 'I know how.' She held his upper arms tightly and spoke in a rapid clear monotone.

'Two years ago Holman had major heart surgery. I heard some people talking. . . . He's fitted with a pacemaker.'

Ginsberg glanced up at the overhead television gantry. He recalled the briefing he'd had from Jeffries before flying to London.

'We want him centre-stage, up there and talking for everyone to see. It's perfect. Millions of witnesses to a death from natural causes. A tragedy, a three-day wonder for the media, and we take the sting out of the tail. Shit, I wish we could've taken Castro the same way.' He'd shaken a cigarette from his packet and laughed at the idea. 'She knows what to do. He gets into his speech, just a few minutes, then' – he'd thumbed a Zippo, kindled the cigarette, and snapped his wrist, closing the lighter with a brisk *clack* – 'like that.'

After a while, they would simply stroll out of the park, leaving the chaos and consternation behind. They were flying out next day, he and Paula. They'd be debriefed in Washington, and that would be the end of things. Ginsberg wondered what she would say. Her mood scared him; she seemed capable of doing anything. As Holman approached the microphone, her face was tense with concentration.

Cauldwell rose on the balls of his feet and flexed his calves a little. He could feel the hardness of the scabbard close to his armpit. He took his eyes off Paula's back for an instant and glanced left and right, wondering where the diversion would come from. He'd seen panic in crowds before – people stampeding to and fro, crashing into one another, heading every which way, stumbling, falling, paying no one else any heed. Perfect.

. . . ignore, at their peril, this demonstration by ordinary men and women. . . . Holman's face was lifted to the microphone. He spoke without notes, his arms lifted as if to embrace the whole crowd, his voice filled with passionate conviction.

In his mind's eye, Guerney saw the faces change. King. Kennedy. Then Holman again. Then Guerney himself. The young man in the garden.

As he pictured that final face, he felt a charge like the slap of backwash on a quayside; his eyes went to Paula and saw her rock forward, almost as if she'd been pushed. The man on her right put a hand on her arm, as if to steady her, and glanced sharply sideways, then leaned and spoke into her ear.

Guerney drew a scene in his imagination. He constructed a garden, a lawn-sprinkler with its chimera of rainbow, a man feeding the hedge-trimmer along the unruly twigs. He set a little girl on the lawn, her eyes fixed on the man. Everything as it had been in the dream. Guerney couldn't tell what the jigsaw pieces meant; he only knew that in some way they spelled terror for Paula, and that they were inextricably confused with what was taking place at the moment, there in the park.

He closed his eyes and his mind filled with effort, as if he were bearing down on a fulcrum-balanced lever and trying to lift the scene into clear view. The shattered spectrum in the arc of water trembled and glowed. All the colours grew in brilliance. The edges of things sharpened, and the features of the little girl came into full definition, as if she had been tuned-in on a screen. Her face was stiff and dark with anger.

Paula was locked on to Holman, her lips slightly parted and curved in a rictus of mirth. Then she swayed slightly and gasped, so that Ginsberg grasped her arm again, looking alarmed. Her free hand went to her throat. Mountjoy looked across. He said: 'What . . .?'

Paula looked again at Holman, this time her face slack with horror. *'Daddy!'* The word emerged as a stifled scream.

410

One or two people round her turned, looking curious or concerned.

There – up there – it was his face – his! – and the whole night-mare was happening again, as though the years had telescoped and he was leaving her once more and she must kill him once more and the nightmare was real, the nightmare was real, and she felt the images rush at her and she understood and spun round, a cry on her lips, together with a name. Guerney!

She spun; and her eye met not Guerney's but those of a man she had never seen before. He was staring at her and holding just one thought, as a man will hold the thought of an ace in the hole; and the thought locked her.

A chill went through Cauldwell. The girl had turned like a compass needle seeking north, and stopped, trembling, when she found his eyes. His cover was his anonymity, yet in some way – *impossible!* – she had singled him out, and the shock was on his face, plain to see.

They looked at one another like parted lovers who find each other, unexpectedly, in a foreign land. Cauldwell saw Paula's lips move, saw one of the men at her side swivel round. It was too late, he knew, for pretence. He paused for only a moment before setting off through the crowd.

Paula swayed. A tide of blackness rushed at her. She had been checked by the man, by the overwhelming thought that he held. She had looked into his mind and found her death there.

A sound like keening came from her; she clutched her midriff, stumbling. Mountjoy caught her as she fell. People nearby leaped back, making room, little cries of alarm coming from those closest at hand. They swayed round her, moving in to look, stepped back, offering advice. They ringed her, making a little clearing where Mountjoy lowered her down.

She was threshing and convulsing. Her eyes showed only the whites. Her head went to and fro, as if she were issuing some frenzied denial, and her teeth chattered. Mountjoy scooped her up and tried to hold her still, but the body in his arms flipped and bucked like a fish. Her breath came in

411

great plosive gusts as if she were holding it until her lungs threatened to burst.

Mountjoy looked up at the ring of faces surrounding them. He was on his own. Ginsberg had gone, pushing people clear as he went after Cauldwell.

Up on the stage, Holman registered the disturbance as a flicker at the periphery of his vision. Someone had fainted. He was far too professional to be distracted. His speech was beautifully orchestrated. Like a conductor, he was nursing the crowd along – now pianissimo, now fortissimo, now moderato. With a deft touch he brought applause, then more as he advanced on his finale.

34

The two men walked briskly, one thirty feet ahead of the other. They jinked through the crowd, both stepping up the pace a little when they began to encounter fewer people, but holding the same mazy line, as if treading some carefully marked route.

Cauldwell was heading south towards the point where the Serpentine fed into the boating-lake. He could see, through the lines of plane-trees and chestnuts, sunlight puddling the surface of the water like spoonfuls of silver. No one was boating. There were twenty or thirty people – no more – strolling along the paths that led away from the lake and just a handful walking beside the water. A small group of riders trotted along the bridlepath at the very edge of the park. When he reached the lake, Cauldwell turned west, allowing himself a quick glance back; Ginsberg was with him, getting ready to close the distance when the moment was right.

She had known him. Somehow she had known who he was. Cauldwell was filled with a huge energy stoked by anger. He didn't know who had done it, or what the purpose was, but he was sure he'd been set up. He had gone to the park believing that no one could possibly know him or guess his reason for being there. Somehow the girl had fingered him. The job was blown, and now this creep was bird-dogging him. Everything was wrong; he was suddenly at risk when risk shouldn't have been a factor. He lengthened his pace, scattering some water-birds feeding at the brink of the lake. A car went past, travelling slowly; an old lady sat on a bench offering chunks of bread to some pigeons that swarmed over her lap and on to her arms. A short way off there was a bridge that carried traffic across the water. Cauldwell strode towards it.

Ginsberg saw his quarry heading towards the Italian Gardens. There were always walkers in the place, and people taking photographs; once there, he'd be difficult to stop. Two or three couples, arm in arm, wandered towards the two men; a small group of people went by on bicycles. Now and again, the wind brought the sound of the PA system from half a mile away on the north side of the park.

Ginsberg decided to close on the man when they came near to the tunnels that led under the bridge. He understood none of it – who this man was, who had sent him – except that he was the enemy. He remembered Paula's face, ashen suddenly, and the way her whole body had begun to shake.

'He wants to kill me.' Her voice had been a bleak whisper, and her legs had begun to buckle. 'He wants to kill me.'

The path divided – a broad walkway alongside the road and a much narrower path that kept to the lakeside and was partially screened by a thin line of trees. It led through the tunnel forty feet ahead. The men were alone. Both began to run at the same time.

Cauldwell went through at a full sprint, out of sight for a few seconds as he followed the tunnel's curve. He emerged running hard, but looking – looking for a place. The path had dropped. On his right was a bank of earth rising fifteen feet to the roadway, on his left some low railings bordering an area of trees and scrub that led down to the lake. He vaulted the railings and put his back to the bole of a plane-tree, screening himself from the tunnel's mouth.

Ginsberg arrived almost at once. The path curved to the right almost immediately. There was no way for him to tell that Cauldwell wasn't still ahead. He went past the tree, then checked. His instinct had spoken to him.

He turned, his hand going between the lapels of his coat, but it was all too late. Bracing himself against the tree-trunk, Cauldwell fired twice, middling the slugs and grouping them so well that the entry-wounds were indistinguishable. The shots sounded like pebbles hurled into the curve of a breaking wave. The first sent Ginsberg back on his heels, the second straightened his body before slamming it on to the ground. Arterial blood geysered up for a brief moment, splashing his clothes and spilling on to the pathway; his leg spasmed and flopped; he slithered a short way as if he were being dragged, then lay still.

Cauldwell cleared the railings and went towards the body. Before he could reach it, two joggers rounded the curve, a girl in a yellow tracksuit, breathing hard, her boyfriend loping easily behind her. The girl almost fell over Ginsberg's outflung arm. She checked her stride with short stuttering steps. They both stopped and looked down, not understanding what had happened for a moment; then they saw the blood-gouts and the agonised cry frozen in Ginsberg's face. Cauldwell stood there, his gun still drawn.

The girl gave a small unearthly *whoop*, stretching both her arms out and walking backwards as if feeling along a passageway in the dark. She made the noise again – *whoop*! She was looking at the gun.

Cauldwell fired twice – a snap shot that struck her high in the chest, a second that smashed her larynx. The boy had turned and started to run. Cauldwell downed him with a bullet that took him in the buttock, then stood over him and put two quick shots into the back of his head. He was thinking of nothing but the need to hurry.

Without fumbling, he fixed the gun back into its spring-clip, then hauled all three bodies up to the railings and tumbled them over. He followed, keeping his eyes on the pathway all the time as he dragged them one by one back into the brush to where the ground sloped away a little towards the water. No one else rounded the bend. He laid them flat, their feet pointing down the slope, each behind the bole of a plane-tree to conceal the head and shoulders from anyone who might look directly left from the path. The torsos were pretty much hidden by scrub, although the girl's yellow tracksuit, besmirched with vermilion, was a bright patch among the leafless branches. Ginsberg was wearing a short dark raincoat over his sports coat. Cauldwell worked it off him, still watching the pathway, and spread it over the girl; then he went up the slope and hopped over the railings once more.

You could find them if you looked. And there was a lot of blood on the path. Cauldwell reckoned on the fact that the path didn't seem to be much used; he reckoned even more on the tendency of city people to mind their own business. Anyone would report the bodies, of course; but the blood would probably be ignored for some while. He figured he might have fifteen or twenty minutes. Enough time to get back to his hotel. He set off, walking rapidly.

He hadn't noticed that the girl wasn't dead when he left. It made no matter. She died twelve minutes later. In that time, five people had walked past the spot, skirting the splashes of blood. The bodies were found half an hour after that.

35

The sound was circling the vault of her head like an echo chasing an echo. It grew in volume as it came back to the source, blaring, fading, then swelling once more as it rose towards her brow.

She opened her eyes. A face hovered above her like a dim moon.

Alan Mountjoy had been powerless to stop them. They had stretchered her back to the ambulance, going at the trot, and slid her in through the open doors, all brisk efficiency. One of them had climbed in with her. 'Do you want to come along?' he'd asked.

Mountjoy had shaken his head – 'Tell me where you're taking her. Which hospital' – then he'd set off at the run, making for the place where they'd parked the car. Ginsberg had been nowhere in sight.

The man smiled. 'You'll be OK,' he told her. 'We'll be there soon.' He straightened the fold of red blanket under her chin. There was nothing to be done; as far as he could tell, she was simply a blackout case. Epileptic, perhaps.

Paula felt the swerves of the ambulance as it raced through the traffic, its siren wailing the two notes that rose and fell in her skull.

There had been the man on the stage. She hadn't killed him. There had been the man in the crowd who carried her death in his mind like a terrible dark secret. But he hadn't killed her. Other people – from her past, from her dreams.

She thought of them, one by one, but it was hard to keep them in mind, so she stopped trying.

The man at her side spoke to her, and smiled again. She smiled back, but meant nothing by it. After a while she closed her eyes, giving herself up to the sense of speed and the endless bray of the siren.

36

'Shouldn't I have heard about this yesterday? Jesus Christ! Pete Ginsberg was my man, you know?' Ed Jeffries looked first at Prentiss, then switched his attention to Ascher for a moment. 'How come he knows? I'm told hours later' – he flung out a hand – 'a *day* later, for Chrissakes. This is shit, you know that, Howard? It's shit.'

Prentiss was impassive. He could see how Jeffries might think it would help to get mad. He sat still while Jeffries paced around the room and sounded off and used Prentiss' first name, which he'd never done before, in the hope that Prentiss might join his conspiracy of anger.

Finally Jeffries flopped into a chair, as if his righteous indignation was spent, sighed heavily, and dug a packet of cigarettes out of his shirt pocket. 'So, it's a foul-up.' He tried for a wearily practical tone of voice that implied *What's new?* and *What's next*? He lit his cigarette and spoke through the exhalation of smoke: 'At least it was *their* foul-up.'

'Was it?' Prentiss asked.

'Sure. Christ, where did it happen?'

'*Why* did it happen?'

'You tell me.' Jeffries waved the cigarette expressively.

'From the start,' Prentiss told him. His voice was very quiet. 'It began to go wrong from the start. The approach to David Paschini, the lack of research, that dumb kidnap; bringing in Guerney as a cover. Some cover!' He paused.

'Things have gone sour, Ed. Guerney's still out there. Rachel Irving's still out there somewhere.' He paused. 'Remember her?' Again, a pause. 'Let me lay it out for you,

419

here. We've got Guerney – alive and missing. We've got Irving – alive and missing. We've got Clive Holman alive and, now, untouchable. We've a dead operative found lying in a neat row with John and Jane Doe – also dead. We've got the Peace Movement asking heavy questions and coming up with their own answers for the benefit of the media, who are having a high old time turning over rocks. Guess what they're finding. They're finding two sets of grieving parents weeping over the bodies of Mr and Miss Ordinary. They're finding, also, an unidentifiable stiff carrying a .38, but no ID – a stiff that no one will talk to them about, because no one knows what the fuck to say. So they're making it up as they go along; they seem to be filing a lot of copy with the word ''assassination'' in it.' Prentiss hadn't raised his voice; he hadn't needed to.

'What else have we got? Well, the Brits up to their armpits in crud – and not too happy about it. Do you believe that? The idea was to *weaken* the movement. Wasn't it?' He waited, as if for a response. 'There are a lot of angry people hearing this kind of news, Ed.'

'I didn't dream this one up – you know that, don't you?' Jeffries stabbed a finger at Ascher. 'Kooks like him came up with this one. OK, it was my show; I was directing. Things went wrong. But not *just* me. Christ, Howard, you brought Cole in.'

A silence drew out. Jeffries fished for another cigarette. The three men sat a while, as if someone had forgotten his lines. Jeffries muttered: 'Christ. . . .'

Finally, Prentiss said: 'It has to be someone's fault. Things went wrong? That's not going to do it. People ask questions at times like these. They want to know how, and why, and who. You see?' He shrugged. 'It has to be someone's fault.'

'You asshole.' Jeffries slapped the table. 'You brought Cole in.' He pointed at Ascher. 'This turkey, this son of a bitch – Christ! – he probably came up with the whole fucking Mickey Mouse scheme.'

'No,' Prentiss told him.

'Someone like him. Some motherfucker, some crazy.' He was shouting.

Prentiss shook his head. 'No,' he said. Then: 'There's nothing I can do, Ed.'

Jeffries looked at him. 'Do I run or walk?'

'There's nothing I can do, Ed.'

Ascher watched the door close. He said: 'In concept, it was brilliant. It was workable.'

Prentiss looked at his hands. 'Sure,' he said.

'You didn't think so.'

'Who cares?' Prentiss sighed. 'You're the expert.'

'Damn right,' Ascher told him. 'We're not backing off from this stuff. The reverse – more money, more research.' He waited, as if to let the information sink in. 'What'll happen?'

'God knows. They're trying to cover Ginsberg; they might make it. Their man – Mountjoy – hadn't a hope in hell of getting any action in time. Some guy found the bodies – his dog.'

'I saw the transcripts. He thinks Cole's gone crazy.'

'What do *you* think?'

'We knew about this thing with her father. She saw it happen, apparently. Then she suffered some sort of collapse. It wasn't too clear, you know? Old records, what the mother could tell us, which wasn't a hell of a lot. Childhood traumas are a dime a dozen. There wasn't anything else. She grew up . . . what can I tell you? She was doing fine.'

'I heard there was a suggestion she killed him.'

'Yeah, I heard that. It's crap.' Ascher's voice was sharp. 'They haven't found her yet?'

'She discharged herself as soon as she got to the hospital. She could be anywhere.'

Ascher nodded. He left the room without saying goodbye. In the street he hailed a taxi and asked the driver to take him to the airport. It wasn't until the cab was in motion that he said: 'Shit. Jesus *shit!*'

The driver looked in his mirror. 'You havin' a bad day,

buddy?' he asked, ''cause I know the feelin'.'

'Just drive,' Ascher told him, 'OK?'

William Prior looked solemn. He waited patiently while his boss finished reading the report Prior had brought with him.

'It's a mess.' The other man threw the papers on to his desk. 'It's a bloody awful mess.'

Prior nodded. 'I'm afraid it is, Minister.' He sat upright, his hands resting lightly on the arms of his chair. And from where I sit, he thought, you've got egg all over your face, you pompous bastard.

The famous actor held the girl close, her head pressed to his chest while he gazed out, mistily, at San Francisco Bay. He kissed the girl and told her that he loved her. It was clear that she loved him, too. The wind lifted her long dark hair.

Then the famous actor was climbing into his car. He wore a purposeful look. He roared away from the kerbside, at the same time radioing his position and the direction he was travelling in. He flipped down the dashboard pocket to check his gun.

Paula thought the famous actor was a pain in the ass. She turned and looked along the beam to the white glow at the projection-point. There came a loud *zip* from the sound-track, then a cascade of images, and the film stopped. People started to slow-handclap the projectionist.

She emerged from the cinema into the late-afternoon dusk, crossed the road at a set of traffic lights and wandered aimlessly towards the nearby road junction, intending to cross again. A thought struck her. She looked at the lights, flipping them to green. Three cars moved away; two made it; the third was hit broadside by a jeep crossing the junction – a shocking *whump*! followed by a ringing of smashed glass. As she left, the lights were running through an endless repetition of their red-amber-green sequence.

For an hour or more, she walked. The things she did made her feel like a prankster. Lights went out. Building protection alarms started up. Telephones rang in empty booths. Trick or treat, she thought to herself.

Now and again she paused, as though someone walking just behind her might catch up and take her arm and guide her to a place she knew. A wind sprang up as the light diminished. There seemed to be a vacancy on the far side of the road, and she realised that she had wandered down to the Thames. Boats decorated with strings of coloured lights went soundlessly back and forth. She felt lonely.

A pub was advertising live music, so she went in and bought a drink and listened to the band. The singer was tall and had long black hair. She made him look at her. It wasn't difficult to do. The music was so loud that it seemed to press on her body. She could feel the bass rising from her footsoles and gathering in little shockwaves at the pit of her stomach.

At the end of the set, the band stepped down off the stage and went to the bar. The singer stood close to her for a moment, then said: 'Do you want a drink?'

'Sure. And some food; maybe later.'

He looked at her more closely, then laughed. 'Yes, OK,' he said. It had happened before. He paid for the drinks. Paula could see that his black hair was shot with streaks of midnight blue.

She lay naked and looked straight up, feeling his hair trail across her breast. When he kissed her it fell over her face like a soft mask.

He moved above her and she forked her legs for him, then quickly stretched her neck and bit him hard on the shoulder. He drew back and yelped. 'That hurt!'

She held him and bit again, harder.

'Shit!' He slapped her, reflexively, a sharp open-handed cuff, and she gasped and drew him inside her.

'Is that it?' he asked, and looked at her face to be sure. He slapped her again and her back arched. 'Is that it?' He felt his body charge with excitement.

Paula closed her eyes and called his name. '*David*!'

* * *

In the small room, with its skylight washed by the glow from passing cars, a jury assembled. Paula looked at their faces and found no pity there. Her father, in judge's robes, waited for the verdict. His skin was mossy from being so long in the ground, and a death-sweat shone on his brow. David Paschini stood before them. The star witness. His eye-sockets churned with maggots. He pointed at Paula. The jury said, 'Guilty,' speaking as one. Her father smiled. There were blood-beads on his lips.

She woke in the dark and found she was crying. The singer put out an arm and caressed her face where the bruises were, then drew her beneath him and eased her legs apart.

'David,' she said, 'David, David, David.'

Though it was too dark to see it, she imagined his face just above hers, the ribbons of flesh, the glisten of wet bone. Maggots fell from his eyes, dropping softly on to her shoulders and neck, leaving delicate trails, their crawlings as soft as the brush of someone's hair on her skin.

They had taken a train, and then, from the country station, a cab. They'd done nothing to cover their tracks; given where they were going, there would have been little point.

The papers were full of the killings. Guerney had read the clues. 'They put a mechanic in for Paula Cole, but didn't tell her minders. Somehow, she identified him – I'm not surprised by that. Then he had to kill the guy who was tailing him.'

'The other two just happened along,' Rachel surmised.

'Yes. Wrong place, wrong time.'

'Why didn't they tell the men who were guarding the girl?'

'For one thing, the mechanic almost certainly wouldn't work that way. They insist on low-risk options. No one knows who doesn't *have* to know. It can foul things up badly if someone's waiting for it to happen; the person gets edgy, starts looking for the moment, gives things away. . . . Also, they'd been with the girl for a while – an affinity grows up. They might have opposed the idea – argued – even tried to find some way of preventing it.'

They were walking up the mile-long track from the road to Druid's Combe. Rachel picked up a fir cone from the verge and rolled it between her palms. 'It would have worked, wouldn't it? If she's got the same powers as David Paschini?'

'Yes. I don't think there's any doubt about that: they'd chosen her for it.'

'The pacemaker would just have stopped.'

'Or become lethally erratic. I don't know.'

'Well,' she said, 'they burned their fingers to the elbows this time. They won't thank you for it.' She shook a few seeds out of the cone. 'Or me.' When he didn't reply, she asked: 'Someone will come here, don't you think? Sooner or later.'

'It's possible. Later if at all. Right now, heads are rolling; people are making for the high ground. They might think of it later.'

'What will you do?'

'Stay here,' he said. 'I live here.'

'I'll leave in the morning – OK?' She dropped the cone on to her foot, lofting it over the hedgerow.

'Yes.'

'I've still got my passport – credit cards – I guess I'll have to use them. Try to make it to Amsterdam, perhaps. I've a friend who lives there.' She spoke as if she were answering questions he'd put to her. She felt a little resentful that he hadn't. A memory came to her of Stella's backward glance as she walked towards the terminal building at Heathrow.

We're both refugees, she thought. My life has come unstitched. I don't know what will happen next.

She left at 8.30 the next day. It was a clear morning, the sky blue, the breeze cold. Guerney had made some coffee, and they drank it in near-silence. Finally, Rachel got up and went to the door.

I care for him, she thought.

He sat at the kitchen table, holding his coffee-mug in both

425

hands, blowing gently at the steam unfurling from the surface.

He could taste on his tongue the word that would have stopped her – could feel its shape and texture. There had been a time when Guerney thought betrayal the greatest sin; he no longer thought that; he realised that concepts like honour and fidelity were meaningless in the face of love or misery or ambition.

All that had passed between Rachel and himself now telescoped, from their first meeting, through the long trusting friendship, to a handful of scenes played out at the house they were now in.

Rachel pitched a snowball at his back, laughing, smothered in white from the fall she'd taken. She turned in the shower, smiling, handing him the bath-brush: 'Do my back.' She knelt under the teeming jets, her dark hair glossy with the sheen of water it carried, and pleasured him like a geisha. She sat close to the fire, wearing his robe as any wife would, and dabbed a potato into the blood-juice from her steak.

Even at the time, he had marvelled – her smiling face, her lust, her easy domesticity. Who would not have believed it? As he'd watched, it had frightened him and angered him, too. He thought now that it was possible for the two to go hand in hand, treachery and joy. Her pleasure at seeing him, her fondness, her moment of childishness, her moment of desire – they could all have been genuine. Perhaps only a fool would confuse betrayal with hatred or indifference.

But there were other risks. They had to do with what he might have to give of himself.

The word stuck in his jaw.

Rachel turned in the doorway, but didn't speak.

'Good luck,' Guerney told her.

He wanted to run, wanted to lose himself in the bare pasture. That could come later. He stacked the mugs, and the pan he'd used to heat the coffee, in the sink, then ran some water over them. The small domestic task seemed bizarre. Then

426

he went cross-country to the village and collected the dog.

'She thought she'd lost you for good,' Mrs Davies told him. 'I was beginning to wonder myself.' She looked at Guerney, full of guileless curiosity.

'No,' he said, 'no – I had to go abroad. It turned into a long trip. I hope she wasn't a nuisance to you.'

'Never,' said Mrs Davies, 'never.' She smiled at him openly, her face free of secrecy or self-interest, the way all truly kind people smile.

That afternoon he left the house, the dog at his heel, and climbed the high pasture. The sun was still bright. The window caught his image, as it always did as he rose towards the skyline or returned from it: the image of a man with his dog leashed alongside him, stepping between the long fur-rows. It mirrored him, together with clear planes of sky and the tall still symmetry of pines. It held those reflections, nothing else.

Guerney felt an edge inside him, his breastbone sharp like a bowsprit. It was as if he might keen in the breeze. His senses were so tuned that his eye found the pheasant in the same moment that the dog stopped and stiffened, her head motionless as the bird filled her vision like something seen at the end of a narrowing funnel. He slipped her at once, feeling, as always, the mixture of emotions that attended the act: exhilaration, sorrow, a makeweight of fear. He watched her brindle flow over the ground as she homed in, a bone torpedo, her prey fixed at the funnel's mouth.

THE END

**THREE MORE GREAT
THRILLERS FOR YOUR
READING PLEASURE . . .**

THE CHINA CARD

by John Ehrlichman

With this startlingly authentic novel John Ehrlichman steps into the front rank of the masters of espionage fiction. At the heart of *The China Card* is the possibility that the Chinese Communists have planted a 'mole' deep within the Nixon administration, within the White House itself. In the hands of an author who *was* one of Richard Nixon's closest advisers, the premise takes on a chilling plausibility that places the President's China 'initiative' in a shocking new perspective.

The China Card is a novel of stunning force in which the reader becomes engaged in the dramatic power plays of history itself.

£3.95

The White House

FALL, 1974

'We did some very good things, Henry. I wonder if any-one will remember them.'

'Of course they will, Mr. President. Within a historical perspective you will be seen as a strong President who brought the nation through difficult times.'

'I wonder; people seem to recall only the worst about a President. Look at what they did to Wilson. Won't the historians dump me in with Harding and Grant? Do you think they will?'

'How can they, sir? There is SALT and China and an honorable end to the Viet Nam war. Achievements like that will not be overlooked.'

'Perhaps you're right, Henry. China is the big one that can't be taken away from us, isn't it? We did that, didn't we? From now on the world is changed because the American President holds the China card in his hand. They have to give us credit for that, don't they, Henry?'

Henry Kissinger nodded slowly. It was idle, Kissinger reflected, to be concerned with history's ultimate judg-ment at the moment when the White House was about to collapse around their heads. 'To a great extent history will be what we make it, Mr. President,' Kissinger replied. 'You will write. I will write. Our colleagues will write. We can do much to direct the historians' vision.'

'That's true, isn't it?' the President said. 'We must be very certain that our friends are encouraged to be among the first to write. What can we do about the others, though? What can we do about Thompson?'

'Not much, Mr. President, beyond what we have done. Thompson is gone. Wherever he is, he fears the Chinese, I am sure. I doubt that he will write a book.'

'Good. It's people like Thompson who could badly confuse historians about the way we opened up China.'

'Yes, Mr. President, he could,' Henry Kissinger agreed. 'He could indeed. But I think the risk is small.'

THE ROPESPINNER CONSPIRACY

by Michael M. Thomas

As topical as today's most worrying financial headlines, *The Ropespinner Conspiracy* is the story of a brilliant and insidious Soviet plot to infiltrate the West's banking system and lead it to self-destruction, aided and abetted by one of America's most prominent capitalists. Here is a novel filled with breathtaking suspense and vivid characters, a tale for our times told with Michael Thomas's elegance, wit and profound insight. And it offers something more: a grave warning (for those who will listen) about the ways in which the West's financial structure has been imperilled by the men who lead it.

£2.95

The place was perfectly situated for the evening's business. It stood almost exactly at the midpoint of the five-mile crescent of the bay; from the air, the sweeping shoreline resembled a crude sickle slicing into the water, marked by a pale, foamy smear where the easy wash of the bay tides met the dark rocks footing the bluffs.

The house sat close to the cliff. It was a loose, sprawling geometry of shingle and clapboard in the middle of what had once been a wide clearing in the surrounding pine forest – a glade, now covered with a roughly cared-for lawn. According to local legend, the Vikings had landed here and been slaughtered on the spot by local Indians, themselves now long since driven off, first by loggers and finally by the insistent encroachment of resort houses.

To sailors entering the bay on a misty day, the forest had an Arcadian, primeval appearance. The tree line formed a seamless viridian stripe along the bluff tops, interrupted briefly by the house and its lawn and then continuing northward again until, at its farther end, the lights of the cottages and the town signaled the indelible presence of civilization.

'I can never look at this without thinking of Locke,' said the elder of the two men standing on the porch. He was a spindly man in his middle seventies, somewhat bent by the years, his angular frame incongruously topped by a fleshy, childlike face.

'Locke?' said his companion. He was a stocky good-looking man, about twenty years younger. As he spoke, his hand rose to his breast pocket and instinctively rearranged a bright paisley handkerchief.

'Yes, Locke. He said, "In the beginning, *everything* was America." '

They were looking seaward from the wide veranda that was the older man's special pride. It was the only addition he'd made to the original plans when he rebuilt the house following the fire.

'Well,' said the younger man, 'the sun's going down. Shouldn't be too long now.' He looked at his watch. 'Wheels up at seven thirty, right? That's what they told you?'

'Yes, yes.' The older man sounded on edge, distracted. He scratched nervously at his tonsure of fluffy white hair.

Twilight was settling on the water. The white lines of the hull and rigging of the sailboat moored a hundred yards out were spectral in the fading light. There were no lights on the intervening bluffs. The other 'cottages' were unoccupied at this time of year and would stay that way until June.

'I just hope people won't notice,' said the older man.

'Notice what?'

'The aircraft. These helicopters make so much noise, you know.'

'Don't be ridiculous.' The younger man heard the impatience in his voice. He paused for an instant to let things settle. Then: 'Look, even if someone happened to pass by, the locals have seen choppers in and out of here for the last twenty years. They won't give it a thought. So don't you either.' He was obviously fond of his companion and prepared to be patient.

'Well, I hope so.' The older man sounded doubtful.

A light breeze off the water stirred the flags drooping from the cross staves of the flagpole.

'Goodness!' exclaimed the older man. 'I almost forgot to take the flags down. And it's after sunset!' He started for the steps.

'Leave it,' said the young man, laying a restraining hand on the other's arm. 'Why bother? It doesn't matter any more, don't you see? Come on, it's getting chilly. I think you ought to go inside. We need you at concert pitch for the next few hours. Are you all packed?'

It was as if he were getting an infirm old uncle ready to go off to the nursing home.

They went inside. At the door, the younger man paused and looked around. Tough country, this, he thought. Tough people. Tough old house. He smiled at his friend's back. And what a tough old guy you've been, he thought affectionately; all steel under those fine manners and intellectual bearing. At least until the last month or so. Well, getting old must be a bitch. The legs go first – and the nerves. Shit, he thought, I'm getting old myself. Almost fifty-seven. Well, not that old.

He took another look around. A hell of a lot had been hatched here, he thought: plans for triumph or tragedy, depending on how you looked at it. His inner eye was cold. There was little or no nostalgia in his own mental storehouse. To him, memory was a kind of inventory, a series of shelves to be checked now and then for goods as needed. Remembrance was just something a man riffled through until he found what he could use to get what he wanted now. The past could be a trap. Look back, and *wham!* – something blindsided you. A man couldn't get where he'd gotten, done what he'd done – what *they'd* done – if he let himself be tied in knots by the past.

'I just think I'll have another look round for that photograph of Grigoriy,' the old man said. 'I can't imagine where it's got to.' He sounded as if he were about to cry.

For Christ's sake, stop whining, thought the younger one. He was tired of hearing about that goddamn photo. He could understand what it meant; hadn't he been hearing 'Grigoriy this' and 'Grigoriy that' for fifteen years now? I know, I know, he thought. Just take it easy. Humor the old fellow.

'You probably left it in Boston.'

'Cambridge.' The old man smiled. 'You never do get it right, do you? No, I'm certain it was here.'

'OK, chief, I yield to your point of order: Cambridge. Go have another look.' He snapped a mock salute. It'll give you something to do, he thought. 'I hope the rest of your stuff is all buckled and zipped. When these guys get here, they're not going to want to stick around for high tea.'

His own luggage – four suitcases, two suit bags, a shoecase, and two briefcases – was stacked neatly by the front door. It was a lot – in spy novels, defectors traveled lighter – but where they were headed was known to be a lousy place for clothes. He was vain about his appearance, so he'd packed enough suits to last the second lifetime to which he was now going.

Ropespinner was over. Complete. Finished. Only the next forty-eight hours remained.

Ropespinner. That was the name – like Cosa Nostra or the Company – that the old man and his Russian pal, Grigoriy Menchikov, had dreamed up, their private code name for what the old man also sometimes called 'our great enterprise of the last thirty years.' The name came from something Lenin had once said: 'Capitalism will sell us the rope with which we hang it.'

Ropespinner: a grand plan to subvert Western capitalism finally and forever. From within: by debauching the banking system that was supposed to be the stable, steady heart of free enterprise.

And they'd done it, by God!

They'd induced the condemned man to plait his own noose. All that was left now was to spring the trap, and that was what they were going to Moscow to do.

His mind jumped ahead to Monday, to the press conference when they'd announce to the world just exactly what they'd done and how they'd done it.

He supposed he'd have to wear the goddamn medal the old man had brought him from Moscow; the damn thing could pull a first-class job of tailoring right out of shape. He'd already planned his getup: the new Holland and Sherry nine-ounce blue-gray pinhead worsted, one of the new shirts from Sulka, and – to add insult to injury – an official bank tie. He'd tried on one of the new suits. The fit was perfect, even if the material was heavier than he usually ordered. Well, winter there was known to be a bitch and, besides, the heavier goods might last longer, maybe the rest of his life.

He looked at his watch – 6:53. He was itching to be off. That was his style. If you come to a decision, then damn it, act on it! Get up and go. No shilly shally!

Goddamn, he found himself thinking, we've really done it! We've broken the goddamn bank! The banks. The entire goddamn Western banking system. The entire goddamn West! And just two guys! Well, three, if you counted Menchikov. Himself out on the front line; the old man working the room; the Russian behind the curtain pulling strings.

Who could have thought it possible? He hadn't – that was for damn sure, and he'd been cut in after it was well under way. Would he have played it differently if he'd been in on the scam from the beginning? He doubted it.

No: he never would have thought it possible, not even now when he looked back and saw for himself exactly what the old Russian had seen way back – when? – '45, '46? How could people, guys who were supposed to be so goddamn smart, be so dumb? What the hell did they think they were doing; where the hell could they think this was taking them, other than right down the toilet? Them and their banks and their countries. The Western governments had cooperated right along, too: Washington and London and Berne. One by one the old barriers had come down, one regulation after another, all toppled in the name of efficiency and competition.

When he looked back on it, it was as if he and the old man had spent thirty years systematically sabotaging a great edifice, like one of those French cathedrals. Planting a charge, sawing a joist halfway through, weakening a buttress. Now all that was left was to push the plunger and detonate the whole mess.

Their Moscow press conference would be the detonator. The goddamnedest show-and-tell the world has ever seen.

He liked the timing. Well, he thought, I would – since it was my idea.

Nine A.M. Moscow time the Monday after Easter. Which meant the big markets in the Far East, Hong Kong and Tokyo, would still be open. Most of Europe would just be waking up; the United States would still be sleeping off the last of its long holiday weekend.

But the financial circuits of the world never slept. This crisis would race along those wires like flame along a fuse, setting off one explosion after another until it all blended into a single great fireball and the circuits melted and the sun went out.

LOST

by Gary Devon

One of the most riveting and tension-filled novels of recent years, *Lost* is the story of Sherman, a deranged and evil boy who will stop at nothing to gain possession of his abducted younger sister Mamie. Accompanied by a vicious, wolflike hound known as The Chinaman, Sherman follows a trail from state to state across the frozen wastes of the eastern American seaboard after the worst blizzard in two decades. Fleeing before him is the woman, Leona, a 35-year-old spinster who has befriended Mamie and two other small and love-starved children, and who will protect them unto death.

Lost is a novel of unbridled menace and breathtaking tension that will engage and terrify you from the first page.

£2.95

Only the sound of his footsteps and the soft padding of the Chinaman's paws broke the night silence. Sherman did not hesitate or look back, striking deftly through the dark countryside. 'Goddam her,' he muttered under his breath; 'goddam her to hell,' the words like a chant, marking his stride. The pills held his pain to a low humming at the back of his brain.

They kept to the high ground parallel to the Scranton road. When the dog wandered down too close to the ditches, Sherman called him and made him come back. Otherwise he let the Chinaman roam. Very little traffic moved on the highway this late at night; for long periods it stood completely empty. Yet he wanted to be sure that their departure wasn't noticed by anyone. He spoke to the dog sparingly and used his pencil flashlight only when he had to – when the darkness of wild bushes blocked his path or the dog slipped into a gully that opened in the ground like a trap.

Moving quickly, they crossed pastures and fences and woods. As soon as the sun came up, Sherman opened his shirt and removed the papers and pictures he'd taken from the Mattingly house. The snapshots, blown up to frame size, had faded to a bronzy orange. The two women, the one he'd just hit and the one who'd taken Mamie, were in both the photographs. He immediately folded them, scored them with his thumbnail, and tore them in two. Then he tore the two halves showing the Mattingly woman into little chunks and threw them to the wind like confetti. In the two half-photos he kept, the woman looked younger than she did in real life. His teeth began to ache from the angry set of his jaw. From his billfold, he removed the print of Mamie's school picture that he'd torn from a newspaper, folded it with the two pictures of the woman, and returned all three, in his billfold, to his pocket.

Methodically he flipped through the sheaf of papers – most of it yesterday's mail, he guessed. All the envelopes had been opened. He separated them quickly, sorting out the circulars and bills and holding the two envelopes addressed to Leona Hillenbrandt in his teeth. The stack of useless material he tore into small pieces and let them dribble and flutter from his hands as he walked. Of the two remaining pieces, one was a letter on good-smelling paper from Cornelia Dunham, Ridgefarm Road, Brandenburg Station, Kentucky. But the other letter, from the Citizens National Bank of Scranton, held his attention and he placed the Kentucky letter inside his shirt.

Sherman tore the bank envelope apart. He paid little attention to the actual writing as he repeatedly formed the woman's name with his lips: Leona Hillenbrandt. Scranton. That had to be where she was taking Mamie. Nothing else made sense. He folded the letter with the envelope and tore them to pieces. The little wad of money he'd found wedged under the Mattingly woman's vase – the three thousand-dollar bills wrapped in a five-dollar bill – remained untouched in his jeans pocket.

It was still very early in the morning when he saw a country gas station far below and wondered if it was safe yet to hitchhike, if he was far enough away from Graylie. He was crossing an area of hills, and had wandered higher from the road than he meant to. While he looked down, two cars moved like minnows onto the asphalt drive, headed in opposite directions. He wanted to be riding in a car. He called the dog and started down the steep embankment.

He counted four cars parked on the grounds, none of them police cars – nothing that looked suspicious. As he and the dog crossed the highway through the morning fog, he saw a clump of road signs. In black letters, one said: SCRANTON 72 MI. The idea of seventy-two miles stretched deep in his imagination and, with it, the minutes ticking away and Mamie slipping farther out of his reach. He pulled a piece of clothesline rope from his hip pocket, tied it to the Chinaman's collar, and they jogged through a display of chalk figures strung out on the ground – reindeer and donkeys pulling carts, and birdbaths – and slipped between the parked cars.

Fog hung in scraps over the road, but the traffic was fairly brisk. As they moved into the shadow of the gas station, a car came in headed north toward Graylie. The attendant ambled from the garage, pumped the gas, and went back to work, frowning at Sherman and the Chinaman as he passed. A lull settled over the station. For several minutes nothing moved on the road.

Come on, Sherman thought, his anxiety mounting. He sat down on the concrete curbing, then stood up and scuffed back and forth.

Two cars came in and stopped on either side of the gas pumps. While the attendant handled the car pointed north, Sherman tapped the passenger window of the one going south, a maroon car. The driver leaned across the seat and rolled the window down a few inches. Sherman asked for a ride to Scranton. The man seemed to consider it, lowered his head as if to decide. 'I need a lift for him, too,' Sherman said. 'He's with me,' and nodded toward the Chinaman. Without answering, the man cranked the window up and turned to stare at the road.

Before the attendant had finished with the maroon car, an old blue coupe had pulled in behind it. Sherman tapped the window glass, and again he thought he might be getting somewhere until he pointed to the big grisly dog; then the driver said, 'Sorry,' and went on studying the map spread on the steering wheel. The car radio was turned low, but the emphatic voice could still be heard: *'Graylie police continue to investigate last night's assault and battery of a local woman, Emma Mattingly, of 210 Columbia Avenue. Mrs. Mattingly has been listed in critical condition. . . .'*

Sherman heard only that much as he withdrew from the side of the car, concentrating on the man reading the map. Fright ran through him like quicksilver. She's still alive, he thought. If she could describe him, it would only be a matter of time before the cops figured out who he was and what he had done – not only what he'd done last night, but all the other nights and other things, the paperboy who'd taken his place, the fire. I should of finished her, he thought; I should of.

Even after the coupe had left, he went on glancing about, alert and cautious. He saw no immediate threat, except the attendant was coming toward them in his blackened coveralls, wiping his hands on a greasy rag. 'You can't hang out here,' the man said. 'You'd better just run along.' The Chinaman clambered to his feet and started to growl, his hackles rising.

'We're tryin' to catch a ride,' Sherman said, pulling the dog's collar, telling the Chinaman to shut up.

'You better catch it someplace else. I want you to clear out of here.' He went inside the garage.

Sherman slowly brushed the seat of his pants. Another car came in headed the wrong way, and the frowning attendant glared at them as he adjusted the pump handle. He had the hood up when a white pickup rolled in, going in the right direction. The driver's window was down, his elbow resting out in the chill November air. Sherman started talking to the man in earnest, telling him he had to get to Scranton because his sister was there and he had to take the dog, and could they ride in the back of the pickup, when the attendant came around the front of the truck. 'If you don't head down that road right now and stop bothering my customers, I'm going to go inside and call the county sheriff.'

Sherman opened his mouth to speak.

'No buts,' the attendant said. 'Either you go down that road right now or I call the cops. Take your pick.'

Tugging at the dog's rope, Sherman tore from the pickup window and marched past the attendant. Angry tears stood in his eyes. He knew when the cards were stacked against him, knew when to keep his mouth shut. He jerked the dog to him, moved down the drive, crossed the highway, and slipped into the ditch so he could let the Chinaman loose. His good hand was curled tight on the blackjack in his pocket. He wanted to take it and beat that sonofabitch to death. He hadn't gone very far when he heard a horn honk and saw the white pickup truck swerve to the side of the road above the ditch. It's about goddammed time, he thought.

He squatted down in a corner of the truck bed, pulling the dog in beside him, and the irregular houses and foothills and pockets of trees wheeled alongside the truck and sank away in an ever-deepening V.

A SELECTED LIST OF FINE TITLES
AVAILABLE FROM CORGI BOOKS

☐ 13139 3	**The China Card**	*John D. Ehrlichman*	£3.95
☐ 13061 3	**Lost**	*Gary Devon*	£2.95
☐ 13270 5	**The Ropespinner Conspiracy**	*Michael M. Thomas*	£2.95